# Nomads of Zyden

Xine Fury

*Nomads of Zyden*

## Contents

**Part 1: The Bond**

## Part 2: The Eyes of O'olos



## Part 3: Beyond Zyden



## Bonus Prequel Stories

*Part 1: The Bond*

## *Prologue*

"They've breached the gates!"

Battle horns blared all throughout Fisher's Rest, drowning out the cries of panicked citizens. Swords clanged, children wailed, and inhuman gibbers echoed throughout the town.

Kya hid under her porch, watching boots run back and forth as the town militia fought off the invaders. Pale, unclad feet joined the fray, and human soldiers fell left and right.

*What are these things?* Kya wondered. It was a peaceful fishing village. They had nothing of value, nothing to kill over. But these attackers fought with a lust for destruction, hooting with delight as they cut down their prey.

The creatures rushed through the town like a tidal wave, losing none of their own as they obliterated the local defenders. Within minutes the town was quiet again. A handful of invaders wandered the dusty street, looking for any humans they might have missed. Black smoke wafted by, carrying the odor of burning wood. Occasionally a survivor would cry out in pain, only to be silenced by the cruel assailants.

*I need to get out of here*, Kya thought. Footsteps stomped on the porch above her, followed by the sound of wood cracking. The creatures were now in her house, most likely looking for more victims.

Kya had been alone when the battle started. Both her parents were fishers, and they would have been out on the lake at this time of day. *I hope they escaped*, she thought. But it didn't seem likely. Her parents would have come for her, despite the danger. She'd have to worry about that later.

Three pairs of white feet milled about in front of the porch. *Go away*, Kya thought. Surely they'd be gone soon. They'd find her house empty, then move on to the next house. As soon as the street was clear, Kya would flee, maybe hide in the forest until this invading army moved on. Then she'd come back and look for her family.

The feet shifted back and forth. Strange voices gibbered at each other. It sounded like one was giving orders. The other two creatures moved on, running in opposite directions.

That left one monster blocking Kya's route to freedom. She heard a sniffing sound, then what she took to be a chuckle. Kya froze in place, not even allowing herself to breathe.

The creature took a step forward, then turned away from the porch. For a moment it seemed to be headed for the house across the street. Then suddenly it turned back around, dropped to its knees, and stared Kya right in the face.

## Tradition

A single figure trudged through the knee-high snow, leaving a trail that quickly filled in behind her. The animal skins she wore offered little protection from the biting winds. Through the blinding snow, she spotted the slightest of movements. The snowbank bulged almost imperceptibly to her left.

Marta stood perfectly still and readied her knife, her mouth already salivating. She hadn't eaten since the previous day, and she hoped her rumbling stomach wouldn't scare away the icevole. They were skittish creatures, and extremely difficult to catch... unless you knew the trick. Marta repeatedly clicked her tongue, perfectly imitating the chittering of the small rodents.

The bulge halted, then began to move in her direction. Marta raised her dagger, ready to strike as soon as the creature was within reach. She realized, a second too late, that the mound of snow was much too big to be an icevole. A huge serpent erupted from the snow, its mouth open wide.

Marta dove to the side, barely avoiding the monster's snapping jaws. She tried to stab it as it went by, but her dagger wouldn't penetrate its thick blue scales. The serpent vanished into the snow again, and Marta squinted to follow its path. She thought she saw it circling to her right, but the thick snowfall made it hard to be sure.

Reacting more on instinct than anything, she sidestepped the next attack right as the creature emerged. It missed her with its bite, but it began to coil around her, closing tight around her legs. She tried to step out of the way, but the serpent was too strong. Her legs were now pinned together, and the monster continued to circle its way up her body.

The serpent was at least twenty feet long, and its body was as thick as Marta's thigh. It was extremely fast for its size, and it was already up to her waist within seconds. Though she'd never faced one of these serpents before, she had the presence of mind to raise her arms so that they wouldn't get pinned to her sides. She stabbed at the creature repeatedly, but none of her strikes left so much as a mark.

The serpent stopped circling when it reached her chest, and once again attempted to bite her. It lunged at her face, and she blocked it with her arm. The serpent bit down on her forearm, releasing its venom. Marta immediately felt her left arm go numb, but she refused to give up. With her other arm she stabbed the serpent in the eye, and this time the dagger went in up to the hilt, killing the monster instantly. It gave one last squeeze that nearly crushed Marta's ribs, then uncoiled limply into the snow.

*I have minutes to live*, Marta thought. The numbness had spread to her shoulder. If it reached her heart, she would die. Fortunately she'd paid attention to her lessons. While this was the first snow serpent she'd faced, she'd learned all about them from her clan. She knew that a snow serpent's blood was a natural antidote to its venom. It was believed that this had something to do with the creatures' mating rituals – two snow serpents would bite each other and lick the wounds before the act, and the rhythmic numbing bursts put them in a procreative mood.

*Focus*, Marta told herself. She could feel the venom spreading throughout her body, and she wouldn't be able to act much longer. The serpent's head now lay a few feet away in the snow, its eye gushing bright green blood. Marta could barely move her legs, but she managed to lean forward and fall so that she landed near the creature's head. Her right arm was now her only functional limb, and even it was starting to lose feeling. She dropped the dagger and pulled the serpent's head to her lips.

She was now completely paralyzed, and she could feel her heart slowing. The serpent's blood burned like firewater as it dribbled down her throat. She felt the sudden urge to cough it back up, but she managed to suppress the impulse. After a few seconds, it barely mattered. She could feel herself choking on the liquid, but she no longer had the ability to cough. Her heart felt even weaker, and her vision was getting cloudy.

Her people weren't exactly scholars, but they were smarter than most outsiders would have thought. Marta knew that the antivenom had to spread through her body to work. She wasn't sure if her current heart rate would be enough to do the job. Worse, her lungs were barely moving at all, and might even be filling up with fluid. Her mind wasn't doing much better, as she felt unconsciousness beckoning her, teasing her, trying its best to pull her into a tight embrace.

*At least I don't have to go through with the ceremony*, she thought. She wondered what death would feel like. The elders spoke of an afterlife where she would meet her ancestors, but Marta wasn't sure she believed that. It was a story that had been passed down for so many centuries that it no longer felt like the information could be trusted. Marta had seen gossip get unrecognizably distorted after only two or three retellings, so it seemed unlikely that a story would remain accurate after so many generations.

*Guess I'll find out soon enough*, Marta thought. There was a three-way race going on in her body, and she wondered which would give out first – her heart, her lungs, or her mind. She hoped it would be her mind. If she was going to die anyway, she wanted to lose consciousness first.

But if anything, she was starting to become more alert. She felt a tingling in her toes, then her fingers. Her heart rate started to increase. She suddenly felt immense pain from the bite in her arm. She tried to scream, but she was choking. She coughed. It was weak at first, but as her strength came back, she coughed louder and harder. When she could move her arms again, she got to her knees and vomited. She continued to cough and vomit for more than fifteen minutes, only taking one short break to wrap up her wound.

*I hate this tradition*, Marta thought as she wiped her mouth. It would have been different if the reward were something she actually wanted, but her prize – the hand of a man she barely knew – wasn't worth the effort. But her clan's numbers were dwindling, and they needed her to contribute her share of offspring to keep her people from dying out.

Though given the events of the last half hour, their marital traditions weren't exactly conducive to the survival of their clan. Before a bride could be married, she had to survive a week on her own, in the harshest wilds on the mountain. She could only bring a dagger and the clothes on her back. She'd have to build her own shelter, kill her own food, and most importantly, stay warm.

The husbands had to endure trials of their own, but theirs weren't nearly as grueling. Marta once asked why women had to endure so much more, and was told that since it was their duty to protect their husbands, they had to prove themselves capable. She'd gone on to ask why the men didn't have to prove they could protect their wives, and was told that the men were already capable. She'd followed up with several more questions about the clan's views on gender equality, only to end up with a month's worth of extra chores.

The numbness was now completely gone, and Marta could breathe normally again. She looked hungrily at the dead snow serpent. Their meat wasn't edible to humans, but that didn't mean they were useless. She stretched the serpent out and rolled it over onto its back, then felt along its stomach for bulges. *There*, she thought, as she slipped her dagger between the scales and cut into the creature's belly. She reached inside and pulled out two partially-digested icevoles. Then she returned to her makeshift shelter and started a fire.

The sun turned the snow red as it set on the seventh day. Marta began the long march back to the settlement. She now wore much thicker furs and some bone armor, thanks to a pair of mountain tigers she'd killed. Part of the tradition was to return with a gift for her husband, and she'd spent the latter half of the week constructing a sturdy shield out of a frost hippo's skull. The shield was roughly three feet high, somewhat rectangular, and the front was covered in snow serpent scales.

The journey back took most of the night, and the sun was beginning to rise when she saw the smoke rising from the village. But it was more smoke than she'd expected. The elders traditionally lit a bonfire on the day of a bride-to-be's return, but from this distance, it looked as if smoke rose from every single house in the village.

Marta picked up the pace, her feeling of unease growing with every step.

She reached the village half an hour later. It sat on a plateau more than halfway up Frostmoor Mountain, and consisted of thirty-two wooden buildings. The fires had burned out, and most of the houses were nothing but piles of crumbling wood and ash.

"Hello?" Marta called out, but all was silent.

She saw no one – living or dead – anywhere she looked. *Maybe they fled the village to escape the fire,* she mused. *But why didn't they send someone to find me?*

The wind changed direction, and suddenly she could smell the overpowering odor of overcooked meat. The stench led her to the burned-out bunkhouse, where the clan's soldiers slept. She gasped as she saw dozens of bodies filling the building. It had to be the entire village. Marta frantically studied the faces of the dead. Most were burned beyond recognition, but she recognized a few.

*My parents are in here somewhere,* she thought, but she couldn't bear to look any longer. She turned away from the bunkhouse and dropped to her knees, weeping. When she was out of tears, she searched the village for answers. She found many signs of battle, but no fallen enemies.

In her absence, some passing army had raided the village and killed every last one of them. *Why us?* Marta wondered. The Frostmoor Clan lived simple lives and didn't hoard wealth. They had no enemies and mostly kept to themselves. There was nothing to gain from their slaughter.

Mountain life was brutal and often short. Her people were taught not to dwell on their emotions. Though Marta mourned in her heart, it wasn't long before her thoughts turned to practical matters. *What now?* she wondered as she rooted through the remains of her home. *I can't stay here. I suppose I'll have to find another clan and see if they'll accept me.*

She knew of a farming community at the base of the mountain. The Frostmoor Clan often traded with them. It wouldn't be easy to adjust to that lifestyle, but at least she wouldn't be alone.

She found a relatively undamaged backpack and began looking for supplies to fill it, to prepare for her journey down the mountain. There wasn't much left, but she packed the backpack with rope, pitons, some dried meat, and a few other sundries. There was a hidden pit under her home where she kept a few supplies, such as a change of clothes and a few weapons.

Her eyes fell on a rolled-up tube of leather. She unrolled it, revealing an exquisitely-crafted sword. It had been in her family for ten generations and was one of their most prized possessions. Her parents had planned to give it to Marta's husband on their wedding day. Now that day would never come, but she wasn't about to leave the sword behind.

She continued rooting through the cache, deciding what to bring and what to leave behind. Soon she came across a small wooden box.

Inside she found a few remnants of her childhood, including her baby teeth and some parchment she'd drawn on as a child. There were a few bits of jewelry, most carved from the bones of her first kill. She brushed these aside and pulled out a small leather bag. She emptied the contents – a wooden ring and a feather quill – into her palm. Both items were infused with magic, and she could feel a mild tingle where they touched her skin.

She took the quill in her right hand and began to draw on her arm. Her body was covered in tattoos, red lines that detailed every significant event of her life. Every dangerous beast she'd ever killed was represented by a hash mark on her thigh. There were also symbols representing each birthday, as well as educational benchmarks. Larger sigils documented events such as Marta learning to swim, her first climb up Grim Peak, and her first monthly cycle. A drawing of a tiger cub represented the birth of her baby brother, and a teardrop beside it signified his untimely death.

Marta now drew a snake and a hashmark on her thigh, to represent the killing of the snow serpent. Then she added a double heart to her bicep to document surviving the betrothal test in the wilds. Finally she drew a burning house on her stomach to represent the destruction of her village. Each tattoo glowed slightly as she drew it, before turning into permanent red lines.

She put the quill back into the leather bag. Then she looked at the ring. It was carved from gray wood, and engraved with holy runes inlaid with silver. It had been crafted by the village shaman on the day she had come of age, and she'd kept it in this bag ever since.

Magic-infused items weren't overly common in the land of Zyden. Enchantment was becoming a lost art, and the Frostmoor Clan had been lucky to have such a talented jewelry smith. The ring's mate – wherever it was now - belonged to Pall, her late fiancée.

The ring had never been worn. It was intended to be placed on her finger during the wedding ceremony, creating a bond that would last a lifetime. Several married couples in the village wore such rings, which allowed them to speak to each other telepathically. The rings were forged in pairs - a single ring without its mate was just a useless trinket.

Marta studied the ring, lost in thought. She'd never wanted to wear it. Pall had been one of the village's greatest warriors, and Marta had been the envy of her peers when they'd been matched. But she'd have gladly let someone else have him. Today, however, she would have been happy to marry him if it meant her people had survived.

Guilt feelings flooded her mind. It was almost as if she had wished for the disaster. *You finally got what you wanted,* she told herself. *Are you happy with the results?* Intellectually she knew it hadn't been her fault. It was sheer coincidence that her village had been attacked in her absence. But she couldn't help feeling like she was somehow responsible.

She slipped the ring on her finger. It was too big at first, but it immediately resized itself for a perfect fit. She could feel its magic, a very slight tingle almost like static electricity. *I never wanted to marry you, Pall,* she thought as she studied the band on her finger. *But you didn't deserve to die.*

*Who said that?* someone answered.

Marta looked around frantically. The village was still silent, and she was still alone. But the voice had sounded as if they'd been right beside her, speaking directly in her ear. She looked back at the ring again. *Hello?* she thought.

*What is this?* the voice replied. *Who's talking to me?*

*Who are you?* Marta asked. *Are you wearing my husband's ring?*

*The voice is coming from the ring?* came the reply. *Is this ring haunted?*

*Were you part of the group that slaughtered my village?* Marta thought.

*Oh no, is the ring cursed? I didn't kill anyone, I swear!*

*Calm down,* Marta thought. *Start from the beginning. How did you get the ring?*

*I'm a slave of the Bonegrinders,* the voice said.

*The Bonegrinders,* Marta thought. *Of course.* They were a tribe of pale-skinned humanoids who raided and killed without mercy. It all made sense now. Bonegrinders turned into dust when killed, so that was why Marta hadn't found any enemy bodies.

*I watched them raid your village,* the voice said. *But I was bound in irons at the time. I promise I didn't participate.*

*Then how did you get the ring?*

*My master put it on me,* the voice replied. *The Bonegrinders like to decorate their slaves with jewelry. It's a sign of prestige — it means you have so much wealth you can waste some on your servants.*

*What's your name?* Marta asked.

*Kya,* the voice answered.

*Where are you now, Kya?*

*In a camp,* Kya replied. *The Bonegrinders are traveling north. From what I've overheard, they're preparing for another raid soon.*

Marta looked at the ring again. *I can find them with this,* she thought. *I can track them down and slaughter the whole lot.*

*They'll kill you instantly,* Kya replied. *They wiped out your village. What chance do you stand by yourself?*

*I'll have the element of surprise,* Marta told her.

*Then you'll get in a couple of kills before they overwhelm you,* Kya replied. *Don't get me wrong, I'd be overjoyed if you won. But I watched them raze your village. Your best warriors fell in minutes. The Bonegrinders are strong and relentless. They fight like animals. What can you do?*

*I can come up with a plan,* Marta replied. *Raise an army. Surround them, take them by surprise.*

Marta thought she heard a sigh. *I'll help you however I can,* Kya told her.

*Then it's settled,* Marta thought. She gathered up a few more supplies, took one last look at the remains of the village, and set out on a path down the mountain.

*Exploration*

"So my friend and I went to a costume party," the jester said. "We agreed not to discuss our costumes beforehand. Imagine my surprise when we both showed up dressed as giant raisins. I guess *grape mimes* think alike!"

Not one laugh, not even a chuckle. The audience stared at him like they were still waiting for the punchline. In a panic, Dobo pulled three balls out of his pocket and started to juggle. His stagehand buzzed around his ear. "You're losing them," Silli whispered, then flew over to the prop box.

*Like I ever had them,* Dobo thought. "But enough about me," he said. "Anyone here from out of town?" Crickets. The audience refused to engage.

Silli rooted through the box until she found an apple, which was almost as large as she was. She also found an egg and a foot-long metal rod that emitted sparks from one end. Using her fairy telekinesis, she tossed them to Dobo one at a time, and he incorporated them into his routine.

Now juggling six objects, Dobo asked the audience, "Does anyone have a small item they'd like to add? How about you, sir?" He nodded to a burly man sitting at the table closest to the stage.

The customer finished his beer in one swallow, then threw the empty stein at Dobo. The jester caught the stein and added it to the juggled objects.

"More!" Dobo said, and nodded to another patron. "How about you, miss?"

"How 'bout this?" the woman slurred. She reached into her bag and threw a dagger at him.

Dobo dodged the dagger, and it stuck in the wall behind him. "Maybe something less sharp? I mean, I've died on stage before, but let's not make it literal. How about you, sir?"

As he juggled, the front door opened and the biggest woman Dobo had ever seen entered the tavern. She was at least six-foot-five and made of pure muscle. She had long auburn hair tied into a ponytail. She wore winter furs and much of her exposed skin was covered in red tattoos. *She's not from around here,* Dobo thought.

He was so distracted that he didn't see the dinner plate come flying toward him. A customer had thrown it for him to juggle, but instead the plate hit him in the chest and he dropped the rest of the objects. Thinking fast, he tumbled backward and performed an impressive acrobatic pratfall. The egg landed on his forehead, eliciting the first real laugh from the audience. "Thank you, that's the show!" he shouted as he stood and bowed. Then he hurried backstage to remove his makeup.

"Good, you're still here," Dobo said as he approached the large woman. She sat alone at a table, brooding. Dobo pulled out a chair and sat down. Silli sat on his shoulder.

"Whatever you're selling, I have no money," the woman replied gruffly.

"Allow me to introduce myself," Dobo said. "Dorian Beauregard the Third. But if that's too much of a mouthful, you can call me by my stage name, Dobo the Dodo."

"Mm-hmm, and the fairy?" Marta asked dully. She was surprised to see that fairies existed outside of children's books, but since she knew so little of the world below her mountain, she'd been taking things as they came.

"My assistant, Sillivene," Dobo said. "I saved her from a cat once, and she hasn't left my side since. I can't seem to get rid of her."

"Hey!" Silli shouted in a high-pitched voice.

"Just kidding, love," Dobo said. "She's a wonderful assistant. Couldn't do my job without her."

Silli smiled at that, then curtsied and sat back down. "Pleased to meet 'cha!" she squeaked.

"Marta," the woman said, though she wasn't really paying attention. She scanned the rest of the patrons as if looking for someone.

"May I ask what brings you to Reuben's Refuge?" Dobo asked.

"I'm trying to raise an army, but so far this town seems to be full of cowards," Marta said.

"And your assumption would be correct," Dobo said. "This town was founded by survivors of the Smythe's Fjord Massacre. Know of it?"

Marta shook her head.

"It was ten... no, eleven years ago," Dobo said. "A legion of invaders devastated Smythe's Fjord, then went on to ravage Willowvane. Some of the townfolk fought back, but were cut down. Those that fled came here."

"Were you one of them?" Marta asked, looking into Dobo's face for the first time. He was about five feet tall and had very prominent ears. There was still a smudge of white paint on his nose.

"No, no, I'm just passing through town," Dobo replied. "I'm on a quest to find an audience who actually finds me funny."

"Then how do you know so much about this town?" Marta asked.

"That's what I do," Dobo answered. "I collect information, tales from far and wide. Someday I hope to be an author. That's why I approached you. You look like you've come a long way. I imagine you have quite a tale for me."

"Hmmph," Marta grunted. "I don't have time for this." She started to stand up.

"Wait, wait," Dobo said. "What if I make it worth your while? I could pay you… not much, but…"

"Unless you have an army, I have no use for you," Marta said.

*Be nice*, a voice said in Marta's mind.

*What?* Marta thought back.

*Be nice*, Kya repeated. *You never know who's going to be able to help you.*

*Can you hear our conversation?* Marta asked.

*No, but I can hear you think your responses, and I can feel your annoyance*, Kya replied.

*He's just a performer*, Marta thought.

*If you're going to raise an army, you need contacts*, Kya told her. *And this is the first person you've spoken to who seemed willing to listen. At the very least he might be able to point you in the right direction.*

"Are you okay?" Dobo asked. "You've been staring into space for nearly a minute."

Marta sat back down. "I will tell you stories," she said. "About my life, about my clan, about why I'm here."

Dobo nodded vigorously and rooted through his coin

purse. "I'll give you—"

"And in return," Marta interrupted, "You will help me gather an army so I can wipe out the monsters who slaughtered my people."

"That's a bit of an ask," Dobo said. "People aren't going to —"

"It's a deal," Silli said, flicking Dobo on the ear.

Dobo shrugged. "Okay, it's a deal."

They made an awkward display of shaking hands. Marta's people shook by grabbing each other's forearms, while Dobo tried to grasp her hand itself. They fumbled for a few seconds before Dobo relented and followed Marta's lead.

"Off to a great start," Silli said with a touch of sarcasm.

*Where are you now?* Kya asked.

*In the back of Dobo's wagon,* Marta thought. *On our way to Oaken Dawn. It's a logging community. According to Dobo, most of the people there are part-time soldiers, making a living during peacetime.*

*Think they'll help you?*

*Dobo sounded doubtful,* Marta thought. *But he still thinks it's our best bet.*

*What do you look like?* Kya asked.

Marta was taken aback. *Why?* she asked.

*Just curious,* Kya replied. *You're my best friend at the moment. I don't even get to talk to the other slaves.*

*I have reddish-brown hair and lots of tattoos,* Marta replied. *I'm not sure what else I can say. What do you look like?*

*Human, brown hair, lots of freckles,* Kya answered. *Probably a lot shorter than you, given what I saw of your people. How old are you?*

*If I live another month, this will be my twenty-third year,* Marta replied. *You?*

*Twenty-one,* Kya replied. *As of two months ago. Normally my family would take me out to a play on my birthday. But they're gone now.*

*The Bonegrinders killed them?*

*I don't know,* Kya answered. *I haven't seen them among the other slaves, so I assume they were ki... ki... I don't think they made it.*

*I'm sorry,* Marta told her.

*I'm going to get some sleep now,* Kya replied.

*Rest well,* Marta thought, and tried to fall asleep herself. It wasn't easy in a moving carriage. She was extremely hot, despite having stripped down to her underclothes. She missed the frigid air of her hometown, but she supposed she'd have to get used to the warmer climate. It wasn't like she'd ever go back to the mountain.

*No... no... leave them alone!* Kya's voice murmured in Marta's ear.

*Kya?* Marta thought loudly. *What's going on?*

*Whu? Oh, I was dreaming.*

*Do you always have nightmares like that?*

*I don't think I've had a good night's rest since my capture,* Kya replied. *It's been four months but the memories are still fresh.*

*I will get you out of there,* Marta told her. *I promise.*

"Not a chance," the foreman said. He was a big man, almost as big as Marta, with chiseled features and a sparse beard. He leaned against a tree with a large X carved on the side.

"But we know how to find them," Marta said. "We can surround them, take them while they're sleeping."

"I've fought Bonegrinders before," he replied. "We'd have to outnumber them ten-to-one before I'd even be tempted.

They're beyond savage."

"Sir," Dobo interjected. "If things go to plan, you will outnumber them twenty-to-one, at least."

"How do you figure?" the foreman asked.

"You're not the only village we're planning to visit," Dobo said. "What if I get signatures from a few more towns, promising that they'll join if it looks like the army will be big enough?"

"I don't know," the foreman said, scratching his chin. "What's in it for us?"

"Survival," Marta said angrily. "If they're not stopped, the Bonegrinders will find you eventually."

"We're pretty out of the way," the foreman said, waving his arms. The logging camp sat in the middle of a thick forest, with miles of trees in every direction.

"So was my village," Marta said. "They had to scale a mountain to reach us. They'll think nothing of a few trees."

The foreman nodded. "You get those signatures and come back. But we won't join unless we're sure we have the advantage."

*What do the Bonegrinders make you do?* Marta asked. She lay in a worker's bunk, as a guest of the loggers. In the bunk above her, she could hear Dobo snoring, sounding not dissimilar to the loggers' saws she'd heard earlier in the day. In the morning they would leave at the crack of dawn.

*Mostly fetch and carry,* Kya replied. *Make their meals, haul their supplies. I'm actually not that much help, to be honest. They just like having slaves because it makes them feel powerful.*

*Do they ever… do things to you?* Marta asked carefully.

*You mean like…* Kya replied. *No, never. They think of us as animals.*

*Do they beat you?*

*They did at first,* Kya answered. *Until I learned to follow their commands. But as long as I do everything perfectly, they don't hurt me… much.*

*Do you speak their language?* Marta asked.

*Some of it,* Kya replied. *I've learned maybe forty or fifty words. Enough to follow orders. Enough to know they're planning an attack. Not enough to know what town they're going to attack.*

*If you find that out, let me know right away,* Marta thought. *Maybe I can warn them.*

*Of course,* Kya replied.

They didn't speak for a while, and Marta assumed Kya had fallen asleep. Marta was still warm. She wanted to remove her blanket as well as her clothing, but that didn't seem appropriate in a bunkhouse full of male soldiers. She was almost asleep when Kya spoke again.

*Marta?* Kya asked.

*Hmm?*

*Do you miss your family?* Kya asked.

*It's a wound in my heart that will never completely heal,* Marta replied. *I'm sure you feel the same way.*

*I can't remember my mother's face,* Kya replied. Though they were speaking telepathically, Marta could hear the anguish in her voice. *I try to think of her, and her face is just a blur. I remember she looked a bit like me, but I can't see her in my mind anymore.*

Marta had no idea how to respond to that. Her people were so stoic that they almost never discussed their emotions. *I'm so sorry,* Marta replied, unable to think of anything else.

*I know you don't understand,* Kya replied. *And that's fine, it's not your nature. I can feel that about you. But my memories are all that remain of my family now. When I forget them, it'll be as if they never existed.*

*A person is more than their face,* Marta told her. *As long as you remember all the good things your mother did for you, she will live on. Remember her laughter, her kindness, and everything she taught you. And if you pass her lessons on to your offspring, she will live forever.*

*Marta?*

*Yes?*

*Do you believe in an afterlife?*

Marta had to think for a moment before answering. *My clan believes that our spirits live on, and that after death we spend eternity with our ancestors.*

*Your clan believes,* Kya repeated. *Does that mean you disagree?*

*I'd... like to believe it,* Marta replied. *But I believe it is unknowable. I can't bring myself to treat it as fact when I only have the word of others to go on.*

*What about faith?* Kya asked.

*I've had faith in many people who were later proven wrong,* Marta replied. *It is human to be wrong sometimes, and I don't hold it against them. But I don't accept everything they tell me as fact, either.*

*I hope my mother's spirit lives on,* Kya admitted.

*Then hold onto that hope if it gives you peace,* Marta replied. *I will even hope it with you.*

*Good night,* Kya thought to her.

*Sleep well,* Marta replied.

## *Ruination*

"See that carriage lying across the road up there?" Dobo asked. The horses slowed to a walk as he tugged on the reins. A woman stood next to the overturned carriage, waving for help.

Marta sat beside Dobo in the driver's seat of the wagon. "Should we help her?"

Dobo shook his head. "It's a ruse," he said. "An ambush. Once we stop, bandits will come out of the woods."

"So you're going to turn around?" Marta asked.

"Wouldn't help," Dobo said. "If these bandits are worth their salt, they've already got people behind us."

"Then we fight," Marta said.

"I like our odds with you here," Dobo said. "But they'll have archers in the woods. I think I have a better idea. Get in the wagon and put on your armor. Silli, plan thirty-seven."

The fairy flitted off of his shoulder and into the back, followed by Marta.

A few minutes later Dobo came to a stop in front of the forlorn-looking woman.

"Help!" the woman shouted. "We were attacked by bandits, and they overturned our carriage."

"Madam, you are in luck," Dobo said. "I happen to be transporting twenty soldiers to join the garrison at Riverton. They should have no trouble righting your carriage." Then he shouted over his shoulder, "Isn't that right, men?"

"Sir, yes sir!" came the reply. Silli used illusion magic to make her voice sound like twenty men.

The woman's eyes widened, and she glanced toward the woods. She made a subtle "stand down" gesture with her hands. "Thank you," she said weakly.

"Send out Marta!" Dobo ordered, and Marta hopped out of the back of the wagon in full battle gear.

The bandit woman stepped back as Marta grabbed the carriage and pulled it back onto its wheels.

"She's the runt of the litter, you see," Dobo explained. "The others are trying to bulk her up a bit, but we're afraid she's never going to measure up to the rest."

"Should be good now," Marta said, as she pushed the carriage to the side of the road.

"Then if you're good, we'll be on our way," Dobo said.

"Thanks again," the woman said, clearly looking disappointed.

"One moment," Marta said, eliciting a confused look from Dobo.

Marta crouched until she was eye-to-eye with the bandit woman. "I see your companions in the woods," she whispered. "I am raising an army to defeat the Bonegrinders. I know you live on the run, but they'll find you too, sooner or later. If you'd like a chance to fight back, there will be a meeting in Riverton later today."

The woman said nothing, but looked lost in thought. Marta climbed back into the wagon and they were on their way.

*So you and the man this ring belonged to… you were engaged?*

Yes, Marta replied. She now sat in the back of Dobo's cramped, prop-filled wagon. In retrospect, Marta was amazed the bandits had fallen for their ruse. There was no way twenty soldiers could have fit in such a vehicle.

They were still an hour away from Riverton. Silli lay on a pillow on the bench across from Marta, sound asleep. The fairy seemed to take a lot of naps, as if each human day was equal to five or six fairy days.

*But you didn't want to marry him?* Kya asked after a long pause.

*How do you know that?* Marta replied.

*It was the first thing you said to me,* Kya told her. *Before you knew I could hear you.*

*Oh,* Marta thought. *No, I didn't love him.*

*I understand,* Kya replied. *My town had arranged marriages as well. Mostly between rich families.*

*Were you betrothed?* Marta asked.

*No, we were poor,* Kya replied. *But there was always a chance one of the wealthy boys would set his sights on me.*

*Did you want that to happen?* Marta asked.

*No, I dreaded the possibility,* Kya replied.

*Why?* Marta asked.

But Kya evaded the question. *Was your fiancée a good man?*

*Yes,* Marta replied. *One of the greatest warriors in the village.*

*Do you think you would have grown to love him?*

*Maybe in a familial sort of way,* Marta thought. *But not as a blanket companion. I just don't… feel that way about men.*

*I see,* Kya replied. *But you would have married him anyway?*

*For the good of my clan,* Marta thought.

*That's… very noble of you,* Kya told her. *I don't know what I would have done. Probably run away from home. And now that my home is gone, I feel so selfish for having felt that way. If I'd married a rich boy, I could have pulled my entire family out of poverty. But it wasn't what I wanted and now they're all gone—*

*Hey,* Marta interrupted. *It wasn't your fault your town got raided.*

*I know, but—*

*But nothing,* Marta told her. *The Bonegrinders weren't summoned by selfish thoughts. And your thoughts weren't even selfish. Only one person can live your life – you. It's not selfish to have your own goals in life. It's not selfish to want more than the fates have in store for you. It's not—*

*Are you trying to convince me or yourself?* Kya asked.

Marta stopped for a moment. *I think we could both benefit from the advice,* she finally replied.

"Are you practicing for a play?" Silli asked, stretching.

Marta realized that she'd been mouthing some of the words as she'd thought them. *We'll talk more later,* she thought.

"It's the ring, isn't it?" Silli asked, stifling a yawn. "I can see its aura. You're talking to someone."

"My friend is a captive of the Bonegrinders," Marta said.

Silli tilted her head. "I think she's more than a friend," she said. "I saw passion in your eyes while you were talking to her."

"I've never even met her," Marta said.

"Oh," Silli said, not looking convinced. "Well, you should tell her that Bonegrinders are allergic to milk. Maybe she can poison them and escape." Then she stretched again and flitted out the front window to join Dobo in the driver's seat.

"Milk," Marta repeated softly, a plan forming in her mind.

The meeting at Riverton went better than expected. Not only did the town militia agree to sign Dobo's document, but a mysterious man showed up who claimed to represent a band of mercenaries. Of course, Dobo and Marta knew that by mercenaries, he meant bandits. But an extra sword was always welcome, and they were happy to collect his signature as well.

From there they rode on through three more villas, where they gathered more support. The more signatures that appeared on Dobo's parchment, the more comfortable the local guardsmen felt in adding their own.

They spent the night in Proudpath, a small village just south of a large forest. The townsfolk were in the process of rebuilding from some sort of disaster, but they nevertheless agreed to add their village to the list.

Unlike most towns they visited, the people of Proudpath didn't seem very surprised to see a fairy accompanying them. Most people didn't believe in fairies, and Dobo often played that up in his stage act. Sometimes he'd present her as one of his illusions, or he'd claim she was a doll he'd enchanted to work as his assistant. But in Proudpath, she didn't even turn any heads.

As Dobo and Marta prepared for bed, Silli told them she needed to run an errand, and she flew out the window with no further explanation. They didn't see her again for the rest of the night.

*I can't do that*, Kya lamented. *Where would I get the milk?*

*Don't the Bonegrinders eat cows?* Marta asked.

*They eat anything that bleeds*, Kya replied. *But it's not like they keep cows here in the camp. When they take down an animal, it's a feeding frenzy right then and there.*

*There goes that idea,* Marta thought. *I was hoping we could weaken them a little before the battle.*

*It sounds like it won't be necessary,* Kya replied. *You seem to be making good headway at raising an army.*

*If they actually show up,* Marta thought.

*They will,* Kya replied.

*What makes you say that?* Marta asked.

*Because people are basically good.*

Marta blinked. *You really believe that?*

Kya hesitated before answering. *I don't know,* she finally replied. *But I really hope so.*

Silli returned at sunrise. She now wore a thin gold necklace with a tiny red jewel. When Dobo asked about it, she simply replied, "My friend gave it to me," and evaded any further questions.

They left right after breakfast, on a path to the town of Fletcher's Dam. They reached it just in time for lunch. Marta was biting into a turkey leg when she heard Kya's voice.

*We're on the move,* Kya reported. *I think they plan to attack a town today.*

*Did you get a name?* Marta asked.

*I heard one of them say Proudpath,* Kya answered.

Marta stood up. "We need to go back," she said. "The Bonegrinders are on their way to Proudpath."

Dobo immediately stood and ran to the town hall. "Send couriers to the following towns," he said, presenting his list of signatures at the administration desk. "They must leave as quickly as possible. Tell them to send their armies to Proudpath."

That evening, soldiers from Riverton, Oaken Dawn, and a few other towns hid in the houses of Proudpath, waiting for an attack. Others climbed the many trees around the town, watching for the oncoming army. The sun went down and the moon rose high in the sky, but there was still no sign of the Bonegrinders.

*Any updates, Kya?* Marta asked as she sat on a bed, surrounded by several soldiers.

*We've been marching all day, but they have me blindfolded,* Kya replied. *I don't know when they're... wait. Something's happening. They're coming to a stop. Now they're tying me to a tree. I think they're getting ready to attack.*

"Spread the word," Marta told a soldier. "The attack is about to begin."

The soldier left the house to report to his commanding officer.

*Something is definitely about to start,* Kya said. *I hear them getting their weapons ready. The commander is issuing orders. I think he's... It's started! They're charging!*

"It's time," Marta said, standing up. She and the other soldiers drew their weapons and filed out of the house.

"Anybody see anything?" a soldier asked. Another soldier signaled one of the lookouts in the trees, but got a negative reply.

*Kya, we don't see anything,* Marta thought.

*I hear battle cries all around me!* Kya replied. *People are screaming! You don't hear any of it?*

Marta's shoulders slumped. *You're not in Proudpath,* she told her. Then she sought out the captains so she could inform them of her mistake.

After another awkward hour, a courier rode up on horseback. "Riverton's been destroyed!" he announced. "The Bonegrinders came out of nowhere. They killed everyone and burned the houses to the ground."

*And all their soldiers were here*, Marta thought, sinking to her knees.

*I'm so sorry*, Kya replied. *I didn't know…*

The captain from Riverton marched up to Marta and slapped her. She didn't retaliate. "You…" the captain stammered, but he couldn't think of a pejorative harsh enough for what she'd done. He took a deep breath and said, "Don't contact us again." Then he ordered his men to their horses to ride back to Riverton.

The other armies left soon after. Marta remained on her knees, eyes closed, her face a mask of pure anguish.

*I didn't mean to —* Kya began.

*Don't talk to me right now*, Marta interrupted, and removed the ring.


Marta woke up at daybreak, still lying in the middle of the street. Farmers carefully stepped around her as they went about their morning routines. The ring lay in the dirt a few inches away. She quickly picked it up and slipped it back on her finger.

*Kya?*

*Leave me alone*, Kya replied.

*I was wrong to blame you*, Marta thought. *It wasn't your fault, and you're hurting just as much as I am. Please forgive me.*

*I shouldn't, but I will*, Kya told her. *I don't really have a choice. You're the only one who can help me. The Bonegrinders are setting up camp. They're even digging a well. They only do that if they're planning to stay in one place for a while. And I think I might be able to tell you where we are.*

*Where?* Marta asked.

*We traveled for about four hours after leaving Riverton. Mostly south, I think. I recognize the Yanree Mountains to the east. It's not far from where I grew up. My parents took me camping in these woods once when I was a child. If I'm right, we're about a mile east of Farside Peak.*

Marta didn't know any of those places, but she knew who to ask. *Let me get with Dobo,* she told her.

She found him performing at the inn. Marta took a seat and waited for his act to be over. This crowd was more enthusiastic than the one at Reuben's Refuge, and he actually finished to a bit of applause.

Dobo spotted Marta and joined her at a table. A few minutes later, a server brought them some breakfast.

"You've got a bit of dirt on your face, just there," Dobo told her, pointing.

Marta dabbed at it with a napkin and discovered that the entire left side of her face was caked in mud. "About last night..." she began.

"You did what you thought was right," Dobo said. "Using the only information you had available. It's not your fault and you know it, but you're going to beat yourself up over it anyway." Silli darted down off of Dobo's shoulder, grabbed a grape off of his plate, and returned to her perch.

Marta nodded. "Thanks for understanding," she said. "Kya thinks she knows where the Bonegrinders are making camp."

"It's not going to be easy garnering that much support again," Dobo said.

"I know," Marta replied. "But I have to try. Not just because I want revenge, but to keep any other towns from ending up like Riverton."

"I'm not much of a fighter, but I'll help however I can,"

Dobo said.

"Contact the armies again," Marta said. "I don't expect them to help us, but if even one joins us, that's more than we had."

The server stopped by to check up on them. "Can I get you anything else?" she asked.

"Could I get a glass of milk?" Dobo asked, and the server nodded. Then she turned to Marta.

"I'm good, thanks," Marta said. Then a thought occurred to her, and she grabbed the server's arm just as she was turning away. "Hold on... milk. Is it possible to get a large amount? Perhaps a jug or two?"

# Retaliation

*I'm nervous*, Kya told Marta.

*Me too*, Marta replied. She was in the back of Dobo's wagon, on the way to the Bonegrinder camp. They'd taken turns driving the cart throughout the day, and now it was almost sunset. Heavy rain poured down on the wagon's roof.

They'd sent couriers to each of the towns listed on Dobo's agreement, and they'd sent even more to some towns they hadn't visited yet. The messages revealed the location of the Bonegrinder campsite and informed them that they would attack at dawn.

*How far away are you now?* Kya asked.

*Dobo thinks we'll get there in a couple of hours,* Marta replied. *Though the rain is slowing us down. We're going to stop about half an hour away from the camp, since we don't know how far out they'll have lookouts.*

*And then what?*

*I'm going to sneak in and poison their well. Then I'll return to the wagon and try to get a few hours of sleep. Hopefully that will give the other armies time to join us. If they're going to show up at all.*

*You're going to sneak in alone?* Kya asked. *Please be careful, the*

*Bonegrinders have very good night vision.*

*Silli's going to cast a spell on me that will make me invisible,* Marta told her. *She says she's never tried it on a human before, but she often casts it on objects for Dobo's act, so it should work just fine.*


Dobo sat in the front of the cart. A small canopy extended from the wagon to protect him from the rain, but he was still soaked. Silli sat on his shoulder, practicing her invisibility spell on a juggling ball.

"Do you think we can trust her?" Dobo asked quietly.

"Marta?" Silli asked, glancing behind them to make sure they weren't being overheard. "Why would she lie?"

"No, Kya," Dobo said. "She was already wrong about Proudpath. What if she's working for the Bonegrinders? For that matter, how do we know she isn't a Bonegrinder herself? She could be leading us into a trap."

"Big trap just to kill a couple of extra people," Silli said.

"Think about it," Dobo said. "We're hoping more armies come to our aid. The more that come, the more towns are left undefended, just like in Riverton."

Silli bit her lower lip. "Hope not. Marta likes her."

"Really?" Dobo asked. "What makes you say that?"

"I watch her when they talk," Silli replied. "Humans have tells. Like the way she smiles and plays with her hair."

Dobo exhaled slowly. "I hope I'm wrong, then."

"Don't worry," Silli said. "You usually are."

Dobo let out a loud burst of laughter, then playfully swiped at Silli as if she were an insect. She buzzed around his head a few times like an annoying fly. When they were done having a laugh, she sat back down on his shoulder.

A couple of hours after sunset, Dobo found a nice hiding spot behind a mossy boulder and brought the wagon to a stop. The moon was bright enough to see by, and the rain had eased into a mild drizzle. Marta gathered her sword and two milk jugs.

"Won't they notice that their water is white?" Dobo asked.

"Hopefully their well will have enough water in it to dilute the milk," Marta said. "And hopefully the diluted milk will still be potent enough to poison them."

"And hopefully they'll actually drink some of it before dawn," Dobo added.

"That's a lot of hopefully," Silli said.

Marta nodded. "Are you ready to turn me invisible?"

Silli frowned. "...Yes?"

"I believe in you, Sillivene," Marta said.

"That makes one of us," Silli muttered, taking Marta's hand. With her hands wrapped around Marta's index finger, Silli uttered a few arcane words.

Marta felt a tingling in her hand that spread up her arm and throughout her body. Her skin became transparent, followed shortly by her muscles and bones. Soon she couldn't see her arm at all. "Did it work?" she asked.

Dobo and Silli both frowned at her. "See for yourself," Dobo said, retrieving a hand mirror from his backpack.

Marta jumped back. Her skin was gone, but her hair and eyeballs seemed to float in midair. She looked down and noticed her armor was still visible as well.

"Sorry," Silli said. "I have to concentrate on each part I want to make invisible. I could make your hair invisible, but your skin would return."

"I could shave your head," Dobo suggested. "And you could leave your equipment here..."

"And face them naked?" Marta asked. "Not a chance. Besides, they'd still see the milk jugs floating in the air. Not to mention my eyes."

Silli let go of Marta's finger, and a few seconds later she became visible again.

"I have a thought," Dobo said, and disappeared into the back of the wagon. When he returned, he was carrying a large, thin blanket.

They draped it over Marta's head, and Silli touched it, repeating the magic words. The blanket became invisible, hiding everything beneath it. The underside of the blanket was still visible to Marta, but it was thin enough that she could see through the weave.

Dobo looked where Marta had been standing mere moments before. All he could see was a spot where the rain wasn't hitting the ground, and the mashed-down grass beneath Marta's feet. "The blanket's technically covering that part of the ground as well, shouldn't that also make the ground invisible?" Dobo wondered aloud. "Shouldn't I see a hole there or something?"

"Never overthink the magic," Silli replied, slipping under the blanket. Then, to Marta, she said, "I will have to go with you, though. I have to keep touching the blanket or the spell will wear off once you get too far away."

"You don't have to if you're afraid," Marta said. "I can always try to sneak in without the invisibility."

"Don't worry about me," Silli said. "If we get attacked, I can fly out of their reach. You can't. You need this."

"I'll stay here with the wagon if that's agreeable," Dobo said.

"Please do," Marta said. "I have enough deaths on my conscience. And keep the horses reined. When you see us again, there's a good chance we'll be fleeing."

And with that, they entered the forest.

*I don't see anything yet,* Marta thought.

*Look for a tall tree with white bark,* Kya replied. *I mean really tall, much higher than the other trees around it. The camp is half a mile north of that tree. Now that the rain's stopped, they've started a campfire.*

"Look for an unusually tall white tree and a campfire," Marta whispered, and Silli nodded.

There was a crunch from about fifty feet away, and Marta froze. She spotted a pale figure between two trees in the distance. She couldn't make out too many details, but the creature was tall, thin, and bone white. As she watched, it scaled one of the trees as easily as one might climb a set of stairs. Then it perched perfectly still on a branch, staring off into the distance.

Marta exhaled a breath she didn't realize she'd been holding. *We must be getting close,* she thought.

Just then another Bonegrinder ran by, passing within five feet of Marta and Silli. Though it was practically a blur, she was able to get a better view as it receded in the distance. The creature was at least seven feet tall, with a bald head and no visible ears. Its reedy physique and ghostly skin made it look like an animated skeleton. It wore minimal clothing – boots, a loincloth, and a sheathed sword.

"There's your tree," Silli said, pointing in the same direction the Bonegrinder had run. They carefully followed until they passed the tree, and soon they spotted a prick of light.

"And there's the campfire," Marta whispered. They continued their approach until they were just outside a clearing. They heard strange voices, a combination of gibbering chirps and low-pitched ululations, sounding like a wild boar's attempt to imitate the forest's usual bird songs and insect chitters. Despite being hidden by the blanket, Marta took a position behind a tree while she spied on the encampment.

Not a tent or bedroll was in sight. Some Bonegrinders slept splayed out in the dirt, while others talked near the campfire. Their faces were skull-like, with sunken-in eyes, slitted noses, and thin lips.

Marta saw a pair of Bonegrinders mating out in the open, while four onlookers watched and seemed to be placing bets. Handfuls of pine nuts changed hands as they pointed and cheered the couple on. Farther away, three humans huddled together, a metal chain leading from their manacles to a tree. Two of the captives were women, but neither matched the image of Kya that Marta had composed in her head.

*Are you chained with another woman and a man?* she thought.

*No, I'm with my master,* Kya replied.

*I don't see you yet,* Marta thought. *Where is the well?*

*North side of camp,* Kya told her. *Right at the edge of the clearing.*

Marta carefully circled the camp. She could see at least thirty Bonegrinders, but she knew more were in the forest. As she picked her way through the woods, she spotted a few more of the creatures sleeping in the trees. Finally she reached the well. It was just a large hole they'd dug in the ground, surrounded by stones and full of muddy water. At first she thought it was a latrine pit, but then one Bonegrinder loped over to the well, dipped in a large copper pitcher, and downed the water in a single gulp.

*Do they make you drink that stuff?* Marta thought.

*That's the least of my problems,* Kya replied.

Marta waited until the coast was clear, then walked up to the edge of the well. She slowly poured both milk jugs into the water. She watched for a moment, pleased to see how quickly the color diluted into the brown water. Then she backed off.

"Back to the wagon?" Silli whispered.

"In a minute," Marta said. She continued to circle the camp, searching for Kya. She passed a pile of sleeping Bonegrinders, another couple that were either mating or wrestling, and three who were feasting on the carcass of a bear cub.

Then she spotted what had to be their leader. He was the tallest Bonegrinder she'd seen so far, and he wore a silver helmet decorated with feathers. His face and body were lined with black tattoos. He sat on a rock, drinking red liquid from a silver chalice. When he set the cup down, a servant refilled it from a jug.

Marta was so busy studying the leader that she barely spared a glance at the servant. It wasn't until the Bonegrinder slapped the woman to the ground that Marta really looked at her. *Kya?* Marta thought, watching her crawl away. She could only go so far, as a chain led from her left ankle to her master's.

*Give me a minute*, Kya replied, wincing. She looked just as she'd described herself – young adult, below average height, brown hair, freckles. But she'd neglected to mention all the scars.

Her arms were covered in deep lines that looked like badly-healed defensive wounds. She had three large marks across her face, and what looked like a burn on her neck.

*I'm getting you out of there*, Marta thought.

*You can see me?* Kya replied. *Where are you?*

*Doesn't matter. I'm going to circle around behind your master and cut your chain. Be ready to run.*

*Wait,* Kya replied. She reached for a nearby wooden rod. Leaning on it for support, she brought herself upright again.

Marta realized with horror that Kya was missing her right leg below the knee.

*I'm not running anywhere,* Kya explained. Deftly bending on the one leg, she picked up the jug she'd dropped when her master had hit her. Then, with a well-practiced display of respect, she shrank from his view and moved to a position behind him. She would wait there until he needed her again.

*They did this to you?* Marta asked, her anger rising.

*A few weeks ago I tried to escape,* Kya replied. *They ate my leg so I wouldn't try it again. Didn't even cut it off first.*

*I'll kill every one of them,* Marta thought.

*I hope you get the chance,* Kya replied. *But now isn't the time. Stick to your plan. Sneak away and come back in the morning with an army.*

*I can't just leave you here,* Marta thought. *Not after seeing this.*

*Tonight's just like any other night,* Kya replied. *The only difference is that you've seen me.*

Just then there was a loud retching sound. Heads perked up all over the camp. A sickly Bonegrinder stumbled toward the leader, then fell on its knees, violently regurgitating the contents of its stomach.

The leader growled, then made a series of clicking sounds.

*What's he saying?* Marta asked.

*He wants to know what's going on,* Kya replied.

The sick Bonegrinder coughed a few times and tried to stand up. Then it fell back to the ground and lay still. A few seconds later, it exploded in a puff of white dust.

The leader pointed to several Bonegrinders and issued a series of commands. They turned and ran away quickly.

*He's putting the camp on high alert,* Kya reported. *They're going to check the well and send scouts to search the surrounding forest. You should get out of here now.*

*Not without you,* Marta replied.

*Just go,* Kya ordered. *You can't help me right now. Maybe tomorrow but you have to survive tonight first.*

"What's she saying?" Silli whispered.

"She wants us to flee," Marta replied.

"Shouldn't we?" Silli asked.

Bonegrinders moved all around them, and Marta had to back against a tree to avoid one of them. Awakened by the commotion, more Bonegrinders dropped down from the trees and joined the search.

"Maybe I can free her while they're distracted," Marta whispered.

"That's insane," Silli replied. "She's right, we have to get out of here. You can play hero tomorrow."

Marta was about to argue, but then she came to her senses. The thought of leaving Kya behind made her sick to her stomach, but it was the only way. "Come on, then," Marta whispered, and they began to sneak around the perimeter.

Then they heard an eerie cheer accompanied by a panicked neighing. Marta stopped and watched as one of the scouts returned, leading a pair of horses.

Marta recognized the horses right off.

"Dobo?" Silli whispered.

The scout gibbered to the leader.

*What's he saying?* Marta asked.

*They found a wagon to the south,* Kya translated. *And now my master is ordering them to tear the forest apart looking for its occupants.*

When the leader was done barking orders, he had Kya bring him his sword. Kya obliged and he took it from her roughly. Then he unshackled the manacle from his ankle and fastened it to an iron loop that protruded from a tree. No longer tethered to his slave, he joined the hunt.

The clearing was nearly empty. Marta counted four Bonegrinders who had stayed behind to guard the camp.

*I can take four,* Marta thought.

*Please don't risk it,* Kya replied.

But Marta wasn't listening. Her sword at the ready, she quietly sneaked into the clearing, stepping slowly and carefully until she stood directly behind one of the guards. She waited until the other three weren't looking in her direction, then she lifted the blanket and stabbed the Bonegrinder in the back. His sword clattered to the ground as he shrieked and turned to dust. The other three guards turned towards him, but Marta was already under the blanket again.

The remaining guards chattered wildly, searching for the attacker. Their attention was focused on the forest, as if thinking their companion had been felled by an arrow. Marta had no problem dispatching another one while it was distracted. Another guard turned at this, catching a glimpse of Marta's boot as the blanket fell back to the ground.

The Bonegrinder screeched and lunged at Marta, who just barely ducked out of the way in time. The blanket fell away as Marta rolled back to her feet. Both guards rushed at her, swinging their swords, and it was all she could do to block both attacks.

Silli flew up into the air, magically summoning a tiny bow to her hand. She fired several luminous arrows at the guards, but they found them more annoying than painful. One Bonegrinder leaped up into the air, reaching for the fairy, and she flitted away just in time.

Marta continued to thrust and parry one guard while the

other tried to swat Silli. Marta's opponent swiped his sword through the air, a swing that would have cut her in half at the waist if she hadn't dodged in time. She countered with a low sweep of her own, but he hopped over it deftly, cackling as if it were a game.

The other Bonegrinder kept slashing at the fairy, but she just flew ever higher to avoid his sword. In a move Silli didn't anticipate, the guard leaped at a tree, planted his feet against it, and launched himself high into the air. Silli tried to fly away but the monster was quicker, and he grabbed her with his free hand. His hand was nearly the size of Silli's entire body, and his fingers closed tightly around her. Only her head and one arm poked out above the creature's fingers.

"I'm sorry," Silli said, looking at Marta. Then she grasped the gem on her necklace and vanished in a puff of fairy dust.

Marta attempted an overhead swipe at her opponent, but he caught the blade in his hand. Black blood oozed from the wound, but he still gibbered gleefully. Then he kicked Marta in the stomach, sending her more than ten feet away. She landed on her back, unarmed and out of breath. The guard dropped Marta's sword, and both Bonegrinders took a few steps towards her.

*I can't win this*, Marta thought. She took another glance at Kya, her eyes filled with regret. Then she turned and fled into the forest.


*Fiddlesticks*, Dobo thought as he watched the Bonegrinders tear apart his wagon. He was well-hidden, and wasn't afraid he'd be found. Several of his magic tricks revolved around hiding in plain sight, so he knew how to fade into a background. He currently hid in a hole in the lee of a large rock, and he was covered in dirt and sod.

But he was worried about Marta and Silli. Something had awakened the Bonegrinder camp, and the creatures were all over the forest, searching for someone. It didn't take a genius to figure out Marta's plan had failed. But the fact that they were still looking gave Dobo hope. It meant at least one of them had escaped.

*They only have to survive until dawn*, Dobo thought. But that was at least five hours away, and with the frenzied way these creatures were searching, nowhere in the forest was safe.


Marta's feet pounded on the forest soil. She ducked tree limbs and brushed leafy vines out of her way as she barreled through the dense foliage, searching desperately for someplace to hide. She was way out of her element here. She might have stood a chance back on the mountain, where she knew the terrain and could use the snow and ice to her advantage. But here it was just trees and more trees. She could no longer tell which direction she was running, and she might have circled back to the camp for all she knew.

She didn't have time to turn her head to see if her pursuers were close, or even to glance at the moon so she could orient herself. For now, all she could do was run.

She burst through more brush and came out face-to-face with a trio of Bonegrinders. She looked left and right for a way out, but there was nowhere to run. She was unarmed, exhausted, and disoriented, but she closed her hands into fists and readied herself for a fight.

Then she felt a large hand grasp her shoulder from behind.

Dobo heard chattering cheers from deeper into the forest, and he knew that someone had been found. He shook his head sadly and climbed out of his hole. The Bonegrinders had moved on from Dobo's wagon, and the remaining scouts appeared to be heading back to the camp.

Carefully watching for more of the vile creatures, Dobo crept back to the remains of the wagon. They'd picked it pretty clean, but surely there was something left he could put to good use. With all the props and illusions he stored within, if nothing else, there had to be an item he could use to cause a distraction.

He dug through the wreckage and emerged with a metal rod. It appeared to be undamaged. He'd often used this device to add a little flair to his performances. The sparks it emitted were just for show, but with a little tinkering...

Dobo's ears perked up. Hearing footsteps from behind, he turned around and gasped.

The camp was alive with activity. All the Bonegrinders were now awake. They stood along the tree line, watching with great interest as two of their strongest warriors carried Marta back into the campsite. She struggled against their grip but couldn't break free. They brought her over to their leader and unceremoniously plopped her onto the ground.

The leader stared into Marta's eyes and made a bunch of clicks and whistles.

*This is the intruder who caused so much trouble?* Kya translated. She was still tethered to the tree, and she watched with tears in her eyes.

The leader smiled and laughed, slapping his knees and

gibbering.

*She will make a great meal for us all*, Kya reported. *Who wants a leg?* she added. Several Bonegrinders raised their hands and gestured at themselves.

Marta got to her feet and pointed at the leader. "I challenge you to a duel!" she shouted.

The leader looked confused, then turned to Kya and chirped. She chirped and clicked back, translating Marta's request into their tongue. The leader spat and gibbered angrily.

"He says you have nothing to offer them but a tasty meal," Kya said. "He wants to know why he should… sorry, this is harder to translate, but I think he's asking why he should even entertain an idea that came from his food."

"Tell him that if he doesn't fight me, everyone in his tribe will know he is a coward," Marta said.

The Bonegrinders stood back and whooped as Kya translated. The leader's eyes grew wide, and he spoke a gibbering reply.

"He says you're not worth the time it would take to stomp on you," Kya said.

But all around the circle, Bonegrinders chuckled and started placing bets. They passed handfuls of dark pine nuts back and forth. The leader noticed this and bristled.

*He knows that if he doesn't accept, one of the others will challenge him for leadership*, Kya told Marta telepathically.

The leader growled and rose to his feet, gibbering angrily.

"Fine, I will tenderize this meat before we eat it," Kya translated.

The leader took his sword in hand. The blade was as long as Kya was tall. Another Bonegrinder handed Marta her sword. A circle formed around the pair, giving them plenty of room.

"So how does this start?" Marta asked. "Does someone yell 'fight' or…"

The leader bellowed and charged at Marta, swinging his sword like a woodcutter chopping into an oak. She fell onto her back and rolled out of the way. The onlookers had to back up even further to avoid the tip of their leader's blade.

Marta scrambled to her feet and tried to get a thrust in, but her opponent had already turned around, and his blade fell in a downward arc. Marta raised her sword just in time to block the blow. The impact was so hard her teeth rattled.

The leader was incredibly fast, and he took swing after swing, giving Marta little time to recover. She parried every strike, but she had no time to counter with thrusts of her own. The leader gradually pushed her backward, and the crowd shuffled with them as they moved.

*He's all power and speed, but no finesse,* Kya advised. *Maybe you can trick him with some fancy maneuvers.*

*I don't have the time,* Marta replied, blocking another thrust.

*Then you have to find a way to use his strength to your advantage,* Kya thought.

*I'm open to ideas,* Marta replied, ducking.

The leader continued to drive her back until she tripped backward, falling over the rock her enemy had been using as a chair. She clambered backward as he brought his sword down. His blade hit the stone so hard that it cracked the seat in two. The leader's sword shook, and it took him a couple of seconds to recover.

Marta took advantage of the opportunity. She telegraphed a thrust to his left side, and the leader raised his sword to block. But she had fooled him with her feint, and swiped at his leg instead. She cleaved him just below the knee, and the limb went flying.

Kya smirked as she noticed the similarity between his

wound and her own. *Don't let up now*, she thought.

The leader howled and grabbed the stump of his leg with his free hand. He dropped to the ground and tried to block Marta's attacks with his sword. But Marta pressed her advantage, cutting off his sword hand at the wrist.

"Tell him I'll let him live if he sets you free," Marta said.

Kya looked skeptical but she repeated the offer. Her master replied quickly. "He's dead anyway," Kya said. "With this failure, someone new will assume command."

Several Bonegrinders stepped forward from the crowd and pulled the leader off the ground. While two held onto the leader's body, another put his neck in a chokehold, then snapped his neck. They dropped his body and it turned to dust before it hit the ground. Then several of the warriors began fighting among themselves. The rest of the onlookers backed off, waiting to see who won the brawl.

*They'll go at it for hours*, Kya told Marta. *This might be our only chance.*

Marta quietly backed her way toward Kya's tree. Then she began to inspect the bonds. The band around her ankle had been sealed with a weld, but Marta managed to pry it open with the tip of her sword. Then she sheathed her weapon and picked Kya up, one arm behind her back and the other under her thighs.

"Marta..." Kya said, pointing at the Bonegrinders.

Marta turned to look. While three or four of them continued to wrestle, the rest of the crowd stared at the two humans. A few began to step forward, their weapons drawn.

"Tell them we had a deal," Marta said, and Kya translated. A couple of the Bonegrinders gibbered and laughed.

"I think the deal turned to dust along with my master,"

Kya said.

"Hold on tight, I'm going to run," Marta said.

But then they heard more footsteps behind them. Marta turned in a complete circle and saw that she was surrounded. She looked down into Kya's eyes, the desperation plain on her face.

"I'm glad we got to meet in person," Kya said, smiling weakly. She leaned up toward Marta's face.

Marta met her halfway. Several Bonegrinders winced in disgust as their lips met.

An explosion sounded from beyond the tree line. Marta and Kya lifted their heads and saw bursts of fire in the distance. Cries of "For Riverton!" sounded all around the camp. The Bonegrinders raised their weapons and prepared for a fight.

A ball of light appeared in the sky, floating above the clearing. It looked like a miniature sun, and though it was only the size of an orange, the light it provided turned night into day. And with this light, Marta now saw a flock of birds approaching from the west.

Only they weren't birds. As her eyes adjusted, Marta realized they were fairies. Dozens, possibly hundreds of fairies. They swarmed into the clearing, firing their weapons at the Bonegrinders. Some were doll-sized like Silli, others were about as tall as Marta's index finger. Some had no wings, but rode flying insects instead. Some were armed with bows while others wielded magic wands. Marta thought she saw Silli among them, but it was hard to tell.

And then the soldiers arrived. They rode in on horseback, cutting down the outer ring of Bonegrinders as they fled the fairy swarm. Marta did a double take as she recognized Dobo riding behind one of the soldiers, firing explosive balls of light from a metal rod.

"Run!" Dobo shouted when he spotted Marta. "Get her to safety!"

Though she was reluctant to miss the battle, Marta carried Kya into the woods. When they felt they were at a safe distance, Marta set her friend down and sat down to rest. Occasionally more horses ran past them on the way to the camp. The riders wore sigils from several different towns. She even spotted the bandits that had almost robbed them.

They were nearly a mile away from the camp, but it was still as bright as daytime. It was hard to see much from this distance, especially with all the trees in the way, but they heard the occasional battle cry and saw little flashes of light from fairy spells and Dobo's wand.

Marta spotted a lone figure headed their way, pushing through the trees and leaping over large patches of undergrowth. She could tell it was a Bonegrinder just by the way it moved, sometimes springing off of trees to avoid the thick foliage. It was still half a mile away, but it was headed straight for them.

And then a dark shape flew overhead. A huge purple dragon dove out of the sky, snatched the Bonegrinder up in its mouth, and bit it in half. Riding on its back was an elegantly dressed woman, about half the size of a human, with iridescent fairy wings.

The dragon flew on to the Bonegrinder camp, where it dove into the fray before returning to the air with multiple creatures in its mouth.

"Glad that one's on our side," Kya remarked.

"I really should be in that fight," Marta replied.

"I think they can handle this one without you," Kya said. "Besides, I need you more." She grabbed Marta by the shoulder and pulled her into a kiss.

The two lay there in the grass, watching the battle from a distance until the actual sun rose.

"So why didn't you tell us you had a fairy army on standby?" Marta asked. The Riverton militia had gifted them a pair of horses. Marta and Kya sat on the back of one, while Dobo rode beside them on another. Silli sat in her usual spot on Dobo's shoulder.

"I wasn't sure they'd come," Silli said. "I don't make promises I can't keep."

"Well, the soldiers sure were glad they showed up," Dobo told her.

"So where are you headed?" Marta asked. "Off to resume your stage career?"

"I'm not sure," Dobo replied. "My whole life was in that wagon. Maybe I just need a clean break. This would be a great time to start over. What about you two?"

"I'll go wherever Marta goes," Kya said. She sat in front, leaning back against Marta's chest. Now she tilted her head to see how Marta would answer the question.

"I've spent all my life on that frozen mountaintop," Marta said. "And I've seen more wonders in the past few days than I ever saw up there. I'd like to see more of this world."

"I'd be happy to give you a tour," Dobo said. "Why, I've seen every town within a thousand miles. There's a festival soon in Sesta that you simply must see. Oh, and I know a carpenter over in Guildport who crafts the most exquisite wooden legs. I'm sure he'd have something to suit Kya. And there's an island winery in Sweetgrape that gives riverboat tours..."

The four friends rode on into the day. Their destination was uncertain, but their bond would last a lifetime.

*Interlude*

"She's a beauty, isn't she?" Dobo said as he put the finishing touches on the lettering.

"Sure is," Kya said, but it was clear she wasn't talking about the same thing. Marta walked by carrying a flask of wood polish, then disappeared behind the trees again. She'd been working on a project for several days, but she wouldn't let Kya see it until it was finished.

"You're not even looking!" Dobo said. He walked over and waved his hand in front of Kya's face, then pointed at the wagon.

"I was with you when you bought it," Kya said. She sat on a tree stump with an unread book about archery in her lap.

"But now she's painted!" Dobo exclaimed. "And I fixed that wobbly wheel! She's like a whole new wagon!"

"Uh, sure," Kya said. "It's really nice."

"Oh, you just don't appreciate fine art," Dobo grumbled.

Truth be told, the new wagon wasn't much to look at. Some of the boards were loose and it creaked a lot as it rolled. It was slightly smaller than the wagon the Bonegrinders had torn apart, though it seemed a little bigger inside simply because Dobo hadn't had the chance to fill it up with junk yet.

And now it had a nice new paint job, bright red and emblazoned with the words:

DOBO & FRIENDS

ADVENTURERS FOR HIRE

It had been a month since the fight with the Bonegrinders, and since then they'd taken on two jobs. Both had paid well, and they'd pooled a portion of the profits to get a new wagon. Riding everywhere on horseback was uncomfortable after a while, and besides, they needed a place to store their belongings.

Maybe they would find a nice town eventually, where they would settle down and make an honest living. But Marta still wanted to see the world and Dobo was thrilled to show it off.

Kya was content to go wherever they went, as she no longer had a family or a place to call home. Her new friends seemed like good people, and how often did one get to hang out with a fairy, anyway? Her relationship with Marta was... well... confusing. She kept getting mixed signals, and she wasn't sure if it was her fault. For someone she could speak to telepathically, it sure was hard to figure out what Marta was thinking.

*Are you still by the wagon?* came Marta's thoughts. *I want to show you something.*

*I was just thinking about you,* Kya replied. *Yes, I'm by the wagon. Dobo's showing off.*

*Be right there,* Marta told her.

A few minutes later, Marta showed up with a bundle in her arms. She sat down next to Kya and unrolled a piece of cloth, revealing a wooden leg. "I just finished carving it this morning," Marta said.

"It's beautiful!" Kya exclaimed.

Dobo frowned as he walked by. "It's good craftsmanship," he acknowledged.

It was a simple peg leg, with a wooden rod about a foot long, attached to a padded cup meant to be strapped to Kya's leg. The wood had been sanded smooth and polished to a shine.

"Thank you both," Marta said. "But you're being nice. I know it's not my best work. I was more concerned with getting it done quickly than making it look good. I just didn't want Kya to keep having to use that crutch."

"Well I love it," Kya said. She leaned over and gave Marta a hug. Marta hugged her back, though not for as long as Kya would have liked.

"We'll get you a better one later," Marta promised as she helped Kya strap the leg on.

Kya stood up and took a few experimental steps. Her balance was a little shaky at first, but she got the hang of it after a minute. "This is perfect," she said. "Let's go for a walk and break it in."

"Good idea," Marta said. "Bring your bow."


It was early autumn, and the fallen leaves crunched beneath their feet as they walked through the forest.

"This looks like a good spot," Marta said. "Have you been reading that book Dobo got you?"

"Not really," Kya admitted. "I keep getting distracted."

"Don't worry about it," Marta said. "Reading's great, but there's no substitute for hands-on practice."

Kya unslung her bow. "If there's any deer around here, we've probably already scared them off."

"Why, are you hungry?" Marta asked.

"Don't I need something to shoot?" Kya asked.

"There's two reasons to fire at a live animal," Marta said. "Either you need a meal, or you're about to be one. Now stand right there."

Marta looked around until she found a tree she liked, then used her dagger to carve an X on the side. Then she returned to Kya and helped her with her stance.

"Now concentrate," Marta said. "Don't release the arrow until you're sure it's going to hit. Archery is more about patience than anything else. Especially for a beginner."

Kya stared hard at the X. A gust of wind blew by, scattering leaves through the air. She had to refocus her eyes once it was calm again. She breathed slowly so as not to shake the bow. Then she let the arrow loose.

It went so wide they never even saw it land. Kya's face crumpled with disappointment.

"It'll take some practice," Marta said. "Nobody ever hits true on their first try. You'll get closer with every shot."

Kya nocked another arrow, patiently focused on her target, and fired. It missed as well, but this time it nearly brushed the tree. Her third and fourth arrows also went wide, but the fifth one hit the tree about a foot below the X.

"See? You're getting better already," Marta said, patting Kya on the back. Her touch sent tingles down Kya's spine.

"Thanks," Kya whispered, retrieving another arrow from her quiver. This time she fumbled with the string and the arrow flipped backwards, twirling through the air and landing somewhere behind her. "Oops," she said, blushing.

Marta chuckled. "You should have seen my first lessons," she said. "I was so embarrassed."

"How old were you?" Kya asked.

"Uh..." Marta hesitated. "Four."

"Four?" Kya asked.

"Almost five," Marta said. "It's dangerous up on the mountain."

"Four," Kya muttered, readying another arrow. Her next few attempts flew way off their mark, but her final arrow hit just above the center of the X.

"Good job," Marta said.

"That one was luck," Kya said. "If I fire enough arrows, of course one or two will hit eventually."

"You'll get better," Marta promised. "Now put down the bow while I gather up the arrows."

Two of the arrows had broken, and a few of them were nowhere to be found. But Marta managed to recover five arrows that were still in good condition. As she picked up the final arrow, she heard a low growl.

"Get... back... to... the... wagon," Marta said as she slowly unsheathed her dagger. She'd left her sword back at the camp.

Kya still didn't see anything. "What's wrong?" she asked. Marta stood twenty feet away, and the way she was moving, they were clearly in danger. Kya followed her gaze until she saw a slight movement. Her eyes had to refocus before she could make it out.

The tiger had brown and tan fur, in vertical stripes that perfectly matched the surrounding trees. There was no telling how long it had been watching them, but now it was positioned to pounce.

"Just go!" Marta hissed, and then the tiger leaped.

Kya reached for her quiver, but it was empty. Then she remembered the arrow she'd dropped behind her. She fumbled around until she found it, half-buried by the leaves.

One paw pressed against Marta's chest, while she fought off its attacks with the dagger. She tried to stab it in the neck but it was much stronger and kept knocking her hand aside.

Then another paw landed on her shoulder, limiting her reach. It opened its mouth and went for her face.

"Hey!" Kya shouted, and the tiger looked up for a moment. She held the bow ready to fire.

While the tiger was distracted, Marta thrust her dagger into its leg. The tiger recoiled in pain and bared its teeth. For just a moment it seemed to ponder its choice of targets, then it pounced toward Kya.

Time seemed to slow down as she let loose her arrow. It torpedoed through the air and hit the big cat right in the eye. And then the tiger landed on top of Kya, pinning her to the ground.

*I'm dead I'm dead I'm dead*, Kya thought, but the tiger wasn't moving. She struggled to work her way out from under its bulk, until Marta pulled the animal aside and helped her up off the ground.

"Are you okay?" Marta asked.

Kya brushed herself off. She had a few bruises, but nothing seemed to be broken. "I think so, what about you?" she asked.

"I'm not hurt," Marta replied, looking the tiger over. It lay on its side, unmoving, the arrow still protruding from its eye. "That was an incredible shot," Marta said.

"Luck," Kya replied. "I wasn't even aiming for its eye."

Marta tussled her hair. "You're a natural," she said.

Kya put her arm around her friend's waist and they walked back to camp.


Dobo and Silli were packing up the wagon as they returned. Dobo raised an eyebrow when he saw their condition. Both looked disheveled, with leaves in their ruffled hair and rips in their clothing. "Archery lessons?" he asked with a touch of skepticism.

"She's very good," Marta said, beaming at her student.

"I'll bet," Silli said with a snort. Dobo snickered and shook his head.

*What are they laughing about?* Marta asked telepathically.

Kya shrugged. *Must be an inside joke,* she replied.

They finished loading the wagon and got back on the road.

*Part 2: The Eyes of O'olos*

*The Ritual*

Two wolves fought under a full moon. They'd been friendly to each other mere moments before, but now they were fueled by blind rage. More wolves joined the fray, and soon the entire pack became a hurricane of gnashing teeth and bloody fur.

The fracas stopped as suddenly as it began. A hooded figure approached, pulling a small apple cart. The confused wolves scattered into the woods as the trespasser went by.

With only the moon to light their way, the figure lurched forward with purpose and confidence, unafraid of the dangers the woods might present. Unseen predators fled at their approach. Even the mosquitoes retreated from their menacing aura.

There was no path, but the figure knew the way. The route was burned into their mind, but even if their memory failed, the voice of Tyk-Shuul guided their actions. *Come to me*, the spirit beckoned. *Come and fulfill your destiny.*

The temple would have been difficult to recognize even in the daylight, as it was overgrown with black moss and twisting vines. The entrance was blocked by a thicket of barren trees. But as this person approached, the vines pulled the trees aside, opening up a path into the ancient structure.

The robed figure pulled the cart inside. Rotting torches burst to life as they entered. The walls were covered in murals depicting war, death, and slaughter. The marbled floors were cracked and uneven. The cart got stuck several times along the way.

Finally the figure approached the altar. Then they picked up the contents of the cart – a young boy, barely eight years old, tied up and gagged. The figure placed him on the altar, then drew a knife.

"Ryveen!" a voice called. A man fought his way into the temple. The vegetation was not nearly as accommodating to his presence, and he had to push his way through several clinging vines. Then he spotted the figure at the altar. "Ryveen! What are you doing with our son?"

The woman drew back her hood. She was only in her thirties, but her haggard face made her look twenty years older. She brushed her tangled black hair out of her eyes, then answered, "What must be done, love."

The man carefully traversed the irregular tiles until he stood a few feet from his wife. He dared not come any closer, as she held the knife above their son's chest. The child's eyes were wide open, and he screamed through his gag.

"Why?" the man asked. "He's our son!"

"I'm sorry, Lorn," Ryveen said. "Tyk-Shuul demands a sacrifice. But worry not, he will go on to a better world."

"Have you lost your senses?" Lorn shouted. "The evil of this place has corrupted your mind! Please, just give me that knife."

"I can't," Ryveen said. "I am but a puppet for the Night

Lord. My life is his to control."

"Ryveen," Lorn said. "It's Tobi. Look at him. Look how scared he is. Remember how much you love him. If you do this, you won't be able to live with yourself."

"Lorn," Ryveen said, her hands shaking. Then she gasped and set the knife down next to her son. "You did it. His influence is gone. Your love has set me free!"

They hugged. "It's you, it's really you," Lorn said. "I was so afraid. You've been acting so strange late—"

And then he felt the knife go into his back. He turned to see Tobi standing on the altar, cackling with glee. Ryveen helped her son pull Lorn onto the slab, where his blood would drain into the intricate grooves carved in the marble.

Ryveen lovingly drew lines of blood on Tobi's face, arcane patterns that would mark him as the vessel for Tyk-Shuul's rebirth.

"The ritual has begun," Ryveen said, as delightfully as if she was telling her son a bedtime story. "Nothing can stop it now."

## The Rescue

*I see him,* Kya reported telepathically. *Stand perfectly still. He's just on the other side of that corner.*

Marta did as she was told. She held her sword at the ready, just waiting for her target to come into view.

*Here he comes!* Kya thought. *Swing! Now!*

The fighter made a horizontal swipe right as the bandit came around the corner. Unfortunately the blade flew just above his head, nicking a few hairs before embedding itself in the wall.

*You might have mentioned he was shorter than me,* Marta thought as she pulled at the sword.

The bandit drew his knife and shouted for help. Marta heard doors open all across the compound.

*From now on, assume everyone's shorter than you,* Kya thought back. They'd hoped Marta would manage to take out the bandits one at a time until she reached the stockade. But now it looked like it was time for plan B.

From her position high up in the tree, Kya could see bandits emerging from every door in the compound. It was dark, Marta had that going for her, but she'd still have an army to face. Alone.

Kya removed a foot-long metal rod from her backpack. Holding it at arm's length, she aimed it at the sky. *What was the magic word again?* Kya thought.

*Little busy here,* Marta replied, swinging her sword at three bandits.

*Never mind, sorry, I remember,* Kya thought. Then she waved the wand and shouted, "Showtime!"

A dozen balls of fire burst from the wand. They didn't land, but rather hung in the sky, each emitting multicolored sparks and making loud popping noises. This caused much confusion in the camp, and several of the bandits fled into the surrounding forest.

Marta now faced four adversaries, but she liked her odds. They attempted to surround her but she wouldn't allow them to get into position. Only one of them had a sword, and it was nowhere near as long as hers, so they had to get close to her to be a threat. And every time one of them stepped forward, she drove them back.

One bandit threw a dagger at Marta's head, but she ducked it while sweeping low, and all four bandits had to jump back to avoid having their legs severed. One stumbled backward and fell on his back. Two more bandits came around the corner.

Seeing her friend in distress, Kya began to climb back down the tree. *Hold on, I'm on the way,* she thought. Her wooden leg slipped a bit against the bark, and she struggled to regain her grip.

*Stay where you are,* Marta replied. *I can handle this. I need your eyes up there. Do you see Dobo yet?*

A voice boomed throughout the compound. "Attention! The Lakehelm Militia has you surrounded. Drop your weapons and surrender now!"

*Ah, there he is,* Marta thought. Her opponents scattered.

Bandits fled all about the camp. The announcement hadn't come from any specific direction, but had resounded evenly throughout the compound. Brigands fled every which way, some running into each other in their haste.

An oblong ball of light flew over the crowd. Wherever it flew, walls of flame suddenly erupted between the buildings. Panicking bandits turned and trampled over each other as they looked for a safe route out of the compound. Had they been in less of a rush, they might have noticed that the flames gave off no heat.

Marta leaned against the wall, calmly watching the crowd rush by. When the coast was clear, she sauntered over to the stockade and sliced the heavy ropes that tied the gate shut. Three prisoners – a man, a woman, and a child – stared at her imposing figure in fear. The pyrotechnic display above reflected off her auburn hair, making her look like some sort of goddess.

"Mayor Gutteridge, I presume?" Marta asked.

"You're not with the bandits?" he replied. The mayor was in his underclothes, as he'd been kidnapped in the middle of the night along with his wife and daughter.

"Freelance mercenary," Marta said. "The council voted in your absence. Hiring me cost a lot less than paying the ransom. Honestly, I don't think they like you very much."

"Nonsense," the mayor replied. "They just know my preference for thrift. Now get us out of here."

Marta led them to the edge of the encampment, where Dobo's wagon waited for them. Marta helped the mayor's wife and daughter into the back. The mayor climbed up to the driver's bench to sit by Dobo.

"Dorian Beauregard the Third," Dobo introduced himself, offering his hand.

"Alistair Gutteridge," the mayor replied, shaking his

hand. "Please, time is of the essence. The bandits could return at any moment. We have to get my family to safety."

"Of course," Dobo said. "But I have to make sure everyone is accounted for." He searched the skies, then fired a flare from a small wand. A few seconds later, a ball of light approached and landed on Dobo's shoulder. As the light faded, the mayor could see that it was a woman, maybe a foot tall, with transparent dragonfly wings.

"You should have seen them run!" the fairy laughed. "They thought my flames were real. Didn't even think twice! I herded them right out of the camp."

"That's... a fairy?" the mayor asked. He reached out to touch her, but she flitted to Dobo's other shoulder.

"Meet Sillivene," Dobo said. "Unless you don't believe in fairies, in which case she's just another of my illusions."

Marta stood by the cart. "Have you seen Kya?" she asked. "She's not answering my thoughts."

"Oh dear," Dobo gasped. "We have to go find her."

"No!" the mayor insisted. "You have to get my family back to town."

"I will find Kya," Marta offered. "You get the mayor back to Lakehelm."

Dobo agreed, and the cart sped off into the night.


*Kya, where are you?* Marta thought. She held her hand against her forehead, in the hopes that it would amplify the magic of her ring somehow. There were only two things that would keep Kya from responding to Marta's thoughts. Either she was unconscious or she had removed the ring.

*Or she's dead,* Marta thought, then quickly pushed the thought away. That kind of thinking wasn't going to help anything. But with all the loss Marta had suffered in the last few months – her husband-to-be, her parents, her friends – it felt like she was just destined to be alone in the world.

"Kya!" Marta shouted. She ran for the tree Kya had been using to watch the bandits. The magical fireballs had fizzled out, but the full moon gave off enough light to see by.

She reached the tree, but Kya was nowhere to be seen. Marta searched the surrounding forest, then got down on one knee and looked through the grass. She was an expert tracker, though she had more experience with snow than with forests. Still, she found matted grass at the base of the tree, and an almost imperceptible trail where something had been dragged across the ground.

She followed it for about fifty feet, around trees and through dense foliage, until she found something that had been left behind.

"Oh no," Marta said, picking up the object. It was a wooden leg. Kya's leg.

Kya would never have left the leg behind on purpose. And she couldn't have made it very far without it, which meant someone had to have taken her. And being unable to run meant it would be that much harder for Kya to escape her captors.

But Marta wasn't going to give up. Stuffing the leg into her backpack, Marta scanned the landscape until she picked up the trail again. Then she ran off into the night.


Six miles from the abandoned bandit encampment, two men sat on a log by a campfire. A third figure, bound in tight ropes, lay limply on the ground nearby.

"Hey, Jynn. What do you think we can get for her?" one man asked, nodding his chin towards their prisoner.

"Don't think she's royalty or anything," Jynn said.

"Doesn't even have two legs. Seriously, Birk, what'd you even grab her for?"

"The camp was on fire, I had to grab something," Birk replied. "She fell out of a tree right in front of me."

"Doesn't mean we have to keep her," Jynn replied.

"Well, Zib said to hold onto her in case she's worth something," Birk said.

"You're an idiot, Birk," Jynn said. "Zib's not coming back. He's been talking about leaving for months, you know that. This is as good a reason as any."

Birk frowned. "Should I cut her loose then?"

"So she can tell the militia everything she saw?" Jynn said. "She's probably seen our faces. We'll be on wanted posters."

"Slit her throat then?" Birk asked, drawing his knife.

"Don't be too hasty," Jynn said, eyeing the woman up and down. "She's skinny and hobbled but a girl's a girl. There'll be plenty of time to kill her, you know… after."

A salacious grin began to spread across Birk's face, but then he jerked his head to the right. "Did you hear something?" He looked around nervously.

Jynn shook his head. Then something stepped out of the woods behind him. A glint of firelight flashed on steel, and Jynn's head went flying. It landed right in the center of the campfire.

Birk shrieked and ran. Marta hurled her sword at him, impaling him in the upper thigh. Then she drew her dagger and cut Kya's bonds.

"Kya, wake up, are you okay?" she asked, gently shaking the woman awake.

"Whu?" Kya asked, blinking. "Where are we?"

Marta hugged her. "I'm so glad I found you. Here, I brought your leg." She got the peg leg out of her backpack and helped Kya put it on.

"Thanks," Kya said.

"I was so worried," Marta said, tightening the straps. "I couldn't hear your thoughts."

Kya clenched and unclenched her fingers. "The ring's gone," she said, holding up her hands.

Birk was crawling away but Marta caught up to him easily. She pulled the sword out of his leg, then turned him over and planted her boot in his chest. With her sword inches from his face, she asked, "Where's the ring?"

"What ring?" Birk asked.

Marta nicked him on the cheek.

"I don't know what you're talking about!" Birk said. "But… Zib! Our partner Zib. He was here with us before. He took her backpack and weapons… I guess he would have taken any jewelry she was wearing."

"Where is this 'Zib' now?" Marta asked.

"I don't know!" Birk said. "He ran off. He's been thinking of leaving us for a while. Said he's found religion or something. He could be anywhere by now."

Kya stood and put her hand on Marta's shoulder. "Let it go, Marta. He doesn't know anything. It's just a ring."

Marta's shoulders slumped. She'd grown accustomed to the constant contact with her best friend. Without Kya's voice in her head, the world felt too quiet.

"You're right," Marta finally admitted. The two turned away from the campfire and headed back into the forest.


Birk watched them vanish into the night, delirious with pain but astounded at his good fortune. He'd been sure they were going to kill him. He still wasn't out of the woods, so to speak, but if he could find a way to bind his leg, he just might make it back to civilization alive.

*And then maybe I'll turn over a new leaf,* he thought. *Zib's right. This line of work is too dangerous.*

The group called themselves the Black Coast Enforcers, and they often presented themselves as champions of justice, an organization dedicated to closing the gap between the rich and the poor. But while that may have been true when the group was founded, today they were just a bunch of thugs. Where they once carefully chose their targets based on the victim's moral failings, now they just robbed whoever was richest and easiest, and their profits no longer went to help the poor.

*This is a sign,* Birk thought. *I should have died tonight, but I've been saved. Forgiven, maybe. If I survive the journey back to town, I will make up for my sins. I'll...*

Crunching leaves interrupted his thoughts. Birk sat up and scanned the forest. A woman entered the clearing, leading a small boy.

"Oh dear," the woman said, pulling back her hood. "Are you hurt?"

"Badly," Birk said. "I was... attacked. By bandits. Can you help me bind my leg?"

"Of course," the woman said. She bent down over the man to examine his wound.

*Another miracle,* Birk thought, laying back on the ground. *It really is a sign.*

"Tobi," the woman said, beckoning her son over.

The boy stood over Birk. He couldn't have been more than eight, but there was something in his eyes that made him seem older. Eons older.

"The forest has been bountiful tonight," the woman said. "Men everywhere. Wicked men, which makes their blood that much more delicious."

"May I, Mother?" Tobi asked, licking his lips.

"I don't know, you've already had three," the woman said in a jestful tone. When Tobi pouted, she laughed. "Of course you may, my son. Every drop makes Tyk-Shuul that much more powerful."

The boy's face took on a horrifying countenance. Birk couldn't comprehend what he was seeing. The child's eyes turned black and his jaw distended, revealing multiple rows of razor-sharp teeth and six or seven wormlike tongues.

Birk knew he had to get away, but he was frozen in fear. The boy stood over him, leering with those empty eyes, his jaw opening ever wider.

Then the face lurched forward, and there was nothing.

## *Lakehelm*

The mayor's office was full of antique books and exquisite furniture. Though Mayor Gutteridge couldn't have slept for more than four hours, he was perfectly groomed and looked sharp and alert.

"Thank you for coming," he said.

"Thank you for inviting us," Dobo said. He and Kya sat on black wooden chairs in front of the mayor's huge desk. Marta stood behind them, with Silli on her shoulder. Dobo had the most experience with official meetings, so he did most of the talking.

"You received your payment without incident?" the mayor asked.

"Paid in full, just as the council promised," Dobo said, patting the pouch attached to his belt.

Mayor Gutteridge nodded. "Are you... planning on staying in Lakehelm long?" he asked.

Dobo had seen this one before. Some towns just didn't trust strangers, regardless of their usefulness. "We'll be out of your hair soon," Dobo promised. "We're like nomads, just seeing the world, making what coin we can along the way."

The mayor frowned. "Would you be willing to stay long

enough for one more job?" he asked.

"We're always willing to help," Dobo said. "What can we do for you?"

"There have been a few murders," Mayor Gutteridge said. "Ritualistic killings. Bodies drained of blood. Strange bites, unlike that of any animal. Runes carved into their skin."

"Do you have any leads?" Kya asked.

"I believe – that is, our leading scholar believes that the markings refer to an ancient cult that worships Tyk-Shuul," the mayor said.

"Tyk-Shuul?" Marta asked. Her eyes widened a little.

"You've heard of him?" the mayor asked.

"No..." Marta said, but her expression said more.

"What is it?" Kya asked. She stood and put her hand on Marta's arm.

"I had a dream last night," Marta said. "I don't remember it. But I know I heard that name in my head."

"That can't be good," Dobo said. He turned to the mayor. "Does this 'Tyk-Shuul' ever possess people's minds?"

"I don't know," the mayor said. "But you should see my scholar immediately. Well, I say scholar, but they're more of a mystic. You will find them at the library. Ask for Esova."

"Esova, got it," Dobo said, standing up. The group left and headed for the library.

"Esova?" the librarian asked. "They'll be on the second floor, Study Room One. But they don't like to be disturbed."

"We're on a mission for the mayor," Dobo said.

"In that case, feel free to interrupt them," the librarian replied.

"You keep saying they and them," Marta said. "Is this Esova a man or a woman?"

"Possibly," the librarian said, shrugging. "But that's their business. If you want to work with them, I wouldn't bring it up."

Marta gave Dobo a confused look, and they started to walk away.

"Wait," the librarian said. "Is that a fairy?"

"Of course not," Dobo said. "There's no such thing. It's obviously a shapeshifted dragon." Then they headed for the stairs.

They were halfway up the stairs when Marta heard the voice. *Tyk-Shuul, I have done your bidding. Five souls devoured last night, just as you asked.*

"What is it?" Kya asked as Marta backed up against the banister.

"Shh!" Marta whispered.

The voice continued. *The cycle has begun, and it can't be stopped. You will arise on the next full moon. But now I seek your guidance. I fear for my safety, and for that of your vessel, my child. Please find us a safe haven to wait out the month. Otherwise, we may have to face the judgment of mortals. I put my life in your hands, you may do with it as you please. Your glory above all.*

Marta took a couple of breaths. "It was the ring," she whispered, holding up her hand. "That must be what I heard last night. Whoever wears it now, they were praying."

"Don't reply," Dobo said. "Let us meet with Esova and seek their advice."

Esova was nearly six feet tall and extremely thin. They wore a long purple robe with a hood. Their face was pale, with sunken eyes and smooth, androgynous features.

"And that was the entire prayer?" Esova asked. Their voice was even and serene, and gave no further clues as to the speaker's gender.

"As best as I can remember it," Marta said.

"Do you believe they can hear your thoughts right now?" Esova asked.

"I don't know," Marta said. "The ring... it's hard to explain... it usually only sends thoughts that are arranged like speech."

"Such as prayers," Esova said.

"Right," Marta said. "But sometimes I pick up Kya's emotions as well."

"Please give me the ring," Esova said, and Marta handed it over.

"Are you going to answer them?" Dobo asked.

"I don't know," Esova said, slipping it on. "But for now, I believe it would be best if I wore it. If they pray again, my knowledge of the Tyk-Shuul cult could allow me to pick up nuances you might miss. No offense."

"No, I understand," Marta said.

"Maybe you could reply and pretend to be Tyk-Shuul," Kya suggested. "Order them to break the ritual somehow."

Esova shook their head. "I believe they would see through that in an instant. If my understanding of the mythos is correct, Tyk-Shuul has already chosen a vessel. An additional voice would only arouse suspicion."

"So what can we do?" Marta asked. "Search the woods for the cultist?"

"No, that would accomplish nothing," Esova said. "Once the ritual has begun, it cannot be stopped."

"But if we kill the vessel..." Marta said.

Esova shook their head. "Tyk-Shuul would find another

vessel. No, I have a special task for you." The shelves behind them were a cluttered mess of books, scrolls, and rolled-up parchment. Esova retrieved a map and unrolled it across the table.

Marta studied the map. It depicted an island continent with the word Zyden written across it. She recognized a few of the towns marked on it, including Lakehelm, Proudpath, and the Frostmoor mountains where she'd grown up.

"Time is short, so I will be succinct," Esova said. "Several hundred years ago, Tyk-Shuul destroyed half the life on the continent of Zyden. He appeared as a titanic monster, able to wipe out entire cities with a sweep of his arm. He commanded an army of snakelike warriors who burned everything in their path. His spawn could infect the minds of their victims, causing them instant insanity. For this reason, the survivors were not believed. To this day, most people believe the devastation was caused by natural disasters instead of the Night Lord."

"So how did they stop him?" Kya asked.

"By summoning a god of their own," Esova replied. "O'olos the Deep Queen, she who slumbers below Center Lake."

"Makes sense," Silli said. "To kill an evil god, you need a good god."

"I wouldn't call O'olos good," Esova clarified. "It is closer to say that we have a common enemy. O'olos cares nothing for the surface realm, so her only goal will be the eradication of Tyk-Shuul. She won't attempt to conquer our world, but she won't make any special effort to protect it, either. I fear their battle will kill thousands, but tens of thousands will die if Tyk-Shuul isn't stopped."

"And… how do we summon O'olos?" Marta asked.

Esova opened a book to a passage that read:

*Seven gems gaze from the deep,*
*They ne'er tire, nor do they sleep.*
*To the sculpture you must pray,*
*Then the Night Lord she will slay.*
*But if you truly wish to live,*
*A noble sacrifice you'll give.*

"But what does it mean?" Marta asked.

Esova frowned. "Have you seen the statue by the lake?"

"The seven-eyed woman with the tentacles?" Kya asked.

"The very one," Esova replied. "A simple prayer ritual in front of the statue should awaken O'olos."

"I feel like there's a catch coming," Silli said.

"...or it would if the statue were whole," Esova continued.

"There it is," Silli said.

Esova scowled at the fairy. "The statue's eyes used to hold glittering jewels, but now they are merely empty sockets. Without those eyes, O'olos is unable to see your prayers."

"So let me guess," Dobo said. "The eyes aren't all sitting in a desk drawer somewhere."

"They were stolen over the centuries," Esova said. "By Tyk-Shuul cultists, and placed in their evil temples."

"...which are scattered across the continent," Silli guessed.

"...and guarded by vicious monsters," Dobo added.

"Did the mayor already tell you this?" Esova asked.

"No, we just know how these quests usually go," Silli said.

"I collect tales," Dobo explained. "There are always patterns to epic stories."

Marta and Kya looked at each other in confusion.

Esova dipped a pen in an inkwell and began circling cities on the map. "The temples were built near these settlements."

"How much time do we have?" Marta asked.

"Twenty-eight days," Esova said. "When the next moon is full, Tyk-Shuul will arise."

"Impossible," Marta said. "Twenty-eight days? It would take at least twice that."

"Let's not be hasty," Dobo said, examining the map. "Some of these towns are only a day's travel apart. And if we take this route..." He traced a line with his finger. "Let's see... we could travel north to Olivetree first... then up to Guildport, over to Sesta... hmmm... then to Proudpath, followed by... ah... Duskmorgue, then head back south to Sweetgrape and Cherrybrook... and finally back to Lakehelm. It almost makes a circle."

"That's still cutting it close," Kya said.

Dobo counted the days on his fingers. "Seven destinations, plus however long it takes us to return here," he thought out loud. "That gives us a little over three days per jewel. I've been to most of these towns. The farthest distance I see is still only four days apart, and there's enough one-day trips to make up for that. It's doable."

"Send two teams," Marta said. "For that matter, send seven teams. With less than a month, there's no reason to put this entire quest on us."

"There is one reason," Esova said. "These temples are impossible to find except for those with special sight."

"I don't have special sight," Marta said. She turned to Dobo. "Do you have special sight?" He shook his head.

"You," Esova said, pointing at the fairy.

"I don't have special sight either," Silli said.

"Oh, but you do," Esova said. "Fairies have a natural talent for detecting magic. These hidden temples emanate a preternatural aura that you will sense from a mile away."

"What am I looking for?" Silli asked, not looking convinced. "Will I see a shimmer, or smell something, or what?"

"When the time comes, you'll know," Esova replied. "Any further questions?"

Kya thought for a second. "Does the statue really need all seven eyes?" she asked. "Surely it can watch us pray with just one or two."

"I don't make the rules," Esova said. "Now make haste. You must return before the next full moon or no power in Zyden will save us."

"Let's get started," Marta said. The party thanked Esova and returned to the wagon.

As the sun went down, Esova locked up the library and returned to their home. As soon as they got inside, they knew they weren't alone. There was an offensive odor in the air, but not like sweat or manure. This scent was searing and otherworldly, conjuring images of the domain of demons.

"Show yourself," Esova said.

A boy emerged from the darkness. His hair was falling out, and his mouth was unusually wide. The child had three eyes in each socket, and none of them looked human. A woman appeared behind him. "Esova," the woman said.

"I don't know you," the scholar answered. "But I know what you are. I demand you leave my home at once."

"I'm Ryveen, and this is my boy, Tobi," the woman said. "Surely you can spare a moment of your time?"

"I have no time for the likes of you," Esova said.

"That's a nice ring," Ryveen said, staring at Esova's right hand. "My lackey gave me one just like it."

Esova took a few steps backward, until their back pressed against a cluttered shelf. "Take the ring if you want it," they said. "Just leave." They felt around behind them, searching for anything they could use as a weapon.

Ryveen stepped around her son and approached Esova. She reached forward and caressed the scholar's cheek. "I just want to know about your meeting earlier," Ryveen said. "My child tells me you've hired some mercenaries."

"Seven eyes, seven eyes," Tobi chanted. "The party's in for a big surprise." Then he giggled maniacally. It was the most unsettling sound Esova had ever heard.

"You can't stop them," Esova said. "You can't even catch up to them. They left town hours ago."

"Do you know the route they took?" Ryveen asked pleasantly.

"I'll die before I tell you," Esova spat.

"No, you'll die *while* you tell me," Ryveen replied. "But how long it takes is up to you."

Esova's hand came to rest on an urn. They flipped off the lid and grabbed a handful of the dust inside. "Enocha vee sinkhara kareech evane," they intoned.

Ryveen just cocked her head, an amused expression on her face. "Should that mean something to me?" she asked.

"I banish you!" Esova shouted, and tossed the red powder at the intruders.

The boy's clothes fell to the floor, now empty. Ryveen gasped. "Where did you send him?"

"To a place so far away he will never be found," Esova said. "A place so cold and cruel—"

That eerie giggling echoed through the house. Esova turned to look at their bedroom door. The door burst open, and the boy rushed forward on all fours. He had even more eyes now, and all of them glared with burning hatred.

He leaped at Esova and bit them on the forearm, severing their hand at the wrist. Esova collapsed to the floor while Tobi ripped into their flesh.

"Slow down, Tobi," Ryveen ordered. "Esova still has plenty to tell us."

*Olivetree*

"Do you sense anything yet?" Dobo asked.

Silli shook her head. As the wagon rode through the outskirts of Olivetree, the fairy concentrated as hard as she could. "Nothing," she said finally.

"Esova said the temples were hidden near these towns," Dobo said.

"But how near is near?" Silli asked. "They said that I'd sense them from a mile away. But what if the temple is more than a mile from Olivetree? And on which side of town do we start our search?"

"Olivetree's surrounded by forests," Dobo said. "We can't waste too much time exploring it. But if there's an evil in the forest, someone in town may have already sensed it, even if they didn't know they sensed it. Let's ask around."

They pulled the wagon into the town square, then boarded the horses at a stable. Olivetree was a sparse town, with wide streets and only a few buildings. They didn't see very many people milling about, even though it was midday.

"There's a sheriff's office," Kya said, pointing across the street.

"Good thinking," Dobo said, heading for the small building.

A sign on the office door stated that it was closed for lunch. Dobo peeked in the window and saw a tiny room with one desk and a single jail cell. "I suppose they don't get a lot of crime here," he said.

"Maybe the sheriff has lunch there," Marta suggested, indicating a nearby inn. It was the largest building they'd seen so far, but it was still smaller than most of the inns they'd seen on their journeys.

"Worth a try," Kya said, and the group went inside.

The inn only had six tables, and most of them were full. Dobo headed to the bar first and got the proprietor's attention.

"Excuse me, good sir," he said. "Is the sheriff about?"

The bartender grunted and nodded toward one of the tables. Two women sat together, talking and eating stew. Neither was dressed in any sort of uniform.

Dobo approached them. "Sorry to bother you," he said. "Is one of you the sheriff?"

"Have a seat," one woman said. She was in her mid-twenties, with dirty blond hair and a slight frame. She wore a plain green dress, with no badge or any other indications of her title.

Dobo and Kya pulled out seats and sat down. Marta remained standing, while Silli rested on Dobo's shoulder.

"Sheriff Mary-Anne Courtney," the blond woman said. "And this is my good friend, Eileen." The other woman, a redhead in a brown dress, nodded politely.

"Dorian Beauregard the Third," Dobo said. "And this is Kya, Marta, and Sillivene."

"You're really the sheriff?" Kya asked.

Mary-Anne nodded. "I know, I get that a lot," she said.

"But we don't get a lot of trouble here. And when we do, we form a posse of hunters to take care of it. 'Sheriff' is more of an administrative term than anything. They gave me the title because I file the paperwork."

"Just between us," Eileen added, "Most of the people in Olivetree can't even read. Is that a fairy?"

"No, the bugs just grow really big in these parts," Dobo replied. Silli stood up and slapped him on the earlobe. Then she bowed to the sheriff and sat back down.

"My mother used to tell me stories about fairies," Eileen said. "You must have come from very far away."

"We're on a quest," Dobo said. "And we could use your guidance. We're looking for an evil temple, somewhere in the forests around Olivetree."

"Well, I don't know about any temples," Mary-Anne said. "But some of the hunters have reported feelings of unease in certain parts of the forest. There's an area to the northeast where the animals seem unusually hostile. I'd ask at the hunting lodge. It's just west of here."

"Thank you, madam," Dobo said. He stood and bowed. "If you'll excuse us, we'll be on our way."


"We call it the Famine Grove," Jhik said. A shadow seemed to cross his face as he explained. "We don't go near it. You can't find much game there anyway, but the animals you do see... they act wrong."

A couple of the other hunters nodded in agreement. A tough-looking woman named Alyza added, "I was attacked by a colony of bush rabbits over there. The guys laughed at me for days."

"It's still funny," Jhik said with a chuckle.

"You wouldn't say that if you'd been there," Alyza said.

"They didn't attack out of fear, or to protect their warren. I could see the murder in their eyes. There was a loathing there, a focused stare of hatred that you'd only expect to see from a person."

"I'd say she imagined it, but I've been there," another hunter chimed in. "There's a mood in the air. It's like the trees themselves are angry."

"Can one of you take us there?" Marta asked.

A couple of the hunters took a step back. Jhik shook his head, and Alyza became fascinated by the dirt under her fingernails.

"We'll point you in the right direction," Jhik said. "You'll know when you're close."

As they were on their way out of the lodge, Alyza tapped Dobo on the shoulder and pointed at Sillivene. "Is that a fairy?" she asked.

"Oh dear, you see it too?" Dobo replied, his eyes growing wide. Then he led his party outside and they headed for the woods.


They'd been hiking for nearly an hour when they felt it. "There," Marta said, pointing to the northeast. It was still a few hours before sunset, but the spot she indicated looked unnaturally dark.

"Where is that shade coming from?" Kya asked. The canopy above that area looked no thicker than anywhere else in the forest.

Dobo looked at Sillivene. "Feel anything?" he asked.

"Let's get a little closer," the fairy answered, looking a bit nervous.

They walked on. A few minutes later, Silli shrieked.

"Silli?" Dobo asked.

"There's something over there," she said. "Don't you feel it?"

"Not yet," Marta said, looking at her friends for confirmation. Dobo and Kya shook their heads.

Silli darted towards Famine Grove and her friends followed. After a couple of minutes, they could all feel the malaise in the air. "I see what you mean," Kya said.

"I felt this way when my village burned down," Marta said. "I could feel the death in the air."

"There's a smell, too," Kya said. "Can you smell it? It's not like rotting, it's just…" she trailed off.

"It's like the odor of gloom itself," Dobo said.

"The temple has to be close," Marta said.

"I don't see any buildings," Kya replied.

"Maybe it's underground," Dobo suggested. "Look for any —"

Silli gasped. "There's sparkles in the air, do you see them?"

Everyone shook their heads. "Where?" Dobo asked.

"Right there!" Silli pointed, looking at her friends like they were crazy.

"What exactly are you seeing?" Marta asked.

"It's like… a house," Silli said, zipping back and forth. "No… a mausoleum. But just the outlines of one. Like if you drew it with green light."

"Can you lead us inside?" Dobo asked.

Silli shivered. "If we gotta," she said reluctantly.

There was a rustling in the trees. A deer came running at them out of nowhere, a buck with huge antlers. No one had time to draw their weapons, and they dove to the side as it charged by. Then it skidded to a stop and turned around, glaring at them.

One look at its eyes and Marta understood what Alyza

had been talking about. It wasn't just hatred, it was intent. There was an intelligence there, perhaps taking a backseat to madness, but intelligence nonetheless.

The deer hurtled forward again, but this time Marta was ready, and she stabbed it as it passed. It was a mortal wound, one that would have felled a tiger, but the buck didn't falter. Nor did it flee. Gushing blood from the massive wound on its side, it turned and charged once again.

Dobo and Kya hid behind trees, but Marta faced the buck head-on. Kya and Silli drew their bows, each getting in a solid hit as the deer dashed by. The arrows didn't even faze it. Dobo retrieved a wand from his backpack and aimed it at the deer.

Marta waited until the buck was only a few feet away, then stepped aside and slashed the animal's neck. It still refused to die, and it rammed her with its antlers, knocking her to the ground. Then the buck reared up on two legs, bringing them down on Marta's chest.

Two more arrows impaled the deer's flank, one much larger than the other. Dobo's wand fizzled as he attempted to launch a fireball. He patted one end a few times, but it still wouldn't go off.

Marta rolled aside and got to her feet. She'd dropped her sword, but she didn't have time to grab it again. The buck came at her, its head down, and Marta grabbed it by the antlers. They wrestled this way for several seconds, the buck pushing forward, and Marta standing her ground. More arrows pierced the animal's side.

The spurting blood became a trickle, and the buck began to tremble and sway. It gave one last weak push, then collapsed on its side.

"You okay?" Kya asked, looking Marta over for wounds.

"It knocked the breath out of me but I'll live," she replied, picking up her sword.

"Let's go inside before anything else spots us," Dobo said, examining his wand.

Silli led them to the front doors. Her friends still saw nothing but forest, and Silli had to guide Marta's hands to the door handles.

"Incredible," Marta said, feeling the handle. "I can feel it, but I can't see it. It's just like when you turned that blanket invisible."

"Whoever did this was much more powerful," Silli said.

The door was stuck, and Marta pulled with all her might. She finally got it open a few inches, and everyone gasped. To everyone but Silli, it was like the opening was appearing in the air itself. Marta put her fingers inside the doorway and pulled with both hands. It finally gave and opened wide.

It was dark inside the temple, and they could only see a few feet inside before it was completely black.

"We'll need some glowstones," Dobo said, reaching into his pocket. He retrieved a handful of rocks and held them in his palm.

Silli flitted over and touched each stone while muttering an incantation. Each stone glowed with yellow light. Dobo tossed one to Kya and another to Marta. Silli didn't need one, as she could make herself glow.

They stood at the entrance for a few more seconds. "If anyone wants to wait outside, I won't blame you," Marta said.

"We're in this together," Kya said. Dobo nodded in agreement.

"Besides," Silli added, "Who knows what other crazy animals are out here."

With Silli in the lead, the group entered the temple.

The hallway was dry and smelled like dust. Their glowstones illuminated dirty marble walls and plain tiled floors. After about twenty feet, the hallway abruptly ended in a steep set of stairs. They carefully descended until they were well below ground level. When they reached the bottom, another short hallway led to a huge open room.

It almost exactly matched what Marta had imagined when Esova first mentioned evil temples. Rows of uncomfortable-looking benches faced an altar carved to look like a pile of skulls. Anatomically correct stone carvings of well-endowed demons leered at them from the walls. One statue in particular caught Marta's eye. It stood with its back to the wall, approximately eight feet behind the altar, and it was the tallest statue in the room.

It had feet shaped like tree trunks, with snake-headed roots protruding in every direction. Its muscular legs had three knees, the middle of which was oriented in the opposite direction. If there were any doubts that the creature depicted was male, they were gone by the time Marta's eyes reached the statue's midsection, where its barbed, erect organ proudly pointed toward the ceiling. Its chest was covered in reptile scales, and its arms were triple-jointed in the same manner as its knees.

But none of that was as horrifying as its face. Its mouth was open wide, with three rows of jagged teeth. It had at least six tongues, all of which ended in open mouths of their own, sporting teeth like lampreys. But the top half of its head was nothing but eyes. Hundreds of eyes adorned its domelike head, covering every inch of its flesh with almost no space in between. The pattern of eyes reminded Marta of a honeycomb, as if a swarm of bees had been using the statue as its hive.

One hand held a dagger with a blade as long as Marta's

sword. The other hand was outstretched with its palm up and its fingers splayed, but from their angle they could only see the back of the hand. The hands were positioned as if the creature was about to stab itself in its palm.

The statue sparked a memory for Marta and gave her an uneasy feeling in her stomach. She was positive she'd seen it in one of her dreams, the night before she gave her ring to Esova.

"Is that Tyk-Shuul?" Kya asked.

"It has to be," Marta said.

"Looks like it's holding something," Silli said, flying higher. "I feel a pulse… something magic." The outstretched hand was about twenty feet above the floor, and Silli rose until she could see the palm.

"Be careful!" Dobo shouted.

"It's a jewel!" Silli shouted. "I think it's the eye of O'olos!" Without another thought, she dove into the palm to retrieve the jewel.

There was a low rumble before the fingers suddenly clamped shut around her.

"Silli!" Dobo shrieked.

Several seconds of terrifying silence went by.

"I've got to get up there," Marta said, digging some rope out of her backpack.

"Maybe I can blast the fingers apart," Dobo said, tinkering with his wand.

"What if it's a puzzle?" Kya proposed. "Maybe there's a lever or something in the room that opens the fingers."

"You look for a lever, I'm going up there," Marta said. She fastened her rope into a lasso, then looked for something to loop it around.

"Throw it around the statue's neck and climb up," Dobo suggested.

Marta shook her head. "The head's too large," she said.

"Then how about... er... that?" Dobo pointed to the rather prominent protrusion below the statue's waist.

"I'm not going near that," Marta said, swinging the rope in a circle. She let it fly, hooking the hilt of the dagger in the statue's other hand. Then she climbed until she was even with the closed fist. She had to swing back and forth a few times to reach the other hand, but soon she was standing on top of the fingers.

She put her ear to the stone. "Silli? Can you hear me?" she shouted between the fingers.

It might have been wishful thinking, but she thought she heard a muffled reply. She tried prying the fingers open, but they wouldn't budge.

"Any luck?" Dobo shouted up to her.

"I think she's alive!" Marta yelled back. "But I can't get the fingers open!"

"Try your sword!" Dobo suggested.

She unsheathed her sword and attempted to drive it between two of the fingers, but they were just too tight. "No good!" Marta shouted. "What about your wand?"

"Still working on it!" Dobo shouted.

Meanwhile, Kya searched the room for anything that might actually be a switch, a lever, or a button. Her eyes fell on one of the demon statues, particularly its tumescent appendage. *Surely not,* she thought.

Instead, headed to the altar. Reasoning that the switch would be used by the high priest in a way that would look like magic to their followers, she searched the base of the altar looking for anything that could be activated by someone's foot.

There weren't any obvious buttons, but she felt around the altar's bas-relief skulls until she came across one that felt loose. She pushed it in until she heard a click.

The fingers sprang open, flinging Marta off of the hand and releasing the fairy. The other hand moved as well, suddenly stabbing the open palm with its dagger. Silli zipped out of the way just in time, jewel in hand.

Marta reached out for anything that might stop her fall, and for one nauseating second, she found herself hanging from the statue's most intimate protrusion. Then she let go and dropped the rest of the way to the floor. Landing on her feet, she went to retrieve her sword, which had been flung in the opposite direction.

"Why does the statue even do that?" Kya asked, watching as the statue reset itself.

"You really don't know?" Dobo replied, and Kya shook her head. "I would imagine it was for human sacrifices," Dobo explained. "You tie someone up and put them in the palm, and depending on which button you press, it either stabs them or crushes them."

"That's just… awful," Kya said.

"You don't know the half of it," Dobo said. "But I'll spare you any further details. I'm just glad Silli wasn't their latest victim."

"Lucky I'm so small," Silli said as she flitted down to Dobo. She handed him the jewel to examine.

"You're sure that's it?" Kya asked.

"Pretty sure," Silli said. "I see a lot of stuff in this room that radiates magic. But it's all green magic. The jewel gives off a blue aura."

"So… green is evil and blue is good?" Kya asked.

"Not exactly but you're on the right track," Silli said. "It's hard to explain but magic has signature auras that capture the vibe of the person who cast the spell. This jewel is the only magical thing that came from outside this temple."

"In any event, it looks like it's the right size and shape to fit in that statue in Lakehelm," Dobo said.

"Good," Marta said, sheathing her sword as she approached. "Now let us be gone so I don't have to look at these statues any longer."

"Yeah, I think they're making Dobo jealous," Silli teased.

"Hey!" Dobo said, swatting at her. He chased her up the stairs and they returned to town.

*I'm too late,* Zib thought. *They've already got the first eye. The sheriff says they left town hours ago.*

*You shouldn't have dawdled,* Ryveen replied. Though she was many miles away, Zib could feel her anger radiate from the ring.

*They had a head start,* Zib explained. *I got here as fast as I could. I didn't even stop to eat. I haven't slept. My horse is exhausted.*

*So catch up to them,* Ryveen thought. *Find them, and use that staff I gave you.*

*I have a better idea,* Zib thought. *What's the third town on the list?*

*After Guildport is Sesta,* Ryveen replied.

*I'll ride ahead to Sesta,* Zib thought. *If I cut through the forest, I can get there while they're still busy in Guildport. Maybe I can set a trap or something.*

*Very well,* Ryveen thought. *But if you fail me again, don't bother to return.*

*Of course, my mistress,* Zib replied. *I will keep you informed.*

Ryveen removed the ring and watched her son play in the dirt. His hands became as rigid as shovels as he scooped soil out of the hole he'd dug. He had to stop when he reached the coffin.

"Just break through!" Ryveen shouted, and Tobi tore

through the pine box with his claws. When he climbed back out of the hole, he carried a skeletal arm in his mouth.

Ryveen beamed at her son with pride. He now had more than twenty eyes, and he was nearly a foot taller than he'd been the day before. *Kids grow up so fast these days,* she thought.

Tobi brought the arm to his mother, and she removed a bracelet from its wrist. "Thank you, Tobi," she said. "That's just what I needed."

## Guildport

Guildport lay halfway up Zyden's west coast. As the wagon pulled into town, their pace slowed to a crawl due to all the traffic. People milled about all around them, carrying boxes to and from the docks. Other wagons blocked the road, waiting to be loaded with supplies. After spending nearly twenty minutes at a standstill, Dobo gave up and pulled over in front of a livery.

"We'll just park here," he said. "We'll pay the fine if it's not allowed."

They led the horses to a boarding stable, then got a feel for the city.

"Same plan as last time?" Marta asked.

"Before we start asking around, I have a surprise for Kya," Dobo said.

"Really? For me?" Kya asked.

"Come with me," Dobo said, and he led his friends to a shop with a pair of wooden statues out front. One was shaped like a bear, and the other resembled an armored knight. Both were exceptionally well-crafted, sanded and painted until they almost looked alive. The sign above the door read "Carrell's Carvings."

More statues were displayed inside the store, some only half-finished. A man sat on a bench, touching up the paint on a life-size carving of a young girl, and for a moment it was hard to tell which one was the statue. The man stood as the door closed, and turned to greet his customers.

"Dorian!" the man said, rushing to shake Dobo's hand.

"Hez!" Dobo replied. "It's good to see you again. These are my friends, Marta and Kya. And of course you know Silli."

"Hezek Carrell," the proprietor said as he shook Marta's and Kya's hands.

"Good to meet you," Marta said.

Hezek eyed the hilt of the sword on Marta's belt. "That's an interesting hilt," he said. "May I see your sword?"

"Of course," Marta replied. She unsheathed the weapon and handed it over.

"Expert craftsmanship," Hezek said, turning it over and over in his hands. "Where did you get it?"

"It's been in my family for ten generations," Marta replied. "It's killed hundreds of dangerous beasts, as well as its share of invaders."

Hezek handed it back. "It's a beautiful piece," he said. "I know a swordsmith who would pay you a small fortune for this weapon."

"I would sooner part with my head than this sword," Marta told him. "When I touch it, I can almost feel a connection with my ancestors."

"I'm amazed it's in such good shape after all these years," Hezek remarked.

"It's been well-maintained," Marta replied. "The hilt has been replaced a few times, and the blade has been replaced at least once."

Dobo bit his lip. He had a philosophical question he wanted to ask, but he decided he'd save it for another time.

"Well, if you change your mind about selling it, you know where to find me," Hezek said.

Marta shot Dobo an expression that seemed to say, *Do we have time for this?*

Dobo picked up on her concern. "I'm afraid we're in a bit of a hurry," he said. "We're on an important mission. But as long as we're passing through…"

"I've got your order ready, just give me one minute," Hezek said. Then he disappeared through a door behind the front counter.

"What order?" Kya asked.

"You'll see," Dobo said, barely able to contain his excitement.

Hezek returned carrying a wooden leg. Kya's mouth dropped open when she saw the fine quality. She looked from the leg to Dobo. "When did you do this?" she asked.

"A couple of weeks ago," Dobo said. "I sent a courier to put in the order. I knew we'd pass through here eventually. It was just good fortune that our current quest brought us this way."

"Have a seat, madam," Hezek said. He slid an ornate wooden chair – no doubt another of his creations – in front of Kya, and she sat down. "Now I can't say it's a perfect match," Hezek explained. "But I followed the measurements Dobo sent me."

"How did you get my measurements?" Kya asked.

"Remember that time you needed a new boot?" Dobo said. "I paid attention while you were being fitted."

"That's so sweet," Kya said. "And maybe a little bit creepy, but mostly sweet."

With Kya's permission, Hezek rolled up her pants leg, then unfastened the straps on her peg leg and set it aside. He made small talk the entire time.

"How did you lose your leg?" Hezek asked.

"It was eaten by a Bonegrinder," Kya replied.

"Ah, yes, that does happen," Hezek replied. Then he picked up the new leg and held it to her knee. It was shaped exactly like a human shin and foot, right down to the individual toes. It had a hinged ankle, giving it a greater range of movement.

"Watch this, you'll love this feature," Hezek said. There was a quick flash of light, and the leg magically attached itself to Kya's knee.

"Wow," Kya said, bending her knee a few times experimentally. "It's enchanted?"

"No annoying straps or braces," Hezek said proudly. "Guaranteed never to come off accidentally."

"I paid extra for that," Dobo said. "The new wagon didn't cost nearly as much as I said it did."

"I thought the wagon seemed overpriced," Kya replied. She stood up and took a few steps. It took a second to get used to it, but it was already much more comfortable than her old leg had been. She walked over to Dobo and gave him a big hug. "Thank you," she said.

Hezek bent down and picked up the old leg. "Would you like me to dispose of this one for you?"

Kya looked at the old leg and suddenly felt a little guilty. Then she turned toward Marta. "You carved it for me," Kya said. She studied her friend's eyes for any hint that her feelings might be hurt.

Marta smiled and hugged her friend. "Your heart is too pure," she said. "I knew the leg was temporary when I carved it. I'm so happy you've found one that suits you better."

"Thank you," Kya said, though something about the hug bothered her. Marta's embraces were starting to feel too familial, like she was hugging a sibling. Then they separated and Kya turned to the proprietor. "I'd like to hang onto it for a while," she decided. "Just in case I need a spare."

"Never hurts to be prepared," Hezek said with a smile. He handed her the peg leg and she stuffed it into her backpack.

"See anything yet?" Kya asked desperately as Silli led them through the swamp.

"You seem anxious," Silli replied. "Are you not having any fun?"

"Says the only one who isn't knee-deep in muck," Dobo grumbled.

"Want to sit on my shoulders?" Marta asked.

"I have more dignity than that," Dobo said.

"But I might take you up on it in a minute," Kya said. She'd bought a new pair of boots after leaving Carrell's Carvings. The old wooden leg wouldn't fit in a boot, so she only owned left boots. But her new leg was designed to work with footwear, so she'd had to do a little impromptu shopping.

And now her new boots were caked in mud. Worse, some of the sludge had seeped over the top of her boots and was now oozing down her pants leg. *I hope this new leg doesn't stain,* she thought.

"Hold on, I think I feel something," Silli said, slowly turning in a circle. The townsfolk had pointed them towards the swamp, but that was as specific as they'd been. The people of Guildport were merchants, not hunters, and none of them had spent much time exploring the marshlands.

"I think I feel it too," Marta said. Just like the forest near Olivetree, there was now a vibration in the air, an almost tangible feeling of violent desolation. "It's like the swamp itself is in a bad mood," she added.

"I think I'm going to throw up," Kya said. Marta patted her on the shoulder.

"There it is," Silli said, pointing towards a grove of trees. The others couldn't see it, but there was a faint green shimmer in the distance.

They were halfway there when the alligator burst through the muck. They'd spotted a few during their trudge through the swamp, but this one was monstrous. It was easily twenty feet long, with barbed teeth and glowing red eyes. It opened its mouth wide and tried to clamp it shut on Kya.

But Marta would have none of it. She pushed her friend out of the way and stabbed the creature in the roof of the mouth. The gator roared, a high-pitched growl that one wouldn't expect to hear from a gator. Then it belched a cloud of rancid green smoke.

Marta felt sick to her stomach, and Kya immediately lost her lunch. The stench was like a boghouse full of rotten eggs, and it was so overpowering that Marta saw stars. She certainly didn't see the giant jaws preparing to swallow her whole. Marta staggered towards the gator's open mouth, oblivious to the danger.

Dobo held his nose and lifted his wand. He launched a ball of fire that hit the monster right in the back of the throat, igniting the gases and filling the monster's mouth with flame. Marta and Kya were knocked backward by the wave of heat that followed, and both landed face-first in the shallow swamp water.

The gator made a weird gurgling sound and swam away.

"Hey, I got my wand working," Dobo said, right before he yelped and dropped it in the muck. The metal rod had overheated and burned his fingers, and now he thrust his hand into the mud to cool it off.

"Do I still have eyebrows?" Kya asked as she got back to her feet.

Marta groaned as she rose from the mud. "We're going to have a talk about that wand," she said.

Silli flitted from Marta to Kya, checking them for burns. She mixed a bit of fairy dust with some mud and said a few magic words. Then she applied the mixture to their blistering skin.

"How'd that thing get so big?" Kya asked, wiping the vomit from her chin. "And did you see its eyes?"

"The temple corrupts the nearby wildlife," Dobo said. "Taints their minds, like that stag in Olivetree. I suppose over time, it causes physical transformations as well."

"Let's just get this over with," Marta said, looking weary. "Silli, point me at that temple."

"At least the statues don't have bippity-boos this time," Silli said, eyeing the stone soldiers. The carvings looked like armored knights, but they had reptilian heads.

"Do such creatures actually exist?" Marta asked, tapping one of the statues with her sword.

"I've heard stories about them," Dobo said. "Snake-headed soldiers who serve evil gods. Some prophecies say that's how the world will end."

"Prophecies are worthless," Marta said. "Either you can change the future or you can't. If you can't, there's no point in knowing it beforehand. If you can, then the prophecy wasn't true in the first place."

"What if the prophecy comes from the gods themselves?" Dobo asked. "Don't think of it as a prediction of the future, think of it as a promise the god is making. A statement of intention. And if it's a dark god with a dark purpose, surely it's useful to know the end is coming so we can stop it?"

"I don't know if I even believe in gods," Marta said. "Some creatures are just more powerful than others. I can stomp on an ant, but that doesn't mean I'm a god. Tyk-Shuul and O'olos are more powerful than us, but that doesn't make them gods."

"That sounds like a semantic argument," Dobo said. "How would you define a god, then, if not by their power?"

Marta had to think a moment. "I don't know," she conceded. "Actual omnipotence would be a good start. If Tyk-Shuul were truly a god, we wouldn't be on a quest to stop him. There would be no point."

"Hey guys, I think I found something," Kya said. She turned a dial that was recessed in the wall, and a stone door slid open.

They gasped when they saw the worship room. It was laid out similar to the one in Olivetree, with several rows of pews facing an altar. But this time the benches were occupied.

Dozens of statues – snake-headed soldiers, like the ones in the hallway – sat in the pews. They rested with their hands in their laps, their heads bowed in prayer. More statues lined the walls, most of them holding books and staffs.

"Anybody else get the feeling these could come to life at any moment?" Silli asked.

"I'm more worried about that," Kya said, pointing behind the altar.

The jaws of a giant stone alligator opened wide, as if daring anyone to enter. The altar sat on the gator's tongue, and as they stepped closer they could see a small jewel resting on the stone slab.

"Soooo..." Silli said. "Those jaws are most definitely going to snap shut when someone grabs the eye, right?"

"If the statues don't kill us first," Marta said. She kept her sword raised, ready to attack anything that threatened her friends.

"What about your telekinesis?" Dobo suggested. Silli often made small objects float as part of their stage act.

The fairy nodded, then flew until she was just outside the jaws. The altar was still about ten feet away. Silli reached out her hand and tried to call the jewel to her.

"It's no good," Silli said. "I don't think the eyes can be affected by magic."

"A lot of magic items are enchanted that way," Dobo explained. "As I understand it, a significantly magical object runs the risk of shattering due to the power it contains. They have to make the item immune to its own power so it doesn't break. This also means it can't be harmed by other spells. Sometimes they even have an aura that disrupts—"

"Sure," Kya said absently. In her mind, she was going through all the items in her backpack, trying to rig a device that could snag the jewel from the altar. She set her pack on the ground and began pulling out objects. She retrieved some rope, her old peg leg, a handful of coins, a change of clothes, a few arrows, and a metal pry bar.

Marta leaned over the lower jaw, reaching with her sword. She stretched as far as she could, but she was still a few feet shy.

Dobo grabbed her around the waist and pulled her back. "Are you insane?" he said. "If those jaws shut while you're halfway in there..."

"I want to try something," Kya said. She held a pry bar tied to a rope. Standing at the edge of the jaw, she threw the pry bar at the altar. It bounced off and she had to pull it back.

"Let me try," Marta said. But her attempts were no more successful.

"Ladies," Dobo said. "I'm a master magician. I can throw a pry bar."

"What does being a magician have to do with anything?" Kya asked.

"Trust me," Dobo said, taking the pry bar from Marta's hands. Then he gave Silli a wink.

He tossed the pry bar, and Silli used her telekinesis to steady it in the air. When it landed on the altar, the fairy manipulated the metal rod until it was lined up with the jewel. Then Dobo pulled the rope.

The pry bar passed right through the jewel without touching it.

"How?" Kya asked.

Marta moved around the jaw, trying to see the jewel from another angle. When she stood directly in front of the gator's head, the jewel vanished.

"Where'd it go?" Silli asked. She flitted back and forth until she was behind Marta. "It's on your back!" she shouted.

Marta turned around and looked up. On the opposite side of the room, above the door from which they'd entered, there was a mirror mounted on the wall. Then she turned around again. "There," she said, pointing.

The true jewel was embedded in the wall, about twelve feet above the alligator's head. "I'll get it," Silli said, and flew up to the jewel.

"Wait!" Dobo said. "Don't forget last time."

"I don't see any fingers, do you?" Silli asked. She grabbed the jewel and tugged at it. "It's really stuck," she said, pulling harder. She thought about going back for the pry bar, but then she gave it one last tug. Suddenly the jewel popped out of the wall. "I've got it!" she announced.

But her victory was short-lived. Brown water gushed from the hole where the jewel had been, and the door began to slide closed.

"Everybody out!" Marta shouted, running for the door. She stopped by the doorway to make sure her friends got through first.

Kya grabbed her things off the floor and followed Marta. Silli zoomed past her as she slid beneath the closing door.

Dobo slipped on the slick floor and fell on his face. He stumbled while trying to get back to his feet. Marta ran back for him and picked him up off the floor.

The door was more than halfway closed. *They're not going to make it*, Kya thought. She looked through the items in her hands and dropped everything but the peg leg. She jammed it under the door to keep it open for a few more seconds. Dobo came sliding through, pushed by Marta. Then Marta began crawling through, but the wooden leg snapped when she was halfway. Kya and Dobo grabbed her hands and pulled, and the door slammed shut just as her feet cleared the doorway.

"The pry bar might have worked better," Dobo said as he helped Marta to her feet.

"I had to think fast," Kya said, stuffing her things back into her backpack.

"You did good, kid," Marta said, pulling Kya into a hug.

Again, it felt like a hug from a family member, and the "kid" moniker didn't help things. *She's only a couple of years older than me*, Kya thought.

"Let's get out of this accursed swamp," Dobo said, and they went back to town.

*Are you in place?* Ryveen asked.

*All set,* Zib replied. *I'll be waiting for them near the temple in Sesta.*

*Good,* Ryveen thought. *Let me know when the deed is done.*

Ryveen slipped off the ring and put it in her pocket. What she was about to do would require concentration, and she didn't want to be distracted by Zib's errant thoughts. Though she'd only possessed the ring for about a week, she'd already empowered the magic to a level the original enchanter hadn't intended. She could even hear thoughts Zib had no intention of sending. If Zib ever planned to betray her, she'd know instantly.

But this unlocked power had proven to be both a blessing and a curse. The previous night she'd made the mistake of wearing the ring to bed. She'd woken up in the middle of the night to thoughts she now wished she could forget.

*The next time you pleasure yourself, take off the ring first,* she'd admonished him. Then she'd added, *And think about someone besides me.*

But now that she'd had time to think about it, she wondered if perhaps his attraction to her might be beneficial. After all, there were few motivators as powerful as lust. If she were to lead him on, he'd be that much more loyal a servant.

She shook the thought away. A week had passed since the first ritual, and a half-moon hung in the sky. Her son grew more monstrous by the day. Silly human feelings like love and lust didn't matter anymore. Zib's loyalty didn't matter either. The transformation would take place regardless of whether Zib took care of those interlopers.

Still, she'd be a fool not to prepare for the worst.

Bracelet in hand, Ryveen once again entered the hidden

temple in the forests of Lakehelm. She'd left her son with a babysitter. Well, someone's babysitter. Tobi had probably eaten the poor woman by now, along with the miserable infant she'd been watching. But Ryveen knew her son. He'd curl up and take a nap after his meal, and he'd stay safe until her return. Even if the parents came home early, Tobi could take care of himself. The last thing Ryveen wanted was to become one of those overprotective mothers who never left their children alone.

Past the altar where the bones of her husband still lay, Ryveen found a secret door. She pressed the bracelet into an indentation on the wall, and a stone slab slid aside.

She carefully climbed down some stairs, using a glowstone for light. When she reached the bottom, a quartet of snake-headed statues flanked the door to the next room.

*Sleeth soldiers*, Ryveen thought. *The minions of Tyk-Shuul.*

She approached one of the statues and held her wrist against its chest. The bracelet glowed for a moment, and some of that glow seemed to get absorbed into the statue. Bits of stone flaked off of the figure until it was a living, breathing Sleeth warrior. And yet it still stood rigid, not because it couldn't move, but because it awaited Ryveen's orders.

She revived the other three statues before she issued her commands. "You will travel to Cherrybrook and wake the Nethursine," she ordered. "Then wait near the temple for the heroes to arrive. Kill them."

*They shouldn't even get that far,* she thought. *But if they do, they'll make it no further.*

With the guardians now gone, Ryveen entered the final door. Torches sprang to life as she stepped inside, illuminating a room as large as a jousting field. Two hundred more statues stood at attention.

*Rest well, my soldiers,* Ryveen thought as studied her future army. *When the moon is full again, Tyk-Shuul will lead you to victory.*

## Sesta

Exploring the town of Sesta was like attending one giant party. Buildings were decorated with streamers. People danced and drank in the streets, while musicians on street corners drowned each other out with their lively tunes.

"Must be their fall festival," Dobo said as they parked the wagon and boarded the horses.

"Where to?" Marta asked, getting out of the back of the wagon.

"Find someone sober?" Kya suggested. "Perhaps a government office or something?"

They walked by a wide brick building. A constant line of people entered and exited the front door. Most of them wore masks. The sign outside read:

CONVENTION HALL

Underneath that, a smaller sign read:

TONIGHT

HARVESTFEST ORGY

EVERYONE WELCOME

"What's an orgy?" Marta asked.

Kya and Silli burst into fits of giggles.

"It's... like a party," Dobo said.

"Maybe we should go," Marta said. "Make some contacts. Someone might know more about the temple we're to face."

"I'm afraid we're a bit overdressed for that kind of party," Dobo replied.

Marta looked down at her armor. "What's wrong with how I'm dressed?"

But by this point, everyone was laughing too hard to answer. Marta's brow furrowed as she watched her friends, wondering what she'd missed.

"I promise I'll tell you later," Kya said.

"Let's just look for a business with a less... lively crowd," Dobo added, and they walked on.


*They're coming*, Zib thought as he hid in the tall grass. He didn't know the exact location of the temple any more than Dobo's party did, but he could certainly feel the evil in the air. All he knew for sure was that they would have to cross the Windsong River to reach the temple, and the easiest way across was the Windsong River Bridge.

And boy were they in for a surprise when they got halfway across.


"This looks like the bridge they told us about," Dobo said. The old covered bridge had peeling red paint and a roof that looked like it had survived decades of bad weather. The sides were constructed of latticed wood planks, spaced so that you could watch the river from the bridge without the risk of falling in.

It was at least a fifty-foot drop to the intense rapids raging below.

"The librarian I talked to thinks the bridge is haunted," Kya said. "She said everyone who crosses it is stricken with dread."

"Then the temple must be right on the other side," Marta said. "See anything yet?"

Silli stared across the ravine, looking for a green shimmer. "Not yet," she reported. On the other side of the bridge, a grassy plain continued for about three hundred feet before the trail disappeared into the trees.

Marta went first, testing the wood to make sure it wasn't going to collapse beneath her feet. "It's old, but it's still sturdy," she said after giving it a couple of good stomps.

They were a third of the way across when they started to feel it. "Yep, there's a temple around here somewhere," Kya said. Then she let out a loud belch. For some reason, the auras that emanated from the Tyk-Shuul temples always gave her indigestion.

Marta patted her on the shoulder. "I feel it too," she said.

"Who's that?" Kya asked. Through the diamond-shaped openings in the lattice, she saw a lone figure standing in the tall grass. He was too far away to make out his face, but he pointed a long staff in their direction. Suddenly he hurled a ball of flame at the bridge.

"Brace yourselves!" Dobo shouted.

The fireball hit the scaffolding somewhere below them. The jolt knocked everyone but Silli off their feet. Before they could get their bearings, more fireballs bombarded the bridge from top to bottom. The flaming bridge collapsed and fell into the river below.

Zib pushed his way through the grass until he reached the edge of the ravine. He peered at the wreckage down below. Violent waves crashed over the wooden debris.

He slipped the ring onto his finger and transmitted two

words. *Job's done.* Then he turned around and walked away.


"I can't keep this up much longer!" Silli shouted. A greenish-yellow dome surrounded the party, protecting them from the rapids.

"Hold it as long as you can!" Dobo replied as he gathered a length of rope from his backpack. "If the shield goes out, we'll be washed away to our doom!"

"Kya, are you okay?" Marta asked. Then to the others, she said, "She's unconscious. I'm not sure if she's breathing."

Dobo tied one end of the rope around a rock that jutted out of the river. Then he tied it around his waist and did the same for Marta and Kya. "When that bubble gives out, be ready to climb," he said.

"Climb where?" Marta asked.

More of the rubble was swept away, and now they could see the sky again. "There's a cave!" Dobo shouted, pointing to a hollow on the inside of the ravine.

"We're going to need more rope," Marta said, gathering some from Kya's backpack. Her friend lay limply by her side, bleeding from several wounds. Marta wasn't sure if she was alive or dead, but she couldn't worry about that right now.

The bubble gave way, and water rushed over them. They trailed from Dobo's rope, swinging left and right as the water rushed by. A wooden board bashed Marta's shoulder on the way by, and she winced in pain.

Silli flew to Marta and took Kya's rope from her, then dashed into the cave. The fairy found a good-sized outcropping and fastened the rope. Then she brought the other end to Marta, who tied it to herself. Dobo cut his original line, and now Dobo and Kya both hung off of Marta, who was tethered to the rock in the cave.

Their weight made the rope cut into Marta's side, but she grunted and climbed, pulling herself forward until she reached the cave. Then she pulled Dobo and Kya in behind her. Once she was sure everyone was safe, she rushed to Kya to see if she was breathing. She got about halfway to her friend before she collapsed.


"You're going to be okay." It was Dobo's voice, coming from somewhere far away.

Marta opened her eyes, but she still couldn't see much. She felt aches and pains from every inch of her body. *And we still have a temple to face*, she thought. She almost closed her eyes again when she remembered her friend. "Kya!" she shouted, sitting upright.

"Kya's fine," Dobo said. "She got a little banged up and took in a lot of water, but she'll be okay."

Marta looked to her left. It was still pretty dark, but she could see Kya lying on her side with her eyes closed. She was breathing normally. Marta crawled over to her and put a hand on her side.

"Where are we?" Marta asked, looking around. She could only see that they were in a rocky tunnel. She thought she saw a bit of sunlight around one bend, but the only other light came from Silli, who kept darting around the corner and returning with more of their supplies. She could still hear rushing water from somewhere in the distance.

"Turns out that cave was deeper than we thought," Dobo said.

"How are we alive?" Marta asked.

"Silli put a bubble around us," Dobo said. "She hasn't really perfected the spell, but it kept us from dying, anyway."

"I'll keep practicing," Silli said as she darted by, dropping some rope as she went. Then she sped farther down the tunnel, into the darkness.

"Where's she going?" Marta asked.

"We're looking for a way out," Dobo replied. "I don't see any way we can climb back up the ravine, but maybe the tunnel leads somewhere."

Kya started coughing. She got to her knees and vomited, then collapsed again. Marta put her hand on her friend's back.

"Did you see who attacked us?" Marta asked.

Dobo shook his head. "It has to be someone who knows about our quest," he said.

"You're not going to believe this," Silli said as she returned. "I think this tunnel is part of the temple. If you go that way, eventually you get to a door. I can't get it open by myself, but it has a green shimmer."

"Give us a few minutes," Kya muttered weakly as she rolled back onto her side.

"Agreed," Marta said, lying back against the wall. Then she closed her eyes and fell back asleep.


They got moving again an hour later. This temple was smaller than the previous ones. It consisted of a single worship room, not much different from the ones they'd seen before. They saw more statues of the snake-headed guards, which – according to the librarian they'd talked to in Sesta – were called the Sleeth.

The altar held three identical jewels, two of which were fake, enchanted to explode if someone were to touch them. But Silli was able to identify the magical trap by its odor, and she recognized the correct jewel simply by looking at its aura.

The hardest part was finding a way out. They knew there had to be more than one entrance, as making worshippers scale a sheer ravine just wasn't a practical way to grow a religion.

"I think I found something," Kya said, pulling a hidden lever behind a Sleeth statue. The floor opened directly beneath her feet, but fortunately Marta was standing right next to her. Marta grabbed her by the arm and pulled her into a hug.

"Yikes," Kya said, staring at the metal spikes down below. They held onto each other for a few more seconds. Kya could feel her friend trembling, which was new. She'd always had the impression that Marta wasn't afraid of anything. "Are you okay?" she asked.

"I almost lost you twice in one day," Marta whispered.

Kya hugged her even harder, then released her. "You're not getting rid of me that easily," she quipped. She tried to sound flippant but she didn't have the energy.

*Is she crying*? Kya thought, studying Marta's face. It was hard to tell. More than an hour had passed since their river escapade, but they were all still pretty damp, and the glowstones provided meager light in the otherwise dark temple.

"Let me take the next lever," Silli suggested. She went around the room, pulling identical levers behind each statue. Most of them opened up more pit traps, but that wasn't a problem for the fairy. The sixth lever she tried opened a hidden door.

The new tunnel led them straight to the surface. They emerged from a small cave just outside of Sesta and returned to town to retrieve their wagon and horses.

Zib emerged from the convention hall just in time to see the wagon go by. *They're alive?* he thought. *Ryveen's going to kill me. But maybe there's still time to do something about it.*

They stopped at a farmhouse for the night. A wooden sign out front read "Trevallane Farms." They let Dobo do the talking, while the rest of the party waited by the wagon.

"The widow Trevallane doesn't trust us enough to let us inside," Dobo said upon his return. "But I talked her into letting us sleep in the barn for the night. She says she doesn't use it anymore, so we can board our horses there as well."

"Very well," Marta said. She'd slept in worse, and she wasn't much for creature comforts anyway. She locked her weapons and armor in the wagon's strongbox, grabbed her bedroll and a glowstone, then led one of the horses to the barn.

Kya took Dobo aside. "Can I talk to you for a moment?" she asked.

"Of course," Dobo replied. Silli flitted back and forth behind him, gathering supplies from the wagon.

Kya chewed on her lower lip. She looked like she was having trouble finding the right words. "It's just..." She took a deep breath. "Would you and Silli mind sleeping in the wagon tonight? I'd like some... alone time with Marta."

Silli happened by at that moment, carrying an apple. She giggled and winked at Kya.

"We're all family here, my child," Dobo said. "Anything you need to talk to Marta about, you can tell all of us."

The fairy put her hand over her face. Then she landed on Dobo's shoulder and whispered something in his ear. Kya's face turned beet red.

"Oh!" Dobo said. "I mean, oh. Of course, of course. The

wagon is perfectly comfortable when it's just me and Silli. Much nicer than some smelly barn. You two enjoy your, ah, alone time. We'll be just fine." By the time he was done talking, his face was red too.

Kya quickly took her bedroll out of the back of the wagon and led the other horse to the barn.

The barn was old but well-maintained. The double doors opened to a breezeway with two stalls, a tack room, and a hay loft up above.

"Where are the others?" Marta asked as Kya climbed up to the loft.

Kya spread out her bedroll next to Marta's. "They're going to sleep in the wagon," Kya said. "They just felt it would be more comfortable."

"But the wagon's so cramped," Marta said.

"Not to Dobo," Kya said. "And Silli can sleep anywhere."

Marta looked a bit skeptical, but she let it go. "If that's what they want," she said.

Kya sat down on her bedroll and patted the space next to her. "Can we talk for a minute?" she asked.

Marta nodded and sat down. "What's wrong?" she asked.

"Nothing at all," Kya said, staring into her friend's eyes.

"That's... good?" Marta replied, looking confused.

"You know, you saved my life today," Kya said.

"You've saved mine several times," Marta replied. "The four of us make a great team. I've lost count of how often we've been there for each other."

"This isn't about them," Kya said. "It's about us."

"What about us?" Marta asked.

"You know... *us*," Kya said, trying her best to look seductive.

Marta's confusion had not abated. Her friend was talking nonsense and looked half-drunk. "Are you okay?" she asked. "You must be tired after everything we did today."

Kya huffed. "I give up. I give up."

"What?" Marta asked, putting a hand on Kya's shoulder.

Kya turned away from her. Her face was flushed again, and she didn't want Marta to see her embarrassment. "It's nothing," Kya said.

"You're my best friend," Marta said. "There's nothing you can't tell me."

Kya felt like she was on the verge of tears. She took a couple of deep breaths to control herself. "Marta..." she began, then paused.

Marta said nothing, and just waited for her friend to continue. She knew she'd missed a social cue, but she wasn't sure what. Her reclusive upbringing often led to these misunderstandings. The Frostmoor Clan had their own ways, which often seemed strange to outsiders.

"When we first met," Kya continued, staring at the ceiling. "We... kissed a few times. Played around. It looked like we were on our way to a whirlwind romance. And then it just stopped."

"Ooooh," Marta said. "I wasn't sure that was what you wanted. We'd just slaughtered an army of Bonegrinders. We weren't in control of our emotions. I'd just lost a family, you were finally free after months of captivity..."

"So it didn't mean anything to you?" Kya asked. "The kisses, the flirting?"

"It meant everything to me," Marta replied. Then she gently turned Kya to face her. "Everything," she repeated, looking into her friend's dewy eyes.

They leaned in towards each other, then hesitated, each half-expecting a knock at the barn door, or a sudden bandit attack, or any one of a thousand possible disruptions.

But no interruptions came. When their lips met, it set off an unstoppable chain reaction of tender caresses and eager gropes, and a cacophony of gasps, moans, and cries of pleasure.

Kya broke away for a moment. "I've never..." she gasped.

"Nor have I," Marta replied. "But I assure you we'll figure it out."

The two fell back into their mindless frenzy of hands and tongues. They furiously removed each other's clothing, then Kya detached her leg and tossed it aside. Marta delicately ran her fingers over her partner's body, but she paused when she reached Kya's right knee.

"You don't need to be so gentle," Kya said between gasps. "Just because I'm broken doesn't mean I'll shatter."

"You're not broken, you're perfect," Marta replied. "And you're mine," she added with a gleam in her eye. She picked Kya up and embraced her petite frame for a moment. Then she tossed her against a bedroll, just roughly enough to show her she meant business.

And then Marta was on top of her, and once again they became a whirlwind of fingers and lips and hot breath teasing each other's most intimate areas.


"Did you hear a scream?" Dobo asked, sitting up suddenly. He fumbled around in the dark for a glowstone.

"It was just the wind," Silli replied with a knowing smile. She lay sprawled across her pillow, reading a tiny book titled "A Fairy's Guide to Protection Spells."

"You're sure?" Dobo asked with a yawn.

"Go back to sleep," Silli said. "You get so cranky in the mornings."

He reclined and rolled onto his side. "Well, just wake me up if anythizzz..." He resumed snoring mid-sentence.

Silli reached over and sprinkled a tiny amount of fairy dust onto Dobo's head. "Just a little something to help you stay asleep," she whispered. After all, there was no telling how long Marta and Kya would be at it.

Kya woke up in the dark, her body half-sprawled across Marta's nude form. Her friend – *Can I even still call her that?* she wondered – was much more comfortable to sleep on than her usual bedroll. She lay there for a few minutes, just enjoying the rise and fall of Marta's chest. She never wanted to move again.

But she gradually became aware of a faint scratching noise. She realized she'd been hearing it for several minutes. The sound had even invaded her dreams, and it was probably what had woken her up. *It's just the horses*, she thought. But the sound didn't come from the stalls below. It seemed to be coming from outside the barn.

*Maybe it's an animal*, she thought. *A fox or something trying to get into the barn.*

And then she heard the horses chuffing and moving around. They usually slept soundly when kept in stalls, but now they seemed restless. Whatever was going on outside, it bothered them as well. *Just go away, fox*, Kya thought, and she tried to tune out the noises. She took deep breaths and cleared her mind. Her consciousness slowly faded and her mind filled with whimsical notions like horseless wagons and indoor outhouses.

But then she heard someone cough, and it snapped her fully awake.

Kya rolled off of Marta and felt around in the dark for her

clothes. She came across her wooden leg and attached it. Then she found a pair of pants and a shirt and hurriedly pulled them on. The shirt was too big – it must have been Marta's – but it would do for now. She considered waking Marta, but she wasn't sure if she'd really heard what she'd heard.

She climbed down the ladder and listened at the barn doors. She didn't hear anything. *Maybe I dreamed it after all,* she thought. *But I won't be able to sleep until I know for sure.*

She opened the door a crack and peered out into the night. It was too dark to see much, so she opened it a bit more. The door let out a creak, and something outside gasped and ran. Kya saw a shadowy form flee around the corner.

*I really should go get Marta,* Kya thought, closing the door behind her as she stepped out into the night. Against her better judgment, she quietly crept toward the edge of the barn. The moon was just a sliver in the sky, and did little to illuminate her surroundings. *Wish I'd brought a glowstone,* Kya thought. She reached the corner and peeked around the edge.

A hand grabbed her by the neck, and another shoved something over her mouth. There was a smell – medicinal, possibly magical – and her entire body suddenly went numb. Then she was out like a light.


Marta stirred to the sound of horses whinnying. "What's bugging them?" she mumbled, then rolled into a more comfortable position. But the horses kept neighing, and she couldn't feel Kya next to her.

She opened her eyes. It was bright inside the barn, too bright. Flickering flames crept up the walls all around her.

"Kya!" she yelled, but her friend was nowhere to be

found.

In one quick movement, she rolled to the edge of the loft and jumped down to the ground. "Kya!" she shouted again. The walls were engulfed in flame, and the smoke made it hard to breathe. She opened both stall doors so the horses could get out, but the outer door was still closed. She tried to push it open but it wouldn't budge. She rammed into it with her shoulder, but it still didn't give.

The horses were panicked, running blindly around the barn, and it was all Marta could do to keep from getting trampled. A flaming beam dropped from the rafters. It landed in the loft, right where she'd been sleeping a minute before.

Marta took another run at the door, but it wouldn't open. *What's holding it shut?* she wondered. With her strength, she should have been able to break through even if it was blocked, but now it was like ramming into stone.

She began searching for a weapon. She'd left her sword in the wagon, but surely there was something in the barn she could use. A horse knocked her over as it bucked at the wall, but Marta got back to her feet and kept looking. Seeing nothing in the stalls, she opened the door to the tack room.

*There,* she thought, just before the ceiling collapsed.


Sillivene woke up to some sort of ruckus. "Are they still at it?" she groaned. It was faint, but she thought she heard Marta calling Kya's name. "Guess so," Silli mumbled. Then she heard some animal noises, which was a bit more disturbing. Curious, she glided over to the wagon's door, where a little window granted her a view of the barn.

"Oh, turdmuffins," the fairy said when she saw the blaze. She flew to Dobo and tried to wake him up. "Dobo!" she shouted, slapping his face. Then she remembered what she'd done earlier. He'd be asleep for at least another two hours.

She opened the window and darted to the barn. The heat was intense as she approached, and she could hear frightened whinnies from within. She was about to pull open the doors when she noticed a glowing green jewel near the handle. It had been placed right on the seam between the double doors, and Silli could feel the magic emanating from it.

*Some sort of enchanted lock*, she thought. She reached out to touch the door but was knocked back a few feet. The doors shimmered with green light.

*I can counter this*, she thought. "Vonek lache corrum!" she shouted, sprinkling some fairy dust on the device. The doors flashed green again but the lock held firm. She concentrated and tried again. This time the jewel went dark and fell to the ground.

"Opheen amotre!" Silli shouted, and both doors opened wide. She flew to the side as the horses burst from the barn. Then she looked inside. A large portion of the ceiling now lay in the middle of the barn, and her friends were nowhere to be seen.

"Kya! Marta!" she shouted, but there was no answer. She tried to go in but the heat was just too intense. *Maybe if I douse myself with a cold spell*, she thought, and tried to remember the incantation. "Esuum Ignee Oor..." she began. More of the roof crumbled, breaking her concentration.

But then she thought she heard a knocking sound from the other side of the barn. It sounded oddly like someone chopping firewood. She flew around the outside to investigate.

Her blood went cold when she saw the figure standing in the distance. Lit by the flames of the barn, the man wore a dark cloak and held a wooden staff. *Is that the same man from the bridge?* she wondered. *Is he following us?* The man watched the barn like a vulture waiting for its next meal to die.

Then Silli noticed Kya's limp form at his feet. "Kya!" she shouted. The watcher turned at her voice and pointed his staff at her. Silli narrowly avoided the grapefruit-sized ball of flame that rocketed toward her.

And then the wall of the barn cracked open and Marta burst through. She was nude, covered in cuts and burns, and carrying a woodcutter's ax. She spotted Kya, then locked eyes with the evil sorcerer. Silli had never seen such a look of fury as the one on Marta's face. The woman's anger was so strong that Silli could feel it in her soul.

Marta charged forward. Her enemy fired another ball of flame, but Marta batted it away with the ax. As she closed the gap, the man held his staff up with both hands in a defensive stance.

"Wait! Please!" the man shouted.

Marta brought her ax down, chopping his staff in half. Then she reversed her swing, catching him right between the legs with the blunt side of the weapon. The man wheezed and collapsed to the ground.

She was about to bring the ax down on his head when Silli stopped her. "Wait!" the fairy shouted. "He might have information we need!"

Marta paused. She was breathing hard and full of rage, and she wanted nothing more than to chop the man in half. But then her eyes fell on Kya and her anger faded. She dropped the ax and fell at Kya's side.

"Is she breathing?" Marta asked, putting her ear to Kya's mouth. She was. Marta could see her chest rise and fall, and could feel her warm breath against her face. Kya was only unconscious.

The man attempted to crawl away while they were distracted, but Marta grabbed the ax and brought it down on his foot. He screamed and cursed, then tried to dislodge the weapon.

"What did you do to her?" Marta asked. She still held her end of the ax handle. When the man tried to touch the ax head, she wiggled the handle, sending fresh waves of pain into his foot.

"It was just sleeping powder, I swear!" the man shouted. "It'll wear off in less than an hour. She'll be fine!"

"Who are you?" Silli asked.

"Zib!" the man shouted, wincing in pain. "Zib Zib Zib!"

"We don't care about your name, you little worm," Marta said, and wiggled the ax again. "She means, who do you work for?"

"I... I work for a dark priestess!" the man said. "She's trying to resurrect Tyk-Shuul! She knows you're trying to stop her, so I've been following your route!"

"Keep talking," Silli said.

"I thought if I kidnapped your friend, you'd get sidetracked trying to find her," Zib said. "Maybe long enough that you missed your deadline. But I wasn't going to hurt her, I swear!"

"Oh, how nice of you," Marta said. "And I suppose you weren't trying to hurt me when you set fire to the barn?"

"I was hoping you'd forget about that," Zib said.

Marta and Silli looked at each other. "He dies," Marta said. She put both hands on the ax handle and pulled it from Zib's foot. He screamed again.

"Wait," Silli urged. "We should tie him up and take him with us. He might know how to get past some of the traps."

"Too dangerous," Marta said. "If he escapes, he'll kill us all."

"We'd keep him chained," Silli said.

"We have no idea what spells he knows," Marta said.

Zib brushed a lock of greasy hair out of his face. "I assure you I don't know any more spells," he said. "My mistress gave me that staff. Without it, I'm useless."

"On that, we're agreed," Marta said, and raised the ax.

Zib held up his hands. "Please!" he shouted.

Marta stopped when she saw his hands. "Where did you get that ring?" she asked.

"Oh, ah, yes, that," Zib said. "I just… ah…"

"Zib," Marta said, remembering. "I thought I'd heard that name somewhere. You were at the bandit camp. The other bandits told me about you."

"Good things I'm sure?" Zib said.

"A bandit and a cultist?" Silli asked. "He keeps busy."

"Hand it over," Marta demanded.

Zib removed the ring and tossed it to Marta. "In exchange for my life?" he asked hopefully.

All three heads turned as they heard a scream. It was the homeowner, Mrs. Trevallane. She was still in her bedclothes and carried a pitchfork and a torch.

"This is going to be difficult to explain," Silli said.

The next couple of hours were very busy. They managed to calm Mrs. Trevallane long enough to tell her all that had happened. The widow insisted on taking Zib to the local magistrate herself, so she could have him arrested for arson. Marta offered to escort her, but she refused. They put Zib to sleep using some of his own sleeping powder, then made sure he was bound securely before they left him in Mrs. Trevallane's care.

Marta and Sillivene rounded up the horses and tended to

their wounds. They had only suffered some minor burns, and they responded well to Silli's soothing spell. The fairy also patched up Marta as well, despite the tough warrior's objections. Kya was the first to awaken, and by the time Dobo opened his eyes around the break of dawn, everyone was dressed and ready to move on.

Sitting up in the back doorway of the wagon, Dobo looked from Marta to Kya. Both sported cloth bandages and several new bruises, though it looked like Marta had taken the worst of it. Then he spotted the smoking ruins of the barn. He looked from the barn to the couple, then back to the barn, his eyes growing wide.

"You two need a safe word," he said. Then they all climbed into the wagon and left for the next town on the map.

## Proudpath

It was a bumpy ride to Proudpath. Dobo drove the wagon as usual. He only let the others drive if there was no other choice. It wasn't that he didn't trust them, but he knew the routes better than they did and didn't want someone to accidentally take a wrong turn. Silli lay on his shoulder, and Marta and Kya sat in the back.

"I need you to do me a favor when we get to Proudpath," Dobo said.

Silli bit her lower lip. She knew what was coming. "You want me to ask the fairies for help," she said.

"I mean, the Fairy Kingdom is right there," Dobo said. "You might as well stop by. Maybe they can spare their army to fight Tyk-Shuul like they did with the Bonegrinders. Or maybe they could send some fairies ahead to the other temples, since they can see them."

"I'll be gone for half a day," she said. "You won't be able to find the temple without me."

"Do you still have that necklace?" Dobo asked.

She'd been hoping he wouldn't think of that. "I do," she admitted. The necklace allowed her to teleport back to the Fairy Kingdom, though it was a one-way trip. If she used it, she'd have to wait for them to reach Proudpath before they could meet up again.

"So it's settled," Dobo said. "You go ahead and use the necklace, see if your people can spare any soldiers. We'll reach Proudpath tomorrow, and you can lead us to the temple then."

Silli nodded and gave Dobo a weak smile. He didn't know the ramifications of what he was asking. She unexpectedly hugged his arm, then she turned and flitted through the wagon's window.

Marta sat on a storage trunk, watching Kya sleep. The floor of the wagon was only big enough for one of them to sleep at a time, though Marta probably wouldn't have been able to sleep at the moment anyway. She turned the ring over and over in her hand, lost in thought.

"Something on your mind?" Silli asked as she rooted through a tiny jewelry box.

"Nothing important," Marta said. She took a deep breath before she continued. "Back when we had both rings, sometimes I could tell what Kya was dreaming. She might think something like, 'The wolves are after me,' and I'd use my ring to let her know she was safe. She'd sleep more soundly after that. It's a minor thing, but sometimes I miss it."

"And where's the other ring now?" Silli asked.

"I assume Esova still has it," Marta said.

"You should put it on," Silli said. "Give Esova an update. Let them know how the quest is going." Then she put on her necklace and darted back out the window.

Marta nodded absently, barely noticing the fairy had gone. "It's not a bad idea," she muttered, and slipped the ring on her finger.

*Esova?* she thought.

A reply came back immediately. *Who is this?*

Marta cringed. Something felt very, very wrong. She expected there to be some difference. After all, Esova and Kya were very different beings. Whenever she used the ring to talk to Kya, she could feel Kya's energy. She'd never be able to put it into words, but telepathy with Kya reminded her of being in a bakery that made sweet pastries.

But this person made Marta think of frozen caves and dead rats. It might have been Esova, but Marta doubted it. She'd only met them briefly, but this telepathic connection felt nothing like Esova's presence.

*Hello?* the other person thought again. *I know you're not Zib, so you must have taken his ring. Which means he failed. And that would mean you're one of the party collecting the eyes of O'olos.*

Marta gasped but didn't reply.

*Oh yes, I know all about you,* the stranger continued. *Let's see… I'm getting a feminine energy, so you can't be Dobo. The ring wouldn't fit a fairy, so you're not Silli. Which leaves Marta and Kya. And I'm getting a warrior's vibe from you. It's good to meet you, Marta. You may call me Ryveen.*

*How do you know all this?* Marta asked.

*Esova told me everything in the end,* Ryveen replied. *Oh, they tried not to talk. They held out for hours. They even uttered an incantation that withered their own tongue, just so they wouldn't be able to speak. But my powers of persuasion won out in the end.*

Suddenly Marta saw an image of Esova in her mind. Their body had been stripped, dismembered, and eviscerated.

Marta's skin went cold and she struggled to breathe. *How did you do that?* she asked. She'd never been able to see pictures when using the ring with Kya.

*I have powers you can't even imagine,* Ryveen replied.

*You're a monster,* Marta thought.

*Wait until you meet my son,* Ryveen replied. *I have a big surprise for you when you get back to Lakehelm. If I were you, I'd give up now.*

*We will stop you,* Marta told her. *I will fight you to my last breath if I have to.*

*Blah blah blah,* Ryveen replied. *Standard hero rhetoric. You're in way over your head here, dearie. Tyk-Shuul will arise on the next full moon, and there's nothing you can do about it.*

*We'll see about that,* Marta thought, and removed the ring. She sat with her head in her hands for several minutes, completely shaken. The image of Esova's broken form still lingered in her mind.

"Hey, are you okay?" Kya asked, sitting up. She stood and sat down next to her girlfriend, putting her arm around her shoulder.

"It's… nothing," Marta whispered.

"It's obviously not nothing," Kya said. "Now tell me all about it."

Marta told Kya everything that had just happened. When she was done, they cried together for a bit. They mourned for a person they'd only met once, but who had nevertheless given their life trying to protect Marta and her friends.

"So this 'Ryveen' person," Kya asked. "She's the dark priestess Zib told you about? The one trying to revive Tyk-Shuul?"

"I believe so," Marta said. "She killed Esova, she sent Zib to kill us, and something is going on with her son. She called him a monster."

"She's using her son as the vessel to revive Tyk-Shuul," Kya reasoned.

Marta nodded. "Maybe we should split up," she said. "Silli and I can take the rest of the temples. You and Dobo head back to Lakehelm and tell the mayor about Ryveen. Maybe he can find her and do… something."

"We're not splitting up," Kya said. "When we get to Proudpath, we'll send a courier with every bit of information we have. But there's no way I'm leaving you to face these temples alone. You need me."

"I need you to be safe," Marta said.

"I'm safer by your side," Kya said. "And besides, you're good with a sword, but you're damn near useless at solving puzzles."

Marta laughed and gave Kya a squeeze. "Very well, you win. I won't try to send you away."

Kya leaned against her arm. "Good," she said. "Live or die, we're doing this together."

The following morning, Kya sat with Dobo on the driver's bench. The muddy road was lined with trees on both sides, but they passed the occasional sign of civilization, such as a wooden hut or a hunter's campsite. It had rained overnight, and now there was a light fog in the air that made it difficult to see too far down the road.

"How are we doing on time?" Kya asked.

"There's no moon tonight," Dobo said. "That means the month is half over."

"And Proudpath is our fourth stop," Kya said. "We're cutting it pretty close."

Dobo nodded. "I know. One bad delay and we've lost. I've been trying to come up with ways to shave a day or two off the trip."

"We could stop camping for the night," Kya suggested. "If we take turns driving, one of us could sleep in the wagon while the others drive all night."

"But then when would the horses rest?" Dobo asked. "I'm already running them harder than I'd like."

"We board them whenever we get to town," Kya objected.

"A handful of hours every two or three days is not nearly enough," Dobo said. "But rest assured, when the full moon approaches, if we're behind, I'll... I'll do whatever needs to be done." A sad look crossed his face.

Kya decided to change the subject. "How much farther to Proudpath?"

"The road should split off any minute now," Dobo said. "Ah, there's a sign now." They passed a wooden sign that read:

PROUDPATH 1 MILE RIGHT

A few minutes later they saw a light in the fog. At first they thought someone was carrying a lantern, but it was too high off the ground. As it approached they realized it was a fairy.

"Sillivene?" Dobo asked as she came to a hovering halt in front of them.

"Good news!" Silli said. "We can bypass Proudpath." She tossed a small object to Dobo and he caught it.

It was one of the eyes of O'olos. "Where did you get this?" Dobo asked incredulously.

"Turns out the fairies knew about the temple near Proudpath," she said. "They destroyed it years ago. The jewel's just been sitting in the treasury."

"Great work!" Dobo said. "What about the other matter?"

Silli shook her head. "They won't help. They're still rebuilding from some battle a few months ago, and they couldn't spare anyone."

"But you told them about the coming of Tyk-Shuul?" Dobo asked.

"Yep," Silli replied. "They said it's all the more reason they need every hand they can get. They're shoring up their defenses. Uh, could we get these horses moving a little faster?"

"Such impatience," Dobo said, flicking the reins. "You just shaved a day or two off our quest. We're going to be fine."

"Still, no reason to dawdle," Silli said. She flew over to the horses and sprinkled a bit of magic dust on them. They picked up the pace with renewed vigor.

"Easy, now," Dobo said. "It's too foggy for a gallop. One sharp curve and we'll go right off the road."

"Maybe just for a couple of miles?" Silli asked. "Until we're well past Proudpath?"

Dobo frowned, then looked at the jewel in his hand. "They… don't know we have this, do they?"

Silli whistled innocently.

"Sillivene," Dobo said.

"It's not like they're going to miss it," she said.

"We're not going to take it back, are we?" Kya asked, looking from Silli to Dobo.

"Of course not," Dobo said. "But I wish you'd found another way."

Silli sat down on Dobo's shoulder. "When I got there, they tried to recruit me," she said. "They ordered me to stay, so I could help them defend the kingdom. I explained that I was on an important quest, but they scoffed at me. They don't think we're going to succeed."

"They'd just let the rest of the world die?" Kya asked.

"They have ideas of their own," Silli said. "But most of them involve protecting the Fairy Kingdom and maybe saving the citizens of Proudpath. They have an alliance with the dragons, but they're mostly trying to divert Tyk-Shuul rather than defeat him. They say he can't be killed, so they're just going to wait it out."

"Cowards," Dobo said.

"I prefer to think of us as pragmatists," someone said.

Dobo and Kya looked left and right, then turned to look behind them. A woman sat cross-legged on the roof of the wagon. She was half the size of a human, with translucent wings and a sparkling dress. Two much smaller fairies flanked her sides, each wearing bark armor and carrying a spear.

"My queen!" Silli shouted, then bowed.

"You're the queen of the fairies?" Dobo asked. He tugged on the reins, bringing the wagon to a stop.

"You may call me Delia," she replied with a nod.

"I'm Dorian," Dobo said. "It's an honor." He tried to do a sort of half-bow while still seated. It looked less like a show of respect and more like he was trying to rearrange his britches because his pants were too tight.

"And I'm Kya," Kya said, not even attempting to bow after seeing Dobo's effort.

"I've come to collect Sillivene," Queen Delia said. "I understand you are on a quest to defeat Tyk-Shuul, but I believe Sillivene would be put to better use elsewhere."

"Surely you can spare one single fairy," Dobo said.

"Our numbers are not what they once were," the queen said. "There was a skirmish a few months ago that left us short-handed. But I will do this for you, Dorian. The Fairy Kingdom will be happy to grant your party asylum if you wish to wait out Tyk-Shuul's rampage in safety."

Dobo shook his head. "I appreciate the offer. But I'd rather go down fighting. What kind of world will we live in if the only survivors are the ones who were too timid to fight back?"

"I understand," the queen said. "I will leave you to your quest. Come with me, Sillivene."

"But we need her to find the temples!" Kya blurted.

"I respect your bravery," Queen Delia said. "But I can't allow one of my subjects to accompany you on a quest that is doomed to fail."

"You helped us with the Bonegrinders!" Kya said.

"This threat is much more dire," the queen replied calmly.

"But that's unfair!" Kya shouted.

While they argued, the backdoor of the wagon opened and Marta walked around to the front. "You must be the fairy queen," Marta said, bowing deeply.

The queen gave her a polite nod. "I was just telling your friends that Sillivene's presence is required at the—"

"I heard," Marta said. "May I speak for a moment?"

Queen Delia blinked a couple of times. She wasn't used to being interrupted. "Go ahead," she said curtly.

"I am Marta, last survivor of the Frostmoor Clan," she began. "My people were isolationists. We bore no ill will towards other clans, we even traded with them, but we never embraced them. We believed in self-reliance. That our ways were pure. We were afraid that if we mixed with other peoples, our culture would become diluted." Marta took a deep breath before she continued. "And then... when death came to our village... there was no one to stand with us."

"I'm sorry to hear that," the queen said, and she looked like she meant it.

"So I set out to see the world," Marta continued. "And it opened my eyes to how much I'd missed, hiding up on that mountain. So many new ways to live, new foods, new people... new love..." She glanced at Kya for a moment, then looked at Silli. "And new species. It's funny, before I met Sillivene, I didn't even believe in fairies. And now... I don't even know how many times she's saved my life."

"Three," Silli said. "Four if you count your social life."

"My point is," Marta continued, "There's a world beyond your kingdom. People aren't more valuable just because they were born in your area. You can wall up your domain and keep it safe while the rest of the world burns in an apocalypse... but why? With no other cultures to appreciate the majesty of your people, what are you living for?"

Queen Delia spent several long seconds dwelling on her words. "There is wisdom in what you say," she finally said. "But... my foremost duty is to protect my people."

Silli lowered her head in defeat. She glanced furtively at the forest as if trying to decide whether or not to make a run for it.

"That said," the queen continued. "...I suppose we can afford to part with one fairy. It's a small price to pay given the circumstances. Sillivene, I formally release you from your duties."

"Thank you, my queen," Silli said, and bowed again.

"And Dorian?" Queen Delia asked.

"Yes, your majesty?" he replied.

"Don't be a stranger," the queen said with a wink. "If your quest is successful, I'd love to see you stop by my palace for a little... celebration."

The queen and her guards disappeared in a puff of fairy dust. There were several seconds of awkward silence.

"So..." Kya said finally. "What's next on the map?"

"Duskmorgue," Dobo replied.

"Sounds lovely," Marta said. "Let us be on our way."

## Duskmorgue

Duskmorgue was not, in fact, lovely. A thick fog hung over the town, making the midday look like late evening. Houses were few and far between, and most of the barren land was filled with cemeteries.

The entire party sat on the driver's bench. It wasn't really wide enough for the three humans to sit comfortably, but Kya sat in Marta's lap. Silli lay asleep on Dobo's thigh.

"Why so many graveyards?" Kya asked.

"The town's surrounded by marshland," Dobo explained. "That's why it's perpetually foggy. They can't grow any crops without sunlight, and no one wants to live here, so they agreed to let some of the surrounding towns use their land for cemeteries."

"So who *does* live here?" Marta asked as they passed a dilapidated house.

"Morticians, gravediggers, people who don't want to be found," Dobo said.

"Sounds dismal," Marta said.

"It's not exactly a tourist trap," Dobo replied. "Though the inn does serve an excellent cup of cinnamon mead. You should definitely get one when we stop to ask about the temple."

Silli yawned and stretched, then took in her surroundings. "Oh neat, you found it without my help."

"What are you talking about?" Kya asked.

"The temple," Silli said. "It's right over there."

Beyond the fence that lined the dirt road, hundreds of tombstones dotted the landscape, interspersed with the occasional mausoleum.

"I don't see anything," Dobo said.

"That crypt right there," Silli said, pointing at a mausoleum. "It has a green shimmer."

"Well, that was easy," Kya said.


"Skeletons give me the creeps," Kya said, warily eyeing a long-dead body.

The mausoleum was bigger than it had looked from the outside, and the walls were lined with open caskets. Everywhere they looked, ancient, cobweb-covered corpses smiled back at them.

"What's wrong with skeletons?" Marta asked.

"They remind us of our own mortality," Dobo replied.

"No, that's not it," Kya said. "Ever since I was a girl I've had nightmares about them coming to life and chasing me."

Marta moved up next to her and gave her a little squeeze. "I understand. I used to have bad dreams about bats. I still cringe a bit when I see one."

"Ah, irrational fears," Dobo said.

Kya gave him a strange look. *We're about to get a lecture, aren't we?* she thought. For just a second she expected Marta to reply to her question, but then she remembered she no longer had the ring.

No one asked Dobo to explain, but he kept talking

anyway. "Skeletons have no muscles," he said. "So even if they could move, they'd be weaker than humans. Their brains have rotted away, so they can't strategize. If a skeleton were to come back to life, it would be inferior to humans in every way. And yet people fear them more than they fear living humans."

"Are you sensing anything yet, Silli?" Kya asked. They checked every coffin and wiggled every candle sconce, looking for a hidden door.

Silli shook her head. "Nothing yet, sorry," she said.

"Maybe what they actually fear is the magic it would take to animate a skeleton," Marta suggested.

"As well they should," Dobo said. "Necromancy is a dark and powerful art, and it should never be taken for granted. But I don't think that's why people fear the dead. In the right hands, magic could also be used to weaponize kittens, but we don't fear kittens."

"Speak for yourself," Silli muttered.

Kya tried to open a coffin in the center of the crypt, but the marble lid was too heavy for her. "Marta?" she asked.

"So what's your... hurgh... theory?" Marta asked as she slid the slab aside.

"As I said, it's a reminder of what will one day befall each and every one of us," Dobo replied.

But no one was listening. Marta, Kya, and Silli stared silently into the stone casket. They'd expected to find a corpse, but instead they looked upon a set of stairs that led down into the darkness.

"The temple's down there," Silli said. "I can feel it."


At the bottom of the stairs they discovered a maze of catacombs. Casket-filled hallways extended in all directions, and even the walls had been constructed from the bones of the dead. A chill air blew through the numerous passages, carrying with it the odor of decay.

"We could be here for days," Kya said, staring down one of the long, twisty hallways. Their glowstones only illuminated the first twenty feet or so. Beyond that, there was nothing but darkness.

"No, it's this way," Silli said. "Trust me." She chanted a minor incantation which caused her to glow extra bright. They followed her away from the stairs, where she took them in a mostly straight line. They had to zig-zag around a couple of walls near the end, but soon they reached the entrance to the temple.

The altar was constructed of human bones, as were the pews and the braziers. Two metal cages hung from the ceiling, both containing skeletons. Behind the altar, a giant sculpture of a skull protruded from the wall. Statues of skeletons stood at regular intervals around the room, some holding unlit torches. In addition to the hallway from which they'd entered, two more doorways flanked the skull sculpture.

"Someone really likes bones," Silli said.

"Those pews don't look very comfortable," Kya added.

"But you have to respect their commitment to a theme," Dobo said.

Marta approached the altar and frowned. "Does anyone see the jewel?" she asked.

The group searched around the altar, the pews, and the statues.

"Can you sense it anywhere?" Dobo asked Silli, but she shook her head.

They searched the other doorways. One led to some storage rooms and a latrine. The other took them to an office.

A rotting desk was covered in faded pieces of parchment. The walls were lined with broken shelves. A stone end table sat in one otherwise empty corner, and a large bowl lay on top of it.

An iron door adorned the back wall. Halfway up the door, a horizontal bar protruded from the steel. Five hexagonal slots were evenly spaced across the bar.

Kya tried to push open the door, but it wouldn't open. She glanced at Marta, who also tried to push it open. When that didn't work, she took a few steps back and slammed into the door with her shoulder. It didn't budge.

Dobo retrieved a pry bar from his backpack and attempted to force the door open.

"Hey, check this out," Silli said. She peered into the bowl in the corner. It was full of hexagonal-shaped gems.

"Is the eye in there?" Kya asked.

"No, they're the wrong shape," Silli replied, rooting around the bowl.

"They look like they're the right size to fit in those slots, though," Kya said.

The gems came in six colors – red, orange, yellow, blue, green, and purple. There appeared to be approximately thirty gems in the bowl. Kya grabbed one of each color and carried them over to the door. Marta and Dobo stood aside as Kya stuck five of the gems in the slots. They fit perfectly, but the door didn't unlock.

"Maybe they have to be inserted in a specific order," Dobo suggested.

Kya removed the gems and tried a different order. When that didn't work, she tried another, and another. "How many combinations can there possibly be?" she wondered aloud.

"Six colors, five slots, that's... seven thousand, seven

hundred and seventy-six combinations," Silli answered. Everyone looked at her strangely. "What?" she asked. "Some of my spells use math."

"Maybe they wrote the combination down somewhere," Marta suggested. She approached the desk and began rooting through the papers. Most of the writing had faded too much to be readable, but she found a few legible documents. She tossed aside several business receipts and a pile of instructions for various ceremonies and rituals.

Then she happened upon a note which read:

I CAN'T OPEN THE VAULT. WHAT IS THE NEW
SEQUENCE? – POPPY

"Did anyone reply?" Dobo asked.

Kya continued trying combinations while Dobo and Marta rooted through the pile, looking for an answer to Poppy's note. After twenty or thirty sequences, Kya's arms got tired and she joined Marta at the desk.

"Can I see that note a second?" Kya asked, and Marta handed it to her. Kya smirked when she saw it. "So," she asked. "Did you notice that 'Poppy' is written in a different handwriting than the original question?"

Marta and Dobo looked at her. "No, why?" Dobo asked.

Kya groaned and started fishing more gems out of the bowl. "Maybe 'Poppy' was the answer to the question," she said. Then she returned to the door and placed five gems in the slots: purple, orange, purple, purple, and yellow.

There was a click from somewhere inside the wall. The door popped open, revealing a small room with several shelves. A few empty iron boxes lay on the shelves, along with a sparkling jewel – one of the eyes of O'olos.

"Let's get going," Marta said, grabbing the jewel.

They were passing back through the temple when they heard it. A low groan from the catacombs, and a burst of cold air that nearly knocked them over. They heard scraping sounds, like bone against stone, shuffling through the darkness of the crypts.

"I knew it," Kya said as she drew her bow. "The second we came down here I just knew we were going to end up fighting skeletons."

"I won't let anything happen to you," Marta said, her sword at the ready.

"Stay calm," Dobo added. "Remember, the dead are just that – dead. They can be animated by magic, but it's no different than animating a doll. And therefore, they should be no scarier."

Kya noticed that Dobo's voice sounded a bit shaky. *He's just as scared as I am,* she thought. Then she put a hand on his shoulder and said, "I'll be brave."

They watched the doorway to the catacombs, waiting for their adversaries to appear. It made more sense to fight them in the temple than in the maze of coffins, where their enemies knew the layout.

There was movement in the shadows beyond the doorway. Something crept closer. The shadows coalesced until they formed a recognizable shape.

The skeletons that burst into the temple were not animated by magic. Each one was entwined with a mass of greenish-orange tentacles that operated the bones like they were puppets. On top of each skeleton's head was a second, smaller head, round and covered with dozens of tiny eyes.

"What are these things?" Kya whispered.

Dobo shook his head. "No idea," he said. "I'm more worried about how many there might be."

Marta rushed forward and sliced a skeleton in half. It

went down easily, and its octopus-like host made a high-pitched keening noise as it bled from its severed tentacles. As the bones hit the ground, the host creature slithered away.

"They're not so tough," Marta reported, taking a swing at the next skeleton in line. But this one grabbed her arm, and one of its tentacles tapped her on the elbow.

Marta screamed. Her arm went numb and her sword clattered to the ground. As Marta knelt to retrieve the sword, another tentacle reached for her head.

An arrow hit the host creature right in one of its eyes, and it backed off, stumbling over a pew. Kya quickly nocked another arrow and fired at the skeleton behind it.

Marta grabbed her sword. She wasn't left-handed, but her right arm was now useless. She took another swing, severing a monster's appendage and causing it to flee. But more kept coming through the door, and the temple was starting to fill up with the creatures.

The party stepped back towards the altar. Marta continued to swipe at any skeleton that came near, and Kya fired arrow after arrow at the horde. Dobo retrieved a small crossbow from his backpack. He wasn't a very good shot, but most of his targets weren't very far away.

Silli pulled a tiny book out of her purse and started reading.

"I'm out of arrows," Kya said. She traded out her bow for a dagger.

"Get behind me," Marta said. She dispatched two more skeletons, but they just kept coming.

"Retreat," Dobo said. Everyone backed into the hallway that led to the storage rooms. Marta stood in the doorway, cutting down any skeletons that got too close.

"Come on, Marta," Kya said. She backed into a storage

room with Dobo, and Marta followed.

"Silli?" Dobo asked.

"Close the door behind you, I want to try something," she said, still flipping through the book.

Dobo started to object, but Marta didn't waste time. She slammed the door and pushed a crate in front of it.

"We left her alone," Dobo said.

"She has a plan," Kya assured him, though she wasn't any more confident than Dobo was.

"I hope she knows what she's doing," Marta said, flexing her elbow. The feeling was starting to come back in her arm.

They heard more shuffling in the hall, then scratching at the door. Marta and Kya sat on the floor with their backs against the crate. Dobo paced back and forth, searching through his backpack for something useful.

And then the scratching stopped. The shuffling receded until they no longer heard anything at all. A few moments later Silli's voice came through the door. "The coast is clear, you can come out."

Marta moved the crate and opened the door. Silli floated there, smiling proudly. Marta looked out into the hallway. The last few skeletons were disappearing into the catacombs.

"What did you do?" Kya asked.

"So I was thumbing through my book," Silli said. She held it up so they could see. The title read "Demons of Zyden."

"Where did you get that?" Dobo asked.

"When I went to the Fairy Kingdom to get the jewel," she said. "Didn't I tell you?"

"No," Dobo said.

Silli shrugged and continued. "So those things are called 'Shuul-spawn.' They start hatching whenever the ritual of Tyk-Shuul is performed. But this is like their larval stage, which is why they can't get around too far without the skeletons. They're not even particularly violent when they're this young. They just wanted us for our skeletons."

"How is that not violent?" Kya asked.

"Believe me, if we ever encounter a full-grown one, you'll see the difference," Silli said.

"So how did you get rid of them?" Dobo asked.

"I sent them to their rooms," Silli said with a giggle. "There's a chant in here that orders them back to their nests so they can sleep until they're needed."

"Is there anything in your book that might help us fight Tyk-Shuul?" Dobo asked.

"That's why I got it," Silli said. "But… nothing so far. I'm only halfway through reading it, though."

They gathered their things and headed back to town.


Later that night, they splurged a little and rented two rooms at the inn. Duskmorgue didn't get very many visitors, so the rooms were unusually cheap. Dobo and Silli stayed in one room, while Marta and Kya stayed in the other.

"What's with the pen?" Kya asked.

Marta was drawing on her skin with her magic quill. "I've fallen behind on my records," she said. "Whenever I accomplish something significant, I draw a symbol on my skin. This one represents the buck we fought in Olivetree. And this is the alligator from the swamps of Guildport."

"What about the lips right there?" Kya asked, pointing to her left hip.

"Oh, that," Marta blushed a little. "That represents our first night together, in the barn of Sesta."

"I'm honored you thought that was worthy of a tattoo," Kya said. "So how come all your tattoos are in the front?

There's plenty of room on your back."

"Because I can't reach my back," Marta replied. "I've drawn my own tattoos since I was old enough to hold a pen."

"I can draw," Kya said. "Want me to record a few events?"

Marta thought it over. "That would be nice," she said, handing her the quill.

"Just tell me what to draw," Kya said.

She listened carefully as Marta instructed her on using the magic pen, then she added the Shuul-spawn to Marta's back. The act felt strangely intimate, and they felt even closer when she was done. Then they used a hand mirror along with the room's dresser mirror to show Marta what Kya had drawn.

"You draw very well," Marta said.

"Would it be okay if I used it on myself?" Kya asked.

"If you like," Marta said.

Kya thought a minute, then added a pair of lips to her right hip to match Marta's tattoo.

"Nice," Marta said.

"And if we touch our tattoos together, it's like we're kissing," Kya said.

"You know what else is like kissing?" Marta asked. "Kissing." She picked Kya up and placed her on one of the beds.


"I knew I should have slept in the wagon," Dobo said, wrapping his pillow around his ears.

"Want some sleep dust?" Silli asked.

"After last time?" Dobo replied. "Not a chance. I'll wake up and the inn will be in ruins."

"Suit yourself," Silli said, and went back to reading her book. The squeals and moans from the adjoining room didn't bother her. Humans gave off an energy when they felt strong emotions, and fairies often picked up on that energy.

One of the reasons the Fairy Kingdom sequestered itself from the human world was because the fairies were too empathetic. Many humans were motivated by greed and rage, and negative emotions made the fairies uncomfortable. Fairies were perfectly capable of getting angry on their own, but their anger was nothing like human rage, the intensity of which was contagious. Fairies who succumbed to human anger often found themselves getting into arguments and fights, and these effects sometimes continued for days.

This was also why fairies were more likely to reveal themselves to children than to adults. Children's emotions were more pure and carefree. They had untethered imaginations and an almost limitless capacity for joy.

In the past few months of traveling through human settlements, Silli had experienced a wide range of emotions. She'd felt anger and jealousy to a degree she'd never felt back in the Kingdom. It was ridiculous how petty humans could be, how mean they were to each other, and how little it took for them to betray one another.

Her friends were better than most, but they were far from perfect. That night behind the burning barn, Silli had felt the full extent of Marta's rage. It was a fury far beyond anything Silli had ever experienced, and she was still amazed that Marta had weathered the emotion without bursting into flame. All that wrath in her heart, and yet, she'd allowed Zib to live.

And now Silli felt the opposite extreme from the room next door. Their joy flowed through the fairy with such overwhelming power that she could barely breathe, and she almost backed away, unable to endure the intensity of their love. She cringed and crossed her legs, tensing every muscle in an effort to resist the waves of pleasure.

But the temptation was just too strong. She peeked at Dobo for a moment. He was sound asleep. Then Silli relaxed and gave in to the sensations that emanated through the wall. Her back arched as she felt the electric tingling of their intimate touches. She floated into the air, convulsing and shivering as their act reached its crescendo. Sparks flew from her body as she climaxed, and then she went limp, crashing back down to her pillow.

"What was that?" Dobo mumbled.

"What... was what?" Silli asked, barely able to find the breath to answer.

"I thought I saw a light," Dobo said.

"Probably just lightning outside," Silli said. "Get some sleep."

"Wake me if there's a fire," Dobo muttered, then began to snore again.

## Sweetgrape

Sweetgrape consisted of two communities. The coastal town of Port Sweetgrape was relatively small and served mostly to facilitate travel to the town proper. Sweetgrape Isle lay off of Zyden's east coast, and could only be reached by boat. Dobo rented a bay at a carriage house in Port Sweetgrape, where he stored his wagon and boarded his horses. Then the party took a ferry over to the island.

It was a beautiful city, with canals instead of streets and numerous gardens throughout. Most of the buildings were made of marble and were covered in ivy. Young lovers took romantic boat rides down gentle rivers while balladeers serenaded them.

The island was home to several wineries, each of which operated its own taverns and restaurants to showcase their products. It was time for lunch, so they entered the first restaurant they saw, a winery-owned pub called the Tasty Vine. As the server brought them their meal, Kya asked her who in town knew the best gossip.

"Oh, that would be Tabitha over at the Crier's office," she replied. "We call her Gabitha. If it's a rumor, she's heard it. If she didn't start it. Is that a fairy?"

"No, he's just really short," Silli said, patting Dobo on the head.

After lunch they checked out the Sweetgrape Crier, the local news outlet. A young boy out front carried a basket of scrolls. "Latest news, sir?" he asked Dobo.

Dobo tossed him a coin and took a scroll. He unrolled the parchment and browsed the headlines. Most of the document reported business profits, recent deaths, and wedding announcements. One winery had recently purchased a competitor. A local barkeep had been arrested for arson. There was a minor scandal in the registrar's office, and a local child had gone missing.

"Interesting," Dobo muttered, but he was less impressed by the content and more by the printing process itself. It featured block lettering as well as artwork. Books weren't uncommon in Zyden, but mass-producing scrolls of this quality on a daily basis? Either magic was involved, or they'd built a contraption that he was sure to find fascinating.

"What sort of device do they use to make these scrolls?" Dobo asked the boy.

"They don't let me in there," the boy answered. Then he looked around like he might get in trouble.

"Don't get too distracted," Silli said as Dobo pushed his way through the front door.

It was chaotic inside. Scribes sat behind dozens of desks, hurriedly writing with quill pens. Other staff members searched through crates full of documents. At one desk, an employee appeared to be interviewing one of the town guards. A man barked orders at various underlings, sending them off in all directions. And somewhere in the background, Dobo heard a rhythmic pounding. Whatever machine they used to print their news scrolls, its vibrations shook the building as it worked.

Workers rushed back and forth in front of the party, none sparing them so much as a glance. Dobo stopped one and asked where they could find Tabitha, and he pointed to a door in the back before rushing off.

A sign on the door read:

TABITHA WRIGHT

CHIEF NEWSATHURGIST

"Chief what?" Kya asked, but only received shrugs in reply.

Dobo knocked on the door, then opened it a crack.

"Come in, come in!" the woman behind the desk called. Tabitha was in her mid-forties and had curly brown hair. She wore a brightly-colored business tunic and had a quill tucked behind each ear.

"Sorry to bother you," Dobo began. "We're—"

"Oh no, you're most welcome," Tabitha interrupted. "I was just about to go out looking for a story, and it looks like one just walked through my door. You're obviously from out of town which means you have a story to tell. The tall woman in particular looks like she's seen a few things, and is that a fairy?"

"Actually she's a—" Dobo said.

"Fantastic, fantastic," Tabitha said, speaking a mile a minute. "I can see the headline right now. 'Fairy Visits Sweetgrape, Blesses Crops With Fae Magic,' what do you think?"

"I don't bless—" Silli said.

"Doesn't matter, it's the headline that sells," Tabitha said. "Now, my intuition tells me you're some sort of adventuring party. Or maybe it's that woman's giant sword. Either way, something is going on here in Sweetgrape or you wouldn't have taken the time to ride the ferry. Now, tell… me… *everything.*"

They spent the next half hour telling her about their quest, Tyk-Shuul, the temples, and the eyes of O'olos. Tabitha took detailed notes, somehow writing with both hands simultaneously. She asked them all sorts of questions, but they got the impression she was writing down what she wanted to hear rather than what they actually said. She was particularly interested in Marta's story, and her former life in the harsh Frostmoor mountains.

"We really can't spend too much more time here," Dobo said. "But do you have any idea where we would find the evil temple near Sweetgrape?"

"It sank," Tabitha said. "Years ago, maybe centuries. It's one of those local legends. Some think it was designed to sink. Perhaps the original worshipers were amphibious monsters."

"There's nothing wrong with being amphibious," Marta said. "When I was younger, I thought I liked both men and women."

Kya put her hand over her face.

"You're smart, I like that," Tabitha said. "But people claim to have seen monsters in the water. Ships avoid that area. Fishermen have no luck there. Smaller boats have disappeared, their crews never to return. If you want a look, it's just off the coast to the northeast. Can any of you breathe underwater?"

Everyone looked at Silli, but she shook her head. "There's a spell, but I haven't tried it. I can only cast it on one person at a time."

"I'm sure you'll work it out," Tabitha said, rising. "Now, if you'll excuse me, I have more stories to chase."

"Can I ask one quick question?" Dobo asked. "What is your printing process? I hear a machine—"

"Trade secret," Tabitha replied curtly. Then she showed them out.

"I'll take you out there, but I won't hang around," the fisherman said.

"But we'll need to wait for her to return," Kya argued.

"Find someone else, then," the fisherman replied.

"What if we just rent a boat and row it ourselves?" Marta asked.

"Looks like we'll have to," Dobo said.

It took some asking, but they finally found someone willing to rent them a boat. When Dobo told him their plans, the boatsman demanded a deposit upfront in case they didn't make it back.

They rowed until they felt the all-too-familiar miasma that seemed to radiate from every temple.

"How long will the spell last?" Marta asked. They hadn't discussed which of them would be taking the plunge, but it was obvious to all of them that it would be Marta.

Silli bit her lower lip as she flipped through her book. "Somewhere between forty minutes and three-and-a-half hours," she answered.

"That's a pretty big window," Kya said.

"I'm not even sure if this is going to work," Silli replied.

"How will I find the temple without your help?" Marta asked.

"One moment," Silli said. Then she dove under the water.

"Don't wear anything too heavy," Dobo suggested. "Leave your backpack here, and only take the essentials."

Marta removed her armor. Now in her street clothes, she stared at the sword in her lap. "I'm not sure if I should take this or not," she said.

"You won't be able to swing it as hard down there," Dobo said. "You'll want to travel light. My suggestion would be to take a dagger and a glowstone."

"What if something big attacks her?" Kya asked.

"Flee," Dobo said. "We're here to collect a jewel, not fight monsters. If something stands between you and the eye of O'olos, and it's too big to fight with a dagger, come straight back here and we'll make a new plan."

Marta nodded. "And if something attacks the boat, don't wait on me. I can swim back to the island."

Silli burst out of the water and shook herself off like a wet dog. "It's pretty easy to spot," she said. "There's a shipwreck down there halfway covering the entrance. Ready?"

Marta nodded and stood up. Silli began chanting in a fairy language, then sprinkled a bit of fairy dust on top of Marta's head. They waited a few seconds, but nothing happened.

Marta frowned. "I don't feel anything yuh... uh... uh... I can't... bree..." She clawed at her neck, and her face started to turn purple.

"Reverse the spell!" Dobo shouted.

Marta shook her head. Small slits opened up on the sides of her neck.

"Get in the water!" Kya shouted. She stood and pushed Marta overboard.

Marta felt instant relief as she plunged beneath the surface. She swam around in a few circles, enjoying how free it felt to swim without having to hold her breath. She popped her head above the water for a moment and gave her friends a wave, just so they'd know she hadn't drowned. Then she dove deeper and began her search.

Marta swam past the temple twice before she recognized it for what it was. Partially obscured by the shipwreck Silli had mentioned, the ancient stone temple was covered in barnacles and seaweed. Glowstone in hand, Marta descended and searched for the entrance. The doorway was wide open, and Marta went inside.

As she swam through the hallways, she tried to calculate how long she'd been underwater. It couldn't have been more than twenty minutes. *I really wish we still had both rings*, she thought. Part of her was glad that her friends would be in less danger this time, but at the same time she was worried she might encounter a puzzle that only the others could solve.

She passed several doorways but continued to swim in a straight line. Most of these temples had simple floorplans, and the main hallway usually led to some sort of worship room. That didn't necessarily mean the jewel was there, but it was often the best place to start.

The hallway led to a large round atrium. The floors featured a mosaic with a sea motif, which depicted giant seahorses engaged in a war against an army of crabs. A large octopus clung to the ceiling. Marta thought it was decorative at first, but then she saw one of the tentacles twitch. She did a triple-take when she realized it was neither a sculpture nor an octopus, but rather one of those Shuul-spawn.

It was much larger than the ones they'd fought in Duskmorgue. All of its eyes were closed, and as far as Marta knew it hadn't spotted her. Marta quickly swam on by, entering another hallway on the other side of the atrium. She spotted a few more Shuul-spawn on the way, none as big as the one in the atrium, but still quite large. If one of these were to take control of a skeleton, the skeleton would have to be at least twelve feet tall.

Finally she found the place of worship. The pews were made of coral, and the altar was carved to look like it was covered in starfish. *And to think they built this before it was underwater,* Marta thought.

Another Shuul-spawn lay across the altar. Marta thought she saw something glittering beneath it, half-obscured by one of the tentacles. She swam as close as she dared, holding out the glowstone for a better look.

It was indeed the eye of O'olos. *You couldn't find a better place to sleep?* Marta wondered.

Most of the jewel was visible. It wouldn't take much effort to wiggle it out from under the tentacle. Marta crept forward – as much as one can creep while swimming, anyway – and drew her dagger. She held onto the altar with one hand, awkwardly holding the glowstone in her palm. With her other hand she touched the tip of the dagger to the jewel, trying to pull it out from under the Shuul-spawn without waking it.

The jewel wiggled a little as Marta nudged it with the dagger. Her face was mere inches away from the Shuul-spawn's bulbous head, but she leaned forward and concentrated on her work. Finally she knocked it free, and the jewel glittered as it floated towards Marta's face. She let go of the altar and grabbed the eye of O'olos before it could get away.

And then she faced dozens of eyes. The Shuul-spawn had awakened, and its many eyes blinked a few times while it tried to comprehend Marta's presence. She turned and swam away, but she doubted she could swim faster than the Shuul-spawn.

The creature emitted a high-pitched squeal that made Marta's teeth hurt. More of the tentacled monsters detached from the walls, many emerging from hidden recesses and seaweed-covered alcoves.

Marta swam with all her might, but the creatures converged on her. In a desperate attempt to avoid their grasp, she threw the glowstone behind her. Most of the Shuul-spawn turned and followed it.

But now Marta was in the dark. She remembered the route; it was a straight shot through the atrium, down the following hall, and out the front door. A little bit of light still trickled down from the surface, and she could just barely make out the tiny doorway in the distance, a faint green rectangle against the black. It looked miles away.

She sheathed her dagger and slipped the jewel into her mouth so she wouldn't drop it. Then she swam as hard as her muscles would allow. She had no idea if she was being followed, or by how many creatures.

She was halfway through the atrium when a colossal tentacle swept by her. It could only have been from the giant Shuul-spawn she'd seen on the ceiling. She swam even harder, barely avoiding a grasping appendage.

She was in the hallway when a tentacle slammed into her side, knocking her against the wall. Marta felt that numbing sting she'd felt back in Duskmorgue, though it didn't seem as potent this time. *Maybe the bigger they are, the weaker their sting,* she thought. But that didn't mean the creature was harmless. More tentacles reached for her, and she backed through a doorway, into one of the side rooms she'd passed on the way in.

It appeared to be a study room, with lumps of rotting driftwood that looked like they might have once been desks. A faint light illuminated the room, coming from a dirty stained glass window depicting an ocean beneath a blue sky filled with birds.

Marta tried to slam the door shut behind her, but between the rusted hinges and the decaying wood, she couldn't even move the door without ripping it apart. More tentacles followed her through the doorway, and she realized she was trapped.

A tentacle wrapped around her leg, and the numbness traveled up her thigh. She drew her dagger and stabbed the appendage. Black blood floated through the water as it withdrew. More tentacles searched for her, but without the monster's eyes, they had to feel around blindly.

Marta turned and punched the window, but she couldn't work up enough force to shatter it. She tried to shatter it with her dagger, but all she managed was to put a large crack in the glass.

More tentacles flowed into the room, followed by the creature's head. It glowered at her with dozens of hate-filled eyes.

It was now or never. Marta stabbed the glass again, this time chipping out a jagged shard. One more hit and the glass finally shattered.

But not the entire window. The stained glass was divided into sections by color, each separated by lead lines. Marta had broken the largest portion of the picture, the part depicting the ocean itself. The rest of the image remained intact.

The opening was slightly too small, but she had to try. Marta grabbed the edges of the glass and pulled herself through the window, briefly getting stuck at her bust, then again at her posterior. She was almost completely out when more tentacles grabbed her by the legs.

And then her breath started to hitch. The spell was wearing off.

*Because I needed more problems*, Marta thought, holding her breath and frantically stabbing at the tentacles with her dagger. They finally let go and she pushed her way to the surface. It was slower going than it should have been because her legs were still numb. Her lungs burned as she desperately pulled herself towards the taunting sky.

And then she broke the surface and gasped for dear life. She spotted the boat and swam as quickly as her arms would let her. Her friends pulled her into the boat and she lay on her back for a few minutes, catching her breath.

"Take us back to the dock," she said. "Before any of those things decide to come after us."

"What sort of 'things' were they?" Dobo asked as he started rowing.

Marta took a few more deep breaths. "More Shuul-spawn," she said. "But bigger. At first, I thought they were octopuses."

"Octopi," Kya corrected.

"Octopodes," Dobo said.

"Squid," Silli offered.

"No, squid aren't the same as octopodes," Dobo told her.

"But the Shuul-spawn aren't either one," Silli replied. "So it doesn't matter which we use to describe them."

"They're closer to octopodes," Dobo countered. "They have round heads and eight tentacles."

"But squid is more fun to say!" Silli shouted.

While they argued, Kya knelt over Marta. "Are you okay?" she asked.

"I'm fine," Marta answered. "I thought I was going to drown back there, but I'm good now."

"Did you get the jewel?" Kya asked.

"Yes, I..." Marta said, then sat up in a panic. She patted herself all over. A look of realization dawned on her face. "I think I swallowed it."

"Ah," Kya said. "Well, you can get it back to us in a day or two."

Marta nodded. "Where to next?"

"I think it was Cherrybrook," Kya said.

"Not quite," Dobo said, turning away from a rather annoyed-looking Sillivene. "There's something I want to check on before we leave town."

The sun was setting when they returned to the Crier offices. A man was locking the front door as they approached. "We have to see Tabitha Wright," Dobo told him.

"She's the only one still in the building," the man said. "Is she expecting you?"

"Oh yes," Dobo said.

The man shrugged and let them in. The front office seemed larger now that it was empty. They still heard the thumping of machinery from somewhere behind the wall.

Dobo knocked on Tabitha's door, then burst in before she even told him to enter. "Have I got a story for you!" Dobo announced.

"Our office is closed," Tabitha said, scowling. Then she smiled and added, "So this better be juicy."

Marta and Kya stepped into the office behind Dobo and they all sat down. Even though Marta had been the one to explore the temple, Dobo told the story, stretching out the details and making everything sound epic. Tabitha hung on every word and took pages and pages of notes.

While Dobo kept her busy, Silli turned herself invisible and explored the back offices. She paused at a locked door marked:

PRIVATE

AUTHORIZED PERSONNEL ONLY

She put her ear up to the door. The mechanical thumping seemed to be coming from the other side. "Vonek lache corrum," she chanted, and sprinkled a bit of fairy dust on the lock. It popped right open and she slipped inside the room.

She gasped at what she saw. Half of the room was taken up by a mechanical device that would have made Dobo drool. Employees fed blank parchment into the device, a large plate came down and pressed against the paper, and printed copies of the Sweetgrape Crier popped out the other side.

But it was the employees that curdled Silli's blood. There were eight in total – four men, two women, and two children. And all of them had Shuul-spawn attached to their heads. Silli recognized both of the children. One was the boy who had sold them a copy of the Crier earlier that day. The other was a girl of about eight. Silli had seen a sketch of her face in Dobo's copy of the Crier, accompanying an article about a missing child.

The employees worked the machine in a trance, one feeding papers into it, another retrieving papers, and two turning some sort of crank on the side. The rest rolled up the finished parchments and readied them for distribution.

Silli reached into her purse and retrieved her book. Then she flipped through the pages, looking for that chant. As she frantically searched for the right page, she noticed that the pounding had stopped. She looked up and saw that everyone was staring at her - both the humans and the creatures on their heads.

*They can see me*, Silli thought. *Even though I'm invisible*. She turned and zipped out the door, followed by a stampede.

"And then she fought a giant Shuul-spawn," Dobo said. "Bigger than this building."

"I'm not sure it was *that* big," Marta said.

"I'm telling it," Dobo replied. "And even though the spell was wearing off, she bravely faced the monster, knowing she might drown before she had the chance to kill it."

"I did more fleeing than fighting, really," Marta said.

"Hush," Dobo said. "So she bravely swang her sword..."

"Swinged," Kya corrected.

"Swung," Tabitha said, still taking notes.

"Dagger," Marta added.

There was a crash from the main office area, followed by a high-pitched scream. Marta stood and drew her sword, then opened the door. Silli was being chased by several people with Shuul-spawn on their heads.

"I'll hold them off!" Marta shouted, rushing past Silli. She took a swipe at the nearest employee, severing the top of the Shuul-spawn's head. The employee, a man of about twenty-five, collapsed to the floor and crawled away.

Now that Marta stood between her and the creatures, Silli started looking for the chant again. Kya stood and readied her bow.

"Did you know about this?" Dobo shouted at Tabitha.

"I don't even know what this is," Tabitha responded. Her face had gone pale and she'd dropped her quill. Her look was one of total astonishment.

Three of the Shuul-spawn released their hosts and flew at Marta. She killed one with a quick swipe and injured another, but the third wrapped its tentacles around her body, making her go numb. Kya readied an arrow but was afraid she might hit Marta.

Silli found the right page and began chanting. More Shuul-spawn detached from their original hosts. One wrapped itself around Kya, and another flew straight for Tabitha's office.

And then, as one, they released their victims and took to

the air. They shivered with agitation, knocking against the ceiling while looking for an exit. One smashed through a window and the rest followed it out into the night.

Marta and Kya lay on the floor while they recovered from their numbness. The other former hosts began to come to their senses and looked around in confusion. "Where are we?" one woman asked.

Dobo and Tabitha stepped out of the office and helped everyone get comfortable.

"Where did these people come from?" Tabitha asked.

"They were operating your printing machine," Silli said. "While being mind-controlled by those things."

"That doesn't even make sense," Tabitha objected. "How did…" Then she thought a moment. "Mr. Orva… He owns the Crier. He's been acting odd lately. A few days ago he said he'd found a way to lower payroll costs while printing even more papers…"

"You seek out strange stories for a living," Dobo said. "That didn't sound suspicious to you?"

"Mr. Orva finding new ways to cut corners?" Tabitha asked. "That's hardly news."

"If he had the Shuul-spawn doing his bidding, he has to be in league with the Tyk-Shuul cult," Dobo said.

"Right," Tabitha said. "If you would do me one favor. Could one of you head to the guardhouse and fetch us some law enforcement?"

"I'll go," Kya said, rising from the floor. Her body was still a little numb, but she could move.

Marta rose as well, and helped Dobo and Silli tend to the recovering victims. Tabitha began searching all the filing crates for more evidence. By the time the guards arrived, everyone was in good shape and ready to press charges.

As a thank you from the mayor, the party was given a free overnight stay in Sweetgrape's finest inn. They picked up a copy of the Crier on their way out of town. The top headline read:

KNILES ORVA, HEAD OF CRIER, ARRESTED ON CHARGES OF KIDNAPPING, FORCED LABOR, AND CONSPIRING WITH CULTISTS

They had breakfast, then took the ferry back to Port Sweetgrape to retrieve their wagon and horses. Then they rode on for a full day and camped overnight. The following morning they had breakfast and continued their journey.

"We should hit Cherrybrook by nightfall," Dobo said. The full moon was four days away, and they'd recovered six of the seven jewels. After Cherrybrook they could return to Lakehelm and complete their quest, for good or ill.

After about six hours on the road, they spotted a man on horseback coming towards them at a full gallop. He pulled his horse to a stop as he reached the wagon.

"Are you headed to Cherrybrook?" the man huffed. He seemed to be even more exhausted than his horse. His clothes were torn and his skin was covered in soot.

"Yes, why?" Dobo replied.

"Don't bother," the man said. "The Nethursine has awakened and razed the entire town."

"The Nether-what?" Dobo asked.

"Just stay away," the man pleaded as he urged his horse into a gallop and rode on towards Sweetgrape.

*That's the one thing we can't do,* Dobo thought as he resumed the drive to Cherrybrook.

## Cherrybrook

*What did you do?* Marta thought. It was the first time she'd put the ring on since the ride to Proudpath.

*You must have heard about Cherrybrook,* Ryveen replied.

*Did you leave anyone alive?* Marta asked.

*How should I know, I'm still in Lakehelm,* Ryveen replied. *But I do know this. Your death awaits you in Cherrybrook. Take my advice and turn back now. There may yet be a safe place for you in this world, far beyond the land of Zyden. Find it and live out your days in peace.*

*I don't run,* Marta thought. *I will face this evil in Cherrybrook, and when I've defeated it, I will come for you.*

*What about your friends?* Ryveen asked.

Suddenly Marta's mind was a collage of images of Dobo, Sillivene, and Kya. *How does Ryveen know what they look like?* she wondered. She'd yet to encounter them in person.

*I see them in your thoughts,* Ryveen answered, though Marta hadn't intended to send the question to her. *But,* Ryveen continued, *Have you seen them... like this?*

Now Marta's head was flooded with new pictures of her friends, only this time they were broken and mutilated, their flesh torn and their faces bloody, their limbs twisted into unnatural angles. Marta shrieked out loud and removed the ring. She sat alone in the back of the wagon, trying to catch her breath. The connection was broken, but those horrifying images lingered.

She couldn't back out now. To do so would mean the death of the world. *But do my friends have to share in that danger?* Marta wondered. She thought on this for a while.

*They'll never agree to split up*, she realized. *But if I find an opportunity to leave them behind, I will take it.*



Smoke rose from the ashes of what had once been an idyllic little town. A beautiful creek flowed past collapsed houses, fallen cherry trees, and the shredded corpses of townsfolk.

"What could have done this?" Kya asked.

"That rider called it the 'Nethursine' but I've never heard of such a beast," Dobo said.

"It wasn't in any of my books either," Silli added.

Marta was silent. The destruction was all too familiar, and images of her own community flashed through her mind.

"So where is it now?" Kya asked. "Seems like we'd be able to see a creature large enough to do... *this*." She gestured vaguely at the debris, then let her hand drop. Her eyes fell on the corpse of a young girl, and the sight made her chest hurt. The child had been impaled by something Kya couldn't identify. It looked like the pointy end of a feather quill, but much larger.

"Maybe it went on to the next city," Dobo said. "Or perhaps it went back to its slumber."

"I can't imagine a single beast capable of this much destruction," Marta said finally. "And yet we're told Tyk-Shuul is an even worse threat."

"Oh, I'm sure there's a connection between the two," Dobo said. "With Tyk-Shuul about to rise, his minions are starting to awaken. The Shuul-spawn, presumably the Sleeth, and now... whatever did all this."

"We should look for survivors," Marta said.

"I agree," Dobo said. "But we can't spend too much time on it, we have a jewel to find."

"If anyone's trapped in the rubble, they could be bleeding out," Kya argued.

"We have to be back in Lakehelm in three days," Dobo countered. "Far more lives will be lost if we miss that deadline."

"Silli, can your magic help us search for survivors?" Marta asked.

But Silli wasn't there. They squinted through the smoke, searching for their fairy friend.

"There," Dobo said, pointing to a bright dot in the sky. Silli circled the town, then returned to her friends.

"I think I see the temple," Silli reported. "...Or what's left of it. It's in just as bad a shape as the rest of the town."

"I'll check it out while you two look for survivors," Marta said. They agreed, and Silli led her to the temple.


"There's just no way to get down there," Marta said, looking at the rubble. "Forget the full moon, I could start digging now and I wouldn't find the jewel until I was old and gray."

"We've come so far, though," Silli said. "We can't just stop here."

"Do you have any sort of spells that can tunnel through rock?" Marta asked.

"I don't think there's one in my books, but maybe if I went back to the Fairy Kingdom," Silli suggested.

"We just don't have that kind of time," Marta said. She sat on the ground and put her head in her hands. *There has to be a way*, she thought over and over. But nothing came to mind. Her body shuddered as a feeling of desperation threatened to overtake her.

She heard a shriek in the distance. *Kya*, she thought, and immediately sprang to her feet. Maybe she couldn't save the world, but she could save her friends.

Kya and Dobo stood with their backs against the wagon, firing arrows and crossbow bolts at the approaching Sleeth warriors. The four snake-headed soldiers spread out, making a semicircle around that side of the wagon as they closed in.

Kya hit one in the eye, but it continued its approach. With nowhere to run, she dropped to the ground and rolled under the wagon. Dobo followed just as the Sleeth rushed forward. Dobo and Kya emerged on the other side, then broke into a run. They heard a shrill whinny from one of the horses as they fled.

Kya ran through the smoking ruins, looking for somewhere to hide. After a minute she realized Dobo was no longer at her side. She didn't want to call out because it would alert the Sleeth. She hid behind the remains of an inn and listened for footsteps.

And suddenly a Sleeth warrior landed right next to her, having leaped from who knew where. It thrust its sword at her, impaling her through the left bicep. Kya cried out in pain and dropped her bow.

The monster withdrew its blade and Kya sank to her knees, gripping her wound. The Sleeth raised its sword, ready to cleave her in two. Kya tensed in anticipation. She was surrounded by detritus, and there was nowhere to run.

And then a blade burst through the creature's chest. The Sleeth buckled to its knees, blood oozing from its armor. Kya now saw Marta standing behind it, once again having come to her rescue. But the Sleeth rose again and faced Marta.

*It survived that?* Kya thought as she watched the two go sword-to-sword.

Marta was the better duelist, but the Sleeth kept shrugging off its injuries. As Marta ducked a wild swing, she countered with a swipe that severed the Sleeth's left arm. The appendage hit the ground with a hollow CLANG, but no blood sprayed from the wound.

"Go for the head!" Kya shouted, finally realizing what she was seeing. The armor was enchanted to fight, but the Sleeth was just a big snake coiled up inside its armor's chest cavity.

Marta hadn't made the same connection, but she trusted her girlfriend's advice. It wasn't easy tricking her opponent into position for decapitation, and the monster parried every attempt at a fatal swing. Then Marta feinted high and slashed low, severing one of its legs. Once again the armor proved to be hollow, but the Sleeth was left with very little maneuverability. Unable to stand up again, it slithered out of the armor, proving Kya's theory correct. It still bled from a few wounds, but it wasn't about to go down just yet. It circled Marta and opened its jaws, rearing back for a strike.

Then it thrust forward at lightning speed, but Marta was half a second quicker. She ducked beneath its bite and drove her sword up through its throat. It was dead by the time it hit the ground.

Marta helped Kya to her feet, but they heard more footsteps approaching. The other three Sleeth had been drawn by the sounds of battle.

But then the ground rumbled beneath their feet. In the distance, where the temple had once stood, a monstrous black shape burst out of the ground. The beast was as big as a barn, but there was too much smoke to make out any details. It sniffed the air and then charged towards Marta.

"Run," Marta ordered, but Kya was frozen in shock. Even the Sleeth halted as if in reverence to the superior being.

As the beast drew near, Marta made out more and more of its features. It looked like a giant bear, but with horns like a bull and the tusks of a warthog. Instead of hair, it had porcupine-like quills. A club-like tail trailed off behind it. Three eyes adorned its horrifying face.

*No*, Marta thought. The middle one wasn't an eye. It looked more like… "The jewel!" she shouted.

The Nethursine lowered its head and charged at Marta. She grabbed Kya around the waist and dove to the side. One of the Sleeth went flying as the great beast barreled past them. Then it turned and swang its massive tail in a wide arc, completely unbothered by trivialities such as who it hurt, whether they were on the same side, and whether or not 'swang' was a word. The other two Sleeth were cast aside like ragdolls.

Marta got to her feet. The beast glared at her and charged again. This time Marta stood her ground, holding her sword directly ahead. Maybe it would trample her to death, but she was determined to slice its belly open as it did so.

And then Silli flew by and plucked the jewel from the beast's forehead. This enraged the monster, and it turned to chase her. It trampled the Sleeth a bit more as Silli darted left and right, teasing the giant creature.

"Get it to come back this way!" Marta shouted, and Silli redirected the Nethursine until it was on a direct path to Marta. While it was distracted by the fairy, Marta ran beneath the beast, carefully avoiding its quills. It roared when she thrust her sword into its gut. No longer distracted by Silli, it reared back for a moment then slammed its full body against the ground in an attempt to crush Marta into paste.

She barely rolled out of the way in time, dropping her sword as she rushed to her feet. Then she ran as fast as she could away from the now furious beast. The Nethursine curled up into a giant ball and bowled after her. It left a quill-filled trench behind as it moved.

The rolling monster was as wide as the street, or Marta would have simply leaped to the side. But the piles of debris meant she would have had to take the time to climb out of the way, and that was time she didn't have. She ran straight ahead, watching the creature's massive shadow loom larger and larger.

A cross street was just a few hundred feet away. If she could make it that far, she'd be able to sidestep the rolling beast. But she'd never make it that far. She could feel the air tremble behind her. Occasionally the tip of a quill would scratch the back of her armor.

And then she spotted an egress. It was a diagonally oriented open doorway, the type that usually leads to a basement. It was still about twenty feet away, but it was a chance.

Another quill scratched her arm as it rolled downwards, and the fresh cut burned. She was out of time. As the doorway came near, she dove into the blackness. The Nethursine missed her by inches as it rolled by.

Marta tumbled down a set of wooden stairs and hit her head on the stone floor. She tried to get to her knees but she was seeing spots, and a wave of nausea overcame her. She lay on the ground for a few seconds, taking slow, deep breaths.

Her eyes finally adjusted to the dim light. The basement had caved in from the collapse, blocking her from moving any farther in. She rested for a few more seconds, and was about to climb back out when the opening was blocked by a shadow. A giant nose pressed itself against the doorway, sniffing. Then the nose shifted to the side and the Nethursine shoved its paw into the hole. It was a tight fit, but it slowly reached for Marta with claws that had to be at least a yard long.

Marta reached for her sword but remembered she'd dropped it. Instead, she dropped to the floor and crawled under the stairs. The paw continued to grope around in the darkness.

Then she heard Kya's voice somewhere far off. "Leave her alone, you… monster!"

Dobo and Silli joined in with cries of "Take this!" and "Here we are!"

*What are they doing?* Marta wondered.

The monster growled in pain and tried to extract its paw from the basement. It couldn't quite get its hand back through, and it tugged several times with no success.

Seizing the opportunity, Marta pulled a broken wooden beam from the rubble, then drove it through the creature's wrist. It roared and clenched its claws, then began pulling even harder to free its paw. But the end of the beam got wedged against the doorframe, and every pull just drove the wood deeper into the monster's wrist.

Whatever her friends were doing to the creature up above, it was working. The Nethursine roared and desperately tried to extract its arm from the hole.

For Marta's part, she kept finding sharp objects and ramming them into the creature's paw. She couldn't exactly do lethal damage from this angle, but if nothing else she could keep the beast distracted while her friends attacked it from a safe distance.

Finally the claws stiffened, then relaxed. There was a thud that shook the basement hard enough to throw Marta off her feet. The arm thrust forward, almost up to the elbow, slamming against the rubble with enough force to bring the rest of the ceiling down.

Marta rolled back under the stairs to avoid the collapse. The Nethursine's dead arm stretched out above her, on the other side of the wooden steps.

When the dust settled, she found she had even less room than she'd had before. She was trapped under the stairs, with a wall of crumbled stone and broken wood blocking her in on both sides. Working by the light of a glowstone, she pulled one rock after another out of the pile and placed them under the stairs. *It's going to take me a year to dig myself out of here*, she thought.

"I think she's over here!" The voice was muffled but obviously masculine.

"Dobo! I'm down here!" Marta shouted.

"I hear her! She's somewhere down below!"

Marta kept moving rocks, making a tunnel. She heard the sound of shifting debris above her as her friends worked their way down to her. After who-knew-how-many hours, she pulled a stone aside and saw daylight.

"I see her!" Silli shouted, peering through the hole. They worked a bit more at widening the tunnel, and finally Marta climbed out of the debris. The sun was starting to set. The monster lay just a few feet away, half its body lying across the building and the other half blocking the street.

"How… how did you… kill it?" Marta asked between coughs.

"We just kept wearing it down with arrows and bolts,"

Kya said.

"And spells," Silli added proudly. "I took out one of its eyes with a magic arrow."

"We couldn't have done it if it hadn't gotten its paw stuck," Dobo said.

"Then we should... probably be... on our way," Marta said, still working the dust out of her lungs.

"Sit down, we have to talk," Dobo said, and everyone sat on the rubble.

"What is it?" Marta asked.

"One of the horses didn't make it," Dobo told her. "And we can't pull the wagon with just one horse. I suppose one of us could ride on to the next town and buy another horse, then bring it back here..."

"...but the next town is Lakehelm," Marta said. "Unless we head back to Sweetgrape, but we don't have that kind of time."

"Didn't we pass a few farms on the way here?" Kya asked. "We could see if one of them could sell us a horse."

Marta shook her head. "Give me the jewels. I will ride the horse to Lakehelm, pray to the statue, and stop Tyk-Shuul. The rest of you can see if there's a farm within walking distance with a couple of horses to sell."

"I'll come with you," Kya suggested. "The horse can take us, we've ridden together before."

"The horse will tire more quickly with two riders," Marta said. "I can get there faster alone."

"By that logic I should be the one to go by myself," Kya said.

"Or me," Dobo said. "We're both lighter than you."

"There may be some fighting when we get there," Marta argued. "You'll need my sword."

"Like we've never survived a fight without you?" Kya

asked. "We just brought down a giant bear while you were stuck in a basement."

"I'm sorry, Kya," Marta said. "I don't wish to devalue your help. I couldn't have gotten this far without you. All of you. But... you know I'm the one who... who..." She paused, trying to think of an inoffensive way to end her sentence.

"You're the hero of the story," Dobo said. "Is that it? You see yourself as the main character in an epic tale, and we're just the supporting cast."

"No," Marta said. "But you have to admit I've been the one to do most of the work," she blurted. She regretted the words as soon as they left her lips. "I mean the swordwork," she added quickly.

"You don't think I've been pulling my weight?" Kya asked. Her face was turning red, but she looked more hurt than angry.

"Of course you have," Marta apologized. "I just want to keep you safe—"

"I'm not some precious piece of art for you to lock in a vault," Kya said. "I'm your partner, and whatever evils we have to face, we face together. And I'm *sorry* if my lazy arse hasn't racked up a kill count to rival yours. Maybe I should spend less time solving puzzles so there's more room in my schedule for maiming."

"I don't think you're lazy," Marta said. "It's just... I'm..." She trailed off.

"The hero," Kya said. "Like Dobo said. Well, I've got news for you, hero. The odds of us stopping Tyk-Shuul aren't great. Even with all four of us. Splitting up right now is the worst thing we can do."

"Then what do you suggest?" Marta asked. "Spend the next three days finding another horse so we can mosey into the burning ruins of Lakehelm?"

"I have a suggestion," Silli said, waving her arms.

"What?" Dobo asked, still glaring at Marta.

"It's almost dark," Silli said. "We rode all morning, fought some snake people and a giant porcupine-bear thing, dug a tunnel... I think we all need a rest. Whatever we do next – find another horse, send a rider to Lakehelm - It'll be easier in the morning light."

"She's right," Marta said. "I'm still coughing up dust, and we're all a bit banged up."

"I suppose," Kya said. "But we still have to discuss this."

They searched the ruins until they found another building with a basement. The house had collapsed but the floor hadn't caved in, so the basement was free of debris. Marta and Kya unfolded their bedrolls on the stone floor. They usually lay them side-by-side, but tonight they placed them on opposite sides of the room. Dobo slept in the wagon along with Silli, with the horse tied up nearby.

Marta made sure her friends were fast asleep before she stole the horse.


"It hurrrrrts, Mommyyyyy..."

Ryveen's eyes widened as Tobi lumbered into the ancient temple, his seven-foot-tall body riddled with arrows and crossbow bolts. He stumbled across the stone tiles until he collapsed right in front of the altar.

"No," Ryveen said, kneeling over her son. "No! No no no!" she shouted impotently. *We were so close*, she thought. *So close.*

As Tobi bled out, Ryveen recognized the fletching on one of the arrows. Her son had been hunted and executed by the Lakehelm militia. Her only son. Only three days away from immortality, and they put him down like a rabid dog.

*There has to be something I can do*, she thought, standing up.

She ran back to the altar and flipped through the ritual book, desperately hoping to discover a loophole, some way to retain the pact.

The transformation was unstoppable. Tyk-Shuul would rise in three days regardless of whether Tobi lived. But now his host would be random, most likely some unsuspecting child of Lakehelm. For Ryveen's pact to work, the vessel had to be of her blood.

In truth, she cared nothing for Tyk-Shuul and the devastation he would cause. It was one of the ritual's side effects she was interested in. The mother of the vessel would be granted near immortality. With Tobi as the host, Ryveen would acquire unfathomable abilities, and she would use her newfound power to conquer the world.

But that was just a dream now. The militia had robbed her of her glorious future. Another child would become the destroyer, and their mother – whether they were currently living or dead – would be destined for a divine rebirth.

*I shouldn't have let him go out alone,* Ryveen chided herself. *He's just a little boy,* she thought, staring lovingly at the monstrous thing her son had become.

A ceremonial dagger lay across the altar. She imagined herself picking it up and shoving it into her stomach. If she couldn't rule the world, she didn't want to be part of the collateral damage. Zyden was about to become a burning hellscape, and a quick death would be preferable to surviving the carnage. She reached for the dagger and ran her fingertips along the hilt.

"Hello?"

Ryveen jumped at the voice, knocking the dagger to the floor. A figure approached, barely illuminated by the torchlight.

"Zib?" Ryveen asked.

"What happened here?" Zib asked. He limped forward but stopped when he saw Tobi's corpse.

"Lakehelm's soldiers murdered my son," Ryveen spat.

"I... I'm sorry for your loss," Zib said nervously. After escaping the cell in Sesta, he'd taken his time returning to Lakehelm. Ryveen's potential ire had slowed his pace. And now he'd arrived at the worst possible time, right after a tragedy that would make her beyond furious. He took a step backward.

But when Ryveen looked at him, she didn't seem very angry. In fact, there was a smile threatening to form at the edge of her lips. If Zib had to guess, it looked like she'd just thought of an idea that would save everything she'd worked for.

"Zib," she said pleasantly. "I need a child."

"Of course, mistress," he replied. "Does Lakehelm have an orphanage, or is there a specific..."

"Hush," Ryveen said. She stepped out from behind the altar and removed her robe.

*Oh*, Zib thought, as she pulled him to the floor.

*Transformation*

LAKEHELM – 5 MI

*Finally*, Marta thought as she passed the wooden sign. She'd spent most of the last two days at a full gallop. She'd barely eaten or slept, and her horse was about to drop from exhaustion. But tonight was the night of the full moon, and there was no time to waste.

She'd almost expected to find Lakehelm in ruins, but it looked just like every other day. It was around midday, and people walked about on their way to have lunch, oblivious to the upcoming apocalypse.

Marta rode straight to the docks and searched for the statue of O'olos. But where the statue had once stood, now there was only a pile of broken stones. She gasped, then grabbed the arm of a passing dockworker.

"What happened to the statue?" Marta asked breathlessly.

"Some vandals destroyed it a couple of weeks ago," the man said, looking at her strangely. "Are you feeling well?"

Marta was tired, distraught, bruised, and dirty from the long ride. Her panic over a simple statue probably made her look insane. She didn't answer his question for several seconds, she just stared into his face with wild eyes. "I'm… fine," she finally said, and let go of his arm. Then she sank to her knees and sifted through the rubble.

*I can't fix this,* she thought. It wasn't like reassembling a dismantled chair. The statue had been smashed into gravel, and there would be no putting it back together again. It was a lost cause.

She sat there for more than an hour, piling up the stones like she was playing in the sand. People stared at her as they walked by, but no one stopped to talk to her.

*I wish my friends were here,* she thought. *They'd know what to do.*

There was a commotion in the distance, from somewhere near the edge of town. *Has the transformation begun?* she wondered. Sundown was still a few hours away, but Marta didn't know all the rules of the ritual. Maybe it only had to be the day of the full moon. Maybe it could happen any time after midday. Maybe it…

And then she saw it. A wagon sped through the streets, not a horse in sight. Dobo and Kya sat in the driver's seat, trying desperately to keep the vehicle under control. They turned sharply to the right, and Marta saw jets of flame spewing from the back of the wagon. Then it turned back to the left, overcompensated, and nearly tipped over. It drove on two wheels for a few seconds before turning back towards the docks.

It skidded to a halt about twenty feet away from Marta. Kya spotted her friend and climbed to the ground. She stomped up to Marta, her face red with anger.

Marta's eyes teared up. "I'm so sorry," she said. "I thought I was doing the right thing…"

Kya's fury melted away at the sight of Marta's desperate expression. They came together in a tight embrace. "You're still a manure-head," Kya whispered.

"Indeed," Marta agreed. "And I'll do whatever it takes to make it up to you, assuming we live long enough. But how did you get here so fast?"

"Take a look," Kya said, and led her to the wagon. Four metal rods were fastened to the back of the vehicle. Marta recognized them as the pyrotechnic wands Dobo sometimes used.

"Like them?" Dobo asked proudly. "They're a combination of my know-how and Silli's magic. See, with the right combination of explosive compounds, and just a bit of fairy dust, I was able to—"

"The statue's been destroyed," Marta interrupted.

"What?" Kya asked. She looked past Marta, over to the docks.

"Should have expected this," Dobo grumbled. "Of course Ryveen knew our plans, why wouldn't she destroy the statue?"

"So what do we do?" Marta asked.

"We go to the library," Kya replied.


"I think it's time," Ryveen said. Her distended belly was obscenely bulbous, easily accounting for half her body weight, and it was covered in dark purple stretch marks. She'd given up wearing clothes the day before, and as of this morning she could no longer stand up. She lay flat on the altar, as it was the only flat surface in the temple, though the symbolism wasn't lost on her. She was indeed sacrificing her body to her Night Lord.

Zib stood by her side, his hand on her shoulder. "Is there anything I can do for you?" Zib asked. His face turned pale as he watched the bulges and knots undulate across her stomach.

"Just be brave," Ryveen said. "Yours is a position of great honor. As Tyk-Shuul's first meal —"

"Meal?" Zib asked. "As in… *meal?*"

"I told you this part already," Ryveen grunted. It was becoming hard to talk.

"You told me I'd have to feed him," Zib said. "I assumed that meant —"

"There's no time to argue," Ryveen shouted. "It's… it's…"

She screamed as a tentacle as thick as her thigh erupted from her nether regions. It was joined by a second tentacle, then two more. Ryveen's screeches reached an inhuman pitch.

*Forget this*, Zib thought, and ran for the exit. He was halfway there when Ryveen's screams abruptly halted, only to be replaced by an unholy growling.

The exit was just ahead. Strange shadows appeared on the walls, and he could hear gurgling and slithering sounds behind him. Then he burst through the doorway and into the twilight. He leaned against a tree for a moment, trying to catch his breath.

*I've got to get out of town*, he thought.

Then a vinelike appendage wrapped around his ankle and yanked him back into the temple.


"Here we go," Kya said, opening a book and laying it flat on the table. The sun was setting, and the four hurried around Esova's office, flipping through books and tossing them aside. Kya's current volume was titled "Legends of O'olos," which sounded promising. She scanned the pages until she found exactly what she'd been looking for.

"So, good news, it looks like it doesn't have to be a statue,"

Kya said. "The eyes just have to be mounted the right distance off the ground, and it has to be near water."

"What about the prayer?" Marta asked. "Is there a specific verse or chant we need to read?"

"Ahhhh... no," Kya answered, searching through the text. "Just make sure the eyes are positioned to see you, then 'assume a supplicant position' and tell her what you need."

"Let's move," Dobo said.


The tree was right on the edge of the lake. Marta used a dagger to carve indentations to hold the jewels. She followed the book's instructions to the letter, arranging the jewels in a V-shape, with the lowest point exactly six feet off the ground.

Once the jewels were in place, Kya dropped to her knees, bowing as she prayed.

"Oh, most powerful O'olos," she said. "We know we aren't worthy, but we beg you for your help."

"Something's coming," Marta said, looking over her shoulder. The crunching of leaves echoed throughout the woods. Marta saw shapes in the distance and drew her sword. "Keep her safe," she said, and ran towards the intruders.

Dobo drew his crossbow and held it ready, and Silli nocked an enchanted arrow against her tiny bow.

"Your greatest nemesis, Tyk-Shuul the Night Lord, will rise again tonight," Kya continued. "He will destroy the land of Zyden if you don't stop him. I know we are ants compared to you, and we are undeserving of your mercy. But... but if you would once again strike down your immortal enemy, it would prove once and for all that you are the superior god. Stories will be written of this day, and your followers will praise your name for years to come. Uh... thank you for... your time."

"Did you feel anything?" Dobo asked and she stood up. "Like a supernatural presence?"

Kya shook her head. "For all I know, I was talking to a tree. Now let's help Marta until—" She started to draw her bow, but suddenly her body was wracked with pain. She convulsed on the ground, coughing and foaming at the mouth.

Dobo knelt and put a hand on her shoulder. "What's wrong?" he asked.

Kya turned and glared at him through seven glowing eyes. When she opened her mouth, her voice echoed like a chorus of howling wolves.

"Where... is... Tyk-Shuul?"

A small army of Sleeth soldiers marched through the forest on the outskirts of Lakehelm. As they drew nearer to the town, Marta burst through the trees, decapitating two soldiers with a single swing of her sword. The nearest soldiers hissed orders at each other and half the contingent converged on Marta while the others continued toward town.

Marta battled furiously, her mind's eye picturing the Sleeth as Bonegrinders, and Lakehelm as her village in the Frostmoor mountains. She took out soldier after soldier, stabbing, thrusting, ducking, and rolling. But soon the earth began to shake. In the distance, trees parted as a giant shape lurched towards them. The Sleeth were just as distracted as Marta by the new arrival.

More trees fell as the Night Lord stomped through the woods on the way to Lakehelm. The sun was almost completely down now, and in the moonlight Marta could barely make out Tyk-Shuul's features.

The creature was at least forty feet tall, his head a dome of eyes, his wide mouth full of triangular teeth. His body looked like a forest of vines had intertwined to form a vaguely human form, and even his clawed hands were just masses of tentacles wrapped together to form wormy fingers.

Shuul-spawn clung to his body like barnacles, helping their master maintain his humanoid shape by wrapping around the loose vines that made up his arms and legs.

All around Marta, Sleeth warriors dropped to their knees, bowing as their master bulldozed his way through the forest. Not wanting to waste the opportunity, Marta decapitated four more Sleeth before they came to their senses and resumed fighting back.

Shouting erupted from the town, and a horn bellowed. As Marta continued taking out Sleeth, Lakehelm militia members flooded into the forest. Then Dobo and Silli joined the fray, firing bolts and arrows at the remaining Sleeth. Marta wondered why she didn't see Kya with them, but there was too much going on to maintain that thought.

The Lakehelm militia fought alongside Marta's party until the Sleeth were all but gone. But they were helpless to stop Tyk-Shuul as he broke through the treeline and approached the town. Lakehelm soldiers surrounded the evil god and fired arrow after arrow, but the Night Lord didn't even flinch. Their swords wouldn't penetrate his skin, and even flaming arrows had no effect.

Tyk-Shuul lifted one massive, tentacled foot and brought it down on top of a barn, then let out a guttural laugh. All over its body, tiny Shuul-spawn detached and took flight, some landing on the panicked militia soldiers.

"Silli!" Dobo shouted. "Do that chant that made them sleep!"

Silli darted forward and started chanting, but the words had little effect. A few of the Shuul-spawn trembled as if they might flee, but none of them detached themselves from their victims.

But then Silli felt an overwhelming sense of rage. She watched as Marta slaughtered Shuul-spawn one after another. The woman's fury was infectious, and Silli allowed it to overwhelm her. The anger invaded every cell in her body, and she glowed with a red light. Then the fairy was off like a fireball, flying straight through the bodies of Shuul-spawn, killing the creatures instantly as she darted from one to the other.

She zoomed over the heads of possessed soldiers, freeing them from their captors as she burned holes through the octopus-like monsters. And then her eyes fell on Tyk-Shuul. *You're mine*, she thought, too furious to think straight. She made a beeline for the Night Lord's head. As she neared, Tyk-Shuul waved his hand and slapped her away. Dobo lost sight of her as she went flying over the trees.

"Silli!" Dobo shouted, and turned to run after her.

"Later!" Marta yelled, grabbing him by the arm.

"But she could be—" Dobo began.

"After the battle!" Marta shouted. "People are dying all around us, and more will die if we shirk our duty!"

More and more Shuul-spawn joined the battle, and half the Lakehelm soldiers fled while others stood their ground. Dobo fired his crossbow, hitting one Shuul-spawn in the eye and sending it screeching away.

Tyk-Shuul stomped on a house, once again shaking with pleasure at the destruction he had caused.

The ground quaked again, only this time the source

seemed farther away, from the direction of the lake. Marta and Dobo turned to see another giant emerge from the trees. The newcomer was just as tall as Tyk-Shuul and also featured an abundance of tentacles, but beyond those similarities they were nothing alike.

From the waist down, O'olos had the body of an octopus, and she slithered through the forest like a swarm of snakes. From the waist up she resembled a human woman, albeit with mottled blue-gray skin and fins running down her arms. More tentacles protruded from her head and dangled down her back like hair.

Her seven eyes were diamond-shaped and crystal blue. The rest of her facial features, her nose, cheeks, and mouth, were...

*Hold on*, Marta thought, studying the behemoth's face. *She looks just like...*

Marta turned and grabbed Dobo by the shoulders. "Where's Kya?" she demanded.

"Later," Dobo said through gritted teeth, mimicking her earlier admonition.

And then Marta understood. Kya had become the vessel for O'olos. "But will I get her back when this is over?" Marta pleaded.

Dobo shrugged. He was still angry with her, but he sympathized with her worries. "I hope so," he said. Then he loaded his crossbow and charged into battle.

Marta stared in awe as O'olos undulated through the forest. She took a less destructive path than Tyk-Shuul had, working with the forest instead of barging through it. Her tendrils reached out ahead of her, gripping trees and pulling her forward, while more tentacles propelled her like slithering snakes. Occasionally one of her appendages would grab a Sleeth soldier and fling it into the lake, or one of her head tentacles would snatch a Shuul-spawn from the sky and pop it into her mouth.

Tyk-Shuul was about to stomp on another house when O'olos grabbed him around the neck. She pulled him back into the forest and began choking him, but he wrestled out of her grasp. Now standing face-to-face, they tore into each other, each grasping and clawing with their many snakelike limbs.

As they pulled each other down into the forest it became tough to discern which deity was which, as all anyone could see was the mass of writhing tentacles that waved over the treetops. Suddenly O'olos went flying through the air, landing next to a building on the edge of town. Tyk-Shuul pounced after her, and they grappled again.

As Marta watched the fight, she realized that O'olos kept pulling her opponent back into the forest, where fewer lives would be lost. *But Esova said O'olos didn't care about the human world,* Marta thought. And then it dawned on her that Kya's influence was still in there somewhere. *How much of her is O'olos, and how much is Kya?* she wondered.

They now fought in the forest again. Marta rushed forward for a better look, and found Dobo standing with dozens of militia members, just watching the battle.

Marta put her hand on Dobo's shoulder. "There's nothing more we can do here," she said. "This is a battle between titans, and our weapons can't even harm them. You should go find Sillivene."

Dobo nodded and ran towards the lake.

Marta sheathed her sword and searched for injured soldiers to aid. She found a man with a nearly-severed arm and helped him dress the wound. Every few seconds she glanced up at the battle, more worried about Kya than what would happen to the world if she lost.

O'olos and Tyk-Shuul seemed evenly matched. The Night Lord fought with intense ferocity, like a rabid animal overcome with bloodlust. The sea goddess was more tactical, delivering fewer blows but making each one count. While Tyk-Shuul tried to tear into her flesh with his deadly teeth, O'olos guided him through the forest, retreating from his blows in a path that must have looked random to her enemy.

In his mindless fury, Tyk-Shuul seized his foe and slammed her into the ground. As they breached the treeline, the Night Lord realized too late that she'd led him to the edge of the lake. Suddenly all her tentacles were wrapped around him, pulling him into the tightest of hugs. O'olos leaned forward and kissed him on the cheek before rolling him into the water.

Marta and the soldiers followed until they stood at the shore. Violent waves rolled in every direction, and the occasional tentacle broke the surface with an explosive splash. This went on for several minutes, and then the lake was calm again.

Marta stared at the center of the lake, hoping against hope that Kya would emerge.

"So... who won?" a nearby soldier asked.

"I don't know," Marta replied.

And then the water erupted. O'olos stood halfway out of the water, holding the head of Tyk-Shuul in triumph. Then she once again disappeared below the surface.

"They were equals on land, but no god is a match for O'olos in her home domain," a familiar high-pitched voice said.

*Silli?* Marta thought. She turned to see Dobo standing behind her. Silli lay in his arms, giving off a faint glow. One of her wings was broken, but otherwise she looked fine.

Marta gave Dobo a hug, being careful not to squish the fairy. Then she turned back to the lake and sank to her knees. Dobo sat down next to her and patted her on the back.

Something glittered on a nearby tree. Marta realized it was the same tree Kya had prayed to earlier. The gems were still in place, and Marta felt like they were watching her.

She remembered the poem from Esova's book. It had said something about a sacrifice. Marta stood and approached the tree. Then she bowed and unsheathed her sword.

"I don't know if you can hear me," she said. "But this sword has been in my family for ten generations. It is the most precious thing I own, and my only connection to the family I have lost. But I offer it to you now." She stood and tossed her sword into the lake. As it hit the water, it shimmered for a second and vanished.

Marta kneeled. "If you could please see fit to return Kya to me, it would mean more than I can ever say. I will give you anything else you want. All that I own, even my life if that's —"

And then the water bubbled. About fifty feet from shore, a woman's head emerged from the water. Marta was on her feet instantly. She dove into the water and swam out to her friend. Then she put an arm around Kya and swam her back to shore.

"I *can* swim you know," Kya sputtered as she sat up on the rocky beach.

Marta looked her over. Kya was nude and her wooden leg was gone, but she appeared to be uninjured. Marta leaned in and hugged her. "I thought I'd lost you," she said.

"I'm okay," Kya said, hugging back.

Dobo rushed up and handed them a blanket from his backpack. Marta put it over Kya's shoulders and hugged her again. The four of them sat on the beach together for several hours.

"How big do you want it to be?" Marta asked.

"Not too big," Kya replied. "I need to save room for all the adventures we're going to have together."

Kya lay face down on a bed while Marta drew on her back. "Eight tentacles, right?" Marta asked as she drew an octopus to represent Kya's epic battle with Tyk-Shuul.

There was a knock at the door, and Marta pulled a blanket over Kya's bare body before she answered it.

It was Dobo, holding up Kya's wooden leg. Silli reclined on his shoulder, still looking a bit tired. "Guess what someone turned in to the lost-and-found?" Dobo asked, handing the leg to Marta.

"Wonderful," Marta said, looking it over. It appeared to have been freshly cleaned. She detected the distinct aroma of the wood oil Dobo often used when maintaining his wagon. "And thank you," Marta added.

"We're going to go downstairs and get some breakfast," Dobo said. "Want to join us?"

Marta looked at Kya, then turned back to Dobo. "I think we're going to skip breakfast today, but we'll catch up with you later."

"Very good," Dobo said. "We'll see you then."

Marta closed the door and returned to Kya's side.

"I actually am a little hungry," Kya said.

"Me too," Marta said. "We'll get breakfast after."

Kya rolled over and sat up. "After? After what?" A playful smile played across her face.

"After we work up an appetite," Marta replied, and leaned in for a kiss.

*Awakening*

*Where am I?*

The world was nothing but a swirling blackness. All of her senses were gone. She couldn't feel anything, hear anything, remember anything. She had no idea who or what she was.

*I can't feel my fingers,* she thought. *Do I even have fingers? Did I ever have fingers?*

As far as she knew, she'd never had a body. Could she have been human in a past life? *What's a human?* she wondered.

She imagined her mind as a bowl, into which the two halves of her consciousness had been poured. One half was a blank slate, completely devoid of memories. As far as it knew, she'd always lived in this void, and the universe had never consisted of anything more. And yet, it seemed to be the half doing the thinking.

The other half seemed to know things. It was the reason she thought in words. It was why she knew what fingers were, even if she couldn't exactly picture them. It was also why she thought of herself as "she" even though the concept of gender meant nothing to her at the moment.

She wanted so much for the two minds to mix, so that her thinking self could access the memories she needed to make sense of things. But one layer sat on top of the other, like oil and water, unable to integrate in any meaningful way.

*I will go insane if I can't remember,* she thought. *Or maybe I already am?* she considered. An eternity of blackness would cause anyone to lose their faculties. And if nothing existed but the void, what did sanity even mean?

*I HAD A SON!* The thought came to her so suddenly and clearly that she wasn't even sure it was hers. It was as if someone else had fired the thought into her brain from a crossbow or...

*What's a crossbow?*

*No,* she told herself. *Don't get distracted. You had a clear thought, hang onto it or you might not get it back. You had a son.*

A picture of Tobi – *His name was Tobi!* – flashed through her mind, the first clear image she'd had since her awakening. And with it came emotions. The warmth of unconditional love. The golden electric tingles of pride. The motivating power of hope. And finally, the icy cold tendrils of loss.

*Loss?* she thought, shivering. Nebulous memories faded in and out around her mind-bowl, and while she couldn't bring any of them into focus, it was enough to fill her with rage. She'd known of her son's existence for exactly eleven seconds, but she was ready to eviscerate whoever it was who had taken him from her.

The fury flooded through her veins. *I have veins now?* It spread throughout her body, returning feeling to her skin, her arms, her legs, her fingertips. She could feel again. Her back was pressed against cold stone. The air tickled her skin. She could smell blood and rotten meat. She could hear breathing. Her own breathing.

She opened her eyes. There was no light. No torches, no moon, not even the glow of lichen. And yet she could see perfectly. She still lay sprawled across the altar of the forest temple. She turned her head to the left, where pieces of Zib - *That's right, his name was Zib! And my name is Ryveen!* – were scattered about the stone floor.

She sat up and gave herself a look. Her body had been split open, from her nethers up to her chest. Her skin was pale and yellow, and she was so emaciated she could see her bones through her skin. Maggots feasted on the edges of her wound.

"How embarrassing," she said. It was the first thing she'd said out loud, and her voice sounded wispy and ragged.

She hopped off the altar and stood up. She was a bit shaky at first, but soon found her bearings. She stared at the gash in her belly, and willed it to close. As she watched, the edges of the wound mended and healed until there wasn't even a scar. Maggots fell to the floor and wiggled around her feet.

Her stomach rumbled. She knelt and picked up a chunk of meat that had once been Zib's thigh. She took a large bite out of the rotting muscle tissue and chewed. Somewhere in the back of her mind she thought she should feel revulsion, but the only emotion she felt was curiosity.

*What am I now?* she wondered. She was breathing, but she didn't feel like she needed to. She could feel her heart beating, but there couldn't possibly be a drop of blood left in her body. She still blinked every few seconds, but she had the feeling that it was only out of habit. She took another bite and idly chewed while she pondered her place in the universe.

She thought of her son again. Her skin became ten degrees warmer as ripples of anger spread through her body. Not all of her memories had returned, but she knew enough. She remembered holding Tobi's lifeless body, though in her mind she still saw him as a little boy rather than the half-god he'd transformed into.

A beautiful little boy... rendered lifeless by a hail of arrows. The arrows of the Lakehelm militia.

*Lakehelm.* More memories flashed through her mind. Had Tyk-Shuul risen as planned? Was Lakehelm still standing?

And suddenly she knew, somehow, that Tyk-Shuul had been killed. All her work had been for nothing.

She threw her head back and screamed so hard that bits of dust shook loose from the ceiling. She wandered around the temple in a rage. She kicked a chunk of Zib into the wall. It splatted across a mural, adding even more gore to an already bloody scene. She brought her fist down on the altar, leaving a visible dent in the stone.

She looked around for something to break. Her eyes fell on a pile of shredded clothing. Her clothing, which she'd had to rip off when her pregnancy made them uncomfortable. Then she spotted the ring lying on the floor nearby.

*That ring.*

She remembered that group of interlopers. The jester, the fairy, the woman with the leg. And of course, the big swordswoman who kept messing up Ryveen's plans. She sorted through her memories, looking for the woman's name.

*Marta.*

Her body heat rose another ten degrees as her anger turned into resolve. They would pay, they would all pay. Where Tyk-Shuul had failed, Ryveen would flourish. She would tear Lakehelm apart... no, that was too easy. She would conquer Lakehelm, drain its resources, and turn it into a monument to her son. And when that was done, she would tend to Marta.

But she wouldn't just kill the woman, where was the fun in that? No, first she would do unspeakable things to Marta's friends. The pain Ryveen felt at the loss of her son, Marta would experience tenfold.

Ryveen's laughter echoed throughout the temple as she formulated a plan.

*Part 3: Beyond Zyden*

*Hunger*

THUNK! The arrow hit the deer right in the neck and it crumpled to the ground. The ranger worked quickly, cutting the animal's throat so it wouldn't suffer. He didn't usually hunt during these hikes, as his job was simply to survey the forest, look for lost campers, and keep track of animal populations. But the deer wouldn't have survived the night anyway, not with its injuries.

Something had torn into the poor animal, something with claws. This confused the ranger, as he'd yet to see any big cats this close to Lakehelm. Tigers roamed the forests to the north, but Lakehelm's woods were mostly home to wolves and deer.

Something rustled in the trees behind him, and the ranger tightened the grip on his dagger. He slowly stood and turned, then searched for movement.

"Excuse me, sir?" It was a woman's voice.

The ranger squinted, looking for the source. "Who's there?" he asked.

A woman poked her head out from behind a tree. "Hi,"

she said. "I'm sorry to bother you, but I need your help."

"You're here by yourself?" the ranger asked.

"My friends were attacked by wolves," she said. "I think they ran back to town, but I've lost my way."

"I'll lead you back," the ranger offered.

"Um, here's the thing," the woman said. "Could I borrow your cloak? I don't have any clothes on." She stepped partially out from behind the tree, just far enough so that the ranger could see her bare leg and shoulder.

"Oh, of course," the ranger said. He sheathed his dagger and removed his cloak, then stepped toward the tree. As he held out the cloak, he asked, "So how did you happen to lose your—"

The woman's hand darted out from behind the tree and clamped down on his wrist. The ranger could see blood all over her fingers, and bits of fur stuck in her fingernails. He pulled away, but her grip was like iron. She jerked him so hard he heard something snap in his arm. And then she planted a foot on his chest and pushed him to the ground.

"I'm sorry," the woman said. "I haven't been myself lately. It's just that I'm so hungry, I lose control..."

The ranger lay on his back, still pinned by the woman's foot. He grabbed her ankle but she wouldn't budge. He looked up at her emaciated form. She did indeed look like she hadn't eaten in weeks. But her mouth and fingers were covered in blood, and fresh blood by the look of it.

"Who are you?" the ranger groaned.

"I'm still figuring that out myself," the woman said. "I can only tell you that I'm not what I was. I am so much more than I was before, but I'm nothing compared to what I will one day be." The woman stared off into space, lost in thought.

The ranger could barely breathe from the amount of

pressure she put on his chest. He pounded on her leg. Then he drew his dagger and stabbed her in the shin. The blade bounced off, unable to pierce her skin. He stabbed her several more times, but she didn't even seem to notice.

He stared up at the mysterious woman. She looked like a living corpse, with yellowing skin and a bony frame. Flies buzzed around her head, and maggots nested in the hair of her nethers. Her face was haggard, her eyes sunken in. She looked both confused and contemplative, as if she were on the verge of answering a question that had eluded philosophers for centuries.

Then the woman's stomach growled, and she seemed to snap back to reality. She looked down at the ranger with a mildly surprised expression, one that said, *Oh, you're still here?*

"Please let me go," the ranger gasped. He knew he was facing something unnatural, a creature he couldn't fight.

"Give me your clothes and I will let you live," the woman said, raising her foot. With her knee raised and her thin frame, she looked oddly like a crane. The ranger slid out of the way but the woman continued to stand that way, perfectly still and balanced. It was as if she simply forgot what her body parts were doing when she wasn't thinking about them.

The ranger removed his boots and vest, followed by his shirt and pants. He tossed them over.

"Underclothes too," the woman said.

"Why?" the man asked. "They'll be big on you."

"Because I don't want to have to eat around them," the woman said.

"You said you'd let me live," the ranger said.

"And I did," the woman said. "I let you live an extra thirty seconds. I hope you didn't waste it."

The ranger turned and ran. He got about five steps before he felt the teeth sink into his back.

"Who's hungry?" Dobo asked as he brought out the serving platter. It was piled high with meats and cheeses, as well as bread, nuts, olives, and cucumber slices.

"What's the occasion?" Marta asked.

"I sold an article," Dobo said. "The Sweetgrape Crier wants to publish my account of Tyk-Shuul's attack on Lakehelm."

"Congratulations," Marta and Kya said together.

"About time," Silli added, and everyone laughed.

Dobo set down the tray and everyone dug in. Silli waited until all the big people's hands were out of the way before she flitted down, balanced a few olives on top of a cucumber slice, and returned to Dobo's shoulder.

The four dined in a room at the Helm's Watch Inn, where they had been granted a free stay for the month. It was the nicest suite in the Inn, with two separate bedrooms and a balcony overlooking Center Lake.

As they ate, they recounted their adventures together, particularly the events covered in Dobo's article.

"So will you be sending them the article by courier?" Kya asked.

"No, I thought I might deliver it personally," Dobo replied. "Just in case the editor has any questions."

"You're hoping people will want your autograph," Marta said. Kya laughed and nearly choked on an olive.

"We're heroes," Dobo said. "What's the point of risking our lives if we don't get a little recognition?"

"So when do we leave?" Marta asked.

"I wasn't going to be so presumptuous as to—" Dobo

began.

"Of course we'll come with you," Kya said.

"We've been living like this for a month," Marta added. "It's the longest we've stayed in one place since I met you. I need to get out and exercise."

"Very well, then," Dobo said. "We leave at dawn."

## Destiny

"Marta."

The voice boomed from the darkness, sounding both strange and familiar at the same time. Marta sat up. The wagon rocked as it made its way north to Sweetgrape. "Did someone call me?" she asked, but she was alone. Kya and Silli rode up front with Dobo.

The wagon's door rattled, like someone was trying to open it. *Bandits?* Marta thought, and reached for her sword. The hilt didn't feel right in her hand. After the battle in Lakehelm, the town's finest swordsmith had gifted her with a new weapon. It was a beautiful blade, and Marta was proud to wield it. But it still didn't feel like hers.

Marta rose into a crouching position, sword at the ready. The wagon lurched, but she kept her balance. The door rattled again, then swung open. But instead of a dirt road, Marta saw a stone path leading to a sunlight-bathed altar. She could feel the wagon moving, but the path remained still.

"Marta," the voice repeated. It was a woman's voice, the voice of an elder.

*Mother?* Marta thought. But that didn't seem quite right.

Then she tried to remember her grandmother's voice, but the woman had died when she was very young.

She felt compelled to follow the path. She hopped out of the moving wagon and approached the altar. As she neared, she realized it wasn't an altar at all, but a stone coffin. The lid was decorated with red paint – to some it might have looked like the tomb had been desecrated, but Marta recognized the symbols for what they were: Tribal symbols, not just of the Frostmoor Clan, but symbols from other tribes as well.

*Whoever lies in this casket must have been well-respected*, Marta thought.

She took a step back when the lid began to move. As it slid off the coffin, the woman inside sat up and turned toward Marta.

"Who are you?" Marta asked. Somehow she was more curious than frightened.

The woman rose to her feet and stepped out of the coffin. She wore battle armor with an insignia Marta hadn't seen since her youth. The woman's wrinkled face was framed by long, white hair. But her eyes... Marta knew those eyes. They were almost like her mother's.

"Are you my... grandmother?" Marta asked.

The woman shook her head, but still did not speak. Instead, she drew her sword.

"I don't want to fight you," Marta said. She knelt and placed her own sword on the ground.

The woman smiled. Then she held her sword across her palms, offering it to Marta.

"You want me to take it?" Marta asked, and the woman nodded. Marta held out her hands and the woman placed the sword in her palms. Then Marta gripped the hilt and studied the blade. She had never seen a weapon so well-crafted. But more importantly, she felt a connection to the sword, much like she'd had with the sword she'd sacrificed to save Kya.

Strange memories flooded her mind. Lessons she'd been taught in her youth, facts about her clan and her lineage. But they weren't just memories. Some of the lessons were things she'd never been taught, information thought lost to time. She saw her mother as a child, then her grandmother, then her great-grandmother, all being taught the history of their clan.

The images went back ten generations, then twenty, thirty, more. She saw the origins of her family line, before they even migrated to Zyden. Hundreds of faces flashed by. She was overwhelmed by a deluge of images, memories that were not her own. Men, women, weapons, armor, ships, villages, battles, flames, blood...

And then it was gone. Marta sat alone in the back of Dobo's wagon. The door was still shut. There was no woman, no ancient sword, nothing but the wooden walls of the cluttered carriage.

She sat for several minutes, trying to make sense of all that she'd seen. *Was that even real?* she wondered.

All she knew for sure was that she needed to go home.


"S-sir, there's a woman here to see you," Rubi said.

"Tell her I'm busy," Mayor Gutteridge growled. His desk was covered in documents, and he couldn't go home until he'd sorted through them all.

"I'm afraid I must insist," Ryveen said as she pushed her way past the frightened assistant.

"I tried to stop her," Rubi said nervously, standing just outside the door.

Ryveen shut the door in Rubi's face. "We need to talk," she told the mayor.

Mayor Gutteridge finished signing a piece of parchment and studied the visitor. She wore an ill-fitting ranger outfit and her mouth was smeared with blood. "What happened to you?" the mayor asked.

"Me? I've never been better," the woman said. "I'm Ryveen. I believe you knew my son, Tobi."

"Doesn't ring a bell," the mayor said. He looked like he couldn't decide whether to be confused or irritated.

"Well, let me refresh your memory," Ryveen said. "A few weeks ago, he was to serve as the vessel for the return of Tyk-Shuul. But then your rangers filled him full of arrows, and I had to create a new vessel. And then you killed Tyk-Shuul, which means now I've lost two children."

"You're the cultist Esova warned me about," the mayor said, rising from his chair.

"Ah, yes, Esova," Ryveen said. "Remarkable person. My son found them delicious. Don't bother calling the guards. They won't be able to help you."

"We'll see about that," the mayor said. He reached into his desk and withdrew a strange weapon. It looked like a small crossbow, but instead of a bolt it held a round glowing stone. "Guards!" he shouted as he held the weapon on Ryveen.

Ryveen yawned and shook her head. "And just what is that thing supposed to be?" she asked.

"A gift from Esova," the mayor said. "They gave me a few enchanted items over the years. For self-protection, you see. I haven't had a chance to try this one out yet, but I'm told it can turn iron into slag. Shall we try it out?"

But rather than shrink away or flee out the door, Ryveen simply chuckled. "Fire if you're going to fire," she said. "Go ahead, get it out of your system."

"Last chance," Mayor Gutteridge warned. He tried to sound threatening, but his voice wavered.

"For the love of Tyk-Shuul, would you just fire already?" Ryveen demanded. "The sooner you pull the trigger, the sooner we can get on with business."

The mayor fired. A white-hot stone launched from the weapon, and Ryveen snatched it out of the air. She studied it in her palm, watching as it burned through her glove. Her hand was unaffected.

"Interesting," Ryveen said. Then she popped the stone into her mouth.

Just then two guards burst in. "Sir," one began, eyeing Ryveen with suspicion. "What do you—"

Ryveen spat the stone out of her mouth. It hit one of the guards in the eye, making a sizzling sound as it melted his flesh. He shrieked and sank to the ground, smoke rising from his face.

The other guard drew his sword and rushed Ryveen. She grabbed his weapon by the blade, yanked it out of his grip, and broke the sword in half over her knee. Then she impaled the guard with both pieces.

"If you need another demonstration, feel free to call more guards," Ryveen said.

The mayor sat back down. "What do you want?" he asked.

"Not much," Ryveen said. "But for starters, you're in my seat."

"So it was a dream?" Kya asked. The four dined at an upscale tavern in Sweetgrape. A server brought them wine and fruit as they waited for their entrees.

"Or was it a vision?" Dobo added.

"I can't say," Marta replied. "If it was a dream, it was the most intense dream I've ever had. But if it was a vision... I may have to rethink my feelings on whether there's an afterlife."

"So what are you going to do?" Silli asked.

"I need to return to the Frostmoor mountains," Marta said. "There is a tomb there I must visit."

"A tomb?" Kya asked. "In your village?"

"No, it was farther up the mountain," Marta said.

"What do you expect to find there?" Dobo asked.

"A sword," Marta replied. "One crafted hundreds of years ago, before my people even came to Zyden. If I interpret the dream correctly, it would have been buried with one of my ancestors, a great leader from the past."

"So you're going to steal from her tomb?" Kya asked.

"Seems a little disrespectful," Silli added.

Marta nodded. "I see two possibilities," she said. "One is that there is no afterlife. If so, then there is no harm in invading the tomb. There are no spirits to offend, no gods to curse me for the desecration."

"We know there are gods, I turned into one," Kya said.

"O'olos is a powerful being," Marta said. "As was Tyk-Shuul. But that doesn't make them gods. Anyone can cause destruction, but a true god creates life."

"What's the other possibility?" Silli asked.

"That my ancestor wants me to have the sword," Marta replied. "It does no good lying underground. But in my hand, it can make the world a better place. Perhaps it's my destiny to use it to save the world."

"...again," Silli added.

"Well, if there's even a chance the world's at stake, we should get moving," Dobo said.

"Thank you, but I must do this alone," Marta said. "You can take me as far as the base of the mountain, but I can't ask you to make the climb. It's too dangerous."

"Excuse me?" Kya said. "Didn't we already have this discussion about a month ago? Where you go, I go."

"There's creatures on the mountain," Marta explained. "Huge serpents, frost hippos, tigers—"

"And together we've faced giant alligators, flying squid monsters, and armored snake-men," Dobo replied.

"That was to save the world," Marta said. "This is a journey of self-fulfillment, a personal mission to retrieve a family heirloom."

"...which you might be destined to use to save the world," Silli said.

"But..." Marta began. She paused, unable to come up with another argument. Finally she smiled, very slightly shaking her head. "I don't deserve such good friends."

Kya put her arm around Marta and squeezed. "No, you don't," Kya said with a laugh. "But you're stuck with us."

"Through thick and thin," Dobo added.

"We won't be able to take the wagon up the mountain," Marta said.

"Understood," Dobo replied.

"And you'll all need winter furs," Marta said.

"I just came into a bit of money," Dobo said, jingling his coin pouch.

"And there's a warming incantation in my spellbook," Silli added.

Marta's shoulders slumped. "Then if I can't talk you out of it, I suppose our next stop is Frostmoor Mountain."

## *Labor*

"Put your backs into it, men!" the foreman shouted, cracking his whip.

"When did he get a whip?" Tethan asked. He made sure to keep sawing as he talked.

"Yesterday, while you were on mining duty," Vekalb replied.

"Why the sudden power trip?" Tethan asked.

"Orders from the mayor," Vekalb said. "Word is Lakehelm's going to get attacked again soon. They need the wall finished as soon as possible."

Just then there was a CRACK sound, and Tethan shrieked. "No talking!" the foreman bellowed.

Tethan's back stung, but he kept working. Soon the tree came crashing down, and the laborers worked together to saw off the excess branches.

Making sure the foreman was out of earshot, Tethan leaned over to Vekalb and whispered, "Are we just going to take this?"

"I am," Vekalb said. "I have to, it's the law. But you know you have an out if you want it."

Tethan understood. Only men could be drafted into heavy

labor duty. Tethan had been living as a man for ten years, ever since his sixteenth birthday. It's who he was, to his very core. He spent all his spare time exercising, and he could out-wrestle any man in Lakehelm. He had an ongoing deal with an alchemist in Guildport. Every month a courier brought him a supply of geeth root, a plant which caused women to take on masculine qualities. In the years since he'd started taking it, Tethan's bust had flattened and his body hair had flourished. He now sported a full beard as well as the body of a lumberjack.

But that didn't necessarily make him a man in the eyes of the law. If he wanted to get out of labor duty, he could simply flash his birth record. Or he could drop his trousers and flash something else.

The women of Lakehelm had also been put to work, but their duties weren't as physically demanding. They'd been tasked with sewing uniforms and sharpening swords, as well as caring for those who were wounded in the mines. It was still a full day's labor, but Tethan wouldn't have to worry about throwing out his back or getting caught in a mine collapse.

*It would be safer work*, Tethan thought. *But do I really want to do that?*

He shook his head and began sawing the next tree. He wasn't about to sacrifice his entire identity just to make his life a little easier. Things would calm down once the wall was built, and once they'd found whatever the mayor was looking for in the mines. It would be a tough couple of weeks, but if anyone could handle it, Tethan could.

*I can't believe I'm knocking on the door to my own office*, Mayor Gutteridge thought as he rapped on the wood.

"Come in," a voice said, and he entered.

Ryveen sat behind the large desk, reading a tome with the words "Legends of the Musgahn" written on the cover. With her other hand, she absent-mindedly carved symbols into the desk with a dagger. The mayor looked on in horror. He loved that desk, and it had cost his constituents a good bit of coin.

"Alistair," Ryveen said warmly. "I assume you have good news for me?"

"The wall should be completed by the end of the week," the mayor reported.

"And the mines?" Ryveen asked.

"They still haven't found it," the mayor said.

"Maybe they're not looking hard enough," Ryveen growled. "Do you have the miners working around the clock?"

"Three shifts, as you ordered," the mayor said. "The mines are never empty."

"And every citizen is contributing their share of labor?" Ryveen asked.

"Every able-bodied adult," the mayor reported.

"I never specified adult," Ryveen said.

"You can't possibly —" the mayor began.

Suddenly Ryveen stood eye-to-eye with Mayor Gutteridge. The mayor gasped; he hadn't even seen her move. "I can possibly," Ryveen said. "In fact, I can definitely. If a citizen is strong enough to lift a pickaxe, I expect them to do so."

"I'll... I'll write the decree," the mayor said, turning back towards the door.

"And mayor?" Ryveen said.

His hand paused on the door handle. "Yes?"

"You seem pretty able-bodied to me," Ryveen said.

The mayor's shoulders slumped as he left the office.

The winds howled as the party trudged up the mountainside. The path Marta followed was nearly invisible from the snowfall. Her people had once kept the way clear, but there was no one left to take on the responsibility. A rope led from Marta's belt to Kya's and Dobo's. Silli stayed tucked inside Dobo's shirt, occasionally poking her head out to see their progress. But whenever she peeked, the view was the same: Blinding snow and mountain peaks that looked identical to everyone but Marta.

"It's only another hour to the village!" Marta shouted. The others barely heard her through the wind. They all wore heavy furs as well as enchanted warming necklaces, but they could still feel the cold biting at their extremities.

Despite Marta's warnings of the mountain's dangers, they'd encountered no animals so far. Their biggest hazard had been the mountain itself, as the others weren't as sure-footed as Marta. Kya and Dobo had each slipped and fallen more than once, and only Marta's strength had kept them from sliding back down the mountain.

"I can see it!" Marta shouted half an hour later. As they neared, Marta saw that it was just as she'd left it. The plateau was peppered with the wooden skeletons of burned-out buildings. The only difference was how little of the buildings could be seen above the snowbanks. Some of the huts were completely covered in snow, while others were only half-buried.

"Let's seek shelter in there!" Dobo shouted, pointing to the least-damaged building in the encampment. But Marta shook her head and led them to a tanning shack instead. It was smaller, and it was missing one wall, but it kept the snow off of their heads. They huddled together and started a fire.

"W-what was wrong w-with the other building?" Kya asked through chattering teeth.

"That's the bunkhouse," Marta said. "It's where the Bonegrinders shoved all the bodies."

"Oh," Kya replied, looking away. Her story was similar to Marta's – both had lost their families to the Bonegrinders, and both were the last survivors of their villages. Kya hadn't yet returned to her hometown of Fisher's Rest. She'd heard reports from couriers; there'd been no survivors. She couldn't bear the thought of going back and seeing it in ruins, or worse, coming across the bodies of her loved ones. She supposed she'd have to eventually, if only for closure, but for now she preferred to remember it as a happy, thriving village.

She couldn't imagine what this was doing to Marta. She moved over until her body was next to her girlfriend's, then put an arm around her. "Sorry you have to see this again," Kya said.

Marta nodded silently.

"How much farther is the tomb?" Dobo asked.

"Two hours, maybe three," Marta said. "But we should probably camp here for the night and continue in the morning. We don't want to be up there when the sun sets."

"I'm so glad you said that," Dobo replied. "My legs are going numb here." He took off his necklace and rubbed it on his thighs.

"I should probably refresh the spell," Silli said, popping out of Dobo's shirt. She touched the stone dangling from Dobo's necklace, and recited some magic words. The amber stone glowed more brightly. Then she did the same for

Marta's and Kya's necklaces. When she was done, she sprinkled a little fairy dust on the fire, causing the flames to nearly double in size. Then she sat on Dobo's knee and enjoyed the heat from the fire.

Marta stood. "You three rest," she said. "I'm going to cover that wall."

"I can help," Kya said.

Marta shook her head. "I'm used to this weather," she explained. Then she stepped outside.

"This can't be easy for her," Kya said once Marta was out of earshot.

"Her body's acclimated to this temperature," Dobo said. "She's probably more comfortable now than she was at ground level."

"I mean seeing these ruins again," Kya explained. "Being reminded of the worst day of her life."

"Oh," Dobo said. He was silent for a moment. Unlike the others, he didn't have a tragic backstory. When he'd first met Silli, she'd been banished from the Fairy Kingdom. Kya and Marta had lost their families. Kya had even lost a leg. But Dobo? He'd had a happy childhood in a moderately wealthy home. He'd only left out of boredom. The town had simply been too small for his ideas. Now he wandered Zyden gathering tales and histories for the books he eventually planned to write.

He wondered if his role as an author kept him from relating to the misfortunes others faced. Too often he witnessed disasters with excitement rather than sorrow, anticipating what he would write about the incident when it was over. He saw the world as a source of great stories, and the greatest of stories were often tragedies. He'd heard that one has to suffer to become a good writer, and that was one thing he'd yet to experience. *But I don't want to suffer,* he thought. *Can I achieve fame as an author without facing loss? Maybe I should cut off a finger or something…*

"You're making it all about you again, aren't you?" Silli asked, staring up at Dobo's thoughtful expression.

"Shut up," Dobo muttered, though he knew she was right.

Marta returned with some animal skins, which she used to cover the open wall. Soon the shack was comfortably warm. Marta took the first watch while the others went to sleep.

Kya was on watch duty when the rumbling started. She touched Marta's shoulder.

"I hear it too," Marta whispered. "Wake the others." She got up and pulled the animal skins aside, then peered into the darkness. It was the middle of the night. The snow had stopped, but it was still too dark to see.

Something moved in the distance. Marta's eyes adjusted until she recognized the shape. It was a steep-goat, a horse-sized goat that often traversed the mountains. Marta's clan once raised them for milk.

But they rarely traveled alone. *Where's your herd?* Marta wondered. She squinted, searching for more goat shapes in the darkness.

Dobo tapped her on the arm. "What is it?" he whispered.

"Nothing dangerous," Marta replied softly. "But I don't see—"

The steep-goat bleated and ran. Another dark shape burst from the snow. The creature caught one of the goat's legs in its jaws, then pulled it back under the snow.

"We're not safe here," Marta whispered.

Dobo and Kya gathered up their belongings and extinguished the fire. Silli landed on Marta's shoulder. As they watched, a squat, bulbous animal emerged from the snowbank, sniffed the air, and disappeared once again. "What is it?" Silli asked.

"Frost hippo," Marta replied. The creatures only hunted in deep snow, so they'd never come into the village before. But with half the encampment buried under the recent snowdrifts, it was no longer a refuge from the mountain's more dangerous creatures.

"Are you going to kill it?" the fairy whispered.

"Only if necessary," Marta replied. The frost hippo wouldn't leave a meal to chase more prey. But they often hunted in packs of two or three. Marta weighed her options. Would it be safer to sneak away and resume their trek up the mountain, or would they be better off waiting until morning? The tanning hut was only partially buried under the snow, but that didn't mean the hippos would ignore it. The creatures were highly territorial, and if they'd claimed the village, they'd kill anything that dared to intrude. But frost hippos slept most of the day. "How long until sunrise?" Marta asked quietly.

Silli rooted through her purse until she found a magic sundial. "It's about three in the morning," she whispered.

"Sun should be up in less than three hours," Dobo said.

"We can't wait that long," Marta replied. "The hippos will find us eventually. If they don't hear us, they'll smell us."

"So we run?" Kya asked.

"I don't think all four of us could outrun the pack," Marta said.

"So we can't leave and we can't stay here," Dobo said. "That doesn't leave room for much."

"I'll have to fight them," Marta said.

"Have you fought hippos before?" Kya asked.

"Only one at a time," Marta said. "But there could be as many as three hiding in the snowbank." Her expression was grim.

"We'll help," Kya said.

"I appreciate it, but I don't think your arrows would pierce its hide," Marta said.

"I have a thought," Silli said.

Three pale-skinned hippos convened under the deep snow, snapping at each other as they tore a steep-goat apart. The largest one played tug-of-war with its mate as they fought over the sweeter parts of the goat's remains. Then their tiny ears perked up. There was a bang overhead. As one, the hippos burst through the snow and followed the light show up above.

Silli flew in a figure-eight pattern, carrying one of Dobo's sparkling wands. The metal rod emitted bright sparks from both ends, fascinating the hippos as it weaved through the air. Then Silli darted off in the opposite direction from the tanning hut, leading the hippos far away from her friends.

She caught up with them at dawn. "H-hope you're h-happy, I'm f-f-freezing," Silli replied as she dove down Dobo's shirt.

"Where's my rod?" Dobo asked.

"They wouldn't stop following me, and I didn't want to lead them back here, so I threw it down the mountain," Silli said, her voice muffled by Dobo's clothing.

"Good work," Marta said. "We'll take a different route down the mountain so we don't run into them again." Her voice took on a strange tone as she said it.

Kya understood. Marta's village was truly lost to her now. Between the snow and the wildlife, the mountain had reclaimed the plateau. Marta couldn't even go back to look for heirlooms. All connections to her past had been erased. The finality of it had to be heartbreaking.

But she soldiered on. "This way," Marta said, leading them farther up the mountain.

The sun was much higher in the sky when they reached the tomb. There wasn't much to see from the outside, just an iron door embedded in the stone wall at the back of a shallow cave.

Marta had to use a pry bar to get the door open. Then the four entered a narrow cavern passage that led to a small round room. Two candle sconces adorned the walls, and Silli flitted over and lit them. It was still dim, but they could see a stone sepulcher standing against the wall, with a woman's body carved on the lid. Shelves around the sides of the room held gold pieces, silver goblets, and ornate daggers.

"Don't take anything," Marta said. Her feelings about the afterlife were still up in the air, but that was no reason to rob from the dead.

"Aren't you here to take a sword?" Silli asked.

"I don't see one," Kya said, looking over the shelves.

"Maybe she was buried with it?" Dobo asked. He eyed the sepulcher, frowning.

"I don't know," Marta said. "But I feel strange. Like... I'm supposed to be here."

"Feel another vision coming on?" Dobo asked.

"Don't fight it," Silli suggested. "Just let it happen."

Marta sank to her knees in front of the sepulcher. The lid slid aside with a grinding noise, and an old woman stepped out. It was the same woman Marta had seen in her earlier vision, in the wagon on the way to Sweetgrape. The woman touched Marta's forehead.

And suddenly Marta *knew*.

She knew histories and legends and family genealogies. She knew intimate details about family members who had died centuries before her own birth. She knew love and hatred and loss. She remembered feuds and battles and assassinations. In the space of a second she attended weddings and funerals, made love and gave birth, grew old and took her first steps. Finally she witnessed a horrible apocalypse, engineered by a woman of pure evil.

And then it was over. The woman returned to her sepulcher and the lid slid closed. Marta fell forward onto her face.

"Marta!" Kya shouted. She and Dobo pulled her off of the floor.

"The woman told me..." Marta groaned.

"What woman?" Dobo said.

"You didn't see the woman?" Marta asked. Her voice slurred like she'd had fourteen ales.

"We saw you kneel," Kya said. "You looked like you were in pain for a moment, then you keeled over."

Marta took a deep breath. "She showed me things," she said.

"What kind of things?" Silli asked.

"...Everything," Marta replied. "I'm going to need a moment."

They sat on the floor and gave Marta time to think. She took a few sips from her waterskin and stared off into space.

After about five minutes of silence, Kya put her hand on Marta's. "How do you feel?" she asked.

"We need to go," Marta replied.

"What about the sword?" Dobo asked.

"The sword isn't here," she said.
"Where is it?" Dobo asked.
"Beyond Zyden," Marta replied.

# Passage

On a quiet road just south of Sweetgrape, a farmer rode an old mare, pulling a small, uncovered cart full of recently harvested vegetables. It was early morning, and he hoped to reach town by noon. In the past he'd always sold his wares in Cherrybrook, but that town had recently suffered a disaster. Sweetgrape was a bit farther from his farm, but the customers were often wealthier, so it was worth an extra day's travel.

He gradually became aware of another set of hoofbeats somewhere behind him. This rider was going much faster, and the clopping grew louder and louder. The farmer pulled his cart to the side of the road, not wanting to be in the way. The road was more than wide enough for two wagons, but given the other rider's urgency, he didn't want to risk a collision.

The farmer watched as the other horse grew near. The rider was just a child – she couldn't have been more than twelve. Her face was bloody, and every bounce of her saddle caused her to wince in pain. She pulled to a stop next to the farmer and slid off the horse. The farmer noticed several wounds on the girl's arms and back. He tried to help her but she brushed his hand away.

"Just hide me," the girl said. Then she slapped her horse on the rump and shouted, "Yah!" The horse ran off and vanished down the road.

The farmer didn't ask her any questions as he helped her hide under a pile of carrots in the wagon. As he got back on his mare, more hoofbeats sounded behind him. Two riders soon pulled up beside his wagon. Both wore the armor of the Lakehelm militia.

"Did you see a girl ride by just now?" one asked.

"Young, injured lady?" the farmer asked. "Can I ask what'cha plan to do with 'er?"

"She's wanted for serious crimes," the second guard replied.

"If you've seen her, we need to know," the first added. His eyes were hard and unsympathetic.

"She went that way," the farmer said, pointing to a side trail that branched off the main road. He knew it led to a dead end after meandering past several farms, but he figured the longer it took the guards to find the girl's horse, the longer it would take them to realize she wasn't on it.

The guards looked at each other, as if having a silent discussion. "No witnesses," one said, and the other nodded. Then the closest guard drew his crossbow and fired. A glowing stone hit the farmer in the chest, burning a hole through his shirt, his skin, and even his bones. The hole in the man's torso widened until he crumpled to the ground, landing in two smoldering pieces.

"I love this crossbow," the guard said as he patted the weapon. He wasn't sure where Ryveen had acquired the item, but it sure was fun to use.

"Get a room, you two," his partner muttered. Then they rode off in pursuit of their target.

The girl waited until she could no longer hear their hoofbeats before she moved again.

"I've never been this far from the mainland," Dobo said, staring off the port railing. "The ocean is so beautiful."

Sweetgrape's docks had long faded from view, and there was nothing but ocean in every direction. The sailing ship was built for cargo, but it had three passenger cabins for those who wished to travel overseas.

"It's really something," Silli replied, though she sounded bored.

"How can you not be in awe?" Dobo asked.

"It's just so... samey," Silli said. "Everywhere you look, the same blue waves."

"The sea holds the greatest mysteries in all of Evrosia," Dobo said. "Anything could be beneath us. Creatures unseen for centuries. The remains of ancient civilizations. Long-forgotten treasures."

"Sorry, I just prefer forests," Silli replied. "At least trees are interesting."

"Feh," Dobo exclaimed.

"Well, I think it's quite a view," Marta said as she approached, walking hand-in-hand with Kya.

They both wore their most comfortable outfits. Marta wore cloth breeches with a loose-fitting top that rippled in the breeze. Her enchanted wedding band dangled from a chain around her neck. Though it couldn't function without its partner ring, it was still a family heirloom and Marta wanted to keep it close to her heart.

Kya wore a knee-length white dress. Most of her outfits hid the fact that she had a wooden leg, but this one did not. Both Kya and Marta seemed more relaxed than they'd been in a long time.

"Any luck sorting out your thoughts?" Dobo asked. "I thought maybe the sea air would help."

"It's certainly calming," Marta replied. "But no. There's just too much. I've been writing down what I can remember, and now my hand's cramping."

"I hope you'll let me read that later," Dobo said.

"Good luck deciphering my handwriting," Marta chuckled.

Kya led Marta to a bench and they sat down. "Do you really think it was your ancestors speaking to you?" she asked.

"I don't know what to think," Marta admitted. "If you'd asked me a few weeks ago, I wouldn't have believed in such a thing. And I still don't know if I do. For all I know, I could be suffering from some head malady."

Kya put her hand on Marta's knee. "I doubt that," she said. "Besides, if you imagined it, how is it that you know things you didn't know before?"

"Do I?" Marta asked. "I could just be remembering history lessons from my childhood. It's all such a jumble. The old woman showed me so much, so quickly, and I can't put the thoughts in order."

"But you know where you're taking us?" Dobo asked.

"A handful of images stand out," Marta said. "Mostly relics and locations. I don't know what evil is coming, but I know what I need to defeat it."

"The sword," Kya said.

"More than that," Marta said. "I'll be facing a foe that can tear me apart with a thought. I'll also need a set of armor, a helmet, and a shield. And they're all buried in different tombs, far from each other."

"So what's the next stop?" Dobo asked.

"The island of Javesia," Marta said. "The ship has a couple of stops to make on the way, but we should reach it in four days."

"Know anything about it?" Kya asked.

"The tomb is somewhere in a jungle," Marta said.

Dobo turned to Silli and asked, "Happy? You're getting your trees."

Silli just smiled and yawned.

Tethan followed the usual path through the mine until he reached his assigned work area. He balked when he saw his new partner.

"What are *you* doing here?" he asked as he grabbed a pickaxe.

"Same as you," Mayor Gutteridge said.

"But you're—" Tethan began.

"I won't have my constituents do anything I'm unwilling to do," the mayor replied. "Remember that next election." ... *If we have one*, he then thought.

Tethan put more energy into his work than ever before. He found it both intimidating and inspiring to be partnered with the mayor. He kept wanting to show off, but he didn't want to tire himself out before the end of his shift.

If nothing else, this proved to Tethan that this extra work was necessary. If the mayor had simply become a tyrant, then he wouldn't be down here in the mines, working alongside the commoners. This meant that the danger was real, and their efforts were not in vain.

*I still wish they'd tell us what we're looking for, though*, Tethan thought. Then he shrugged and kept on swinging the pickaxe.

*And just who is this*? Tabitha wondered as she entered her office. She'd left the door locked the night before, she was sure of it. But now a girl sat in front of her desk, covered in dried blood and looking like she might fall over at any moment.

"Tabitha Wright?" the girl asked as the reporter entered.

Tabitha closed the door behind her and locked it. "How did you get in here?" she asked.

"I've been here all night," the girl said. "I had to sneak in after dark. I have a master key, see?" She held up a silver key that shimmered in the light.

"And where did you get that?" Tabitha asked as she sat down behind her desk. She pulled several sheets of parchment out of her desk along with a pair of quill pens.

"My father's the mayor of Lakehelm," the girl said. "My name's Alysia."

"Good to meet you, Alysia," Tabitha said. "And what brings you to the Sweetgrape Crier today? I take it you have some juicy news for me?" She held a pen in each hand, ready to write down every word that came out of the girl's mouth.

"I need your help," Alysia said. "Lakehelm's been taken over by a bad person. My father helped me sneak out, but the townspeople are being forced to work day and night. He wants me to get the word out, maybe raise an army. But that's not all…"

"Raise… an… army…" Tabitha repeated as she furiously transcribed Alysia's words. "What else?"

"He wants me to find a woman named Marta Frostmoor," Alysia said.

"I know her," Tabitha said. "Her friend Dorian sold me an article recently. 'The Battle of Lakehelm: A Triumph of Good Versus Evil.' One of our best-selling issues."

"Do you know where she is now?" Alysia asked.

"Unfortunately I do," Tabitha replied. "And if you'll excuse the expression, I'm afraid you've missed the boat."

## *Javesia*

The coastal village of Traedyuh was the only settlement on the island of Javesia. As Marta and her friends disembarked, they had to dance around several busy dockworkers to reach the town proper.

Most of the buildings were constructed by wrapping vines around living trees, and then shoring up the inside with sticks and mud. It was warm on the island, much too warm for Marta's tastes. But the others seemed to be taking it well.

"I've heard of this place, of course," Dobo said. "Most of the citizens are explorers. They spent their days roaming the forests, searching for ancient temples. Then they come back to town and sell their finds."

"How long will the boat wait for us?" Kya asked.

"It won't," Marta replied. "From what I understand, ships come and go all day long here. Once we've found what we're looking for, we'll book passage on another ship to take us to the next island."

"So how do we find the tomb?" Silli asked.

"We'll need to hire a guide," Marta replied.

As it turned out, guides were a thriving business in

Javesia. The minute Marta expressed interest in entering the jungle, local entrepreneurs climbed over each other to offer their services. Some didn't even ask for money up front, but rather demanded a cut of any treasure the party might find. Some of the potential guides rubbed Marta the wrong way, and she didn't trust that they'd have her best interests at heart.

They went with a man named Keez. He was almost as tall as Marta, and every bit as muscular. He had short red hair and pale, freckled skin.

"Ready for adventure?" Keez asked as they walked through town. Marta had changed into her armor, while Dobo and Kya wore rugged explorer's outfits they'd bought in Traedyuh.

"Hardly," Marta replied. "I'm afraid we're not your typical clients. I'm seeking a very specific artifact."

"I shouldn't tell you this, but I doubt there's much left to find out there," Keez told her. "The people who lived here before, centuries ago, they were called the 'Wildbark' clan. They left all sorts of artifacts behind. But the last few years there's been a boom of treasure hunters, and I'm afraid the island's just about picked clean."

The word "Wildbark" echoed through Marta's head. It brought up images of jungle warriors clad in animal skins and covered in tattoos. She felt a kinship with these people, and she wanted to know more about them. But the memories just wouldn't come. Somewhere in her mind she saw a bookshelf with volumes labeled Wildbark, Seaborn, Sandstone, and Musgahn. But try as she might, she couldn't open the books and read them.

"Is something bothering you?" Kya asked.

Marta shook her head. "Just... trying to remember something," she replied.

Keez was still talking. "But sometimes people get lucky," he said. "I just have to warn you, a lot of the island's visitors don't make it back alive. But you look tougher than most. Do you know where you want to start?"

Marta fumbled through her backpack and pulled out a piece of parchment. "Have you seen a cave that looks like this?" she asked.

It was a crude drawing, depicting a cave with a triangular entrance. It was surrounded by rock formations, including one that was shaped like a horse's head.

"Saberfang Cave," Keez said. "Where did you hear about it?"

"That's my business," Marta said.

"Hmmm…" Keez replied. He looked thoughtful for a moment, then studied Marta as if appraising her toughness. "It's not going to be easy," he finally said. "Several people have died trying to figure out its secrets. But I'll be happy to guide you there for, say, fifty percent of the take."

"That's robbery," Dobo growled.

"It's fine, Dobo," Marta replied. "We're not in this for the treasure. There's only one artifact that I'm interested in. Anything else is yours to keep."

"You're okay with him robbing your ancestor's grave?" Kya asked.

"This entire island is a desecrated gravesite," Marta replied. "A few more trinkets can't make it any worse."

"Madam, you have a deal," Keez said.


Nake Thornbow, captain of the Lakehelm guard, watched his troops train for an upcoming battle. He was proud of the work they'd put in. Lakehelm wasn't known for its military, but they'd held their own against the forces of Tyk-Shuul, and they'd be even more prepared for the next conflict.

*I just wish I knew what they'll be up against,* he thought.

"Lakehelm will soon be under attack," the mayor had said. "I can't tell you more just yet."

It wasn't like the mayor to be so secretive. Did he not know either? And if that was the case, why was he so sure the town was in danger?

Just then a woman came running up to him. Nake recognized her as Rubi, the mayor's aide.

"Excuse me, sir," Rubi said. "The mayor wants to see you."

*Maybe now I'll get some answers,* Nake thought as he followed her to the mayor's office.

He opened the door expecting to see Mayor Gutteridge, but instead, a woman sat behind the mayor's desk.

"And you are?" Nake asked.

"Ryveen," the woman replied as she rose from the desk. She crossed the office and stroked Nake's cheek. "I've been working with the mayor on a special project," she purred. "I'm sure you're wondering why we've been overworking your poor troops."

"They can handle a little overtime, ma'am," Nake replied proudly. "But yes, it would help to know what they're training for."

"Understandable," Ryveen said. "Just look into my eyes and I'll tell you everything."

Nake gave her a strange look. It didn't feel like she was taking this meeting seriously, but there was something hypnotic in her voice and he found himself unable to turn away.

Then Ryveen's eyes changed. For just a moment, Nake thought he was looking into a snake's eyes. And then part of him faded away - he wasn't sure which part, but he no longer cared if Ryveen took his troops seriously or if she was legitimately working with the mayor or if she had Lakehelm's best interests at heart. Suddenly Nake knew that he loved Ryveen, more than any man had ever loved a woman, and he would send every one of his troops to their deaths if it meant keeping Ryveen safe.

"You're going to have the most powerful army on the planet," Ryveen said, her voice as soothing as a warm bath.

"The most powerful," Nake repeated. His voice seemed to come from some far-off place.

"And they will do whatever I tell them," Ryveen said.

"Anything," Nake agreed.

"They will die for me," Ryveen said.

"If it keeps you safe," Nake droned.

"Good," Ryveen said. "Now do me a favor and send in your second-in-command."


The trek to Saberfang Cave took most of the day, and they spent much of it traipsing through mud, climbing rock walls, and navigating narrow ledges. The cave entrance lay on the other side of a twenty-foot ravine, and they had to construct a makeshift bridge out of fallen trees to reach it.

Marta was the first to climb across. She had a rope tied around her waist, so the others could pull her up if she fell. When she reached the other side, she tied the rope around the ears of the horse-shaped outcropping. Her friends tied the other end of the rope to a tree, and the rest of the party crossed one at a time, using the rope for support. Silli hovered by each of them as they crossed, ready to cast a protective spell if they fell.

The cave itself was plain. By the light of their glowstones, they followed the tunnel for about twenty feet, where an iron door prevented them from proceeding further.

"There used to be some golden pots in the hallway here," Keez told them. "And a couple of statues. Like I said, picked clean. No one's gotten through the door, though."

Marta studied the door. It looked similar to the one in the Frostmoor tomb, but this one was etched with the image of a shield. The shield was divided into four sections, and each had been marked with a different rune. Marta removed the prybar from her backpack.

"Wait," Keez said. "I've heard about this one. If you try to force the door open, poison darts fly out of the walls." He held his glowstone next to the wall, pointing out dozens of holes that went from floor to ceiling.

"Maybe we could cover the holes?" Dobo suggested.

"Hold on," Marta said, studying the shield. "I know what these runes mean. They were in my visions. I think they represent the seasons."

"So maybe you have to touch the runes in a specific order?" Kya suggested.

Marta frowned, lost in thought. She tried to remember anything in her visions that might help her.

"What's this writing?" Silli asked. She flitted over to one of the cave walls, her natural glow lighting up the words carved in the stone.

Dobo followed her and studied the letters. "It's not any language I've ever seen," he said. "Marta?"

Marta turned and gasped. "I remember," she said. "It's the old tongue. My mother taught me that language when I was very young. We stopped using it long before I was born, but some families still taught it so we wouldn't forget our history." She lowered her voice and added, "...which I did."

Kya gave her a reassuring hug. "So can you read it?"

Marta frowned and looked over the words. "It's been a

while... 'Only... those of... blood will know. Spring to Fall... Summer to...' and that last word is either 'Winter' or 'asparagus.'"

"Let's go with Winter," Kya suggested.

"So this island's 'Wildbark' clan... they were your ancestors?" Silli asked.

"I wasn't sure before, but the writing would seem to prove it," Marta said. "I know my tribe was nomadic before we settled in the Frostmoor mountains. But offshoots of our clan must have settled elsewhere."

"I should write a book about your clan's history," Dobo said, jotting down some notes.

Marta stood in front of the metal door. "I want everyone to stand back," she ordered. "If darts are about to fly out at me, I don't want them hitting anyone else."

She waited until everyone was back near the cave entrance, then pressed the runes in the order she'd read. The metal door popped open, and everyone went inside.

The tomb looked similar to the one in Frostmoor Mountain. A sepulcher lay in the center of the room, and a shield lay on top.

"That's the relic," Marta said, touching the shield. It was ice blue, roughly three feet tall, with a flat top and rounded edges that came down to a point. It was solid metal but textured to look like scales.

"I thought it was going to be a sword," Kya said.

"I don't know which artifact we'll find in which tomb," Marta said. She picked up the shield and put her arm through the straps, getting a feel for the item.

Keez looked around the room. "There's nothing else of value in here," he said.

"We'll still pay you," Dobo said.

"Not enough," Keez said. "That shield is pristine. I can get thousands for it, maybe more. Hand it over."

Marta shook her head. "You will be well-compensated, you have my word. But this belongs to my family line."

Keez reached behind his back and pulled a metal wand out of his backpack. He pointed it at them like it was a weapon.

"And that is…?" Dobo asked.

"I've found relics of my own," Keez said. "This is an ancient magic wand, capable of emitting jets of flame once a day. Give me the shield, or I'll burn you to cinders."

Kya turned to Silli and asked, "Is he bluffing?"

"The wand is definitely magic," the fairy confirmed. "I see its aura."

"You three leave, I will deal with Keez," Marta said.

"No one's going anywhere until I have that shield," Keez said. "I can kill you all now and take it, or you can give it to me and I'll leave you here to find your own way back. At least if you hand it over, you'll stand a chance. Which is it going to be?"

"No," Marta said, drawing her sword. Dobo and Kya reached for their weapons as well.

"You had your chance," Keez said, and flicked the wand. A huge burst of flame emitted from the tip.

Marta instinctively held up the shield. The flames filled the room from wall to wall, enveloping everyone within. For several seconds, the entire cave was an inferno of angry orange light, accompanied by the smell of cooking meat.

And then it dispersed. Marta and her friends huddled behind the shield, completely unharmed by the fire. Keez had not been so lucky. His charred remains lay across the stone floor, his face locked in a rictus of agony.

"What just happened?" Kya asked.

"The shield protected us somehow," Marta said.

"I saw the flames all around us," Kya said. "But they just... stopped a few inches away. Like we were in a bubble."

Dobo took the wand from Keez's dead grasp. "This could be useful later," he said, stuffing it into his backpack.

It took a bit longer to get back to town without a guide, but they made the trip without incident. Then they booked a trip to their next destination, the Island of Kosis.

## *Kosis*

"Did your visions tell you anything about Kosis?" Kya asked. This ship was much smaller than the previous one, and had little room for passengers. They'd had to agree to sleep in a storage room to come along. The party currently sat on crates on the main deck, watching the island grow larger as they approached.

"Only that it's a small island with lots of ponds," Marta replied.

"The captain told me more than that when we booked the trip," Dobo said. "Hardly anyone lives there, and those that do make a living selling water from the island's largest lake."

"What's so special about the island's water?" Silli asked.

"Probably nothing," Dobo said. "But the locals claim it's a cure-all. Gives you energy, fights off disease, that sort of thing. Charlatan flimflam designed to take advantage of the gullible."

"You don't know," Kya said. "With all the magic we've seen, there could be something to it."

"Don't hold your breath," Dobo replied.

The ship docked and Marta's team disembarked. Six

thatched houses sat near the docks, but there were no more buildings beyond that point. Dobo asked one of the local residents if they knew of any tombs, but no one was aware of any such thing. The locals permitted them to explore, but warned them not to contaminate the lake.

"I suppose we just have to go look," Marta said.

"Maybe a vision will kick in," Kya suggested.

Beyond the docks, the island was mostly sparse grassland, with a few trees and the occasional hill. They wandered for about an hour, skirting the edges of lakes and ponds as they went.

"I don't see a lot of places to hide a tomb," Dobo remarked.

"Nor do I," Marta admitted. "Sillivene, do you see anything magical?"

The fairy shook her head. "Nothing," she said. "Except for that lake over there." She pointed to one of the larger pools. It was the only lake they'd seen with a fence around it.

"The lake?" Dobo asked, and the party ran to the fence. It was a simple, waist-high wooden fence. Intermittent signs warned them to keep out.

"It's just a faint shimmer," Silli said. "This must be the lake they sell all the water from."

Marta climbed over the fence and peered into the water. It was crystal clear, and she could see all the way to the bottom.

"See anything?" Kya asked, climbing over to join her.

Marta shook her head. "It sparks a memory, but I'm just not sure."

Dobo stayed outside the fence, keeping a lookout for any natives who might object to their investigation. Meanwhile, Silli buzzed over the lake, looking for the source of the magic.

"I think it's strongest at the bottom," Silli said as she

returned to Marta. "Whatever's down there, its magic is affecting the entire lake."

Marta stripped down to her underclothes and set her things aside. "I'm going down there," she said. "Silli, do you still remember that water-breathing spell?"

"Give me a moment," the fairy said, as she dug a tiny book out of her purse. "Now remember, it's kind of random how long it lasts. And you won't be able to breathe air until it wears off."

"Can I make it wear off early?" Marta asked. "I don't want to be stuck down there any longer than I have to be."

Silli flipped through the spellbook. "Umm... yes," she said. "If you want to end the spell early, just say 'weriam finet.' Are you ready?"

Marta nodded. "Go ahead," she said.

Silli said a few magic words and sprinkled some fairy dust on top of Marta's head. Marta dove into the lake just as the gills opened on her neck. Then she swam to the bottom and felt around the floor of the lake.

As she sifted through the silt, her fingers brushed something metal. She moved her finger along the edge until she found a corner, then wiggled her fingers under the plate.

*Pull it open,* a voice told her. Marta's eyes widened. The ancestors were speaking directly to her.

But the plate wouldn't budge. She squatted on the sandy floor and used both hands to pull. Finally the metal plate flew aside, revealing a square-shaped hole in the lake bottom. She stared at it for several seconds. She wondered if she should resurface and let her friends know what she'd found.

*Go in,* the voice said. Not one to disobey her ancestors, she swam into the hole.

"Hey, get away from there!" the dockmaster shouted. He and his fellow islanders all held crossbows at the ready.

"I do apologize," Dobo said. "My friends and I were just overeager to see your operation."

"We told you not to contaminate our lakes," the dockmaster said. "Come with us. You will remain at the docks until it's time for you to leave."

Kya climbed back over the fence and joined Dobo, and Silli trailed along behind.

"Wasn't there one more of you?" one of the islanders asked.

"She wandered off," Dobo explained. "Don't worry, I'm sure she'll meet us at the docks."

The dockmaster looked suspicious. "None of you swam in the lake, did you?"

"Wouldn't I be wet if I had?" Dobo asked.

The dockmaster looked him up and down. "Good," he finally said. "That water can heal you if you drink it. But if you submerge yourself in it, it can be deadly."


"Shift change!" a guard shouted.

Mayor Gutteridge tossed his pick aside and joined the line of workers headed out of the tunnel. More miners passed them on their way in, fresh and ready to work. The mayor was a little bothered by how eager they seemed. They'd adapted to this new way of life a little too easily, and the mayor wondered if it was more than just a sense of duty that drove them. He'd lied to gain their support, telling them that Lakehelm was in danger. But a lie could only get you so far. This newfound energy was more than loyalty, it almost seemed…

*Supernatural*, the mayor thought. Was Ryveen somehow controlling the citizens' minds? It wouldn't be the strangest thing she'd done. The mayor knew she was powerful, but how powerful? Just what were her limits?

*I could always just ask*, he thought. As evil as Ryveen was, she was surprisingly honest at times. She liked to brag about her schemes, especially when she knew there was no way to stop them.

Though he wanted nothing more than to return home and go to sleep, he decided to stop by his office instead. It was late in the day, but he knew Ryveen would still be there. She rarely left.

He entered the town hall and knocked on the door to his office. When there was no answer, he opened the door and went inside.

Ryveen sat cross-legged on the floor, staring off into space. Her mouth moved as if she were talking to someone, but he couldn't quite read her lips.

"I'm sorry to disturb you," the mayor said after clearing his throat.

The woman didn't reply, she just continued to stare at the wall. Her eyes had rolled up so far that he could only see the whites.

*She's in a trance*, the mayor thought. *She has no idea that she isn't alone.*

Possibilities whirled through Mayor Gutteridge's mind. He couldn't waste this opportunity. But what could he do? He'd already tried to kill her with an enchanted crossbow. She'd shrugged off the magical ammunition like it was a marshmallow.

Still, immunity to one thing didn't mean she was immune to everything. He'd squirreled away more than one magical weapon over the years. There was an enchanted dagger hidden in the bottom drawer of his desk, specifically designed to bypass magical barriers. Never taking his eyes off Ryveen, he crept over to the desk, opened the drawer, slid aside the false bottom, and retrieved the dagger.

The mayor stood behind Ryveen, dagger held in both hands. Then he brought it down as hard as he could, right between her shoulder blades. It cut through her ranger's uniform like butter, but the glowing blade wouldn't pierce her skin. In a panic, the mayor stabbed her over and over, leaving the back of her outfit in tatters.

"A bit lower and to the left," Ryveen said. "I have an itch."

Mayor Gutteridge leaped back and the dagger tumbled out of his hands. It landed point down on his desk and easily sank into the wood, all the way to the hilt.

Ryveen stood and turned toward the mayor. "I hope this has been educational for you," she said. "Now that you know you can't harm me, you won't try it again, correct?"

The mayor sat down on his desk, nodding. "Point taken," he said.

"I'm not convinced," Ryveen said. Then her pupils turned to slits and her voice took on a deeper, echoing quality. "Hold the dagger to your throat," she said.

"What?" Mayor Gutteridge asked. "No, I'm not going to —" But his hand acted independently of his mind, and before the words were out of his mouth, he realized he was already holding the blade inches from his neck.

"I'm going to ask you some questions now," Ryveen said. "If you answer honestly, you'll leave this office on foot. If you lie, you'll leave this office in pieces. Understand?"

"Yes," the mayor replied.

"Good," Ryveen said. "First things first. Where did you get these magic weapons?"

"Esova," the mayor answered. "They owned several

magic artifacts. They gifted me with a few for self-defense."

"Yes, you told me that already," Ryveen growled. "But where did Esova get them?"

"I don't know," the mayor said. The dagger moved another half-inch towards his throat. The heat from the blade blistered his skin. "I really don't know," he added. "Esova was a very private person. They said they'd taken an oath of secrecy to some magic guild. They said that magic should be kept rare, and that it was too dangerous to fall into common hands. Thousands of years ago—"

"I know the story," Ryveen interrupted. "Some ancient weaponsmith forged magic weapons for an entire army, and they overtook the continent. Then power-hungry generals turned the weapons on each other. When the dust settled, they locked the weapons away in an underground vault. Do you happen to know where the vault is?"

"Of course not," the mayor said. "I doubt the legends are even true."

Ryveen chuckled. "Oh, they're true," she said. "And what's more, I believe Esova knew where the vault was. I don't usually regret killing people, but I wonder if I was too hasty in eviscerating your mystic. Oh well, live and learn."

The mayor's hand shook as he tried to put his arm down. "Even if you're right, you'll never find it," he said. "People have searched for centuries."

"Let me tell you what I believe," Ryveen said. "I believe there was more than one vault. A major armory, and many smaller caches. I believe Esova raided one of the smaller vaults. That's where they found your dagger, as well as that cute little crossbow of yours. You know, the one I gave to the soldiers I sent after your daughter."

"Wait, what?" the mayor asked.

"Oh, you didn't know about that?" Ryveen said. "I

assumed you were the one who smuggled her out of town. She's probably dead by now."

"Please, no," the mayor said.

"Well, it's out of my hands now," Ryveen said. "I haven't heard any updates, so there's a chance they still haven't found her. But they will."

"Call them back," the mayor begged.

"I don't even know where they are at the moment," Ryveen said. "They could have chased her all the way to Northpoint for all I know. It's a pity, really. If she'd stayed in town, I could have used her as a bargaining chip. Now all I've got is your wife."

"Don't bring her into this," the mayor said.

"That depends on you," Ryveen said. "Try my patience again, and you'll be holding the dagger to *her* throat. Just imagine... It's one thing if I kill her, but it'll be so much funnier if I force you to do it. Do you under —"

She stopped mid-word, and once again stared off into space. Mayor Gutteridge found himself back in control of his arm. He set the dagger down on the desk.

"Leave me," Ryveen whispered as she returned to her position on the floor.

The mayor quietly slipped off the desk and out the door.

The underwater tunnel stretched on for hundreds of feet. Marta swam furiously, hoping the spell wouldn't end early. She came to a bend in the tunnel and swam upwards until she emerged in a small cave. She wheezed for a few seconds before she gasped the magic words, "Weriam finet." Then the gills closed and she was able to breathe normally again.

*Getting out of here might be a problem,* she thought, staring down at the tunnel from which she'd emerged.

But that worry would have to wait. She removed a glowstone from her pocket and looked around. Another metal door blocked her passage, but it opened easily. A helmet sat atop this tomb's sepulcher. It was silver and blue, with a scale pattern that matched the shield. Marta touched the helm, and another flurry of images went through her mind. She saw a tribe of mariners, hardy seafaring folk who built villages on rafts and lived on a diet of fish and underwater plants.

*The Seaborn,* a voice said in her ear.

"What does the helmet do?" Marta asked.

As if in answer to her question, the tomb began to fill with water. Marta pulled the door shut, but water continued to seep in. *I need to leave,* she thought. She remembered how long she'd had to swim to reach the tomb. It had taken her at least ten minutes, maybe longer.

*I can't hold my breath that long,* she thought.

Then the voice spoke to her again. *Put the helmet on.*

She did as told. The helmet was loose at first, but it magically tightened until it was comfortably secure. The room seemed brighter with the helmet on, and she found that she no longer needed the glowstone to see. She shoved it in her pocket and opened the metal door again. The water was now up to her waist. She steeled herself for the long swim, took a deep breath...

...and realized that she no longer needed to breathe. It was a strange feeling, and she would have had a hard time explaining it to anyone else. Though she held her breath, cool air continued to flow in and out of her lungs. *Where is the air coming from?* she wondered, but the question would have to wait. The water now reached her neck. She submerged and swam back through the tunnel.

The way in had been dark, illuminated only by her

glowstone's meager light. But now the tunnel was much brighter, and she could make out details she hadn't seen on the way in. Before she'd thought the tunnel was just a natural cave formation, but now she saw carvings on the wall, depicting the Seaborn tribe engaged in activities such as dancing, praying, and sailing.

*Maybe this tunnel wasn't always underwater,* Marta reasoned. *Or did my ancestors wear this helmet to make these carvings?*

She'd been underwater for at least ten minutes, but she felt no urgency, no reason to rush. She took her time and studied the images as she swam. She ran her fingertips over the carvings, hoping to feel a stronger connection to her people. There was something overwhelming about touching history, knowing these images had been chiseled so long ago, by people who shared Marta's blood. It was the Seaborn clan's way of communicating with the future, and it was a pity these messages had to stay hidden underground.

*No one else will ever see this,* she thought. The realization made her sad, but also a bit elated. It was like knowing a secret, a piece of information just for her. In a strange way, it made her feel important.

Then she reached the end of the tunnel and swam to the surface of the pond. She gathered up her things, noting that her friends were no longer nearby. *I hope they're not in trouble,* she thought. The sun had set, but to her it was still as bright as day. It was strange, she could tell what time it was by the color of the sky, but she had no trouble seeing in the dark.

Marta got dressed and returned to the docks. Kya and the others were fine, though they'd been worried about her.

"Nice helmet," Kya said. "How do you feel?"

"Better than ever," Marta replied, confused by the concern on Kya's face. "Why?"

"The dockmaster said the water would kill you," Dobo told her.

"I feel fine," Marta said. "Are you sure he wasn't just trying to keep you away from it?"

"Or maybe you're immune to the water's effects," Silli suggested, looking Marta up and down. To her fairy eyes, the helmet and shield radiated a magical glow. But Marta's body shimmered as well. Maybe it wasn't as bright, but it was enough to get her wondering. Had the magic of the relics rubbed off on her, or was this the result of swimming in magical waters?

Dobo took his friends aside, making sure the islanders couldn't overhear. "Something has occurred to me," he said. "If the magic of the helmet is what gave the water its purported benefits, then we may have just put these people out of business."

Marta nodded. "Then let us make haste," she said.

Another cargo ship arrived an hour later, and they paid extra to book passage on it. From there, they changed ships three times until they found one headed for their next destination, the coastal city of Tkeatek.

## *Tkeatek*

SPANG!

The pickaxe chipped through the rock and hit something metal.

"I think I've found...," Tethan began, but the mayor shushed him.

"Quiet," Mayor Gutteridge hissed. "This is what she wants."

"What who wants?" Tethan asked.

"Start working on a different spot," the mayor said. "Pretend you never found this. If Ryveen—"

A taskmaster approached, brandishing a bullwhip. "Everybody out of the tunnel," he ordered.

The mayor cursed, but Tethan just looked confused. They joined the crowd as dozens of workers made their way out of the mines. Once they reached the surface, the mayor began to turn away but Tethan grabbed his hand. "What's going on?"

Mayor Gutteridge pulled Tethan aside, then looked around for listeners. They were surrounded by chattering miners, half-drunk with elation from getting off work early. The crowd gradually dispersed, with most of them heading for the tavern.

The mayor led Tethan behind a storage shed. When he was satisfied that they wouldn't be overheard, he looked Tethan in the eyes and said, "If you can find a way out of town, you should take it immediately."

"Does this have something to do with what I found?" Tethan asked.

"Everything," the mayor replied. "I'm not in charge anymore. Lakehelm's been taken over by a madwoman with godlike powers. We need to get people out."

"Fleeing is for cowards," Tethan said. "If what you say is true, we have to stay and fight."

"We can't," the mayor said. "She's just too powerful. I've tried—"

"Oh, Alistair!" The woman's voice carried over the crowd of cheering miners.

"Just go," the mayor said, then turned away and went to find Ryveen.

"I hear you unearthed something," the woman said as Mayor Gutteridge approached.

"It's probably nothing," the mayor replied. "Just a mineral deposit, I'm sure."

"I don't know, I have a good feeling about this one," Ryveen said. She was in a giddy mood, and she couldn't stop smiling.

On Ryveen's orders, the mayor led her and a pair of her most trusted guards through the mine until they reached the chamber where Tethan had made his discovery. The rock had chipped away, revealing the corner of a metal plate.

One of the guards handed the mayor a pickaxe. "Unbury the rest," he said.

But Ryveen held up her hand and pushed the mayor

back. "I'll take care of it," she said. Then she punched the wall. Rocks flaked away, revealing the rest of the metal hatch. It was perfectly square, about four feet on each side, with ancient writing etched across it.

Ryveen ripped it open and peered inside. Then she got down on her hands and knees and crawled through the hole.

"Now's our chance," the mayor whispered to one of the guards. "Slam the door, brace a beam against it. We can be rid of her forever."

"Why would I do that?" the guard asked in a monotone voice. "Ryveen loves us. She loves all of us." He stared at the hatch with an unfocused gaze.

"Snap out of it!" the mayor ordered. "What has she done to you?"

"I'd do the same to you if I didn't need your mind intact," Ryveen replied, sticking her head back out of the hatch. "Now come here, I want to show you something beautiful. Bring a torch."

The mayor reluctantly crouched and followed her through the hatch.

"Wow," the mayor said. He wished they hadn't found it, but he had to admit it was a breathtaking discovery. The ancient armory contained hundreds of weapons racks. Some displayed swords and daggers with enchanted blades that still glowed after centuries of gathering dust. Others held crossbow-like weapons loaded with magical ammunition. There were even a few pieces of siege equipment, large ballistae capable of hurling magical bombs.

"These weapons haven't seen the light of day in over a thousand years," Ryveen said. "But soon they will cover the land in fire and death. Zyden will fall, then all of Evrosia. The world will bow down before my army."

"You know, getting a pet is also fulfilling," the mayor suggested. "Or maybe a hobby. Have you tried glass-blowing?"

"I don't think small," Ryveen said, delicately touching the mayor's neck. "I never have. Why should I? I have the world at my fingertips, and you would have me playing arts and crafts?"

"It can't last forever, Ryveen," Mayor Gutteridge said. "Maybe you'll conquer Zyden, maybe you'll even branch out to the rest of the world. But you'll always want more. Ruling the world won't be any more fulfilling than ruling Lakehelm. Just quit while you're ahead, before you make any more enemies."

"The enemies are the point," Ryveen said. "The more I destroy, the more I am known. The survivors will know me as a goddess!"

"Why not be known for kindness, instead?" the mayor asked. "With your power, you could save thousands of lives. Cure diseases. End famine. Help the poor. History would remember you as the greatest healer who ever lived. Now *that's* a goddess."

"This conversation has become tedious," Ryveen said. "Go home, Alistair. I wish to bask in the glory of my armory, and your whining threatens to sour my mood."

"If you change your mind, I will help you," Mayor Gutteridge said, then climbed back into the tunnel.

"Sentimental fool," Ryveen muttered. But she forgot him moments later. She grabbed a crossbow off its rack and fired it at the floor, creating a crater five feet deep. She giggled with glee, then danced around the armory like a child in a toymaker's shop. She tossed the crossbow aside and retrieved a pair of swords. She swiped at imaginary foes and executed ungrateful citizens, then commanded armies to march on rival kingdoms.

Then she lay on her back and reveled in her success, her mind abuzz with plans of world domination. Aroused by visions of death and bloodshed, she performed obscene acts of self-gratification with the hilt of a magic dagger. When she was satisfied, she fell asleep cuddling an enchanted sword.


"Say it again?" Kya asked.

"Tkeatek," Marta repeated.

"Tuh-Kee-uh-tek?" Kya asked.

"Close enough," Marta replied. "It's a desert on the continent of Nokorr."

"A new world," Dobo said. "I never thought I'd set foot on a different continent. And to think just a few months ago, I was the one showing you around Zyden."

Two weeks had passed since Kosis, and as much as they enjoyed the sea air, they couldn't wait to see land again. They docked at a trading port on the south coast of Nokorr, then hired a carriage to take them to Tkeatek. They rode northeast for two days, watching out the windows as the grass gave way to sand.

"You're sure this is where you want to be?" the driver asked as they climbed out of the carriage. The city looked hostile and primitive. Citizens with cloth-wrapped faces repaired their weathered stone huts with clay paste, while harsh winds created little sand tornadoes that danced down the street.

"We'll be fine," Marta said as she paid the driver.

"Where to?" Dobo asked as he watched the carriage take off down the road. He missed it already, and couldn't wait to get indoors.

"Let's try that place!" Kya suggested, pulling on Marta's hand. The building she indicated was a bit larger than the others, and had a faded painting of a lizard on one wall. They weren't sure what kind of business it was, but it was better than being outside.

It turned out to be a restaurant. The easiest meat to harvest in the desert came from large reptiles, which they were surprised to discover were quite delicious. It was, however, the first restaurant they'd been to where the water cost more than the meal.

"So is your intuition giving you any hints about where to go next?" Dobo asked as he picked the meat off a lizard leg.

"No, but the man tending bar did," Marta replied. "He said there were some ruins just east of town. He called it 'The Old City.' No one goes there now. They said it's crawling with rathuriks."

"What's a rathurik?" Kya asked.

"He wouldn't say," Marta replied. "He just laughed and said I'd know it when one ate me."

"They don't really like visitors here, do they?" Silli asked.

"I doubt they get very many," Dobo replied. "It's not exactly a vacation spot."

"Hopefully we won't have to stay very long," Marta said. They finished eating and prepared for a walk. Taking a cue from the locals, they each bought cloth coverings for their faces. Marta, however, found that hers wasn't necessary. Even though the helmet didn't cover her eyes, it still seemed to protect her from the sand somehow. It even dimmed the sand's blinding glare.

The Old City was less than a mile away, but it took longer than it should have to make the walk. The sand was full of hidden sinkholes, and more than once the wind picked up until it was impossible to see. By the time they reached the ruins, they felt as if they'd been walking for an entire day.

A row of conical stone pillars rose from the sand, spaced roughly fifty feet apart, looking like the teeth of a giant carnivore. As they got closer, they realized that each of the pillars was a small building.

"Which one?" Dobo shouted over the loud winds.

"The closest one!" Kya insisted, and they all agreed.

The structure featured a rusted metal door, partially blocked by sand. Marta pulled it open and they all fled inside. Then Marta closed the door behind them.

"Glowstones, Sillivene," Dobo said, holding out a small rock. Silli sprinkled a little fairy dust on Dobo's rock, then did the same for Kya. Marta hadn't even realized it was dark inside. The round room was empty except for a trapdoor in the floor.

"Might as well see if it goes anywhere good," Kya suggested, pulling on the iron ring and revealing a spiral staircase that descended into darkness.

"Shall we?" Dobo asked.

"It's better than going back out there," Silli replied.

Marta led the way. The stairs ended in a hallway. As they walked through the narrow passage, they found more staircases leading back to the surface.

"I guess it didn't matter which entrance we took," Kya said.

The hallway turned a few times until they reached a large open foyer. The room had a high ceiling and featured dozens of doors leading to more hallways.

"This could take a while to explore," Dobo muttered.

"There's words above each door," Kya said, pointing. "Can you read them, Marta?"

Marta studied the ancient writing. "Exit... Offices... Records... Restaurant..."

"Any of them say tomb?" Dobo asked.

"Did you just hear something?" Silli asked.

They all stopped talking and listened closely. Something thudded from far away, but it was impossible to tell which hallway the sound had come from. Everyone stood perfectly still.

Marta very slowly drew her sword, but she kept reading the signs. "Mausoleum," she finally whispered, pointing at a door. The group tiptoed towards the doorway. They were almost there when a creature burst from one of the hallways.

The monster was about the size of a horse. It had the body of a crocodile, but with six spider-like legs. Its tail curved like that of a scorpion, complete with a stinger the size of Marta's sword. Its eyes were round and bulbous like an insect's, and it was covered in rough, sand-colored scales.

"Get behind me!" Marta ordered as it skittered towards them. It struck at her with its stinger, but she blocked it with her shield. Then two more of the creatures entered the atrium from other hallways.

Marta continued to raise her shield, but now she had to block strikes from three different directions. Back in Javesia, the shield had protected them with an invisible barrier, but Marta saw no evidence of such a thing at the moment. She wondered what the rules were — would the barrier automatically activate if a sting threatened to come close? She didn't want to experiment to find out.

"I'm guessing these are rathuriks," Dobo muttered as the party backed towards the mausoleum. Kya drew her bow and Dobo readied his crossbow, and both fired several shots at the creatures. Unfortunately their arrows and bolts wouldn't penetrate the rathuriks' thick scales. Silli flew up above them and fired a few magical arrows from her tiny bow. Her shots at least made the monsters flinch, but they didn't seem too bothered by them.

Kya and Dobo retreated into the mausoleum. Marta backed up toward the hallway, fending off the rathuriks as she protected her friends. Then two of the stingers struck at once, but she was only able to block one of them. Marta shrieked in pain, then backed the rest of the way into the mausoleum.

Dobo remembered the wand he'd gotten from Keez. He retrieved it from his backpack and gave it a flick, causing a burst of flame to erupt from the end. The rathuriks backed off, making insect-like screeching sounds. But then the wand was spent, and the creatures advanced once again.

The party turned and fled. The next door was closed but unlocked. Once they were through, they slammed the heavy iron door and placed a crossbar over it. The monsters scratched at the door but couldn't push it open.

"Your arm," Kya said.

Marta's arm was starting to swell where the stinger had pierced it. "It's noth… noth…" Marta began, but fell to her knees and vomited.

"Silli?" Dobo asked.

The fairy dug through her purse and found a pouch of salve. Then she rubbed it on Marta's arm and sprinkled some fairy dust on it. "I don't know if this will work, but it's all I've got," she said.

"Have to keep going…" Marta said, trying to get to her feet.

"You need to rest," Kya told her.

"The voices are telling me to press on," Marta argued.

"Just sit for a minute," Dobo said. "There's no reason to rush." He and Kya gently pushed her down as she tried to stand.

"No, I'm fine," Marta rasped. Her speech was becoming slurred, and she had trouble focusing on her friends' faces.

"You've been poisoned," Dobo said. Then he turned to Silli and asked, "Is there an antidote in any of your books?"

Silli rooted through her purse and flipped through some books. "Give me a minute," she said.

Marta shook her head and rose to her feet. Dobo and Kya tried to hold her down but she shook them off. "I might not... have much time..." she said.

"You're in no condition to—" Dobo began.

"I know what I'm doing!" Marta shouted and staggered down the hall. "The voices say... they say..."

The others gave up trying to stop her, and followed her instead. Silli continued looking through her books but didn't have much luck. She found a recipe for a scorpion venom antidote, but she didn't know if it would apply to these creatures, and she didn't have the ingredients it would have required anyway.

Marta took several turns, guided by voices the others couldn't hear. Then she reached a familiar-looking metal door and pulled it open.

On top of this tomb's sepulcher lay a single metal gauntlet. "Just one?" Kya asked when she saw the item. "How many tombs are we going to have to visit to get the whole set?"

Marta collapsed, and her friends rushed to her aid. "Her face is turning green," Dobo said.

"We can't stay here," Kya said. "We have to get her back to town. Maybe they have an antidote."

"At this rate she'd be dead by the time we got there," Dobo replied. "And how are we going to drag her past those monsters?"

"The glove," Marta said weakly. Drool dribbled out of her

mouth as she spoke.

"You're going to be okay," Kya told her. "It can't end here. Not like this." Tears streamed down her cheeks as she held Marta's hands.

Marta brushed Kya's hands away and reached toward the sepulcher. "Give me... the gauntlet..."

"If you think it will help," Dobo said as he picked up the glove. He felt electric tingles in his fingers as he passed it to Marta.

Marta donned the glove and flexed her fingers. Silver scales traveled up her arm and over her shoulder, then spread across her entire body. Within seconds she wore an entire suit of armor which matched the style of the helmet and shield.

"Her color's coming back," Kya said.

Marta closed her eyes and took a few deep breaths, then rose to her feet. "I feel... much better," she announced.

Dobo looked her over. Her face was back to normal, and she no longer swayed where she stood. "Amazing," he said. "Do you think this armor has healing properties?"

"It would seem so," Marta replied. She touched where she'd been stung. She couldn't see the wound as it was covered up by the armor, but she could no longer feel any pain or swelling in the area.

Kya looked Marta up and down. She looked like a king's royal guard, not the barbarian-like warrior she'd come to know. "How do you take it back off?" she asked.

"I don't know," Marta replied. "I suppose I just..." As she thought about removing the armor, the scales receded until it was once again just a gauntlet. The wound on her arm was completely gone.

"Astounding," Dobo said, touching her bare arm. "And you're sure you don't feel sick?"

"I've never felt better in my life," Marta said. "But I am anxious to get out of here. Are all of you ready?"

Everyone agreed and they left the tomb. Getting past the rathuriks was much easier now that Marta had the armor. Their stingers couldn't pierce the silver scales, so Marta no longer had to focus on defense. She attacked the creatures with such fury that her friends turned pale. When the final rathurik turned to flee, Marta pursued it and hacked off each of its legs before driving her sword through its eye.

"That was... violent," Dobo said when it was over.

"*You* didn't feel its sting earlier," Marta said icily.

Dobo looked at Kya with a raised eyebrow. Kya shrugged and looked confused.

Silli took a more direct approach. "Hey, is the armor affecting your mind?" she asked.

"I can feel the blood of my ancestors flow through me," Marta replied. "They guide my sword, enhance my skills..."

"Yeah, you looked like you lost it for a minute back there," Kya said.

"They were great warriors, unmatched in battle," Marta replied. "But they always fought for a better world. I promise you, I will not forget who I am."

Kya wasn't sure she believed it, but she decided not to argue. They returned to Tkeatek and hired a wagon to take them out of town.

## *Veantra*

"We just want to talk," General Tysus shouted. He held an enchanted horn that amplified his voice so that it could be heard across the moat and through the wall. *And when did Lakehelm get a moat, anyway?* he wondered. He hadn't visited Lakehelm in several months, but the town looked like it had gone through years of growth. The wooden fence was twenty feet high and spiked along the top, and a forty-foot wide canal circled the town. Much of the town's surrounding forest had been cut down, presumably to build the wall.

"Go away," Mayor Gutteridge shouted back from atop the wall. "You have no business here."

But Tysus stood firm. Behind him, forty soldiers on horseback held their bows ready. "You're a good man, Alistair," Tysus shouted. "I've known you for a long time, and I trust you. But disturbing rumors have reached my ears. We hear you're building an army. That you plan to expand to the north, and you intend to wipe out anyone who gets in your way. I can't believe that of my old friend. Please assure me that these rumors have no merit."

"Please," the mayor shouted back. "I don't want to see

you get hurt…"

"Oh, let me talk to him," another voice said. The mayor disappeared behind the wall. A woman in a black dress took his place. "You may call me Ryveen," the woman said. Her voice boomed across the moat without the need of any magic items. "Lakehelm and its army are under my control."

"What are your intentions?" Tysus asked.

"I only want what's mine," Ryveen replied. "Lakehelm, Zyden… the rest of Evrosia. Nothing big, really."

"I represent the combined militias of Guildport, Olivetree, and their outlying communities," Tysus shouted. "Know that if your army attempts to march north, we will consider it an act of war."

"Only consider it?" Ryveen asked. "How indecisive. I give my word to you, General, that when I decide to wage war, there won't be any doubt in your mind."

"Is that your intention, then?" Tysus asked. "To start a war?"

"And if it is?" Ryveen asked.

"I give you fair warning," Tysus said. "I have contracts with thirteen towns. You are but one. You can't hope to win against—"

"Oh, this is boring," Ryveen said. "Kill them."

Dozens of Lakehelm soldiers popped up behind the wall. They fired their crossbows, sending hundreds of glowing orbs at Tysus and his soldiers. Explosions rocked the road, tearing the riders apart along with their horses. It was over after the first volley; Tysus didn't even have time to issue an order.

"I suppose we're at war now," Ryveen remarked as she descended the stairs to ground level.

Mayor Gutteridge just gaped at her as she walked away.

*There has to be something I can do,* he thought. But he was all out of ideas.

Veantra was a thriving city with a well-educated population. It was bigger than any of the towns in Zyden, with hundreds of clay brick buildings alongside well-maintained roads and parks. While it was still technically in the same desert as Tkeatek, the city's irrigation system was so well-designed that one wouldn't have known.

Marta got a few funny looks with her shiny helmet and shield. The citizens of Veantra didn't tend to walk around armed, much less dressed for war. But no one tried to stop her, either.

"Have you seen any guards since we've been here?" Dobo asked.

"I think there was one at the city entrance," Marta replied.

"They must not get a lot of trouble," Dobo reasoned.

Getting information about the local tombs was as simple as asking at the nearest library. The librarian pointed them to the city planning section, where dozens of shelves held rolled-up maps.

"I think this is the tomb," Kya said, pointing to a spot on a map of the undercity. Several tombs, catacombs, and underground cemeteries dotted the map, but Kya pointed to the oldest one. Each construction was labeled with a build date, but the tomb Kya indicated was labeled "pre-Veantra" with three question marks.

No one tried to stop them as they descended into the undercity, through the catacombs, and to the ancient tomb. As usual, a metal door opened to a round room containing a sepulcher. But this time, nothing lay across the lid.

"Where's my artifact?" Marta asked.

"Someone must have taken it," Kya replied.

"It would have been stranger if they hadn't," Silli said. "I mean, sitting out here in the open all these years? We didn't even have to fight any monsters."

"Let's go back to the library," Dobo suggested.

It took several hours of browsing, but eventually they found a book full of archaeological records. The tomb had been uncovered two decades earlier, and the contents had been transferred to a museum on the other side of the city. By the time they reached the museum, it was already closed for the day.

"We'll have to break in," Marta said.

"Will you listen to yourself?" Kya asked. "We're the heroes, remember? We're not here to break the law."

"It does seem like these relics are a bad influence on you," Dobo added.

"And if we walk in there in the daytime, do you think they're just going to hand the relic over?" Marta asked. "We're going to have to steal it either way. At least it will be easier while they're closed."

"I'm not comfortable with this," Kya said.

"This artifact was crafted by my people," Marta said. "I have a greater right to it than anyone in this city. Why is it legal for them to steal it from my ancestor's tomb, but it's illegal for me to reclaim it?"

"We could at least try to get it legally first," Kya said. "Maybe there's some sort of proof-of-ownership document you can fill out."

"Kya, I adore you, but you are naïve," Marta said. "If we reveal our interest in the item in advance, then not only will they say no, but they'll know it was us once it's stolen. And it means waiting an extra day, which is time we may not have. The voices tell me that the evil grows ever stronger. I don't know how much time is left, but I do know I'll need this relic to save the world."

"I'm not so sure about these voices," Dobo said.

"They haven't steered us wrong yet," Marta replied.

They knew they couldn't talk her out of it. They waited until the middle of the night, when the city was quiet. Then Marta pried open the museum's back door with a pry bar, and the party followed her inside.

The museum had three floors. A registry book on the first floor listed the locations of all the museum's artifacts. It was too dark for most of the party to read, and they didn't want to use their glowstones for fear of being discovered. But Marta's helmet allowed her to see as if it were daylight, and she found the listing without much trouble.

"Second floor," she whispered. They crept up the stairs and followed the signs. Then the voices took over and guided Marta to her target. The party came to a stop in front of a five-foot-high pedestal, which displayed a longsword in an ice-blue sheath. A plaque on the pedestal read:

Ancient Sword

Date Unknown – Pre-Veantra

Believed To Belong To The Musgahn Tribe

"Musgahn Tribe," Marta said reverently. There was no glass, no barrier, nothing to prevent Marta from just reaching out and grabbing it. *The people of Veantra sure are trusting*, Marta thought as she reached for the hilt.

Then her fingers brushed a nearly invisible string and several torches burst to life. "Is someone in here?" a voice called from the lower level.

Marta grabbed the sword and rushed down the stairs. Crossbow-wielding guards blocked all the exits.

*Kill them*, a voice said in Marta's ear.

"I will not," she muttered. But she did unsheathe the sword. The blade was made of blue steel, with runes carved on one side.

"Put down the sword and come with us," one of the guards ordered.

"The sword belongs to me," Marta replied.

Dobo and Kya climbed down the stairs behind her. They couldn't seem to decide whether to draw their weapons. Silli hid inside Dobo's shirt.

"This is your final warning," the guard said.

Marta activated her gauntlet, and armored scales appeared all over her body. "Your weapons can't hurt me," she told them.

"But they can hurt us," Kya said. "Would you really let us get killed in the crossfire?"

"Just stay behind me," Marta said.

"No!" Kya shouted. She stepped in front of Marta and approached one of the guards, her hands raised. "My friend is a descendant of the Musgahn Tribe," she said. "The sword is her birthright. We'll do whatever it takes to prove her claim to the artifact."

"Well that does make a difference," the guard said, lowering his crossbow. "We wondered if any of you were left. The museum has been prepared to offer it to any of your tribe who came to claim it. I just wish you'd come at a more reasonable hour."

"Really?" Marta asked. "You're just going to let me take it?"

"Of course not," the guard said. "There's a process. In the morning, we'll wake the magistrate and the research committee. They'll ask you some questions and have you fill out some paperwork. If they believe you, they'll let you keep the sword. Either way, you'll pay a fine for breaking into the museum."

"That's more than fair," Dobo said.

Marta sheathed the sword and handed it to the guard. "So be it," she said.

The interview went better than expected. The scholars of Veantra were fascinated by the story of Marta's life and her quest to retrieve the other artifacts. They asked her all sorts of questions about her tattoos and her childhood in the Frostmoor mountains. They were so pleased to have new historical information to add to their archives that they waived her fine. Convinced that she was telling them the truth, they allowed her to take the sword. Marta and her friends took another carriage back to the southern coast of Nokorr, then booked a ship to Zyden.

"I owe you another apology," Marta said.

"Yes, you do," Kya replied.

They sat together on a bed in their cabin, on a passenger ship headed for Sweetgrape. Marta's artifacts lay sprawled across the other bed.

"I'm afraid I've been a bit... driven the past few weeks," Marta explained.

"I know," Kya replied. "You've been treating us like we're in the way, just more obstacles to slow you down. There's a voice in your ear, telling you where to go and what to do, and I'm not entirely sure it has your best interests at heart."

Marta shook her head. "My best interests are inconsequential. My ancestors only care about defeating a great evil, one that threatens the entire world."

"Do you know that, though?" Kya asked.

"They've been right about everything," Marta replied. "They knew where to find the relics. They showed me my clan's past."

"That doesn't make them all-knowing," Kya said. "The scholars in Veantra also knew a lot about your clan, but they're not gods."

"What are you suggesting?" Marta asked.

Kya leaned against Marta's shoulder and put a hand on her thigh. "I don't know," she said. "Something about this doesn't feel right, but I can't say why. Just promise me that whatever happens next, you'll keep your eyes open."

"You have my word," Marta said.

Kya nodded quietly. She trusted her partner, but she wasn't sure how much influence these voices had over her. If the ancestors demanded something terrible, would Marta be able to resist?


*She'll be returning soon*, Ryveen thought with glee. The final piece of her plan was about to fall into place. She had powers beyond those of mere mortals, and now she commanded a legion of mind-controlled slaves, armed with magical weapons. There was only one thing left she needed, and she didn't even have to work for it - it was about to fall right into her lap.

## *Showdown*

The party disembarked at Sweetgrape, took the ferry back to the mainland, and retrieved their wagon and horses from the stables.

"Where to?" Dobo asked, holding the reins. He hadn't been in the driver's seat in weeks, and he couldn't wait to be on the road again. Marta climbed up and sat next to him, while Kya loaded a few things into the back.

"I don't know," Marta answered.

Silli buzzed around the horses' heads, making sure their bridles were secure. "You don't know?" she asked as she flitted by. "We did a lot of traveling to end up at 'I don't know.' Aren't the voices telling you anything?"

"I only know that I'll need the artifacts to combat a rising evil," Marta said. "I don't know when or where this evil will appear, or even what form it will take."

"Well, we've got to go somewhere," Dobo said. "Why don't we take a trip over to Guildport for supplies?"

Just then a young courier came running up to them. "Don't go yet!" the boy shouted. "I have a message for you!" He reached up and handed Dobo a piece of parchment.

"What is it?" Marta asked, leaning over to look.

"It's from Tabitha at the Crier," he said, quickly reading over the text. "She says Lakehelm's been taken over by an evil overlord. They need our help."

"Tell Tabitha we'll head straight there," Marta told the boy. He nodded and left.

"Guess we have a destination," Dobo said, and they set out for Lakehelm.


"Snap out of it!" the mayor said, slapping Tethan across the face.

"But I have to protect Lakehelm," Tethan replied, and went back to chopping the log.

The night before, Tethan had been caught helping a few citizens escape from town. A couple had gotten away, but most of them had been captured and taken to Ryveen. Mayor Gutteridge had just learned of the incident this morning.

"This isn't you," the mayor said. "Listen to me, Tethan. Tethan! Look at me!"

But Tethan just kept chopping. The mayor grabbed his arm and tried to pull him away, but Tethan pushed him aside and continued his work. Half the forest had been cut down, but Ryveen wasn't satisfied. She wanted the walls thicker, taller, and at one point she'd even used the word "spikier."

"How can I get through to you?" Mayor Gutteridge asked, but Tethan didn't seem to hear him. Whatever Ryveen was doing to people's minds, the magic was powerful.

*I can't believe I'm going to try this*, the mayor thought. But he needed help, and Tethan knew which citizens could be counted on to oppose Ryveen.

As Tethan brought his ax up, the mayor rushed forward

and lay across the log, right in the path of the ax. Tethan brought the ax down, but stopped himself midway.

"Mayor?" Tethan asked, tossing the ax to the side.

"Are you back?" the mayor asked.

"How did you know that would work?" Tethan asked. He blinked and shook his head, as if he were waking up from a nightmare.

"I didn't," the mayor said. "But a heart as pure as yours can't be used for evil."

"What do we do now?" Tethan asked. All around them, more blank-faced workers chopped logs, carving them into spikes that would be used to fortify the wall. None of them seemed to notice the conversation between Tethan and the mayor. There weren't even any taskmasters about, as they were no longer necessary.

"We fight back," Mayor Gutteridge said. "Even if it costs us our lives."

They pushed the horses harder than Dobo would have liked, taking turns at the reins while some of the party slept in the wagon. Despite their best efforts, it still took five days to make the trip from Sweetgrape to Lakehelm.

"Just a few more miles," Dobo said soothingly to the exhausted horses.

"What's that?" Kya asked, pointing to something in the road ahead. It was the middle of the night, and there wasn't much moonlight to see by. Silli flitted forward, her natural glow illuminating the upcoming obstacle.

"It's a body," she said as she returned. "It looks burned."

"Wake Marta," Dobo said, and Silli flew through the wagon's window. They'd decided that Marta would take the final sleep shift before Lakehelm, as she would need to be well-rested once they arrived.

The closer they got to Lakehelm, the more bodies they found. The debris consisted of both soldiers and horses, their corpses violently ripped apart by an unknown force. The soldiers wore uniforms from several different towns, and their bodies were in various states of decay. Some had clearly been there longer than others.

"What do you suppose happened here?" Kya asked.

"Looks like they marched on Lakehelm and failed," Dobo replied. "Several times."

"I know but..." Kya replied, then paused. "What could have done this to them?"

"Let me out here," Marta ordered through the window. Dobo brought the wagon to a stop.

"Time for a plan?" Dobo asked as Marta emerged from the back. She was dressed in her new armor and sword, the silver-blue gleaming even in the darkness.

Marta shook her head. "No plan," she said. "I'm going to walk straight up to the gate and ask to see whoever's in charge."

"Look at all this destruction," Kya said, waving her hand at the remains of the soldiers. "Whatever did this had to be magical. How do you know it won't go right through your new armor?"

"Why else would my ancestors have sent me to retrieve these relics?" Marta asked. "They knew I'd need them to fight back. Therefore, my armor must be able to withstand whatever magic I'm to face."

"You're taking a lot on faith," Kya said.

"It's not 'faith' when the ancestors actually talk to me," Marta replied. "I understand your worry, Kya. But it's not as if I'm praying to the sun or sacrificing livestock to a lifeless statue. Why should I doubt the power of the spirits who sent me on this quest? As far as I'm concerned, they've proven themselves several times over."

"I suppose you have a point," Kya said, though the concern hadn't left her face. "Will you at least allow us to stand beside you this time, or are we about to hear another speech about it being too dangerous?"

"I had another plan for you three," Marta said. "While I confront the overlord, the rest of you find another way into town and help however you can. See if there's prisoners to free, start a riot, whatever you can do."

"So you can go be a big hero without us getting in the way," Kya said. "Again."

Marta looked hurt for a moment, then angry. "I apologize," she said icily. "But this is the way it needs to be. I can't fight as effectively if I'm worried about your fate."

*Ignore her*, whispered the voice in Marta's ear. *She will forgive you later. Right now you must hurry.*

"She's hearing it again," Dobo said, recognizing Marta's far-off expression.

"What are they telling you?" Silli asked.

"They told me I must make haste," Marta replied. Then she turned and ran towards Lakehelm.


*When did they even have time to do this*? Marta wondered as she saw the eyesore of a fence. She felt a knot in her stomach, a growing certainty that she was walking towards something uniquely evil.

As she reached the moat, the drawbridge lowered and the portcullis raised. Marta continued through the front gate. Two guards approached. Their weapons were not drawn, nor did they give her any orders. They flanked Marta's sides and guided her through the town, never saying a word.

As they walked, Marta saw many townsfolk at work, fortifying the walls and building new structures. None of the workers made eye contact, nor did they show any curiosity as Marta passed. The guards took her by a field where a platoon of soldiers stood at attention, unmoving, unblinking, and probably unthinking. Marta gradually realized they were taking a roundabout route through town. Wherever the guards were taking her, they'd been instructed to show off first.

After nearly half an hour of walking, they arrived at the city council meeting hall. The doors opened to a large open room that was usually full of tables and chairs, but the hall was currently unfurnished.

A woman stood in the center of the room. She had pale skin and wore a blood-red blouse with black leather pants. Her face was thin with sunken-in cheekbones, like that of a woman on the brink of starvation, but her eyes were full of life.

"Marta, it's a pleasure," the woman said.

Though they'd never met face-to-face, Marta recognized her voice immediately. "Ryveen!" she shouted. "I should have known it was you."

"I suppose you're here to thwart my evil plan and vanquish me to the netherworld," Ryveen said, sounding bored.

"Or you could surrender right now," Marta replied.

"Says the mouse to the tiger," Ryveen said. "You can't begin to imagine my power."

"Oh, but I can," Marta said, drawing her sword. "That's why I came prepared. I wear the sacred artifacts of my people. Even you can't harm me through this armor. Even you can't stand up to this sword. Even you—"

"Yes, yes, I know all about the relics," Ryveen said. "Who

do you think guided you to them?"

"What?" Marta asked.

"I can't believe you didn't figure it out," Ryveen said. "Those voices in your head? All mine."

"No…" Marta said. "It wasn't you, it was…"

Ryveen held up her hand, showing off her ring. "I've been speaking to you through this," she said. "Again. You didn't see that coming?"

Marta touched her chest just below her throat. Somewhere under her armor, the matching ring still hung on a chain around her neck. "But I—" she began.

"Yes, I know, you don't even wear it around your finger," Ryveen explained. "I've improved my attunement to the ring. As long as it's on your person, I can speak to you."

"But why?" Marta asked. "Why would you send me hundreds of miles away to find the equipment I'd need to defeat you?"

"Because I wanted the relics for myself, and I didn't want to get my hands dirty looking for them," Ryveen replied. "Seriously, do you expect me to take over the world dressed like this?"

Marta's eyes narrowed and she raised her sword. "Good luck taking them from me then," she said.

"Aw, that's sweet," Ryveen replied. "Good luck to you too. You're going to need it in a moment."

Marta swiped her sword through the air, her blade on a course to meet Ryveen's neck.

"Stop," Ryveen said. Her pupils turned to slits, and the whites became yellow.

The blade stopped mere inches from Ryveen's neck. Marta couldn't will herself to finish the strike.

"Give me the sword," Ryveen said. Unable to stop herself, Marta sheathed the weapon and handed it over. "And the rest of the relics as well," Ryveen added.

Marta complied. The armor retracted back into the glove, and Marta handed it to Ryveen along with the shield and helmet.

Ryven donned the items and activated the armor. "How do I look?" she asked.

"How did you do that?" Marta asked.

"Oh, right, you would ask that, wouldn't you?" Ryveen said. "I suppose it started when I died. See, I'd made a deal before my death, and I came back with all sorts of new abilities. I'm still discovering some of them. I don't even need these relics to conquer the world. But at least if I have them, no one can use them to challenge me."

"This whole time…" Marta huffed.

"I know, that was the best part," Ryveen said. "I gave you faith, made you believe in the power of your ancestors. Turns out the way to a warrior's heart is through their dogma. Maybe I should start a religion."

Marta shrieked and tried to tackle her, but Ryveen stood as immobile as a statue. Marta clawed at the woman's eyes and throat, but her fingers wouldn't scratch Ryveen's skin. Marta pounded on her until her fists were bloody, then stopped to catch her breath.

"You done?" Ryveen asked.

"Not… as long… as you live," Marta said between heavy breaths.

The door opened and three guards walked in, dragging Kya behind them. "We found this one sneaking around outside," one guard said.

"Perfect timing," Ryveen replied. "What about the jester and the fairy?"

"Still looking, but we'll find them," the guard said. "What do you want me to do with this one?"

"Leave her here," Ryveen said, grasping Kya's arm. "I just thought of a new game."

The guards left and shut the door. Kya struggled, but Ryveen's grip was like stone.

"Who is this woman?" Kya grunted. She punched Ryveen in the face, but only hurt her hand in the process.

"It's Ryveen," Marta replied.

Kya's eyes widened. "The mother of—"

"Thank you for reminding me," Ryveen said, pulling Kya closer. "I'd almost forgotten the role you played in killing my precious child."

"Let her go," Marta said. "Do what you want to me, but let Kya live."

"You talk as if you actually have bargaining power," Ryveen said. "Now shush for a minute, I'm trying to think of a game. Something where you'll suffer slowly. What if I ask you questions, and every time you get an answer wrong, I cut off part of your girlfriend?"

"No!" Marta shouted. She tried to pull Kya free, but Ryveen's grip remained strong.

"You're right, that one's only fun for so long," Ryveen said. "How about, 'Two Truths and a Lion?' That's where I ask you personal questions, and if you don't answer honestly, I drop Kya into a lion pit. No, how about good old-fashioned darts? I throw, Kya catches. With her face. Or maybe—"

A boom sounded in the distance. The building shook, and orange light flickered in the windows. Ryveen released Kya as she ran to the window.

"Come on," Marta whispered, ushering Kya to the door.

But then the door opened and a guard entered. "Ryveen! Someone's set fire to the storage shed!"

"Well, find them and kill them!" Ryveen shrieked, only

half-turning around.

The guard left, and once again Marta and Kya crept toward the exit. But Ryveen moved like a blur, and suddenly she was standing in front of the door.

"Going somewhere?" Ryveen asked.

"You look like you have your hands full," Marta said. "You don't need us getting in the way." Shouting could be heard outside.

"Nonsense, I always have time for my special guests," Ryveen said. She tried to sound flippant, but Marta could see the concern on her face.

There was another explosion, one that rattled the windows of the meeting hall and temporarily turned night into day. Marta held Ryveen's gaze for a few seconds, but Ryveen turned away.

"Official business," Ryveen said, opening the door. "But this isn't over." She vanished into the night.

Marta and Kya followed her out the door. Dobo came running around the corner a few seconds later, followed by the mayor and a man they didn't recognize. More men and women ran back and forth through the streets, some dressed in soldier uniforms and carrying weapons. Marta could barely hear above all the shouting.

"What's going on?" she asked.

"A lot," Dobo told her. "The mayor was sneaking people out while we were sneaking in. We ran into—"

"We need to hurry," the mayor interrupted, leading them away from the meeting hall. He explained more as they ran. "Ryveen found a cache of magic weapons and transferred them to a storage shed. Tethan here detonated it."

"That magic ammunition rocked the whole town when it went up," Tethan added proudly.

"Ryveen's been controlling people's minds," the mayor

explained. "But we've found ways to snap them back to reality."

They turned a corner and arrived at a wide field full of tree stumps. Soldiers were everywhere. Some stood in a trance while other citizens pleaded with them, dangling various trinkets in front of their faces. Other soldiers looked like they were just waking up from a bad dream.

"We've found that if we show them sentimental objects like—" Tethan started to explain, but then he interrupted himself. "Whoah… is that a fairy?"

Silli flitted over the heads of the entranced soldiers, sprinkling bits of fairy dust on them as she passed. Each one blinked a few times, looked confused, then relieved. Silli noticed her friends and flew over. "I'm almost out of fairy dust, but I'll wake as many as I can," she said.

"Good job," Dobo said as she flew off. Then he turned to the mayor. "How else can we help?"

"Just be ready for a fight," the mayor answered. "Ryveen will go on a rampage when she sees what we've done. I fear our entire militia won't be enough. That woman is invincible."

"Even more so, now that she has my armor," Marta said.

In the distance, they heard a scream so loud it shattered windows. "Who did this?" Ryveen's booming voice reverberated throughout Lakehelm.

And then there was a cacophony of shrieks and cries that sounded closer and closer to the clearing.

Marta stared in horror as Ryveen dashed through the crowd, sword drawn, cutting down random citizens on her way.

"Kill her!" Mayor Gutteridge shouted, and the soldiers within earshot drew their crossbows and fired. But the bolts bounced harmlessly off her armor.

Tethan and the mayor each wielded enchanted crossbows from the armory, and they fired their magical balls of light at the advancing woman. Their shots made blinding explosions as they hit Ryveen's shield, the backsplash injuring several bystanders. But Ryveen was unaffected.

She came to a stop in front of the mayor. "You betrayed me," Ryveen growled. More crossbow bolts bounced off her back, but she didn't seem to notice.

"I was never on your side in the first place," Mayor Gutteridge replied. His voice shook but he stood firm.

"Fine," Ryveen said. "I don't need an army. I can tear this world apart by myself."

A soldier swiped a sword against her neck, but the blade bounced right off. Ryveen quickly turned and stabbed him through the stomach. Then she turned back to the mayor.

"Please stop killing my people," the mayor begged. "Your quarrel is with me. Punish me, leave Lakehelm, conquer the world if you must. But I can't bear to watch my citizens die."

Ryveen seethed. "Stop... telling me... what to do!" she shrieked, then drew back her sword, ready to cut Mayor Gutteridge in half.

"No," Marta said, pushing the mayor aside. "You know you want me most of all. You and me, one on one, right now."

"Marta, no," Kya said, grabbing her girlfriend's arm. But Marta pulled away and glared at Ryveen.

"I don't mind killing you first," Ryveen hissed.

"Take my sword," Tethan said, handing it to Marta. The blade gave off a hint of yellow light, and Marta could feel the weapon's magic vibrate in her hand.

Ryveen and Marta stood face-to-face, less than five feet apart. The crowd formed a circle around them, giving them plenty of room to swing their swords. Ryveen was fully armored in magical relics, while Marta wore a simple cloth shirt and leather pants.

"I'm going to cut you limb from limb," Ryveen said. "But I won't kill you, no. I'll keep your dismembered body alive, at least long enough to watch your friends die in the most horrible ways you can imagine."

"Are you just going to talk, or are you going to fight?" Marta asked.

Ryveen bellowed something unintelligible and raised her sword high above her head. Marta lifted her sword to block the downward blow, but Ryveen's blade sliced through hers like it was bamboo.

The sword finished its arc and struck Marta in the forehead. But rather than cutting into her skin, it came to a rest and would go no further.

"What?" Ryveen asked, withdrawing the blade. Then she slashed sideways, striking Marta across the arm. The blade cut through her sleeve, but again it wouldn't penetrate her skin. In a fury, Ryveen pulled away and stabbed Marta in the heart, but her foe remained undamaged.

"I don't believe you're—" Marta began.

But Ryveen went berserk, stabbing and slashing Marta over and over. Bits of cloth went flying, and when she was done, Marta's shirt was in tatters. But not a drop of blood had been spilled.

"What is this trickery?" Ryveen asked.

"The relics were created by my clan, for my clan," Marta said. "The enchanters didn't want them to be used on members of the Musgahn tribe. That sword can't harm me, and that armor won't protect you from me." To demonstrate, Marta thrust her broken sword forward. The scales that made up Ryveen's armor moved aside, opening a hole over Ryveen's chest. But the blade still wouldn't puncture her skin.

"Fine," Ryveen said, tossing her sword aside. Then she dropped the shield, removed her helmet, and deactivated her armor. She threw the gauntlet onto the ground with the rest of the relics. "I don't need this junk anyway. I can kill you with my bare hands."

Then she pounced, tackling Marta to the ground. Though Marta was bigger, Ryveen was much stronger. She straddled Marta's prone form and tore into her with both hands. Marta tried to block Ryveen's blows, but the madwoman fought with relentless ferocity.

Marta's face became a bloody mess, and she fought to stay conscious. Then Ryveen pulled back and thrust her hand into Marta's chest. Marta could feel Ryveen's fingers close around her heart, squeezing it with a vicelike grip.

And then Ryveen made a "gurk" sound as a blade poked through her chest. Her face lost its remaining color, and she slid to the side and onto the ground. Kya stood above Marta, holding the relic sword, its blade now stained red.

Marta gurgled and began choking on her own blood.

"Quick, put the gauntlet on her," Dobo said.

Kya dropped the sword and pushed Marta's hand into the gauntlet. Nothing happened at first. Blood spurted from Marta's chest, and she didn't appear to have the awareness required to activate the gauntlet.

"Marta, please" Kya said, leaning over her. "Hurry, use your armor." But Marta just jerked and lay still, releasing one last gasp. With tears in her eyes, Kya leaned in and kissed her on the lips.

Marta's fingers twitched. Kya pulled away as scales crawled up Marta's arm and across her body. The bruises and cuts on Marta's face faded and healed. Then Marta started coughing. Kya helped her roll over as she hacked up more blood.

"What… happened?" Marta said between coughs.

"I think we won," Kya replied.

Marta rolled to her knees and stood up shakily. Then she pulled Kya into a tight hug. All around them, people cheered.

Upon Ryveen's death, the rest of the entranced townfolk regained their faculties. Ryveen's body lost its supernatural durability upon her passing. The people of Lakehelm burned her corpse into ash, ground her bones into powder, and scattered the dust to the winds. Then they gathered up the remaining magic weapons and locked them in the mines once again. Marta offered to add her relics to the vault as well.

"Won't you need them?" Dobo asked. "You worked awful hard to get them."

"No one needs to be that powerful," Marta replied. "As long as I have them, there's a risk that they'll be taken from me. At least this way I'll know where they are if I ever need them again."

Once all the ancient weapons were locked in the vault, including Marta's artifacts, the mayor ordered the mine to be destroyed. With a few well-placed explosives, the mine collapsed, burying the entrance to the vault. Those who knew the location of the cache were sworn to secrecy.

The mayor offered Marta's party a large reward and a permanent house in Lakehelm. But Marta turned him down.

"We'll stay for a few months before moving on," Marta told him. "But I'm not ready to call anywhere home just yet."

Dobo agreed. "We're nomads," he said. "And there's a big world out there, just waiting to be seen."

"But there is one thing you can help me arrange," Marta told the mayor, and the two got to work making plans.

It was the biggest wedding Lakehelm had ever seen. The entire town came out to see Marta and Kya exchange vows, as well as a few out-of-towners such as Sweetgrape's celebrity reporter Tabitha Wright, and Guildport's Hezek Carrell, who'd carved Kya's leg.

Alysia Gutteridge scattered flowers down the aisle, which was a wide dock on Center Lake. She was followed by Dobo, who escorted Marta and Kya to a platform out on the lake, where the mayor officiated the ceremony.

The weather was perfect - the sky was a bright blue and there was a gentle breeze that kept it from getting too warm. The odor of fresh pastries wafted over from the meeting hall, as the town's best cooks prepared for the reception.

Marta wore her clan's traditional betrothment armor, which she'd crafted herself from the bones and hide of a white panther. Kya wore a simple yellow wedding dress she'd inherited from her mother. During the month since Ryveen's defeat, the party had traveled to Kya's hometown of Fisher's Rest. While much of the town was in ruins, they'd managed to find a trunk in the remains of Kya's childhood home, containing a few family heirlooms along with the dress. Kya felt a long-missed connection to her mother when she put it on. It was almost like her mother was there with them, watching them get married.

*And maybe she is*, Kya thought.

They didn't memorize any vows. They each spoke from the heart as they expressed how much they meant to each other. Each cried as the other spoke, as did many of those in attendance.

Then Sillivene flitted across the dock and handed each of them a magical ring, the same pair of rings that had brought them together in the first place. As they placed the rings on each other's fingers, they once again gained the ability to speak to each other telepathically.

*I love you*, was the first thing Kya heard as the rings went on.

*Always and forever*, she replied.

Then they kissed, a kiss unlike any they'd shared before. Their thoughts became as entwined as their fingers, their minds a jumble of images and feelings until they couldn't tell whose thoughts were whose.

It was during that kiss that they knew. No matter what else the future had in store for them, no matter what foe they encountered, be it dragon, Bonegrinder, or would-be goddess... they would always face those challenges together.

Always and forever.

*Bonus Prequel Stories*

## *Banishing Act*

*This is the life,* Silli thought as she yawned under the silkleaf blanket. Then she rolled over and fell back asleep. A mosquito the size of her head buzzed around her ear, tickling her with its proboscis.

"Stop it," Silli said weakly, but the insect wouldn't stop pestering her. "I *will* swat you," she threatened, but she knew it was an empty threat. The taskmaster was a grig wizard who commanded every bug in the palace. Right now all of the Queen's servants would be suffering the same fate as Silli.

"Five more minutes?" Silli pleaded, but the mosquito refused to leave. "Fine," Silli said, and rolled out of bed.

The palace floor was covered in fae-grass, and she loved the feel of it between her toes. She poured herself a glass of honeydew juice, spiked with a bit of zip-bean to help her wake up. Then she headed down the hall to the group shower.

The other pixies laughed and talked and teased each other, but Silli just stood in the corner and washed. She'd never been very good at making friends. She could crack jokes with the best of them, but she just never seemed to understand where to draw the line.

"Hey Flitta," one pixie said. "Nice butt. Oh wait, sorry, that's your face!"

"Good one, Piri," Flitta laughed. "Hey, I heard you singing in choir last week. You couldn't carry a tune if it had handles."

Piri burst out laughing, and the two continued to one-up each other as they washed.

*I made the same joke about Piri's singing last week, and she damn near bit my head off*, Silli thought.

Once she was clean, Silli returned to her nook and put on her servant's uniform. It was sewn from bright yellow leaves with a pair of walnut-shell pauldrons. Then she rushed to the cafeteria.

"The Queen will awaken in ten minutes, so eat fast," Beeto warned. Silli's supervisor had green skin, the legs of a grasshopper, and no sense of humor whatsoever.

Breakfast consisted of gnome-apples, grapes, and a selection of chopped nuts. Silli shoveled her food down her throat so she wouldn't be late. She'd been on the palace staff for over a month, but it was to be her first day as one of Queen Delia's personal aides.

She was still chewing as she zipped down the hall toward the Queen's chambers. The Queen liked to be awakened precisely at the crack of dawn so she wouldn't waste a moment of daylight.

"My Queen," Silli said as she entered Delia's bedchamber. The Queen stretched as she sat up in bed. Silli rushed to her side, along with another assistant by the name of Niva. Queen Delia was roughly three feet tall, more than triple the height of her assistants, and one of the most beautiful creatures Silli had ever laid eyes on.

Silli and Niva each grabbed one shoulder of the Queen's robe and lowered it across her shoulders. The robe was made of the rarest semi-transparent spidersilk, and it was luxurious to the touch. Then they escorted the Queen to her personal bath, where they removed the robe and helped her into the bronze tub. *She couldn't walk five feet in the buff?* Silli wondered.

Niva assisted the Queen with washing, while Silli operated the tub's "fizz-therapy" function. As Silli turned the crank, heated bubbles rose up through the water.

"A little faster," the Queen ordered, and Silli turned the crank harder.

*Can't they come up with a spell for this?* Silli wondered, already starting to run out of breath. But she'd already asked Beeto the same question a few days earlier, and he'd warned her not to take any shortcuts.

Silli watched as Niva ran a soapy coral sponge up and down Delia's arm. *That would feel so good right now,* Silli thought. Her own arms were already burning and sore from turning the crank.

"That feels nice," the Queen said as Niva washed her other arm. Then, to Silli, she ordered, "More bubbles, please."

*Are you kidding me?* Silli wondered, turning the crank even harder. Her arms were about to fall asleep. Then she remembered a spell she'd just learned a few days earlier. "Perpetius Motios," she whispered as she sprinkled a bit of fairy dust on the crank.

"What was that?" Queen Delia asked.

"Sorry, I burped," Silli said.

She let go of the crank and watched as it continued to rotate by itself. And then it picked up speed. Silli watched in horror as it spun so fast it became a blur. In the tub, the bubbles came faster and larger and hotter.

"What's going on?" Delia asked, looking alarmed.

The tub soon resembled a pot of boiling broth, and the Queen screeched as she fluttered out of the tub, her legs reddened from the heat. "What did you do?" the Queen asked, standing over the crank.

As soon as the words were out of her mouth, the crank shook itself loose and flew across the room, smashing a makeup mirror. Then the tub erupted, spewing boiling water up to the ceiling and drenching the entire room.

Niva quickly cast a soothing spell on her sponge and rubbed it along the Queen's legs and rear. Delia glared at Silli with bared teeth.

"Get out," Queen Delia ordered, and Silli darted out the door.


"Get off the stage, you dipwit!"

Another unsuccessful performance. His jokes bombed, he dropped a ball while juggling, and they didn't even laugh at his pratfalls. *My act needs something*, Dorian thought. He returned to his wagon with his head hung low.

*At least I got paid*, he thought as he transferred a few gold coins into a strongbox. The wagon was cramped, with prop boxes stuffed against every wall and costumes hanging from the ceiling. He'd managed to stuff a tiny desk into one corner for his writing.

He liked being an entertainer, especially on the rare occasions when he was on fire. There was something about those nights when he vibed with the audience. There was an energy there, a collective mood that almost felt like magic.

But tonight hadn't been one of those nights. And as much

as Dorian liked performing, he didn't feel it was his calling. In his heart, he was a collector. He gathered lore: stories, legends, historical accounts, myths, and data. Someday he hoped to publish his findings in a series of books. He could see it now:

A Grand History of Zyden: A Treasury of Facts and
Legends

By Dorian Beauregarde the Third

Volumes 1-50

Maybe fifty was a bit optimistic. Regardless, he planned to work on this project for the rest of his life. But to gather the information he needed, he would have to travel all over the continent. Of course, no one was going to pay him to ride around Zyden gathering stories. Hence the stage shows. He enjoyed traveling, even if he was a bit lonely at times. He wished he had a partner, maybe a stagehand to help him with his magic tricks, but he didn't want to subject anyone else to his erratic lifestyle.

The performances didn't pay much, but they came with perks. The inns in which he performed often gave him a free meal with every show. Some even gave him a room if they weren't booked up. It was nice to sleep somewhere besides the wagon now and then.

Dorian jotted down some notes about his current stop. Sesta was a festive town, hosting multiple parties every night, some of which were quite debaucherous. He had to admit that he'd been tempted to attend one of the events. But he didn't have money to throw away on fleeting pleasures, at least not at the moment.

When he was done writing, he set the paper aside to dry. Then he studied his map. At dawn, he'd be on his way to a small village called Proudpath. Hopefully their audiences would have a sense of humor. And if not, maybe they'd at least have some good stories to tell.

*Guard duty, I can't believe it*, Silli thought, standing at attention.

It was humiliating. She'd spent two days in a cell while a magistrate deliberated on whether she'd been trying to assassinate the Queen. She finally managed to convince them that she wasn't a killer, she was just exceptionally incompetent. And now she was out on a work release program, pending further investigation.

One little mistake and she'd traded a cushy job at the palace for standing still all day and watching a wall. She was going to miss the soft bed at the palace. It was much nicer than the leaves they used in the barracks. She'd also miss the hot showers and the fresh food. At the moment she even missed the inane banter of her coworkers. Anything was better than Thrawby's criticisms.

"You're slouching, Sillivene," Thrawby said as he stomped by. He was a muscular brownie with blonde hair. He was the same height as Silli but he didn't have wings. As he inspected his troops, he wielded a rapier which he swept about dangerously as he talked.

"Sir, sorry, sir," Silli replied. "I didn't sleep well. Sir."

The other fairies in line struggled to keep a straight face. Unlike Silli, it wasn't their first day.

"I don't tolerate whining," Thrawby growled. He pointed his rapier at the wall. The magical barrier around the Fairy Kingdom was invisible to non-fae, but Silli saw it as a wall of wavy yellow lights. "That barrier is our greatest defense against monsters. Without that wall, dragons could just walk on in, causing all manner of destruction. Is that what you want, you worm? Is it?" His sword swished through the air until it was half an inch from Silli's nose.

Silli nearly jumped backward but managed to keep still. "Sir, no sir," she said timidly.

"I can't hear you," Thrawby said.

"Sir, no sir!" Silli repeated more forcefully.

"When I ask a question, I expect more than a whisper!" Thrawby said.

"Sir, yes sir!" Silli shouted. "But have you thought about having your hearing checked? Um… sir?"

Thrawby darted forward until he stood nose-to-nose with Silli. "What was that?"

"Sir, I was just concerned, sir," Silli said. "Hearing loss is no joke. It could get you killed. If a dragon snuck up on you… Sir…" She trailed off as his face reddened.

"Do you think you're funny, little worm?" Thrawby asked.

"Sir, no sir," Silli replied.

"Tell us a joke then," Thrawby replied, sweeping his rapier in a wide arc. "Make us all laugh."

"Sir, I don't know any jokes, sir," Silli said.

"Oh suddenly the comedian's out of jokes?" Thrawby asked.

"Sir, I'm not a comedian, sir," Silli said.

"Oh I think you are," Thrawby said. "And I want you to get it all out of your system now, before we go any further. Go ahead, worm. Make me laugh."

Silli was at a loss for words. She couldn't believe how far this had escalated. Was this a test? Did he actually expect her to tell a joke? Or was she supposed to stay quiet?

Thrawby stared at her, waiting. The silence was getting more uncomfortable by the second.

*I have to say something*, Silli thought. But her mind went blank. She couldn't remember a single joke she'd heard in her entire life. She thought back to her time in the palace. In the showers, one of the other pixies had said something…

"Nice butt, sir," Silli said. Unable to stop herself, she added, "Oh, wait, that's your face. Sir." Her face reddened.

Thrawby looked like his head was about to explode. The other pixies took a step back and braced themselves. Silli had never been so embarrassed. She wished she could turn invisible.

And then she remembered she could.


Dorian turned off the main road and onto the trail that led to Proudpath. The woods were thicker here, and the tree branches curled over the path until they intertwined above Dorian's head. It looked like a tunnel to another world, and he found it both unsettling and inspiring. *I have to put this in a book someday*, he thought.

Now and then he thought he saw strange lights from deep within the forest. *The fireflies are out early*, he thought. Though given how much the forest canopy blocked the sunlight, he supposed the fireflies could be forgiven for getting a little confused.

Dorian stopped now and then, letting his horse rest while he enjoyed the spooky atmosphere. He gathered up a quill, some paper, and a crossbow in case any dangerous animals showed up. Then he reclined on the roof of his wagon, where he spent an hour dreaming up scary stories and dark poetry. He had no set schedule, nowhere he had to be in a hurry.

*What's that?* he thought, sitting up and squinting. A few of the fireflies were behaving strangely. They didn't blink but rather flickered a semi-constant yellow. Five or six of the lights seemed to be chasing another one.

He couldn't always tell how far away they were, but

sometimes they vanished behind trees that were hundreds of feet away. Sometimes the fleeing light would disappear for a few minutes, and the rest of the lights would wander around in confusion. Then the fugitive would reappear and the chase would be on again.

"Fascinating," Dorian whispered, writing down some notes. They couldn't possibly be fireflies. Were these the will-o-the-wisps he'd read about in fairy tales when he was younger?

The fleeing light started to come closer. Dorian ducked as it broke through the tree line and zipped over his head. For just a second he got a clearer view of the creature. It looked like a tiny woman with dragonfly wings. *A fairy?* Dorian wondered. Then it vanished into the forest on the other side of the trail.

The pursuers balked when they neared the tree line. Dorian suspected it was because they spotted his wagon. Even though he couldn't make out any details, he could almost tell what they were thinking by their body language. *They don't want to be seen by humans*, he thought. The lights hung in place for a few more seconds, then turned around and went back the way they'd come.

Dorian stayed a bit longer, hoping to spot more supernatural creatures, but the forest was now silent.

*I don't know where to go*, Silli thought as she crawled through the grass. She wasn't safe in this forest. She couldn't fly anymore – shortly after escaping the pixie guards, she'd had a run-in with an owl. She'd scared it off with a spell, but not until after it bit one of her wings. It would take a couple of days to heal. Until then, she was on foot.

The village of Proudpath was just ahead. She couldn't ask

any humans for help. It was forbidden to confirm the existence of fairies, and while Silli probably wouldn't be allowed back into the Fairy Kingdom any time soon, she still felt obligated to follow their rules. Besides, many humans were scary brutes who killed for sport.

*Maybe I can find a barn or someplace to hide until my wing heals,* she thought. An owl hooted somewhere overhead. Silli tried to turn invisible again, but she was out of fairy dust. She could generate more naturally, but it would take a while, and she didn't want to spend another minute in the forest.

The sun was setting, and villagers began lighting torches and candles as they locked up their businesses and returned to their homes. Silli waited until the coast was clear, then ran across a field until she reached a house. She put her back against the wall, watching the skies for birds of prey. Through an open window above, she heard the sound of a knife banging on a chopping block. The odor of cooking meat wafted out to her nostrils. Fairies didn't typically eat meat, but the spices smelled heavenly.

Silli slid around the side of the house, waited for more people to walk by, and then ran to another house across the street. She hadn't used her legs so much in years, and she was starting to get tired. *Why do humans build their houses so far apart?* she wondered.

She spotted a barn behind the house. There was a wagon parked next to it, with the words "Dorian's Traveling Show" painted on the side. She realized she'd just seen that wagon an hour or so earlier when fleeing her coworkers.

*Traveling show?* Silli thought. *Maybe I can sneak aboard when it leaves town.*

She approached the wagon and climbed up one of the wheels, but she couldn't find any way in. The back door was locked and all the windows were shut. She gave up and jumped down to the ground, then proceeded to the barn.

The barn door was shut, but it didn't completely touch the ground. She got a little muddy as she slid under the door, but given the other indignities she'd suffered over the past few days, it barely even bothered her.

She looked around to make sure she was alone. A few horses stood in the stalls, and she heard snoring from somewhere up above. *A human?* she wondered, looking up at the hay loft. She couldn't see anything, but wherever they were, at least they were asleep.

She searched for a safe place to sleep for the night. She couldn't sleep out in the open, what if a human came in? Nor could she sleep in one of the stalls, where she might get stepped on by one of the horses. The tack room was closed, but she thought she might be able to squeeze under the door again.

As she crept through the breezeway she felt a sudden chill, like she was being watched. No, not just watched, stalked. *It's just your nerves*, she told herself. But the feeling wouldn't go away. She thought she saw movement. A shadow. She turned and saw a pair of yellow eyes staring at her in the dark. She had just enough time to scream before the creature pounced on her.

*What is that caterwauling?* Dorian wondered as his eyes fluttered open. He'd rented a farmer's barn for the night, hoping to get a good night's sleep. The wagon wasn't uncomfortable, but any time he had the chance to sleep somewhere less cramped, he took it. Especially if it was reasonably priced. The farmer had only charged two copper for the use of his entire barn, allowing Dorian to board his horses and himself for less than most towns would have charged for the horses alone. He loved a good deal.

But it wasn't such a good deal if he couldn't get any sleep. Dorian crawled to the edge of the loft to see what the commotion was. It was dark, but he could just make out an overweight housecat playing with a smaller animal.

Except it wasn't an animal. Dorian squinted and then gasped. A doll-sized woman shrieked as she fought off the cat's sharp claws. Dorian climbed down the ladder and shooed the cat away. The woman was curled up in a ball, weeping. "Are you all right, miss?" Dorian asked. She was covered in mud, her clothes were torn, she had several large cuts, and two of her wings were broken.

*Wings*, Dorian thought. She looked just like the fairy he'd seen on the way into town. Already he'd started to convince himself he'd imagined it, that he'd been tired from riding all day and mistaken some fireflies for something magical. But he couldn't deny what now lay in front of him.

"Are you a… fairy?" Dorian asked.

"No, I'm a loser," Silli whimpered. "Just go away and let me suffer in peace. Or better yet, stomp on me really hard, so I don't have to face judgment from my queen."

"Now there, there," Dorian said. "Things can't be that bad, can they? Let me help you."

Dorian reached down and picked her up, then carried her outside to his wagon. She didn't protest or try to escape. He lit a lamp and dug through his things, looking for medical supplies. He applied some salve to her wounds and bandaged them up.

"What's your name?" Dorian asked as he worked.

"Sillivene Dimplecheek," she replied. "But you can call me Silli. Who are you?"

"Dorian Beauregarde the Third at your service," he replied.

"That's kind of a mouthful," Silli said. "Mind if I call you

Dobo?"

"Dobo?" Dorian asked, and Silli nodded. A lightbulb seemed to go off above Dorian's head, despite it being a few centuries too early for lightbulbs.

"You're looking at me funny," Silli said.

"Sillivene Dimplecheek," Dorian said. "How attached are you to this village?"

"Not very," Silli replied.

"How would you like to go on the road with me, and see the world?"

"I'd very much like to get out of here as soon as possible," Silli replied, nodding vigorously.

"And... how do you feel about stage comedy?" Dobo asked.

Silli shrugged. She'd never really gotten the hang of humor. She'd certainly been the source of laughter on many an occasion, but on purpose? Not so much. But maybe humans would be more appreciative of her unusual wit.

"I suppose I can learn," she said.

Dorian shook her tiny hand between his thumb and forefinger. "You're going to love it," he said, and they started hammering out the details.


"Behold!" Dobo announced as he waved a wand over a covered cage. "Tonight I bring before you a creature from the deepest mystical wilds. A being of such mystery that entire books have been written about her existence. A thing of wonder so unique—"

"Get on with it!" a tiny voice yelled from within the cage. The audience laughed.

"Then without further ado, I present to you, the magical, the mystical, the mythological... Sillivene the fairy!" Dobo pulled the cage away, cover and all, leaving Silli standing on the pedestal… in her underclothes.

"Hey!" Silli shouted, feigning embarrassment. "You pulled away one cover too many!" Applause and laughter erupted throughout the inn.

"Sorry, sorry," Dobo said. He reached into the cage and pulled out a tiny dress. Silli touched the cloth and it wrapped itself around her body. "Now say hi to the audience," Dobo said.

"Hi to the audience," Silli repeated with a curtsey. More laughter ensued.

"This is the real deal, folks," Dobo said. "Mythology made material. Literally a fairy tale brought to life."

"And I can dance, too!" Silli shouted, going into a whimsical shuffle.

The audience roared. In the back row, a short, hooded woman watched the show in silence. Those around her assumed she was a child, but in truth, she was the oldest person in attendance.

"That's just a puppet, right?" someone nearby whispered.

"I think it's done with mirrors," another said. "There's a woman behind the curtain, and we're seeing her reflection somehow."

But the hooded woman knew the fairy was real. She watched as the duo juggled, performed simple magic tricks, and told bad jokes. She never clapped, but she did chuckle a few times. Halfway through the show, she stood and left the inn.

"Some show tonight, eh?" Dobo said as they climbed into the wagon.

"We had 'em in stitches," Silli replied.

"It was all you," Dobo said, changing out of his jester outfit. "You're a natural at comedy."

"I learned from the best," Silli said, though she was a bit distracted. Something had been placed on top of her pillow. *An envelope?* she thought. It hadn't been there before the show.

"Well, I don't know about you but I'm beat," Dobo said. "I'm going to get some shut-eye."

"Go ahead, I might be up for a little while," Silli replied.

As Dobo tucked himself into his bedroll, Silli grabbed the tiny envelope and fluttered out the window. She sat on the roof of the wagon and opened the letter.

"Sillivene, I had the pleasure of attending your performance this evening. While I can't say the humor was to my taste, I'm glad you have found a place where you belong. Your partner seems to care for you very much, and it's good that you've made a friend in this harsh world. I don't see you as a threat to the Fairy Kingdom; if anything, your show encourages skepticism by presenting the audience with an illusion to disprove. Please continue to keep the Kingdom a secret, and I won't send anyone to collect you. Officially you are banished, but don't hesitate to return if an emergency should arise. Good luck with your future endeavors. - Queen Delia"

Silli read it three times before putting it back in the envelope. *Banished,* she thought. She hadn't planned on going back any time soon, but the word was still a punch to the gut.

And yet, the letter seemed more positive than negative, and it cheered Silli up to know she had the Queen's approval. She flitted back through the wagon's window and lay down on her pillow. Dobo's snores echoed throughout the vehicle, but Silli found the rhythmic sound oddly comforting. The wagon wasn't huge, but it had everything she needed. A roof, a friend, a purpose. She yawned and stretched across her pillow.

*This is the life,* Silli thought as she fell asleep.

## *Fairy Dust*

*Author's Note: This story originally appeared in the collection "Geek Cutes," but takes place in the same universe as Nomads of Zyden.*

The wind flowed across the plain, gently tickling the grass and barely disrupting the many sets of butterfly wings as they flitted from flower to flower. On first inspection, a casual observer might simply have said "Wow, the bugs sure grow big around here," before continuing to enjoy the breeze. But a closer look would have revealed much more fascinating creatures: tiny winged people, happily singing while tending the garden.

These were the fairies, the magical fae folk, carefree lovers of life, simple-minded protectors of nature. These minute hovering gardeners went about their work with extraordinary zeal, and our hypothetical observer would have wondered if this was work or recreation. There were thirty-one of them today, following their usual routine, each focused on their specific job. An insect-like grig tilled the soil with the help of a large stag beetle. He was followed by a wingless brownie, who dug small holes in the loose dirt. A highly-energetic pixie planted palm-sized flower seeds, carefully burying one at a time. A nixie then walked by sprinkling water over the dirt. Finally, a tiny sprite sprinkled fairy dust over the planted seeds, which insured quick growth. This chain of workers was mirrored throughout the garden, each group concentrating on a different species of flower. A single dryad supervisor walked among them, stepping carefully and monitoring the quality of their work.

They sang as they worked, a freeform, wordless tune that conveyed the joy in their hearts. For them, all was right with the world, and they were one with nature. The flowers that grew would be used for potions and nectar, and would eventually yield seeds so they could plant even more flowers. The fairies would always be able to rely on their crops, and they always gave back more than they took. Such was the pleasure they took in the cycle of nature, that they were never short of volunteers for the job. For as Delia the Fairy Queen was fond of saying, "Mini hands make light work."

THUMP!

The singing stopped. Thirty-one sets of ears perked up.

THUMP!

Thirty-one heads looked up from their flowers, searching for the source of the noise.

THUMP! THUMP! CRACK!

A tree fell over in the distance. The fairies turned in that direction just in time to see a great reptilian head burst through the treeline.

"It's a red!" shouted a pixie, and the gardeners scattered. A few fairies succumbed to fear and fled into the forest, but most went for their weapons. As the dragon pushed past the last few trees and entered the clearing, he was greeted by a swarm of tiny arrows. Most bounced harmlessly off his crimson scales, but a few managed to slip beneath them and pierce the monster's skin. These pinpricks were no more than a nuisance, however, and the dragon responded with a large belch of flames.

Any dragon was bad enough, but a fire-breathing red was particularly unwanted by this plant-loving group. The dryad supervisor now fled in terror, having been turned into a living torch by the monster's breath. She nearly reached the treeline before collapsing into a heap of kindling. Two nixies tried to put her out, but it was a lost cause. "Charge!" yelled a fearless brownie, leading the remaining gardners-turned-warriors toward their enemy, while a few sprites and pixies chanted out protection charms.

The dragon was outnumbered, but it was much more powerful than the tiny army it faced. It was sure to be a short battle.

Some distance away, Queen Delia emerged from her bath. She was beauty and grace personified, born of pixie but sired by a human. Such pairings were rare, and physically impossible without growth potions or other magic. It was a union that seldom produced offspring, and such progeny were often well-gifted in magical ability. The Queen was much taller than most of her subjects, nearly half the size of a human, with a pair of translucent golden wings that glittered in the light.

As she crossed her chambers, two sprite attendants dried her skin with an oakleaf towel, and perfumed her perfect body with lilac essence. Then the sprites helped her into a robe of the finest golden silkleaf, which matched the color of her wings. A third attendant entered with a plate of assorted ripe berries, along with a cup of the finest mix of nectar and honeysuckle juice. The Queen took a small sip from the cup, and strode over to the balcony.

Fairies didn't hoard wealth any more than dragons planted gardens. But the Grand Oak Palace was exquisite nonetheless. Built atop the oldest, tallest tree in the forest, the wooden palace was formed from the living tree itself. The pinnacle of dryad construction, the palace hadn't been built so much as grown. The floor was composed of closely intertwined branches, which curved sharply upwards to form the walls. The branches were so well-knit that they even held in a layer of dirt, upon which more plants grew. The Queen's chambers more closely resembled a park than a bedroom, complete with stone paths and chirping birds.

From a distance, the palace was virtually invisible, though the tree did stand out simply by virtue of being so tall. From the balconies, the Queen could see her entire kingdom. The treehouses of Fairy Haven, the peaceful Nixie Lake, Grig Burrows, the beautiful Fairy Gardens... The Queen stopped. There was a thin black line rising from the gardens. She chanted a spell, causing her eyes to glow brightly. Now she could see the gardens more closely, and what she saw terrified her. Fire and smoke, and the occasional flash of red scales. The Queen turned quickly, calling to her attendant. "Kora... Ah!" She had turned to find herself staring directly into Kora's huge eyes, startling her until she realized that the attendant was actually hovering on the other side of the room, enlarged only by the Queen's vision spell. It would have been funny if not for the emergency.

"Kora, send a squad to the garden. We have a Code Red."

"Red? Right away, Mum." The sprite flitted out the door. The Queen didn't watch her go, instead turning back to the view from the balcony. Kora knew the drill. The squad would be dressed in fireproof gear, carry cold-enchanted weapons, and the squad's wizards would have freezing spells ready to cast. Additionally, a nixie cleanup crew would be on standby to put out the garden. And when it was over, the Magic Council would investigate the magical barrier which - usually - prevented dragons from crossing into the Fairy Kingdom.

The fairies had dealt with this before; they knew what to do.

Another burst of smoke and fire blossomed from the dragon's mouth. A tiny sprite managed to survive the flames, having protected herself with an incantation. Her success was short-lived, however, as a huge clawed foot came down on top of her. She was killed instantly, leaving nothing but a cloud of sparkling fairy dust, which swirled and danced away as it mixed with the smoke from the blazing garden.

"Fall back! Fall back!" yelled the final surviving pixie, retreating to the cover of the forest. One of her legs was badly burned, and her leafy skirt was on fire, but she ignored both in favor of firing more arrows at the great lizard. Below her line of fire, she could see a pair of sprites fleeing in her direction, and a nixie trying to drag a mortally wounded grig out of harm's way. The brownies were long gone, their fearlessness leading to their early deaths in the battle. The pixie nocked another arrow, gritting her teeth in anger. She knew it was a losing battle, but she intended to go down fighting.

Suddenly it got very cold. A huge gust of wind blew through the garden, and the sky darkened. Fluffy snowflakes fell lazily to the earth, mixed with light freezing rain. The rain quickly grew in severity, until large chunks of ice were falling from the sky. There was a loud shout of "Charge!" and twenty fairy soldiers entered the fray. The frontline consisted of ten brownie swordmasters, carrying shields enchanted against fire. Behind them was a line of eight pixie archers, firing powerful enchanted arrows at the dragon's most vital areas. At the back of the squad stood two pixie wizards, responsible for the sudden change in weather. All the soldiers were wearing the exquisite golden uniforms of the Queen's elite guard, with bright red shoulder pads to indicate that the uniforms were enchanted against fire.

The dragon could not last long against such a group. Its most powerful weapon was effectively useless against the soldiers, and so the dragon had to rely on tooth and claw. He was still the strongest of the combatants, and could easily tear a fairy to shreds. But his opponents were simply too small and quick for him. They deftly dodged his claws, ducked his attempts to bite them, and leaped over the sweeps of his tail. And for every swipe he missed, his own hide was punctured by dozens of tiny arrows, his belly pierced by tiny blades, and his head bashed by flying icicles. When a well-aimed arrow caught him in the eye, he knew he'd had enough. He turned and fled back out of the grove, taking the same path of fallen trees he'd forged on his way in. But the soldiers weren't about to just let him get away. They followed the beast through the trees, easily keeping up with the tiring monster. They reached another clearing, and the dragon finally collapsed. The fairies formed a large circle around the helpless beast, and quickly executed him.

Never ones to waste good spellcasting components, the two wizards started passing out vials, which the soldiers began filling with dragon blood. Once all the blood had been drained, the wizards cast a spell to dissolve the body. One of the archers fired a flare arrow into the sky, which signaled the nixie cleanup crew that it was time to head for the garden. Wounds were bandaged, arrows were retrieved, and finally the soldiers lined up to head back to the Garden.

Suddenly, they found themselves surrounded. All around the clearing, dragons faded into existence. Two more reds, a green, a yellow, a blue, and two purples - the last two responsible for the powerful invisibility spell which had allowed for their dramatic entrance. Before the soldiers even had time to be surprised, the dragons opened their mouths and let loose blasts of deadly breath.

The Queen watched it all through a small scrying orb. Her twenty best soldiers... no, not just soldiers, these were also her friends. Two of them had even been her blanket companions in the past. But she had no time for tears. "Kora!" she called. Before Kora could even respond, the Queen commanded, "Code Rainbow."

The first dragon had been a ruse. She'd thought it was a random rogue, who'd blundered through a weak spot in the barrier. But packs of dragons tended to stick with companions of like color. This had to be a coordinated attack, planned in advance by the Dragon War Council. This meant that the dragon sorcerers had discovered a counterspell for the barrier. Worse, it probably meant that more dragon packs had made it through. The Queen rushed back to her balcony.

And there it was. More columns of smoke drifted skyward, at key points throughout the kingdom. The invasion had begun.

On the Southern border of the Fairy Kingdom, there rested a small village called Proudpath. To the local farmers, the existence of fairies was a topic of frequent discussion. Living so close to the fairy regions meant that there had certainly been more sightings than in the average town. Just a few weeks prior, a pair of children had been lost in the woods, only to be guided back to safety by a kind sprite. And there were many more such "fairy tales." A mortally injured villager was healed by a tiny angel, strange lights scared a pack of wolves away from a young girl, and even the local shoemaker had received mysterious help when he became too ill to keep up with his business. But the debate was still there - were these truly fairies, or help from the gods themselves?

In truth, the villagers enjoyed the mystery. It was fun watching the fireflies off in the woods at night, and wondering if they were truly insects or actually fairies. It made for great campfire talk, and gave them material for bedtime stories.

Today there was to be no mystery. As the dragons advanced through the village, indiscriminately smashing houses with no more remorse than they had for the trees, the fairies fought back in full view of the frightened villagers. The fae folk were all the more careful with innocent humans about. The dragons showed no such consideration, and that gave them a tremendous advantage. The fairies were beaten back, wounded, and chased into the forest by their enemies. The surviving humans watched helplessly as the final dragon marched out of Proudpath, pursuing the fae into the woods. On a better day, the villagers might have taken up arms against the dragons, but at this moment they were in no shape for battle.

"Take me to Torrentia," the Fairy Queen ordered. She was quickly escorted from the palace, through the surrounding grounds, and to the caves. A guard saluted as she strode past, and two more guards opened the door to the prison for her. On one side of the giant cell, two sleeping dragons snored loudly. In the opposite corner, a woman sat on the floor, examining her fingernails. The Queen entered the cell, and the inmate rose to meet her.

"My Queen," Torrentia said, doing a mock curtsy. In her current human form, Torrentia was much taller than the Fairy Queen. She was beautiful, but it was a harsher kind of beauty, much different from the Queen's delicate features. She had angular cheekbones, dark eyes, long silver hair, and grayish skin so pale it was almost translucent. She wore a flowing dress that appeared to be made of silver scales. Torrentia faced the Queen with a sarcastic half-smile, showing no fear of her captor.

"Torrentia Wyvernica Demonicus," the Queen acknowledged, not the least bit intimidated by the woman.

"Queen Rainshower Sunbow Moonbeam," the woman replied.

"That was three queens ago," Queen Delia answered.

"My apologies. Shows how long I've been locked up here... and you fae folk do look so alike to me," Torrentia said wryly. "So... to what do I owe the—"

"I have not the time for pleasantries," the Queen interrupted. "As much as I hate to do this, I need your help."

"Go on," the woman said, but her smile told the whole story. She already knew of the attack.

"Drive them off," the Queen demanded.

"And my incentive?" Torrentia's tone was playful, and it was obvious she knew what the Queen would offer.

"Your freedom, of course," the Queen answered.

"And the full terms of this freedom?" The woman looked down at her wrists, which were bound with glowing magical loops.

"You will order the dragons out of my kingdom. If they do not obey, you will use deadly force."

"Against my own kind? I think n—"

The Queen would not be interrupted. "Once the dragons are gone, you will immediately return to your den in the Northern Regions. You will stay in the Northern Regions, and never trouble my kingdom again."

"How do you expect to enforce that?"

"By your word," the Queen replied. "Your bracelets are bound by my magic. If you give me your word, and truly intend to honor that promise, then the bracelets will come undone. If you intend to deceive me, the binding spell will continue."

Torrentia looked thoughtful for several seconds. "Very well," she said finally. "You have my word. I will fix your little dragon problem, and return to my homeland for good." As soon as the words were out of her mouth, the bracelets vanished.

"Torrentia," the Queen said, "Don't even think about tricking me. Remember I possess the ClearSky Blade."

"But not one of you can wield it," Torrentia replied with a sly smile. "Save your empty threats. I will do as you asked, and you will not see me again."


Minutes later, a woman walked out of the cave, into the bright day. She hadn't seen sunlight in decades, and it took her eyes several seconds to adjust. She stretched her arms towards the sky, and her transformation began. Within seconds, the huge silver dragon was ready to take flight. Behind her, the Fairy Queen and her escorts stepped out of the cave.

"I hope I've done the right thing," the Queen said.

A group of four dragons, all of different colors, left a trail of destruction on their way to the Grand Oak Palace. They stopped as a winged shape flew over the top of the cliffs. A silver dragon swooped down in front of them, hovering in their faces. She wasn't quite as large as the other dragons, but she still had a presence that awed them. She hissed in dragon-speak, "Retreat! Return to the Dragonsands!"

Two of the dragons looked at each other, considering her words. Finally the green one answered, "We will not! Victory is in our grasp!"

"Then, die!" shouted the silver dragon, opening her mouth wide to show her wicked fangs. Faster than the dragons could follow, the silver dragon bit into the green dragon's neck. A blue dragon started to come to her rescue, when he was suddenly struck by a huge bolt of lightning. The silver dragon flew backward and muttered an incantation. The sky went black. Acid rain, massive hailstones, and rapid bolts of lightning all fell from the sky, bombarding all dragons present.

Torrentia, the Great WeatherWyrm of the Northlands, had decades of power stored up, and she loosed all of it on the dragon army. Those that weren't killed fled for their lives. When Torrentia was satisfied that she'd fulfilled her part of the bargain, she glared at the Grand Oak Palace, uttered a curse in dragon-speak, and flew off toward the Northern Regions.

The sun set, turning the world a furious orange as the day struggled to hold on to the light. The last of the surviving dragon invaders had long since retreated, and Torrentia was halfway back to her den in the north.

The Fairy Queen finally completed the last of the protection spells. She had worked hard on improving the Great Barrier, and was confident that this time there would be no counterspell. This time the Barrier could not be disrupted, circumvented, or avoided. Of course, that's what she'd said the last time.

Confident she'd done all she could, the Queen and her escorts teleported back to the palace. Many fairies would be working through the night collecting dragon blood and disposing of corpses. The next month would be a busy one for the entire fairy community. There were trees to replant, a garden to regrow, not to mention helping the Proudpath villagers with their damage. The Queen herself would have a full schedule inspecting their work. And of course, there would be a mass funeral for all those lost today. But things would return to normal, as they always did.

"Why would anyone want to be a brownie?" Honeycomb asked, struggling to pick up a wooden beam.

"That's not what I said," Thistle replied. "I said I am one." She flitted over to Honeycomb's side, helping her lift the beam.

"But you're clearly not," Honeycomb said. "You have wings. And glowy skin. And boobs."

"On the outside, yes," Thistle said. "But in here, I swear I was meant to be a brownie." She pointed to her head, causing her to lose her grip on the beam. She quickly put both hands back under the wood.

"Why though? Pixies are so much better. We can fly! And we have magic dust!" Working together Honeycomb and Thistle moved the beam to the side of the dirt road. They were about to grab another beam when they heard one of the villagers cry. They rushed over to see what the matter was.

"I can't stop the bleeding!" a woman cried. She was cradling a small boy, and using a piece of burlap to stanch a wound on his arm.

"Let me have a look," Honeycomb said. The villager looked afraid – she still wasn't used to the presence of the fae folk – but she let the pixie see. Honeycomb spread her fingers and said a few magic words. Glittering powder burst from her palm, landing on the child's arm. The wound glowed for a moment, then closed.

"Oh thank you!" the woman said, and hugged her child. The two pixies flew off, looking for more flotsam to clear.

"Let's see a brownie do that!" Honeycomb said.

"I know, I know," Thistle replied. "But you don't understand. I never said brownies were better than pixies. I didn't just wake up one morning and say, 'I wish I couldn't fly anymore.' But when I look at my reflection, I just look wrong to me. It's like I'm seeing someone else."

"Well, I think you're crazy," Honeycomb said, dragging a broken wagon wheel away from the road. "But that's probably why we get along so well. Do you want me to start calling you by a different name?"

"I haven't thought of one yet," Thistle replied, "But you'll be the first to know if I do."


"Tell me more about your kingdom," the old woman said. She'd been mortally wounded during the invasion, but she would live, thanks to Honeycomb's healing hands. Still, her recovery wasn't going to be a walk in the park. Magic could only do so much, and the greatest healers were back in the

Fairy Kingdom, busy tending to their own wounded.

"What would you like to know?" Honeycomb asked, pouring some water into a wooden cup. Honeycomb looked like a young woman with blond hair, but she was less than a foot tall. Her transparent golden wings held her aloft as she flitted about the room, retrieving various salves and herbs.

"What's your name?" the woman asked.

"Honeycomb," she answered. "And this is Thistle," she added, gesturing toward her friend. It had been a long day, and most of the fairies had returned to their kingdom. Only Honeycomb and Thistle had remained behind to wrap up some loose ends.

"Beautiful names," the woman said. "I'm Amalla." She paused for a few moments, trying to decide what she wanted to ask first. Thistle pressed a wet rag to Amalla's forehead. Finally the old woman asked, "Are all of you girls?"

"Most of us," Thistle said.

"The sprites and pixies are girls," Honeycomb added. "Also the nixies and dryads. The grigs and brownies are boys, though."

"What's the difference between a pixie and a sprite?" Amalla asked.

"Sprites are smaller," Thistle said. "Like bug-sized. And kind of nuts."

"Thistle," Honeycomb said, stifling a laugh. It was true, though, just rude to point out.

"How do you... make more pixies?" Amalla asked. She was trying to ask a delicate question without offending them.

"Sex," Thistle said bluntly. "Surely you've heard of it?"

The old woman laughed at Thistle's brashness. Now that

she knew she wasn't going to offend them, she was more frank herself. "So the pixies and sprites mate with the brownies and grigs?"

"Pretty much," Honeycomb confirmed. "Brownies have offspring with pixies or nixies. Sprites have offspring with grigs, 'cause they're smaller. Sometimes other pairings happen, thanks to magic and such."

Amalla kept asking questions, and the two answered as best they could while making her comfortable. They told her all about fairy society and biology. When she finally fell asleep, the two pixies gave some instructions to her caretaker, and flew back to the Fairy Kingdom. It was starting to rain.


Kra-koom! The Grand Oak Palace shook at the peal of thunder. A flash of lightning immediately followed, and for a moment, the Queen's bedroom was as bright as day. It had been raining since dusk, and the rainfall had grown heavier by the hour. Queen Delia rolled over and looked at the time. Across the room, a magical sundial sat on a stone pedestal, glowing throughout the night. It was well after midnight. She closed her eyes again, but another report sounded, even louder this time. The room shook, and a mirror tumbled off her dresser.

"Candlebright," the Queen said, and several candles lit up around the room. She tossed her spidersilk sheets aside and got to her feet. Then she reached for the thin dress hanging on her bedpost, and slipped it on over her head. She knelt and examined the shattered mirror. She'd once heard of a human superstition about broken mirrors and bad luck. While the fairies didn't share that fear, they had their own little rituals regarding shattered glass.

A mirror shattered by lightning became a powerful divination tool. It had to be an accident, however. The magic somehow "knew" if a mirror had been intentionally placed in the path of a storm. Not that it mattered in this case, as this mirror had been broken by thunder, not lightning. But was that close enough?

The mirror had fallen face down. As the Queen turned it over, for just a second, she saw a face that wasn't her own. Torrentia laughed at her from the broken shards, her face fractured and multiplied, a dozen sets of evil eyes fixing her with a triumphant glare. And then she was gone. Queen Delia didn't know if it had been her imagination or an actual portent.

The tree shook again, and this time the thunder and lightning came together. Five quick booms, each accompanied by blinding flashes of light. The Queen rose, backing away from her window. Three more crashes sounded, three more bursts of lightning. She heard yelling from outside her door, and quick footsteps. There was a knock at her door. They didn't wait for her to answer, but burst in.

"My Queen!" a brownie guard said. "We must get you to safety now!"

As the residents of Fairy Haven looked on in despair, the kingdom's largest oak became a lightning rod, struck over and over by angry fingers of electricity. It burst into flames, which burned despite the impossibly heavy downpour. The lighting strikes became stronger and more frequent, stabbing at the tree with sizzling knives, tearing it apart with claws of light. Within minutes, the grandest tree in the forest, which had stood for more than a thousand years, toppled to the ground.

From her enormous throne room in the Great Cavern of the Charred Mountain, the Dragon Queen Torrentia watched it all on her quartz scrying stone. She laughed maniacally, her face turning purple. Nearby, her two drake guards watched her uncomfortably, worried for her sanity.

The previous Dragon Queen, Lizbethia, still hung from enchanted manacles on the opposite wall. She'd ruled for more than fifty years, having taken over after Torrentia's capture. But she'd been no match for Torrentia's power, and the returning queen had made short work of her upon her arrival.

Both queens were currently in their human forms. Lizbethia was covered in horrific wounds, many of which would have been fatal to a lesser being. But she clung to life, dizzy, thirsty, her head pounding, her arms numb. The enchanted manacles would keep her alive, even as Lizbethia begged for death. She wouldn't heal, nor would she perish; she would simply remain in this near-death state for as long as Torrentia found it entertaining.

"If... you... wipe them out..." Lizbethia said, straining to speak, "You... won't have... dust..."

Torrentia thought on this. It was a good point. The dragons used fairy dust for certain spells and rituals, just as the fairies used dragon blood for some of theirs. It was the primary reason the dragons attempted to raid the Fairy Kingdom. If not for the animosity between the two cultures, it could have been a symbiotic relationship.

"Well, they started it," Torrentia replied. She didn't know if it was true, but it's what she'd always been taught. The dragons and the fairies had been at war for centuries, and while no one could remember exactly how it had begun, both sides refused to take the blame. "They'll pay for those years I was locked up," Torrentia said. "I'll decide when they've had enough."

"But the nursery..." Lizbethia gasped. Torrentia knew what she meant. The dragon population was dwindling, mostly because they had a low birth rate. Dragon eggs required fairy dust to incubate. It was said that in ancient times, fairies and dragons had lived and worked together. Some even believed that the two species had created the world together, with the dragons carving out the mountains and rivers, while the fairies created the forests and animals.

Torrentia stood, walked over to Lizbethia, and stroked her chin. "Don't worry, Liz," she said. "I'm sure a few fairies will survive. They'll flee, regroup, start a new kingdom elsewhere. But they'll never question our superiority again." She turned back to her quartz stone. More bolts of lighting pounded at the fallen tree, and the fires were spreading through the forest.

Once again, Torrentia threw back her head and laughed.

"This one," Honeycomb said, pointing to a stump. Working together, Thistle and Honeycomb rolled the stump to the side, exposing a hole in the ground. A small swarm of sprites emerged from the hole, thanking the two pixies for freeing them. The hole was nearly flooded; they'd arrived just in time.

It was daybreak, though you could barely tell due to the heavy storm clouds. The lightning had let up a bit since the fall of the Grand Oak, but the rain was just as strong as it had been all night. Honeycomb thought about the human village nearby. Were they getting flooded? They were still recovering from one disaster, another this soon was just too much. But Honeycomb forced herself to let go of these thoughts; she had her own people to think about right now.

The pixies were covered in mud, not to mention splinters and cuts. They couldn't fly in the pounding rain, so they'd had to search for survivors on foot. They were also running low on magic fairy dust. "This must be what it's like to be a human," Honeycomb said, digging through some fallen branches. Her muscles ached, and she wished she could sit down and rest a bit. "Or a brownie," she added, glancing pointedly at Thistle.

Thistle just shrugged, pulling aside a large branch. In addition to being landbound, brownies couldn't generate fairy dust. Sure, they could cast spells, but not innately. They had to study to use magic, same as any human wizard. If Thistle ever, somehow, got her wish, she'd be giving up a lot. But again, it wasn't a want, it just... was. Walking around on two feet, using her muscle more than her spells, it felt right to her, somehow. She was tired and bleeding, but right now she felt more like herself than she had in a long time.

Pushing aside a large rock, they uncovered the entrance to a grig den. These poor grigs had not been as lucky as the sprites. The den was completely flooded, and several lifeless bodies floated on the surface of the water.

There was no time to mourn. The two pixies rushed to the next pile of detritus, looking for more survivors.


Nearly two hundred brownies crowded into the cavern, and more were on the way. The line led to a simple table, on top of which lay a sword. Queen Delia stood behind the table, clearing her throat. She'd spent all night on the run.

She was wet, cold, and injured, but there was no time for rest now. Every minute she hesitated, more would die.

She looked terrible. Her clothing was in tatters, her hair was full of twigs, and one of her wings was broken. But her audience still gave her the same reverence as always, and became completely silent when she tried to speak.

"Thank you for coming," the Queen said, and then went into a coughing fit. Three sprites carried over a wooden cup full of warm honey nectar. While the Queen drank it, another sprite touched the Queen's throat, which glowed for a moment. This annoyed the Queen, but she didn't say anything. She'd been waving off healers all morning. She wanted her healing sprites out in the kingdom, helping survivors.

"I know many of you would rather be out helping your loved ones, and I'm sorry to keep you," the Queen said. "But this is a matter that takes precedence over all else. Fifty years ago, Torrentia was captured using the ClearSky Blade. The wielder was mortally wounded in the fight, and he will forever be remembered as a hero."

She took another drink. "It is said that Torrentia can only be killed by another silver dragon, but it's also said that she's the last of her kind. The ClearSky Blade was forged from the tooth of a silver dragon, and it is believed to be the only weapon in existence that can defeat her." She gestured toward the blade, but didn't touch it.

"The blade holds a powerful curse. It can't be wielded by anyone but a brownie, as even touching the hilt will kill most fairies. Even brownies can't hold it for long, as it causes them horrendous pain until they pass out. Only one brownie in a generation can wield it properly. The chosen one."

She cleared her throat, and took another sip of nectar. "That's why you're here. Some of you have tried to wield the blade before, but perhaps this time you'll—" She coughed some more, and the sprites brought her a fresh drink.

When she spoke again, she sounded less regal, and more desperate. "This has to work," she said. "The storm will continue until it wipes us out, unless we kill her. One of you *has* to be this generation's chosen one. Whichever of you manages to defeat Torrentia, you will forever be known as a hero. In addition, you will become my new king."

The brownies lined up in front of the sword. As the first one approached, the Queen's attendant announced his name. "Curloyle Verdane," she said, looking into a small crystal ball. Curloyle nodded respectfully to the Queen, then reached for the sword. He gripped the hilt, and attempted to lift the blade. He tried to look triumphant as he held the sword aloft, but he couldn't hide the pain in his eyes. Curloyle collapsed to the floor and crawled away, the sword clattering at the feet of the next brownie in line.

"This is a dumb idea," Honeycomb said.

"I have to try," Thistle said, donning a robe. With her wings flat against her back, the heavy cloth made it difficult to tell she was a pixie. Her face and hair were filthy from all their rescue work, which helped the illusion.

Honeycomb shook her head. "The blade will kill you."

"So will not knowing," Thistle countered. "This is just something I have to do."

Honeycomb nodded. "I understand. Well, no, not really. But I know you, and I know you have to be you."

Thistle leaned forward and kissed her on the lips. They felt sparks between them; actual, visible sparks, the kind that only appear when fated fae couples kiss. They should have been surprised at the revelation, but it felt so right, that neither questioned it.

"I hope you find out what you need to know," Honeycomb said as she pulled away.

Thistle just nodded. She pulled her hood up over her head, and began walking toward the cavern.

Honeycomb watched her go, worried that it might be the last time she saw her.

No one questioned the robed brownie with the obscured face. Everyone in line was disheveled and in various states of dress, and besides, their attention was on the sword, not the crowd. It wasn't until Thistle was tenth in line that she realized she might be in trouble. One of the Queen's attendants, a pixie wearing the robes of a seer, held a crystal orb. As each brownie approached, she called out their name.

*I'm going to get in so much trouble*, Thistle thought, looking around nervously. She considered making a break for it, but she had to see this through. She wondered if she'd be sentenced to hard labor. But for what crime? Trying to save the kingdom? The Queen was too busy with the current crisis to start throwing out punishments for no reason. *Besides*, Thistle thought, *If the sword rejects me, I won't survive long enough to get punished.*

She watched as the brownies in front of her each tried to wield the blade, only to drop it, shrieking in pain. Finally it was her turn. The sword sat before her, halfway off the table from where the previous brownie had dropped it.

"Thistletta Rosebush," the attendant said aloud, then did a double take.

The Queen looked at Thistle strangely. "Please remove your hood," she said.

Thistle complied, revealing her face to the shocked Queen.

"Please let me try," Thistle begged.

"I know you want to help," Queen Delia said. "But it will kill you. I'm sorry, but you'll have to leave."

Thistle nodded, and started to turn away. Then she stopped, rushed to the table, and grabbed the hilt before anyone could stop her.

Queen Torrentia was growing bored. The scrying stone continued to show scenes of violent weather. But the fae folk had taken refuge in caves, where Torrentia's storms couldn't reach them. Sure, there was some entertainment value in watching their treehouses topple and their gardens flood, but the best part was over. The Queen had gone underground, beyond the reach of Torrentia's scrying stone.

She passed the time by throwing daggers at Lizbethia. The woman couldn't die, but she could still scream in pain whenever a dagger hit a particularly tender spot. Whenever she ran out of daggers, a drake servant would pluck them out of Lizbethia, and return them to a box at Torrentia's side. But even this was getting boring. The Dragon Queen considered finishing Lizbethia off, but she knew it was something she could only do once, and didn't want to lose her favorite toy. She decided she'd wait until the Fairy Queen was in her custody. Oh yes, she would make a fine replacement.

"My Queen," said a drake guard, shaking Torrentia out of her reverie. She glared at the interruption, but nodded for him to continue. "We have visitors," he said. "Representatives from the Fairy Kingdom wish to negotiate."

Torrentia laughed out loud. "Negotiate," she repeated, twisting the word with her tongue. "This should be fun. Is the Queen with them?"

"No," the guard said. "Two pixies, and four brownie guards. And they've brought the blade."

"The ClearSky blade?" she asked incredulously. The guard nodded. "Make the brownies wait outside," Torrentia said. She couldn't take the chance. "But send in the pixies. Let's see what they have to say. This should be fun."

The guard nodded and walked away. A few minutes later, he returned with the two pixies. They carried a large, folded leaf, which was wrapped around a sword.

"A gift, for me?" Torrentia asked, her eyes on the sword.

Both pixies bowed. "Queen Torrentia Wyvernica Demonicus," one said, "I am Honeycomb Leafwillow, and this is Thistletta Rosebush. We've been sent by Queen Delia to negotiate. If you will end the curse plaguing our kingdom, we offer you the ClearSky Blade."

"My, my, the Queen must be desperate indeed, to part with such a rare weapon," Torrentia said. "Or maybe she realized it was useless to her, since none of you can wield it."

"Nevertheless, it is yours," Thistle said. "You just have to remove your curse."

"Very well, I accept," Torrentia said. She had no intention of ending the curse, but these two didn't need to know that. Once she had the sword, she would slay these visitors and punish the Fairy Kingdom even more. She nodded toward the sword, and held out her hand.

Thistle flew forward until she hovered just a few feet away from the Dragon Queen. She unwrapped the leaf, but rather than hand over the sword, she grabbed it by the hilt. Thistle now assumed a battle pose, and glared at the evil queen. "This is your last chance," Thistle said. "End the curse, or I will end your life."

Torrentia's expression didn't change, but she did take a step back. "That must be a fake," she said. "No pixie can wield that weapon."

"I'm no ordinary pixie," Thistle said. "But if you don't believe your eyes, I'll be happy to give you a demonstration." She swiped the sword through the air a few times, leaving faint blue lines in the air. Though the pixie was dwarfed by the Torrentia's human form, Thistle showed no fear, and returned the Dragon Queen's glare with fire in her eyes.

For just a moment, a visage of fear crossed Torrentia's face. But then she laughed, shaking her head slowly. Something changed in the room. The air itself seemed to come alive with energy. "You may hold the weapon," she said. "But do you have the skill to use it in battle? I think not."

"Try me," Thistle said. She kept a brave face, but she could feel the hair rising on her neck.

"Be careful what you wish for," Torrentia said, then suddenly thrust her hand forward. A blast of electricity flew from her fingertips, a bolt every bit as powerful as the ones that had toppled the Great Palace. The room flashed with blinding blue light, and even Torrentia had to blink a few times before she could see again.

Thistle remained where she'd been, hovering a few feet away. Her blade now glowed bright blue, with sparks of electricity popping and crackling around it.

Torrentia opened her mouth to say something, but no words came out. "Guards," she finally managed to squeak. "Kill them."

Thistle pointed her sword at one of the guards. A bolt of lightning blasted him, leaving nothing but a smoking corpse. The remaining guards turned and fled.

"Traitors!" Torrentia shouted. Then, to Thistle, she said, "Maybe we can negotiate after all. I'll draw up a peace treaty. Just let me go get my pen." Then she turned and ran.

A jolt of lightning hit her in the back, and she tumbled onto her face. As she got to her knees, her head turned toward Thistle, her face contorted with fury. As the pixies watched, she grew, doubling in size, then tripling, her silver dress merging with her skin, covering her in shiny scales. When the transformation was complete, she filled the cavern, her head nearly touching the high ceiling. The silver dragon stared at Thistle with contempt, and let loose with her lightning breath.

The air crackled around Thistle, and it was hard to breathe, but the sword continued to protect her. She could feel the weapon's power growing in her hands, and the energy seemed to flow through her body. Her blood felt like it was boiling, but she felt no pain, only power. She let loose the blade's energy, firing a blast so powerful the ground shook.

Torrentia was sent flying across the cave, where she hit the wall hard. That burst of energy would have turned a lesser dragon into ash, but she managed to shrug it off. "Fine," she said, in a deep, gravelly voice, "We'll do this the hard way." She leapt forward with surprising speed, and attempted to bite the pixie. Thistle just barely got out of the way in time. The two fought back and forth, Torrentia dodging the pixie's stabs, and Thistle keeping away from those mighty jaws.

Honeycomb watched from across the room. She wanted to help her friend, but she had no weapon that could harm the dragon. She heard a groan to her right, where Lizbethia still hung from her magical chains, several daggers protruding from her body. Honeycomb debated for a few seconds, then approached the former dragon queen.

"Ow!" Thistle shouted, as the dragon backhanded her across the room. She hit the wall, then tumbled to the ground. She rolled to the side just as a massive foot stomped beside her. Not wanting to waste the opportunity, Thistle stabbed Torrentia in the foot. The silver dragon roared in pain, withdrawing her foot.

As powerful as the ClearSky blade was, Thistle still had her work cut out for her. The blade protected her from lightning, which was a lifesaver, but its blasts weren't powerful enough to penetrate the dragon's scales. And while it was the only weapon capable of piercing Torrentia's hide, Thistle was having a devil of a time hitting anything vital. The dragon was unbelievably fast, and it stayed on the offensive. Thistle barely had time to dodge the creature's bites, much less find a weak spot to target.

Torrentia let loose another breathful of lightning, and Thistle barely brought the sword up in time to block it. Then the dragon spun, whipping her massive tail at the pixie, once again knocking her against the wall. Thistle got to her knees, dazed from the impact. Her sword had clattered away somewhere to her left, but she kept her eyes on her enemy. She was seeing double, and she had to blink a couple of times before she could tell which dragon was the real one.

Except they were both real. The silver one charged toward her, but the purple one stood still. "Torrentia!" the newcomer bellowed, and the silver dragon turned.

"Lizbethia," Torrentia growled. "How did you get loose?"

"We have a new treaty with the fairies," Lizbethia replied, nodding toward Honeycomb. "If you wish to avoid execution, you will surrender immediately."

Torrentia chuckled, a noise that sounded like an avalanche. "That is not within your power," she said. "But if you want the throne, come and take it." As if to hammer home the threat with a visual aid, she reached forward and grasped her human-sized throne, snapping it off its dais.

The purple dragon screeched and rushed forward, her fangs going for Torrentia's neck. The two wrestled, causing the cavern to shake. Honeycomb watched the fight in awe. It was like being witness to a battle between gods, the kind of match that could reshape the world if it went on long enough.

The titanic reptiles tossed each other against the walls, rocks falling with every impact. Finally Torrentia got her jaws around Lizbethia's neck. Just as she was about to bite, she cried out in pain. She turned her head to see Thistle standing on her back, the ClearSky Blade buried hilt deep between the silver scales. It wasn't a lethal wound, but it hurt more than anything Torrentia had ever felt. She released Lizbethia and moved her head towards the pixie, her massive jaws open wide.

And then Thistle released the blade's electricity. Still buried in the dragon's skin, the lightning flowed through Torrentia's body, burning her from the inside. The silver dragon wailed, an unholy, ear-splitting shriek that echoed throughout the cavern. Smoke rose from her mouth, and her eyes burst like overripe melons. Finally her head hit the floor, and her breathing stopped.

Lizbethia reverted to her human form, and Honeycomb sprinkled fairy dust on her wounds. The three headed back toward the cavern entrance, so they could inform the drakes of the change in leadership. The drakes were more than happy to follow Lizbethia again, as she'd been a much kinder master in their eyes.

The brownie guards were let into the cavern, and the drakes set up a table where the visiting fairies could parley with the new Dragon Queen. "A flying brownie, I thought I'd seen everything," Queen Lizbethia said, studying Thistle with admiration.

"I'm just a pixie," Thistle said, her voice tinged with disappointment. "I don't know why the blade chose me."

Lizbethia shook her head, and her eyes glowed for a moment. "You only see things as they are," she said. "I see things as they were meant to be. You have the soul of a brownie, make no mistake about that."

"You really think so?" Thistle asked.

The Dragon Queen nodded. "Tell me," she asked. "If you could transform, so that your body matched your mind, would you?"

"In a heartbeat," Thistle said. "But no such spell exists."

"Maybe not that *you* know of," Lizbethia replied with a wry smile.

One month later, there was a celebration in the village of Proudpath. The townsfolk had prepared a banquet in the center of town, and everyone feasted together – humans, fae folk, and even Lizbethia, in her human form. Queen Delia sat next to her, the two still hammering out the details of their trade agreement.

Honeycomb and Thistle sat next to each other, locked in intense conversation, barely even noticing the world around them. Thistle was completely a brownie now, from head to toe, and he'd never been happier. The transformation spell had used a combination of fairy dust and dragon blood – Torrentia's blood, to be precise – and the change was permanent. Thistle felt like he was finally experiencing life for the first time, instead of just watching the world through someone else's eyes.

The Fairy Queen had offered Thistle the throne, but he'd turned it down. He'd experienced a rebirth, and he didn't want to waste this new life writing decrees and ordering people around. Besides, he didn't want to have to marry the Queen. While Queen Delia would certainly make an ideal partner – she was intelligent, beautiful, and full of grace – Thistle's heart already belonged to another, and he stared into her eyes now.

Sparks flew again as Thistle and Honeycomb kissed. The rest of the table seemed to fade away, the sounds of raucous celebration becoming a distant hum. Their kiss was so strong, their connection so intimate, that they could feel each other's heartbeats. For just a moment, Thistle believed he could even hear Honeycomb's thoughts.

Life wasn't back to normal, and things might never be the same again. Rebuilding the Fairy Kingdom would take months if not years. There were other dragon factions, beyond Lizbethia's control. And dragons weren't the only monsters out there.

But right now, at least for Thistle and Honeycomb, the world was as perfect as it ever would be.

*Author's Notes*

This book takes place in the same universe as the short story "Fairy Dust" in the collection "Geek Cutes." You shouldn't need to read the one to understand the other, but for the record, the timeline order is "Banishing Act," then "Fairy Dust," then the bulk of this novel.

...If you want to call it a novel. So far I've published eight books, and I don't know that I'd call any of them novels, even the ones that say "novel" on the cover. Almost everything I write reads like a collection of short stories, mostly due to my short attention span. Even this one is more like three novellas in a trench coat.

But I write what I write. Of all the books I've written, this was the most fun, and I hope you enjoyed reading it. Please check out some of my other books if you like LGBTQIA+ sci-fi and fantasy.

Special thanks to Kaius Coolman, KJ Martin, Alan K. Garrett, and all the voices in my head (except Steve).

- Xine

## *About The Author*

Xine Fury is a brain piloting a skeleton wrapped in a flesh suit.